LAWYERS, GUNS AND MONEY

By

BOB MAYER

www.bobmayer.com

Lawyers, Guns and Money by Bob Mayer

ISBN: 9781621253372

Dedication:
To two men I had the privilege of serving with:
James O'Callaghan and David Boltz.
Rest in Peace in Valhalla.

Send lawyers, guns and money
The shit has hit the fan
Lawyers, Guns and Money: Warren Zevon

Sample Praise for Bob Mayer's thrillers:

Eyes of the Hammer (Green Berets)
Stephen Coonts: "A scorcher of a novel. Mayer had me hooked from the very first page."
WEB Griffin: "Exciting and authentic. Author Mayer, a Green Beret himself, gave me a vivid look at the world of the Army's Special Forces. Don't miss this one."

The Line (Shadow Warriors)
Publishers Weekly: "Mayer has crafted a thriller in the tradition of John Grisham's *The Firm*."

Dragon Sim-13 (Green Berets)
Kirkus Reviews: "Fascinating, imaginative and nerve-wracking. Mayer's tough, businesslike soldiers again include a tough, businesslike female."
Publisher's Weekly. "A pulsing technothriller. A nail-biter in the best tradition of adventure fiction."
Journal of US Special Operations: "This is one book you can trust."

Synbat (Green Berets)
Kirkus Reviews: "Action packed entertainment."
Assembly Magazine (Association of Graduates, West Point): "Mayer has stretched the limits of the military action novel as this is also a gripping detective story. Mayer brings an accurate depiction of military life to this book which greatly enhances its credibility."

Lost Girls (The Cellar)
Publishers Weekly: "Excellent writing and well-drawn, appealing characters help make this another taut, crackling read from Mayer."

Eternity Base (Green Berets)
Midwest Book Review: "Unlike most military stories this will appeal to general audiences as a fine thriller. Highly recommended, indeed."

Cut Out (Green Berets)
Kirkus Reviews: "Sinewy writing enhances this already potent action fix."
Southern Book Trade: "Clancy, Coonts and Brown might have the market cornered when it comes to hardware, but Mayer knows what

all Infantry types will tell you: it's the soldier who makes all the difference."

Bodyguard of Lies (The Cellar)
"Heart-racing, non-stop action that is difficult to put down."—Mystery News
"Thelma and Louise go clandestine."—Kirkus Reviews

The Rock
Kirkus: "A crackling science thriller in the vein of Crichton."
Publishers Weekly: "The best combination of science fiction and technothriller this year."

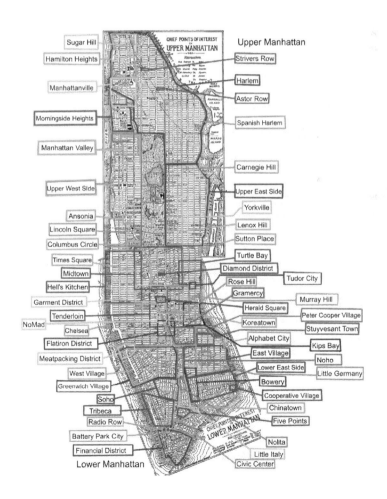

Thursday Night, 4 August 1977

UPPER BAY, NEW YORK HARBOR

The Statue of Liberty's torch, flickering in the dark and shrouded by rain, could be an invitation or, more realistically, a warning. Since he was piloting a boat, William Kane, who was fond of maps, likened Lady Liberty these days to those sea serpents drawn on the blank spaces of ancient charts with the dire warning: *Here there be monsters! Stay away!*

Three weeks earlier the city had been savaged by massive rioting during the nightlong Blackout on the 13th of July, an explosion on top of a decade of a slowly filling cesspool of blight and decay. There were many who felt New York would never recover and that the Blackout had been the death knell. They compared it to the fond memories of the '66 Blackout as proof the city had gone to hell.

Kane, who was also a student of history, was rather ambivalent about the memories and the projections. New York City had survived many trepidations and would plod into the future in one form or another. Being practical, he used glimpses of Lady Liberty's torch to the southwest to fix the boat's position in the rotten weather, drawing a mental line from it to the muted glow of the Twin Towers of the World Trade Center to the northeast. He twitched the dual throttles to keep the forty-two-footer in position, the eastern point in a triangle with Liberty and Ellis Island equidistant to the west.

"That's the subway," Kane nodded his head, indicating a barely visible dark mass in the harbor.

"Excuse me?" The man Kane had labeled Money, since he wasn't big on remembering names, had been a pain ever since boarding, ordering him about as if Kane were a servant, which technically was true, given he was on the job.

Money was seated in the plush chair to Kane's left rear. The Actress was in the chair next to him. Money was from Texas, a point he'd made within the first minute. He wore tailored jeans, a starched white shirt under an expensive sports jacket, alligator hide boots and a black Stetson crowning silver hair.

Kane's attire wasn't in the same income bracket, or fashion consciousness, with his dyed black jungle fatigue pants, grey t-shirt and unbuttoned blue denim shirt, sleeves rolled. He wore scuffed jungle boots, bloused inside the cuff of the pants with boot bands. A forty-five-caliber pistol rested in a supple leather holster under the denim shirt on his left hip, two spare magazines behind it on the belt, a commando knife in the small of his back and other assorted weapons secreted here and there.

"Ellis Island," Kane explained the comment as he released one of the throttles and pointed. "Most of it's built with fill from subway excavation. Originally, it was only three acres, but landfill expanded that to over twenty-seven. On top of old oyster beds. The island wouldn't exist without the subway and vice versa."

"Doesn't look like much of anything," Money said. "My waste yard on the ranch has more acreage. My people were in the States long before Ellis Island let in the riff-raff." He checked his watch as if he had an important date, beyond the beautiful woman seated next to him who'd been vaguely pitching him a movie concept since they pulled away from the Battery on the southwest shore of Manhattan. "This is bullshit," he muttered.

The Actress reached out and put a hand on the Money's arm. "See? History. That interests people. That's our film's motif and—"

Money cut her off. "You know what the blackout did to *Superman*? How far over-budget that is?"

"That's because of Brando, not the city," the Actress countered. "And that's not a New York movie. They only shot a couple of weeks at the Daily News as a stand in for the Daily Planet. The rest was filmed elsewhere. *Saturday Night Fever* is under budget."

Money wasn't impressed. "A dancing movie with that disco bongo drum crap. It's buying a stud-bull that can't get it up. It'll disappear without anyone noticing it was ever made. Along with that *Welcome Back Kotter* kid they cast." He waved a dismissive hand. "The city's a pigsty." He indicated Kane. "We need a man with a gun just to go out on a boat. Are there pirates out here?"

Kane wasn't sure if the question was addressed to him, the Actress or rhetorical. His default mode was silence although he found the concept of pirates in New York Harbor intriguing. He remembered Brother Benedict mentioning pirates being part of the city's history. Captain William Kidd had used the harbor as his base for a while and had something to do with Trinity Church, which still overlooked Wall Street. Given the reaction to the Ellis Island/subway reference, he doubted Money would be interested in exploring history any further.

"And there's that loony, Son of Sam, shooting people," Money continued his New York City tirade, interrupting Kane's musings on Captain Kidd. "You know how much securing a set for three months at all the locations in that script would cost?"

The Actress, a voluptuous blonde wearing a low-cut dress that displayed her assets, and whose name Kane also couldn't remember although it rhymed with something, which he also couldn't remember, made a tactical shift in her pitch. "Perhaps if I show you the storyboards? They're below in the bedroom."

Money showed more interest in the possibilities below than above deck. The two descended via the hatch to Kane's left, Money leading. The Actress gave Kane a wan smile and rolled her eyes which earned her some points with the former Green Beret. She slid shut the teak door.

Kane peeled back the stained Velcro covering the glowing face and checked his watch. Adjusted the engines and wheel, pointing the yacht north into the outgoing tide combined with the flow of the Hudson River. He considered dropping anchor, since he had no idea how long 'going over the storyboards' would take and he was to the west of the shipping channel.

Kane focused on the faint silhouette of the Statue of Liberty to the port side, dredging up all sorts of history about it and the island upon which it was perched.

Kane cocked his head when he heard a muffled yelp for help. He sighed and headed below. Turned at the bottom of the steps toward the aft cabin. He passed through the Actress's scream as he slid open the door to the cabin. The Actress was on her back on the bed, scrambling to free herself, obviously panicked, naked from the waist up. Money lay on top of her, also with his shirt removed.

"Okay, sir, leave the lady—" Kane began, but sensed movement to his right and brought that arm up in a reflexive high block, partly deflecting the sap aimed at his head. The lead-filled leather weapon struck him a glancing blow and he staggered back.

Kane dropped to the deck, sweeping the attacker's legs with his left leg. As the man went down, Kane was on top of him, repeatedly smashing his elbow into the attacker's face at close range. The man scrambled to get away from the furious assault.

Kane let him, getting to one knee and drawing the forty-five, thumbing off the ambidextrous safety as he brought it level.

A muzzle flashed in the open aft sliding door and a bullet snapped by Kane's head accompanied by the sound of the gun firing. The shooter was behind and below the Sap Man, standing in a boat bobbing behind the narrow dive deck, which helped explain the miss. Kane fired, but the escaping sap-man was in the way and the round hit him in the shoulder, punch-spinning him out of the door and into the rubber boat.

An outboard engine roared to life.

Two flashes and the crack of shots from the boat. Bullets hit the ceiling above Kane. Crouching, he sidled left, weapon at the ready.

The engine accelerated.

Kane approached the door on an angle. Peered around, muzzle leading. The zodiac accelerated to the west, a dark figure at the driver's console, a wounded man in the back, and a third figure kneeling and aiming a gun this way, but not firing.

Kane brought the forty-five up, but spun about as he sensed someone behind him.

His finger twitched but he didn't fire at the Actress. He turned back, but the boat disappeared between the Statue of Liberty and Ellis Island in the rain and dark smudge of the Jersey shoreline.

"Fucking New Jersey," Kane muttered.

"Help him," the Actress said. She'd pulled her top up but that seemed to be the extent of her recovery.

"What happened?" Kane checked Money. It was obvious that Sap Man had hit him. Kane also noted the not inconsiderable pile of white powder on the small table next to the oval bed.

"I saw that guy coming up from behind and tried to warn Mister Crawford," the Actress said. "Did you shoot him?"

She was several lines behind in the script, but at least Crawford was stirring.

"I shot one of them." Kane felt along the wound on the older man's head. "His skull isn't busted. He's lucky."

"You really shot someone?" the Actress asked. "That was *really* loud! Really, really loud!"

Kane pulled off his denim shirt and used it to staunch the blood from the wound. "There's a first aid kit in the cockpit. Get it."

"Did you kill them?"

"First aid kit. Now!" Head wounds could be bad bleeders, a fact Kane had first-hand knowledge of given the old scar just above his right temple and extending underneath his thick, dark hair.

Crawford's eyelids flickered. "What the tarnation? Who slugged me?" He tried to sit.

Kane noted an old wicked scar on Crawford's abdomen, just below the rib cage. There was a faded eagle, globe and anchor tattoo on the older man's right shoulder.

"Easy," Kane said. "Stay down for a minute."

The Actress returned holding the kit. "Here."

Kane ripped open a gauze pack.

"I think I'm going to be sick," the Actress said.

"Head's over there," Kane said.

"What?"

"Bathroom," Kane amplified. He turned to the older man and replaced the shirt with gauze. The blood was mostly staunched, the laceration minimal. "You have a thick skull, Mister Crawford. You'll be okay. What day of the week is it?"

"Huh?"

"Day of the week," Kane repeated.

"Friday."

"Date?"

"Four August.

"Year?"

"Nineteen-seventy-seven. What in tarnation is going on?"

Kane didn't stop him from sitting up. "You don't have a concussion. You're probably gonna have a bad headache for a bit." Kane checked the carpeted floor. Wet spots where the intruder had been. Kane walked to the sliding door leading to the dive deck. Some blood spatter on the deck. The attackers must have rowed up in the dark from directly behind since he hadn't heard the engine. "You got enemies?" he asked Crawford.

"Sure, I have enemies. No one worth their salt doesn't have enemies." Crawford tried to retrieve his shirt from the deck, but couldn't make it. "A man who doesn't have enemies isn't a man."

Kane handed the shirt to the older man. "Enemy enough to want to kill you?"

"What happened?" Crawford demanded as he buttoned.

"I've got to radio the NYPD harbor patrol," Kane said.

"Whoa, buckaroo, hold your horses!" Crawford tried to stand, leaned right, and fell onto the bed. He held up a hand. "Just give me a sec, hombre." He slowly sat up, one hand on the bulkhead. "*What happened?*" he demanded in a voice used to being obeyed.

Kane gave a brief summary of recent events.

Crawford didn't interrupt. It took Kane under twenty seconds.

"No body?" Crawford asked.

"One of them is wounded," Kane said. "There's three bullet holes in here."

"The holes can be patched," Crawford said.

"Get to the point, please," Kane said to Crawford.

"I'm not going to get stuck in this hell's half acre over a little blood on a boat and some bullet holes," Crawford said. "I've got important business to attend to in the morning before I fly home."

"I just shot someone," Kane said.

"Not well enough. He's still breathing."

Kane didn't respond.

"They came at us," Crawford pointed out. "I doubt they'll be going to the police. Let sleeping doggies lie." He reached down and was able to pick up his Stetson without falling over. "Besides, you want to get the police involved in this, William Kane?"

Kane remained still, waiting for the inevitable.

Crawford felt his head, grimaced in pain. His hand came away sticky with blood. "Guess I won't be wearing my hat for a bit." He smiled crookedly at Kane. "Oh yeah, cowboy, we're all in this together."

"You were a Marine," Kane said.

"And you were Army," Crawford said. "Green Beret, right?"

"Your scar?"

"Jap bayonet on Makin Island."

"You were a Raider," Kane said.

For the first time Crawford seemed impressed. "You know a bit of history, eh?" He pointed at Kane with the hat in hand. "You got at least one scar I can see, compadre. And some fresh ones on your wrists and neck. I don't know what you got into recently but it wasn't pretty." Crawford shook his head, but stopped and winced. "Let it go. There'll be a tidy bonus in this for you. Take the boat back to the marina."

"You know who it was," Kane said.

"I don't have a blessed clue who it was," Crawford said. "But don't worry. My people will find out. Let them take care of it. New York cops couldn't find their behinds with both hands.

Plus, all they're worried about right now is that Son of Sam bastard."

The Actress came out of the head and stood close to Crawford. "Are you all right?" she asked him, putting a hand on his shoulder.

"Fine, darling."

Kane indicated the cocaine. "Is that why?"

"It doesn't put a pretty shine on things," Crawford admitted. "But there's nothing to prove you didn't supply it."

"Please," the Actress pleaded. "I can't get in trouble."

"I shot someone," Kane said, but as he spoke the words, he knew they meant nothing and he was the one behind the script now.

"It's a done deed, cowboy," Crawford said. "And remember. We're the witnesses. We can remember it one way or the other." He looked at the Actress. "You're with me on this, darling, aren't you?" It was more a threat than a question.

She gave Kane an apologetic look and nodded assent.

"Right," Kane said. "The marina." He headed for the bridge.

*****

It was still a dark and stormy night, which was a cliché, but clichés are truisms and Kane didn't have many of those in his life so he took it at face value. The rain made the current job easier as he scrubbed blood off the dive deck. Another positive was that the drizzle was warm.

He'd docked at the pier from which they'd departed and where Crawford's limousine had been waiting the entire time. Crawford had thrust five thousand in crisp, new hundreds, still bank banded, into Kane's hands without comment, before heading to the limo. The Actress, whose name he still couldn't recall, had scurried after him, barely getting inside before the door was slammed shut and rubber burned as it peeled away.

He considered calling Toni, his boss for this job, and telling her about the evening's events, but he wasn't certain what to make of it, so tomorrow would be soon enough. He pulled out a flashlight and shined it on the deck to check his work. Clean of blood.

There were scuffmarks in the decking that no amount of scrubbing was going to fix, although some of them were old. The boat was a rental, via Toni, and he figured he'd gone above and beyond this evening. She could deal with the owner and the bullet holes and the marks. It was likely the boat had seen worse damage from partiers.

He sat down, feet dangling over the edge, just above the polluted water of the Hudson River, not exactly feeling like Huckleberry Finn on the Mississippi. Unconsciously, he ran his hand along the scar on the side of his head.

It didn't make sense. One of the intruders had a gun, but the one who'd come in had used a sap to attack Crawford. If the goal had been killing, the gun should have been first. Or both should have had guns. Unless a kidnapping? Crawford? The Actress? Or had the sap guy been in the cabin first, the gun man providing cover from the boat, and Crawford and the Actress interrupted something?

Kane glanced over his shoulder. Went to where the initial attacker had come from the side. There was a hatch there which led to the ladder descending to the engine room. It was unlatched. Kane pushed it open and flipped on the light.

The bomb was just inside, on the edge at the top of the ladder. A red light was flickering on top of the bundle of C-4, then it turned green.

Wednesday,
19 November 1967

HILL 875, DAK TO, VIETNAM

"Benedicat vos omnipotens Deus, Pater, et Filius, et Spiritus Sanctus."

"Amen," Kane *whispers under his breath while he studies the topographic map spread on top of his rucksack with his platoon sergeant.*

"Finding God in the foxhole, L.T.?" Sergeant Carter asks.

"He's omnipotent," Kane says. "He can find me if He wants to. Even here."

Forty feet away, Father Watters winds up the abbreviated service, holding his hands over the cluster of paratroopers kneeling on the jungle floor around him. "Ite, missa est. Go forth. And be safe, my sons."

The most important aspect of the mass in the midst of the jungle, as far as Kane is concerned, beyond the comfort it gives those who believe, and those who don't but wish they could, is the large number of soldiers in the cluster. More than ever before. An indicator of the pervading fear that this op isn't going to be an easy one.

"Hey diddle, diddle, right up the fucking middle," Sergeant Carter complains about the operations order in a low voice only Kane can hear. "They teach that at West Point?" Carter is from Detroit, made his latest rank in Germany and this is, surprisingly for the stripes, his first tour in Vietnam. But he gets some experience points for his tough childhood.

"They taught us Caesar, Napoleon, Grant and MacArthur, to name a few," Kane says. "They all did right up the middle one time or another." And Kane remembers from his lessons that Grant in his memoirs regretted only one order out of all the carnage he commanded in the war—the final, frontal assault at Cold Harbor; right up the middle.

Kane looks at the objective; he can see as far as the dense surge of green that marks the base of Hill 875. "Not much choice."

"Why are we taking the hill, sir?" Carter asks.

"Because it's there." Kane regrets the flippant answer. Carter, and the rest, are putting their lives on the line. He tries to explain. "A Special Forces CIDG company made contact on the hill. The general wants us to take it." As far as the plan, Kane isn't thrilled. Two companies, Charlie and Delta up, with Alpha in the rear, two up-one back, classic army tactics since men had been whacking at each other with swords. Except the NVA are anything but classic.

"Why not just blast it with arty?" Carter asks.

Kane tires of the questions to which there are no answers. After five months Kane is a veteran. He has more time in-country than Carter and most of the men in the reconstituted company of mostly replacements.

Kane looks at the trail that runs through the position. They'd marched on it this morning and the attack is going to follow it up the hill. "I want an OP with an M60 behind us," he orders Carter.

Carter frowns and Kane knows he's thinking his platoon leader is putting a valuable machinegun pointing in the wrong direction. But memories of Ranger School always hover in Kane's brain. He can practically hear Chargin' Charlie Beckwith screaming: 'Don't be stupid!'

"Get the OP out with a 60 and check the men, sergeant."

Kane was moved to Alpha company after the disaster at Hill 1338 in June. He's the senior platoon leader in the company. It's disconcerting that he's commanding Ted's old platoon but no one in it remembers Ted.

Kane is a very different man from the one who'd experienced his first combat that day. Physically, the change is startling. He's lost weight that hadn't been apparent he could lose. He has practically no body fat, his body is all lean muscle. But it's in his mind that he's changed the most and the window into it, his eyes, are deep and withdrawn.

As Carter heads one way, Kane goes to the other end of the platoon. He kneels between two men. "Canteens full?"

Both young soldiers nervously nod, eyes wide.

Kane looks over their gear. Both are FNG, fucking new guys. Kane doubts either of them shave. He inspects their weapons. "Listen to your squad leader. He'll take care of you. Do what he says and you'll be fine."

The FNGs nod.

Kane moves down the line dispensing advice and as much encouragement as he can muster, which is almost nonexistent.

Why are *they taking this fucking hill?*

Because it's where the enemy is.

*****

Fierce fighting ahead has been going on for an hour at the head of Alpha company. They'd been going uphill behind Charlie and Delta which have been engaged for even longer. In trail position, Kane's platoon has not made contact yet. But that changes in an instant.

Bugles blare behind them and Kane instantly knows what that means. It's a trap.

The sound of the firing intensifies. Kane recognizes the sound of B-40 rockets and recoilless rifle fire, which means the NVA are dug in. Jets scream overhead, dropping heavy bombs on Hill 875. Artillery fills the gaps between air strikes.

Kane is behind a log, firing his M-16 on semi-automatic, actually aiming. He sees the enemy occasionally, a rarity. Khaki figures flit among the undergrowth and broken jungle. He implicitly understands they can also see him, but he's always known they can see him. It is usually their advantage having the Americans blundering into them. But now they're attacking.

He hits some of those figures, but it's not something to spend a moment on in the heat of battle.

Keep shooting. Issue orders. Hold it together. Updating the company commander on the radio.

Kane glances left and right, checking his men. Two soldiers are fetaled in their hole, not firing. "Carter!" Kane yells, getting his platoon sergeant's attention. He points at the two.

Carter slithers through the mud and undergrowth to the hole.

Kane can barely hear the radio over the sound of battle; the new company commander is calling in fire. Danger close. 'Grab them by the belt buckle'. That's the NVA's tactic to reduce the American's artillery and air power superiority. Get so close to the Americans it can't be used.

Except in the direst of circumstances.

NVA pour out of tunnels and advance through the jungle.

This isn't the Sky Soldier plan.

This is the NVA plan, long prepared, waiting for the Americans to blunder into the trap. The paratroopers are in the midst of tunnels and bunkers and long-planned fields of fire. Surrounded. Charlie Beckwith would be swearing up a storm at the stupidity.

The NVA charge, some of them screaming, some insanely laughing, firing their AKs. To the left, a platoon CP, command post, is overrun, all the Americans killed at close range.

The company commander is standing, firing his pistol into the air to keep men from running; to prevent a complete rout.

Kane drops a magazine, slams another home. Eighteen rounds, he thinks as he starts firing, one part of his brain counting rounds, most of it considering the diminishing tactical options. The perimeter is dissolving, men fading uphill toward the dubious safety of Charlie and Delta.

"Hold the line!" Kane screams, but his voice withers beneath the screaming of bullets, artillery and jets.

There are too many NVA.

An M60 machinegun is firing nonstop thirty yards away, farther down the trail at the OP. It's the only thing saving Alpha from being completely overrun. Someone is making a stand.

For the moment.

"Hold the line!" Kane yells.

The handset jerks out of Kane's hand. He turns to see the cause. Blood is pumping from the ragged, gaping hole in the center of what used to be the RTO's face.

The RTO's wound saves Kane's life as a round snaps underneath the front lip of his helmet and plows along the right side of his head and punches a hole through the rear of the helmet.

Stars explode in Kane's brain and he's knocked off his feet, steel pot flying.

Kane falls on top of his RTO. Kane is barely conscious, his head ringing. Although his ear is only inches from the soldier's mouth, he can't hear the man's desperate, whispered prayers. He does feel the RTO's final breath.

Kane's blood mixes with the RTO's.

Kane looks up. Jungle, a tiny patch of sky, the canopy shredded by the artillery. Blue sky. A bird flies past. Kane envies it. He can't get his body to respond. A fire alarm is ringing in his head.

The sky is blocked by a brown face. Strangely, the Vietnamese smiles, revealing a gold tooth in the center. The Vietnamese says something but Kane can't hear him. He can only see the lips moving.

Bullets snap overhead. Artillery thunders. Kane hears that distantly, on another stage. The M-60 is still burning rounds, a last stand.

He's going to die. He knows it. The Vietnamese looming over him is going to kill him, just like Ted. He pulls his West Point ring off. Drops it into the blood and piss-soaked mud.

The brown face disappears and Kane feels a tug on his LBE. He's being dragged. Uphill.

He realizes the man is a Montagnard CIDG. Kane tries to help, to push with his feet, but his body isn't working.

The M-60 goes silent.

"Friendly!" the Vietnamese is calling out and Kane finally hears the word.

They're passing bodies. American corpses litter the trail that runs uphill toward Charlie and Delta.

"You not too heavy," his savior says, pauses, smiles once more. He raises his voice. "Friendly!"

Bullets going in both directions crack past the retreating Americans. Alpha has fallen apart.

Kane wants to stand, to issue orders, save his platoon, save the company. Save his men. He can't get to his feet.

He's pulled once more. Through the mud, broken vegetation. Over an eviscerated body smearing blood and gore.

"Friendly!"

They pass between two wide-eyed, frightened paratroopers. They're pointing their M-16s downhill. This is the perimeter of Charlie and Delta.

Another five meters. Stops. The brown face is in front of him again. Grabs him by the shoulders and sits him against a tree, facing uphill. Fingers probe the side of his head. He can barely feel them.

"My arm! My arm!" someone is screaming close by. "Where's my arm?"

Artillery. Bombs explode, the earth shakes.

What circle of hell is this?

"Mom. Mom. Mom." *The voice is insistent.*

Kane wishes it would stop. His right eye fills with blood. The casualty collection point is thirty feet away, near the company CP. Too many bodies. Too many.

Father Watters pulls a paratrooper to the collection point. Someone tries to get him to stop, to make him get down, but Watters shrugs him off and heads back to the perimeter.

"Dai Yu?"

Kane focuses on the CIDG.

The man taps his chest. "I'm Thao."

"Thao," *Kane whispers.*

Thao points at the wound. "Lot of blood, but head strong. You be okay."

"'Okay'?" *Kane repeats.*

A chopper flits overhead, cases of ammo and medical supplies tossed out, and away fast, bullets following, tattooing the metal.

Kane puts one hand against the tree. Tries to get to his feet, collapses.

Thao points to the casualty collection point. "I get bandages. You stay. Okay?"

"Right." *Kane's not sure he actually says the word. Everything is echoing.*

Thao scampers off, dodging wounded, empty ammo cases, the dead, broken tree trunks, discarded helmets and other debris of war.

His men need him. Kane has to get back in the fight. He tries to wipe the blood out of his eye but his hand has little strength.

Thao is back. "Easy, Dai Yu." *He wets a piece of cloth with his canteen and wipes Kane's face, surprisingly gentle amidst all the violence.*

Thao has a syringe of morphine.

"No," *Kane tries to wave it off. He has to stay alert. Lead his men.*

He doesn't feel it when Thao hits his thigh with the morphine.

Thao clears Kane's eye of blood. Father Watters is on his knees fifteen meters away, cradling a dying soldier in his arms, his head next to the man's ear, whispering Extreme Unction.

A jet screams by, angled across the axis of the hill, drops its bomb. Danger close.

The ground convulses. More screams.

"Weapon," *Kane says to Thao.* "My weapon."

Thao nods. "Many weapons here. Wait, Dai Yu." He doesn't have to go far. He returns with a blood smeared M-16.

Thao points toward the sound of the bugles and the AKs and the screams. "I get more wounded."

How can anyone be alive there?

How can anyone be alive here?

Kane grasps the M-16, uses it as a crutch to get to his feet. The surviving officers are gathering near the casualty collection point, coordinating the defense. Kane takes a step in that direction. Feels a whisper of something along his spine. Stops and looks up.

A jet is inbound. But it's coming from the wrong direction, along the axis of the ridge instead of across like the others.

The last thing Kane sees, silhouetted against the flash of the exploding bomb, is Father Watters making the sign of the cross over a dying soldier.

Friday Morning, 5 August 1977

MEATPACKING DISTRICT, MANHATTAN

Kane placed the five spot on the table in the corner of the diner while he put his green, stained map case bag against the wall.

"How are the hands?" Morticia asked as she placed a cup of coffee and glass of water with two ice cubes in front of him. She's been working at Vic's Diner for sixty-two days, which sometimes seemed like an eternity to Kane, given her constant suggestions on how to upgrade the place once she'd found out Kane and Thao, the cook, owned it.

"At the end of my arms," Kane said. He held them up to prove his point, exposing the pinkish scars on his palms from the rope burns acquired in the old Nabisco Factory three and a half weeks earlier. There were also marks around his wrists from the handcuffs by which he'd initially been hung. The ring of red around his neck from where he'd subsequently been hung was almost gone. He'd had better nights.

He had a bronze Montagnard bracelet around his right wrist along with a watch on a wide green nylon band secured with Velcro and a flap covering the face so that the glowing hands couldn't be seen at night unless it was peeled back. The band was smudged and no matter of soaking or washing would get the bloodstain out, not that Kane had any desire to since it was a connection to his best friend, dead ten years.

"Still the funny man," Morticia said. "Not." Six feet tall, she sported a long black wig with a silver streak in it. She wore a tight black dress on her slim figure. It went to her ankles and when she walked, it appeared more of a glide. "The leg?"

"Healing," Kane said. "It hurts when I laugh."

"Then you're not suffering," she said.

Kane feigned mock outrage. "Hey, I tried."

"Yeah. Okay. A point." She put a folded meal ticket on the table. "From Thao, as usual. Don't you have a phone at home? Do you have a home? Or do you live in a cave?"

Without waiting for an answer, she moved on to serve a quartet of meat truck drivers entering for breakfast after their late shift delivering fresh cut to butchers in the outer boroughs. There were several ladies of the night at the end of their tour of duty eating at the counter. Thao, the cook and Montagnard who'd saved Kane's life in Vietnam, appeared out of the kitchen to top off their coffee and bring them the plates he'd just prepared.

The diner boasted new covers for the booths; red with white stripes. Kane couldn't quite recall what color the old ones had been, other than worn and torn. He didn't like the new ones; too stiff and too bright. Kane and co-owner Thao had drawn a line in the tile on one of Morticia's prime ambitions for the diner: renaming it. The faded signs facing Gansevoort and Washington, the southeast corner of which the diner was perched, would remain the same:

VIC'S DINER
GOOD FOOD!

There was a new jukebox, which didn't make sense to Kane since who wanted to listen to music in the morning? It was quiet at the moment, which proved his point. He'd drawn her attention to that several times before her glare made it a negative return on the effort.

Kane was seated in the rearmost booth, adjacent to the kitchen door. From this perch he could see the booths along this wall, the counter and through a window in the swinging door into the kitchen where Thao worked the stove. Most importantly he could survey both outer doors, one on either street.

Kane unfolded the ticket revealing a short message encrypted in two five letter blocks. Kane took the moleskin notepad out his shirt pocket. Opened it to the trigraph and ran the letters through it using the diner's sign as his and Thao's personal one-time pad.

TONIA TTENW INDOW SONTH EWORL DXXXX

Not exactly the biggest secret when and where to meet Toni and in need of encrypting. Kane sometimes wondered if Thao did it as training, since he had the trigraph memorized or to keep Kane fluent in his old Special Forces skills. He struck a match from the book next to the ashtray and burned the ticket, stirring the remnants to dust in the tray, part of his morning blocked in.

It was the only thing on his schedule other than his usual run over the Brooklyn Bridge to Gleason's gym to work out.

The Kid came in the Gansevoort door, smiling, but watchful. He was accompanied by a rare sound: a train horn from the elevated High Line, the end of which was caddy-corner from the diner. Traffic was down to a couple of times a week on the dying, elevated rail line that ran along the lower West Side of Manhattan.

"May the Force be with you," he said to Kane as he tossed the *New York Times* on the table and pocketed the five-dollar bill. He was eighteenish, wore jeans, construction boots, and a checked lumberjack shirt with no sleeves and open most of the front, exposing a skinny, hairless chest.

"Morning," Kane said. "Going to drizzle all day?"

"It's already clearing out," the Kid said. "The sun will come out eventually."

"No doubt. Seen Wile-E?"

"Nope." The Kid sought to explain. "Junkies ain't normal. You gotta understand they go down a hole and don't appear for a while."

"I do understand," Kane said.

The Kid frowned at that but didn't pursue.

"Certain you don't want the job?" Kane asked for the sixth time in the three and a half weeks since the initial offer. "Wile-E's been AWOL for a week. I think Thao was getting used to the help."

The Kid avoided Kane's eyes. "I'm still thinking on it."

"All right," Kane said. "It's yours whenever thinking comes to a conclusion."

"Yeah," the Kid said. "Hey, you got someone else doing it anyway."

"He's temporary," Kane said. "He's going into the Army in a bit. We could use more help."

"Okay," the Kid said, uncommitted. He beat a hasty retreat out the door he'd come in.

"Stop hassling him," Morticia said, seemingly always within hearing distance.

"It's not hassling someone to offer help," Kane protested. "And you were worried Wile-E and the Kid would cut into your tips. We don't have either."

"But we got your cousin, Riley. He's a good worker."

"Right," Kane said.

"This glamorous life isn't for everyone," Morticia said. Then she turned serious. "I am worried about Wile-E. I've asked around on the street. Nobody's seen him."

"I checked his old haunt on the West Side Highway last week," Kane said. "No sign." He was referring to the abandoned section of the West Side Highway just a block to the west, past the High Line. The main car artery on this side of Manhattan had been closed from the 23rd Street exit south after a truck fell through the northbound lanes in 1973. The proposed replacement for the highway, Westway, had partially been the cause of Kane's confrontation with Sean Damon, an Irish gangster/political fixer who had expected to control the contracts to the proposed one-point-five-billion-dollar project. Damon was no longer among the living after the events at the old Nabisco Factory, next to the High Line.

"Check up there again," Morticia said.

Kane raised an eyebrow. "Yes, ma'am."

"Please," she added.

"Right." Kane nodded good morning at Dave Riley, his younger cousin, as he hustled by with a plastic tub, and began clearing off a table.

"What did you mean when you told the Kid you understood about Wile-E?" Morticia asked.

"That's none of your business."

"You're awfully snippy this morning," Morticia pointed out.

"I had a tough evening last night," Kane understated.

"Partied too hard?"

Kane stared at her.

Morticia pivoted. "Since you didn't like my previous name suggestions how about the Chat-n-Chew?"

"It's the morning," Kane said. "You see many people chatting in here?"

"Some of 'em. Thao talks to the customers when he does the counter. I converse with you when I have to."

"You don't have to right now. Besides you're either chatting or chewing, not 'and'. It's impolite. Then it would be chat or chew and we want 'em chewing."

"Ha!" Morticia snorted and glided away. She angled to the Gansevoort door as a tall and wide black man in a tailored suit entered.

"Morning, Omar!" she called out, loud enough for Kane to hear. She gave Omar Strong a peck on the cheek as she went to the counter to get a cup and the pot and he headed directly for Kane.

Strong was a homicide detective formerly with Manhattan South but currently reassigned to the Omega Task Force pulled together to capture Son of Sam. A former Marine, he was broad and solidly built. As he slid into the booth across from Kane, he took up most of the space.

"Still master of all you survey?" Strong asked.

"Doubtful," Kane said. "There's dissension in the ranks."

Strong laughed. "She just wants to make the place classier."

"Like the neighborhood?" Kane leaned forward and lowered his voice. "What's her real name? You gotta know by now."

Strong batted the question back over the table. "What happened to you during the Blackout? The hands? Neck?"

Kane sighed.

Morticia slid up, putting a cup in front of the detective and pouring. "Can I get you breakfast, sweetie?" she asked him. "The usual?"

Strong shook his head. "Got to get out to the Island and work. My day to bring the donuts, so the car is loaded with them."

"You're joking, right?" Kane asked.

The look Strong gave him indicated he was not.

Morticia pouted for a moment, then returned to work as several customers entered.

"Anything on Wile-E?" Kane asked.

"I've got important things to deal with," Strong said. "Searching for a junkie isn't high on the priority list."

"He's a veteran. First Cav."

"You told me. There's lots of veterans out there on the street, in case you haven't noticed. But yeah, I put the word out at the precincts in lower Manhattan. Anyone sees him, they'll call me."

"Thanks."

Strong got to the real reason for his visit. "There was a fire on the top floor of a building in the old Nabisco Complex during the Blackout. The one closest to the waterfront. On Tenth Avenue."

"Nice segue," Kane said. "Lots of fires all over the city that night. Lucky anything's left standing."

"True," Strong acknowledged, "but FDNY finally got around to digging through. The fire had burned out on its own during the Blackout so it wasn't a priority. They discovered there were incendiary devices used as initiators. They also found teeth and bone fragments."

"Could be homeless," Kane said. "My uncle is on the job at the house on 138th in the South Bronx and says that happens all the time. Owners torch their place for the insurance. Don't know or don't care if someone's squatting."

"Except," Strong said, "no one's filed for insurance and the Fire Department hasn't figured out who the owner is beyond a holding company named Trinity Holdings. But I made a few calls and checked the plates on a fancy car parked in the loading bay of the building. Registered to Sean Damon. Who has, coincidentally, been missing since the Blackout. Along with his Unholy Trinity. What amazing coincidences, don't you think?"

"They're missing but has anyone been missing them?" Kane asked.

"This isn't the wild west, Kane. Vigilantism doesn't cut it."

"Are you accusing me of something?" Kane asked.

"What did they do to you?" Strong asked. "The hands. The wrists. The neck. The burn on your leg? All occurring on the night of the Blackout?"

"Morticia tell you that?"

"She told me the little she knows. That Thao and Wile-E and that Kid brought you back from outside the Nabisco Factory in bad shape. It doesn't take a rocket scientist to connect the dots."

"Why are you here?" Kane asked. "You just said you were busy with Son of Sam. He killed another woman Sunday. Wounded the guy pretty bad. Lost an eye, didn't he?" He tapped the *NY Times*. "I did read that in the paper. Plus, you got donuts to deliver."

"I know what Son of Sam did," Strong said. "This time we have some real witnesses."

"Good. But he's still out there."

"We're going to get him," Strong said. "There's some details we're untangling. Something will pop out of them." He glanced to make sure Morticia wasn't listening in and lowered his voice. "There was something else found in the wreckage. Something that elevates this to another level and *that's* why I'm here. To give you a heads up. There were weapons. M-16s. Over two hundred. For your information, and warning, the FBI has taken over, shutting the NYPD out."

"I assume the weapons are no longer functional since they were in the fire," Kane said. "You know the M-16. Made by the lowest bidder with plastic pieces and parts. In '67 we had the early version. Weren't they fun? I preferred the M-14. Better range, bigger round. You hit something with that it stayed down. And it worked when you needed it to."

Strong stared at him, waiting.

Kane leaned forward and spoke in a harsh whisper. "We've agreed on truth, not the law, and I'll go as far as I can with the truth on this. You can close the book on Damon and the Trinity. As a bonus, you can also close the book on the killings where the women's heads were burned and decapitated. You've seen those pictures on the board in the 109 Precinct, right? The multiple murders no one is investigating? I know they were just hookers, but they were people too. The man who did that won't ever be doing it again. Oh, yeah, you can also close out the Cibosky case. The guy who killed him is dead, too. That make you feel better?"

Strong leaned back in the booth. "Damn, Kane."

"Yeah."

Strong frowned. "I don't have Damon or his guys pegged as doing that to hookers."

"Wasn't them," Kane said. "Damon and his guys did other stuff. Worse."

"Then who was it?"

"Nobody who matters any more. And the M-16s were heading to Ireland. A lot of bad shit was terminated that night."

Strong began shaking his head.

"Do you feel any better?" Kane asked.

"No. It causes me great unease and puts me in a very awkward position."

"Nicely phrased," Kane said. "'Awkward'? You wanted truth. You got it, but not enough that you need to do anything. As I was recently told, let it go. And you wouldn't be in this position if you hadn't come in here this morning asking questions you shouldn't have wanted answers to. Why'd you ask?"

"I was hoping—" Strong began, but stopped.

"Hoping for what? That God sent an avenging angel down and smote Damon and his murderers?" Kane continued. "You think you understand but you have no clue how bad Damon and his guys were, Strong. Worse than your nightmares. They were pure evil. They killed a lot of people in terrible ways in that building."

Strong put his large, scarred knuckle hands flat on the tabletop. Remained still for several moments. "Told you when we first met that you were a shit storm, Kane. You're doubling down on that."

"I did that a long time ago," Kane said "We need a storm every once in a while, to clean things out. It's natural law." He stared into the detective's eyes. "You going to let the Nabisco fire go?"

"I wasn't in it to start with," Strong said. "Given the weapons, it's the FBI's province. But they don't have much to work with other than the serial numbers. Just thought I'd give you a friendly heads up. You're welcome."

"I appreciate it. I didn't torch the place. Damon didn't want to leave much behind if the place got compromised. He had thermals set around the outer wall."

"That what you call it? 'Compromised'?"

"He was doing very, *very* bad things in that place. And he had it rigged to burn so his cremation was self-inflicted."

"Was his death?"

"In a manner of speaking. And, truth, Omar, I swear I did not kill him."

"You're full of shit."

"You wanted truth. *That's* truth."

"And if Damon and his Trinity weren't doing those multiple hooker killings?" Strong asked. "Who was that? Who killed Damon? Who killed Cibosky?"

"No one of consequence. Someone whose own mother wouldn't miss him."

"How's your conscience?" Strong asked.

"My conscience has been crowded with worthwhile people for years," Kane said. "People who should be remembered. It's got no room for those worthless assholes."

Strong slid out of booth. Towered over Kane. "I have to catch a killer. The legal way. But let me tell you something, Kane. This won't turn out well if you continue down this path."

"Every path I see ahead of me goes the same way," Kane said.

"Where's that?"

"You know. Murphy's Law. What can go to shit, will."

"You need help, Kane." Strong pointed at his head. "Real help." He nodded at Morticia on the way out.

She made a beeline to Kane. "What did you say to him to piss him off?"

"I actually gave him good news," Kane said. "He'll understand that soon."

"You're a piece of work, Kane."

"Yeah, I know. And you don't mean it in a good way."

"Depends on the day of the week. Today. Nope."

WEST SIDE HIGHWAY, MANHATTAN

Upon leaving the diner, Kane delayed the workout and took a detour over to the West Side Highway, next to the closed northbound ramp on 19th. He walked around the barriers. The ramp merged with the road in the center, rather than on the side, a strange quirk that contributed to the highway's negative reputation. When he reached the elevated roadway, he turned south. He pulled the moleskin notebook out of the breast pocket and did a quick check for particulars.

Nature had taken root on the stretch of abandoned roadway with grass and bushes struggling to survive in the gutters on either side. A derelict wall of plywood bisected the abandoned roadway. Kane slid through. A section of the northbound side was gone.

Beyond was a makeshift camp for the homeless. Tarps, tents, even cardboard boxes to provide shade were scattered about.

"Hey, Mac." Kane greeted the same old man he'd met on his first trip here a month ago, when he'd initially tracked Wile-E down after the junkie had held up a pizza place on the West Side while Kane was waiting on a slice.

Kane had no idea if 'Mac' was a real name, but he'd heard someone else call him that and written it down in his notebook full of 'particulars'; this one on the page titled WILE-E. There wasn't much more on the page other than 1st Cav. The grizzled veteran sat in a rusting and tattered folding chair staring at a smoldering fire and a #10 can hanging over it from a tripod. He sported a dirty white beard and long hair and wore stained, rummaged clothing. He glanced up at Kane. "Hey, young fella." His voice was rough, gravelly. He held out his hand, palm up.

Kane gave him a fiver.

"Aint seen 'im since last time you checked," Mac said as he stuffed the bill into his pocket.

"I know a guy at the Soldiers and Sailors Home," Kane said. "I can get you a bed for a couple of nights. On the arm."

"I'd need cab fare," Mac said.

Kane peeled twenty from his money clip. "Tell the guy at the desk Will Kane sent you."

"Roger that." Mac didn't seem enthused.

"You going there?" Kane asked, scanning the area, just in case Mac was wrong, but that was doubtful since he seemed the linchpin to this community.

"Nope. Just wanted the extra money."

"Why not?"

"And leave all this?" Mac was incredulous.

"Hot shower. You can do laundry."

"I'd just get dirty again." He looked up from the can. "Why do you care about Wile-E? What's he to you? Were you in the same unit?"

"Same war," Kane said.

The old man harrumphed and spit, indicating what he, a World War II veteran, thought of Vietnam. "Lots of guys in the same war. Bunch of vets end up here. My war, Korea, Vietnam. We had a guy from the Great War, but he died a few months ago. Whatever the next one will be, they'll end up here. You gonna save them all?"

"Nope."

"Damn right."

"But I did just offer *you* some help," Kane pointed out.

"Yeah," Mac grudgingly admitted. "You know what happened to Wile-E?"

"What do you mean?"

"In the war? What happened to him?"

"No."

Mac spit again, this time close to Kane's boots. "But you're trying to help him?"

"Why do I have to know what happened to someone to give them a hand?" Kane asked. "He wants me to know, he'll tell me."

Mac looked up at him and his eyes were bright blue above the gray beard. "Were you actually in the shit?"

"Yeah."

"You tell people, civilians, what you saw?" Mac asked.

"They wouldn't understand."

Mac nodded. "But soldiers. Those of us who were in the fight. We do."

"What happened to him?" Kane asked.

Mac leaned forward and peered into the can. "Know why he's called Wile-E?"

"Second-hand," Kane said, having just read that info on the page in his notebook. "I was told it was because he chases the heroin."

"Ha! See? Think you're so smart. You don't know shit. Got nothing to do with that. That was what he was called in his unit."

Kane grabbed a milk crate and sat next to Mac, ignoring the odor. "Educate me, sir."

Mac shot him a piercing look, trying to ascertain if Kane was serious. "He had a partner. Coyote. They were close."

"What happened to this guy, Coyote?"

Mac looked at him as if he were an idiot. "You think they called some soldier, Coyote? You got shit for brains?"

"Okay, who or what was Coyote?"

"A dog. They were a team. Wile-E was Coyote's handler. Tracking dog. Part of some special unit. Went way out there in the boonies looking for the bad guys."

"Tough job," Kane said. "Dog teams like that were usually on point. Most dangerous place to be."

"Yeah," Mac said. "Wile-E says they were good and I got no reason not to believe the man. Said they were together over ten months. Hell, we stayed for the duration in my war. Stayed until we won the damn thing."

"Vietnam wasn't technically a war," Kane said. "Generals didn't know what they were doing. Nor the politicians. We just fought for each other."

"That's every war," Mac agreed. "But got to fight until only one side is standing. Otherwise, why are we fighting?"

"You've got a point," Kane allowed.

"Wile-E, he fought with Coyote. Said the dog saved his life a bunch-a-times. Saved guys in his unit. Coyote led them to a lot of the enemy. Wile-E says the damn dog even got a medal one time. Can you believe that? A dog getting a medal?"

"Did Wile-E get one?"

"He didn't say. That's why I believe him. Talks more about the damn dog than hisself. And I hear him sometimes. When he aint in his right mind. Talks as if the dog is there." Mac looked off, eyes a bit misty. "He says the dog got wounded. Shot, right in front of him after it had warned them of an ambush. Just a few feet away. But he couldn't get to it. And the fucking Japs, they let it lie there, whining, trying to draw Wile-E and his guys out. He had to listen to it die slow."

Kane didn't bother to correct the war's enemy.

"Saw the same once," Mac muttered. "'Cept is was a sergeant. Lay there screaming for help, but no one could get to him. He was an asshole, but still. Was tough listening to a man dying slow and not being able to help 'im. If he hadn' been an asshole someone probably woulda shot him out of his misery." Mac checked the can and it must have to be to his satisfaction as he used a piece of cloth to tip it and pour some coffee into a cup. Took a sip and sighed.

Kane waited for more, but it appeared the old man's train of thought had run out of steam.

"I appreciate you trusting me with that," Kane finally said.

"Huh?" Mac frowned. "Yeah. Losing that damn dog messed him up bad. Hell, I lost friends I don't miss as much as he misses that dog. But, you know, dogs are different, I guess." He pointed. "He's in his lean-to."

Kane glanced over at the corrugated metal leaning against the outer guard of the roadway on the southbound side. "You said he wasn't here."

"I lied."

"For the money?"

"Wasn't sure if you could be trusted," Mac said. "And the money. And he asked to be left alone for a while. But maybe you're for real." He turned back to his perpetual #10 can.

Kane walked to the lean-to and knelt at one end. The smell was terrible, similar to the first time he'd tracked Wile-E down a month ago. "Hey." He reached in and shook Wile-E's shoulder.

"Heard you been looking for me," the veteran muttered. "Heard you talking to Mac. Was trying to decide if I should crawl away, but I'm too damn tired."

"Morticia's been worried about you," Kane said. "You just disappeared on her."

Wile-E slithered out of the lean-to. He wore torn jeans and a t-shirt that had once been white but was tending toward the other end of the color spectrum. Wile-E blinked in the light; eyes not quite focused. "Morticia's been worried about me?"

"Yeah. She keeps asking me to check on you. She's been on the street looking."

Wile-E looked away, toward the Hudson River. "She shouldn't do that. The street's dangerous. Tell her not to worry."

"It's her thing," Kane said. "She's a worrier. You tell her. But you should probably get cleaned up first. I told Mac about Soldiers and Sailors. You two can go together."

Wile-E looked over at the old man. "He's a tough son-of-a-bitch. Always has the coffee warm for whoever wants it."

"You should get some," Kane said.

"It's terrible coffee."

"I used to chew the grounds from the C-rats while on recon," Kane said. "Got to be better than that."

Wile-E nodded. "Not by much."

"What years were you First Cav? They saw some shit, especially early in the war in the Ia Drang."

"That was before my time," Wile-E said. "'68. Helped the Marines at Khe Sanh. That's the only reason Mac talks to me, and he won't admit we broke the siege for them. Plus, his brain is a little fuzzy." Wile-E laughed. "Tough old guy." His face abruptly shifted. "Then we went into the A Shau. That was fucked."

"Mac told me about Coyote," Kane said. "Sorry."

"Ah, shit. He shouldn't have told you that."

"He didn't mean any harm."

"I know. I just, I don't know. I mean a fucking dog shouldn't mess someone up this much. We lost a lot of guys in the unit."

"It's different for everyone," Kane said. He held up his wrist, showing the watchband. "My best friend. Found his body along with most of the men in his company. Some of them, they'd tried to surrender, but you know how that went. It was bad." Kane forced himself to put his hand on Wile-E's shoulder. "Nothing wrong with feeling what you feel. But the smack doesn't help." He removed his hand.

Wile-E nodded. "I go on and off. Been cleaning up for a few days now. I shoulda stopped by the diner. I told you I'd do the job. I like to keep my word. A man's word gotta mean something."

Kane waited for more, but nothing was forthcoming. Finally, he said: "You know the drill. Tell the guy at Soldiers and Sailors my name. He's got rooms for both you and Mac." He started to leave, then paused. "I'm not hassling you, but your job is still open at the diner if you want it. Morticia and Thao miss you."

TOWER ONE, WORLD TRADE CENTER, MANHATTAN

"Bullet holes?" Toni asked.

"We don't get a swanky table?" Kane asked as he joined Antonia Marcelle, known to everyone except her mother and court documents as Toni. She was waiting at the bar in Windows on the World on the 107th Floor of Tower One of the World Trade Center. It was the northern tower, offset to the west from its companion. Kane was oblivious to the envious glares from other men as he sat next to her but he was very aware of his field of fire and possible exits.

"Do you own a suit jacket?" Toni asked. She had lustrous, thick black hair that curled and twisted its way to her shoulders in a seemingly random pattern. Combined with her olive tinted skin and long legs, she was a presence in whatever room she occupied, even here, high over New York City, with the spectacular ninety-mile view in all directions through the tall windows. She was several years older than Kane's thirty-two, the sister of his Beast roommate, Ranger Buddy, and best friend, who was interred in Section XXXIV in the Academy cemetery.

"Doubtful," Kane said. "I'm not sure what happened to the one I was issued as a cadet and I lost my Dress Blues."

"No jacket, no table."

"Don't they loan them?" Kane asked.

"Give me a break. You're sweating, Will. Did you go to the gym and run back here from Brooklyn?"

"I gotta work out," Kane says. "I go a little crazy if I don't."

"We wouldn't want you crazy, would we?"

Kane looked around. "Vic's has more ambiance."

"Don't you mean ambivalence?" Toni gave him a sideways look which terminated that avenue of dialogue. "Bullet holes? Did the party get out of hand?"

Kane reached into the map case hanging on his right hip and retrieved the bundle of money Crawford had pressed on him. He put it on the bar in front of her.

The bartender averted his eyes from the cash. "May I get you something to drink, sir?"

Toni had a tall flute in front of her. Kane checked his watch. "Coffee, black, glass of water with two ice cubes, please."

"Right away, sir." The bartender moved off.

"You didn't need to do that." Toni indicated her drink. "I'm a grown up."

"It's still morning."

Toni held up a long red fingernail at the end of a long finger. "Don't start with me. And wearing that—" she indicated the Velcro covered watch—"how can you do it? Don't you remember Ted every time you check the time?"

"That's why I wear it. If we don't remember the dead, remember their names—" Kane stopped. "Sorry."

Toni waved it off. "I know." She pointed at the money. "What's with the cash?"

"Crawford gave it to me to not call the cops."

"Did he pull a six shooter and go cowboy on you?" Toni asked.

Kane nodded to the south, where they could see to the horizon underneath the dark clouds. A line of rain was moving to the west "The city, before there was a United States, bought the island to quarantine smallpox victims."

Toni glanced at the magnificent view of New York Harbor. "What?"

"Liberty Island," Kane said. "It was originally part of a group of small islands among shallow oyster beds. The Indians used to harvest them. So did the early Dutch settlers. But landfills destroyed that. It was named Bledloe Island and—"

Toni cut him off. "You do that when you don't want to answer me. Go all Brother Benedict on me with city history."

"During World War One Germans infiltrators blew up an ammo depot on Black Tom Island on the Jersey side and damaged the Statue."

"Fascinating." Toni began tapping her fingernails on the bar as the bartender brought Kane his coffee and water with cubes.

"I know you're doing *that* to irritate me," Kane said, "but sometimes there is a method to my stories."

Toni stopped tapping.

"The bullet holes were not made by Crawford or the Actress or me." He dropped the two cubes in the coffee.

"'The Actress'?" Toni repeated. "She has a name. Truvey. That's her stage name."

"Truvey what?" Kane asked.

"Just Truvey. It's her shtick. She didn't tell you her name?"

"I'm sure she did," Kane said.

"And she didn't immediately add that it rhymed with groovy?"

"I have a vague memory of that." Kane tapped his shirt pocket where he kept a moleskin notebook. "I wrote it down."

Toni shook her head. "Seriously, Will. You are out to lunch sometimes. Who else was on the boat? Or were the bullet holes there when you signed for it? What happened last night?"

Kane quickly summarized events of the previous evening, ending with the light flicking from red to green.

The end brought a strong reaction from Toni. "What the fuck! What happened then?"

"Nothing," Kane said. "The blasting cap hadn't been inserted into the explosives or wired to the detonator. Crawford and Truvey's tryst interrupted the perpetrators."

"Stop talking like your Uncle Nathan, the detective," Toni said.

"You want me to talk like my Uncle Conner?"

"God forbid."

The bar tender approached with a couple of menus but was stopped cold by Toni's raised hand. He quickly retreated.

"Who were they?" Toni asked.

"No idea," Kane said. "Have you heard from Crawford?"

"Not a peep."

"He said he was sending his own people to deal with it which makes it sound like he has an idea who it was. He was acting weird. As if he were waiting on somebody. That's the extent of my knowledge. I started the evening feeling like I was some sort of pimp and ended it almost getting blown up. Oh yeah, the bomb was attached to a radio-controlled detonator. That's why the light changed. If the fuse had been hooked up, it would have gone off. Twenty pounds of military grade C-4. We'd have been splinters."

Toni ignored the pimp jab and started tapping again as she gazed out the window, eyes not quite focused. Kane recognized the look, restrained his irritation at the tapping, and took a sip of his cooling coffee.

After a long thirty seconds of nail drumming, Toni delivered her summation. "It doesn't add up."

"Nope."

She stopped the fingernails. "What are *your* problems with it?"

"Why a bomb?" Kane said. "Why not just shoot Crawford? They knock him out so they can blow him up? Seems overly complicated."

"Unless they wanted people to think it was an accident," Toni said.

"Maybe."

"You said the blast would have wiped out the boat, right?"

"Yeah."

"What about the wreckage? Would it sink? The remains get swept out to sea? Leave no trace?"

Kane had already thought about that. "I don't know. The tide *was* going out and it's not like NYPD sweeps the water. There are enough bodies in the East River that there are probably wise guys with cement shoes on the shoulders of earlier wise guys with cement shoes. I'll have to check."

"Or it could be blamed on an engine explosion," Toni said. "An accident."

"Maybe."

"There's another possibility," Toni said.

"What?"

"That you were the target," Toni said.

"Still overly complicated," Kane said. "And why would someone want to kill me?"

"Jesus, Will. Your Blackout night stunt?" She turned on her stool toward him. "What happened to Damon? He hasn't been seen since then. Along with his Trinity. Last I saw of you that day you were going to meet him and it didn't look like it was going to be a happy chat. In fact, you said I'd never see you again. But you called me the next day and said everything was fine, which is total bullshit given your neck and wrists. I've asked and you've stonewalled me. What really happened?"

"Best you not know."

"And Quinn?" Toni asked. "He's been gone since that night also."

"Sofia Delgado tell you that last one?" Kane asked.

Toni kept her focus on him. "What happened to them?"

"Omar Strong asked me the same this morning," Kane said. "Except the part about Quinn, but he doesn't have the same inside channel to the Cappucci family that you do. Is Sofia pining for her missing lover? Speaking of lovers, the two of you been cozying around in Studio 54 lately?"

"I'm being very patient here, Will," Toni said tersely. "Why was Strong asking you?"

"Seems some corpses were found on the top floor of one of buildings in the old Nabisco complex. Burned up in a fire the night of the Blackout. There were lots of fires that night."

"*What* did you do, Will?"

"You're the lawyer, Toni. You know better than to ask questions you don't already have the answer to or don't want answered." Kane paused. "But you know the answer, don't you?"

Toni let out a deep breath. "Sweet Jesus. All five?"

Kane nodded. "And all of Damon's films. Gone."

Toni blinked. "Just you? Or did Thao help?"

"Again. Don't ask questions like that." Kane took another sip of his luke-warm coffee. "Just the way I like it. Thao wasn't involved."

"How did Strong react?" Toni finally asked.

"I wasn't as explicit with him, but they discovered a shipment of weapons among the debris. Two hundred and forty M-16s. It's no longer NYPD's province. The FBI is taking lead but they're not going to learn much. Probably trace the serial numbers on the M-16s and find out what armory they were stolen from. Beyond that, what's there to pursue? The bad guys are dead.

"Strong said he didn't think there wasn't enough left of the bodies for an ID. But they'll eventually figure out that Damon owned that floor since his limo was in the loading bay in the basement. Strong seemed disinclined to want to learn more or pursue, but he was not pleased with me. I think that's the best course of action for everyone. I'm certainly done with it."

Toni swallowed and nodded. She looked at her drink for several moments before speaking. "Thank you, Will. And you're right. We shouldn't talk about it." Toni regrouped. "What are we going to do about last night?"

"I'll see if I can get a line on the detonator," Kane said. "Demo guys sometimes leave a signature and I know a really good one to ask. That's all I have. Maybe you can find out through your contacts whether anyone has shown up in an emergency room with a forty-five slug in the shoulder and a broken nose?"

"I'll do that." Toni grabbed his forearm, pulling him toward her. "Really, Will. Thank you." She got off her stool and hugged him.

"You are most certainly welcome," Kane said into her hair, smelling the same perfume that had been on her brother Ted's letter that first night in Beast Barracks in 1962. He let go and they both sat.

"Will the FBI be a problem for you?" she asked.

"I don't see why. Nothing links me to the place."

"Who knows you were there?"

"Thao," Kane said and then he realized Wile-E and the Kid. And Morticia. And Pope most likely. That was the problem with associating with people. But only Thao knew what had happened in the building.

"Who were the M-16s for?"

"The IRA."

"They'll want to know what happened to their guns," Toni pointed out. "And Damon. He was important to them."

"Again. Nothing links me to that place." Kane thought about the duffle bags full of cash and decided that wasn't a piece of information he needed to contribute.

"Still," Toni said, "you have potential enemies in the IRA even if they don't know about you. Before that, you had the CIA bugging your apartment. You haven't kept me up to speed on your life."

"Ditto," Kane said. "I did this gig as a favor to you."

"Let's not get into it," Toni said. "Please, come downstairs and see the offices," she begged him. "I'll show you the one for my head of research." She indicated the windows. "It's got an unbelievable view."

"I got shot at and almost blown up doing you a favor," Kane said. "Imagine the excitement I'll experience working full time."

"Oh, screw you. Your life would be dull without the excitement."

"How is your father taking you splitting from his firm?"

"We haven't spoken since I left."

"At all?

"No."

"In other words," Kane said, "he's not taking it well. And he's probably not happy about Damon disappearing. His Westway deal hinged on Damon. Are you out of that?"

"I was never in it," Toni said.

"Your father called you into that meeting with Damon," Kane reminded her.

"You don't believe me?" Toni shook her head. "Damon wanted me there at the start to make a point to my father and I. Once they got ready to talk Westway, I was dismissed."

Kane knew what that point was and it was best not to pursue. "Good."

Toni took a deep breath. "It's hard to believe Damon's really gone. He was—" she shook her head. "A demon hovering over our lives. A malevolent cloud."

"He was evil," Kane understated.

The moment was broken by the bartender daring to intrude. "Ms. Marcelle?" He had a phone in his hand. "It's your office." At her nod he plugged it into a jack underneath the bar and slid it across.

"How does Mrs. Ruiz know the exact moment?" Kane asked, referring to Toni's secretary.

"ESP," Toni said. She picked up the receiver. "Yes?" A slight pause and then: "We'll be down right away."

"'We'?" Kane asked as she hung up.

"Crawford's guy is here."

"'Guy'? He said he was sending his people, plural."

"Apparently he misspoke. Put it on my tab," she told the bartender.

Kane indicated the banded money.

"Take it," Toni said.

Kane put it back in the map case and followed her to the elevators.

"Now you'll finally make your visit," Toni said.

"Right."

"I really could use you."

"Stop hassling me," Kane said as they entered the elevator.

Toni shot him a look. "What?"

"Something someone told me to say when someone asks the same thing too many times."

"I'm offering you a good deal."

"That's what I said and was told it was hassling."

The elevator halted just a few floors below the restaurant and Toni led the way. "We're facing north."

"I like the south view," Kane said. "The harbor, the Statue, Ellis Island. Did you know—" He gave up when he saw she wasn't listening.

Toni opened a door and they entered a foyer that allowed an unobstructed view through to the windows facing north. Manhattan stretched into the distance, the Empire State Building centered right. Lower than where they stood. To the northeast was the Bronx, where Kane had grown up. Beyond it in the haze was Westchester. To the north the George Washington Bridge arced over the Hudson River. Northwest, the Palisades guarded the shoreline of New Jersey. And somewhere in that smudge on the horizon on the west side of the river, fifty miles north, was West Point, Kane's alma mater.

Toni halted and faced him. "You were saying?"

"Not bad," Kane admitted.

Mrs. Ruiz, a matronly woman who'd worked for Toni at their former firm, held court at a u-shaped desk centered in the foyer, chatting amiably with a man dressed in black boots, worn, faded jeans, an un-bloused brown shirt and sporting long, straight dark hair tied in a pony tail that extended to just below his collar. When he turned to face them, he revealed a narrow, sharp face and bronze skin. He was six-two, lean, and sparkled dark eyes. He had an old brown leather satchel in one hand. He wore a silver and blue turquoise necklace around this throat.

"My, my," Toni murmured as she missed half a step.

Mrs. Ruiz stood up, flustered. "Ms. Marcelle, this is Mister Yazzie." She was smiling, something Kane wasn't sure he'd ever seen Ruiz accomplish.

"Ma'am." Yazzie nodded and held out his hand.

Toni took it. "Welcome to New York, Mister Yazzie."

"A pleasure to meet you," Yazzie said. He turned. "Captain Kane."

Kane shook his hand. "I'm not in the Army anymore." He noted the bulge of a weapon on the man's right hip and something else on his left. There was a shade in those eyes that resonated with Kane, but not in a positive way.

"Our service stays with us," Yazzie said.

"Stays or sticks?" Kane asked.

"Shall we talk in my office?" Toni suggested.

Toni led the way followed by Yazzie and Kane. Toni indicated the square table with four chairs. Crawford's 'man' took the chair Kane would have, facing the door.

Kane paused at the only item mounted on the wall: a West Point saber inside a wood case backed with black velvet. The saber was drawn and resting on two small hooks, the scabbard just below it. Three medals—purple heart, bronze star and Vietnam service ribbon were pinned to the velvet under the blade along with a combat infantry badge. A metal scroll at the bottom:

THEODORE JOSEPH MARCELLE
CLASS OF 1966 USMA

Below it was a battered, black footlocker with MARCELLE, T.J. LIEUTENANT stenciled in faded white paint. Kane turned from the saber. "Ted would be proud," he said to Toni, indicating the office. "That you're making it on your own and away from your father."

Toni nodded, swallowed hard. "Thank you."

He indicated the footlocker. "Your dad gave you Ted's locker and his medals?"

"After I took the saber, he sent it over," Toni said.

Kane pulled out a seat and Toni sat. He claimed his own directly across from Yazzie, putting the map case on the floor.

Toni pulled on her professional mask. "What can we do for you, Mister Yazzie?"

"Just Yazzie, Ms. Marcelle," he said. "My people use one name."

"I go by Toni."

Yazzie nodded. "Toni, then." He turned to Kane.

"You can call me Captain."

"Don't be a dick, Will," Toni said.

"Kane works. My people use one name too. Unless there's two of us in a room at the same time, but that's a rare event and even then, we don't speak so it's never an issue."

Yazzie shrugged. "Kane." He shifted to Toni. "Boss Crawford wants me to follow up on the events of last night."

"'Boss'?" Kane asked.

"We all call him that on the ranch," Yazzie said.

"Subtle," Kane said.

Yazzie stared at him for a second too long before facing Toni.

"I just heard what happened," Toni said. "I'm not appreciative of the fact that Mister Crawford threatened my employee."

"I'm in the room," Kane said.

Yazzie didn't turn from Toni. "His hasty action was necessary, but he did compensate Mister Kane for the misunderstanding."

Toni smiled. "Yes, I know of the cash payment. Will didn't hide it from me. You underestimate."

"Did he just insult me?" Kane asked.

Yazzie shook his head. "I'm sorry we're getting off to a difficult start, Toni, but it's an uncomfortable situation."

"Three shots in my direction," Kane said. "It would have been a lot more uncomfortable if one of them had hit."

"But yours did?" Yazzie asked.

"See," Kane said, "your tone indicates that's a question. You're barking up the wrong tree, hombre. Didn't Crawford relay to you what I told him occurred while he was not particularly conscious and lying on top of a half-naked woman not his wife?"

"Boss's wife passed some years ago," Yazzie said.

Kane drew his forty-five and put it on the table. "I'll show mine if you show yours?"

Yazzie looked at Toni but she didn't indicate one way or the other. He pulled a Browning Hi-Power out of the holster on his right hip and put it on the table, muzzle facing away.

"Thought cowboys used revolvers," Kane said.

"I'm not a cowboy."

"My bad," Kane said. "Bow and arrow?"

"Your humor escapes me," Yazzie said. He indicated the .45. "Old school."

"Reliable," Kane said. "What kind of name is Yazzie?"

"One that has a long and honorable lineage."

"Will," Toni warned.

"What's on your left hip?" Kane asked. "Extra mag?"

Yazzie unclipped a device roughly five inches long by two wide by one deep. It was shiny metal and *MOTOROLA Pageboy II* was written on it.

"I've heard of those," Toni said. "Do you mind?"

"Go ahead," Yazzie said.

Toni examined it. "What kind of range does it have?"

"Far enough," Yazzie said. "Especially here in the city with retransmitters on tall buildings. On the ranch, we've built towers to cover it all."

"Excuse my ignorance," Kane said, "but what is it?"

"A pager," Toni said. "A way of getting hold of someone remotely. It what, beeps?" She asked Yazzie.

"Sounds a tone," Yazzie took it from her and clipped it on his belt. "A caller can also leave a short voice message."

"What good does that do?" Kane asked.

"If someone wants to get a hold of me or let me know something important," Yazzie said, "they page me."

"Sounds like you're on a short leash," Kane said.

"That's one way of looking at it," Yazzie said. "I prefer to view it as granting me freedom. I'm not tied to a phone or desk."

"I've been thinking of getting some for the office," Toni said.

"Count me out," Kane said. He indicated the gun. "I'm not thrilled about you coming to Toni's office armed."

Yazzie spread his hands in apology. "You're correct. I've appeared impolite, especially since you've graciously granted me this meeting on little notice." He nodded at Kane. "Can you please tell me what happened last night in your own words? I find it's best to get things first-hand. Especially since, as you note, Boss Crawford was not fully conscious for a key portion."

"Hold on." Toni interrupted "Before we make any statements, we're going to need a certified document from Mister Crawford regarding—" she paused as Yazzie reached into his satchel, retrieved a binder and removed a legal document and handed it to her.

Toni scanned it, then nodded. "Vague enough not to cause problems for Mister Crawford but specific enough to keep Will clear of anything from Crawford's end."

Yazzie held up a finger. "We cannot, of course, vouch for this Truvey woman's recollection of events with regard to your employee."

"Have you talked to her?" Toni asked.

"Yes," Yazzie said.

"Crawford pay her off, too?" Kane asked.

"Our business is our business," Yazzie said. "We're content about her on our end, but we can't vouch for her on your end."

"Forget about the paper," Kane said. "Is *Boss* Crawford going to stick with the facts?"

"He wants no part of this made public so there will be no facts to stick to."

"We're just supposed to take your word on that?" Kane said. "Honest Injun?"

"Boss is a trust-worthy man," Yazzie said, his voice tight.

"Because he cuts your paycheck?" Kane asked.

"Because he's my foster father," Yazzie said. "I've known him my entire life."

"You call your dad, boss?" Kane asked. "Does that cause psychological issues?"

Yazzie ignored the comment.

Kane continued. "*Boss* leveraged me into committing a crime by not reporting the shooting."

"Which makes him complicit," Yazzie said. "Correct, Toni?"

"Yes," Toni said.

"Was he more concerned about the cocaine?" Kane asked.

"There was no cocaine," Yazzie said.

"Right," Kane replied.

"Tell the story, please," Toni prompted Kane.

He quickly recounted what had happened. Yazzie didn't make any notes or ask a question until Kane was done.

"Where is the bomb?"

"I've got it," Kane said. "Gonna have an expert look at it. Try to get an idea where it might have come from."

Yazzie nodded. "Could you keep me apprised of that?"

"That's my business," Kane said.

Yazzie considered him for a few seconds. "I could reach into this pack and put twenty thousand in cash on the table. However, I fear you would take that as an insult, Kane. What would—"

Kane cut him off. "You didn't say please."

Yazzie smiled, revealing very white, even teeth. "My apologies. Could you *please* keep me apprised concerning what you learn about the bomb?"

"Surprised you didn't ask me to turn it over," Kane said.

"This is your land," Yazzie said, indicating the view out the window. "My resources are limited. Also, given your background, I believe you would have access to someone with excellent bomb expertise."

"What do you know of my background?" Kane asked.

"Enough," Yazzie responded.

"You didn't put the money on the table," Kane said.

Yazzie did so, four bundles identical to the one from the previous evening.

Toni spoke up. "Do you have suspicions about who did this? An enemy of Mister Crawford?"

"Boss has several enemies capable of nefarious deeds," Yazzie said. "My brothers are investigating them."

"'Brothers'?" Kane asked.

"Yes," Yazzie said, without explanation

"Then what are *you* investigating?" Kane asked.

"The event," Yazzie said. "Wherever that leads."

"Meaning?" Toni asked.

"That it's possible Boss wasn't the intended target," Yazzie said. "There were two other people on the boat. If one of them was the intended, then we no longer need be concerned about a reoccurrence."

"Will *you* keep *us* apprised of your progress?" Toni asked.

Yazzie nodded. "Of course." He took two of the four bundles off the table and put them in the satchel. "Who knew Boss Crawford was going to be on the boat?" he asked Toni.

"Me," Toni said.

"You didn't tell Mister Kane beforehand who the passengers were?" Yazzie asked.

"I *am* sitting here," Kane said. "No, she didn't. Just where the boat was to be picked up, what time to be there, and that I was to take some people out for a cruise around the Statue of Liberty and wherever else was desired."

"That's your job here?" Yazzie asked. "Boat driver?"

Toni interjected. "Mister Kane is head of research and security. He was doing me a favor."

"Who would want to kill Boss Crawford?" Kane asked. "It would help to get an idea."

Yazzie shook his head. "I'd hate to cast aspersions without proof. This incident is rather unexpected."

"For unexpected you got here pretty quickly," Kane pointed out. "And had legal paperwork drawn up. And already talked to Truvey."

"Boss Crawford owns several planes. I was on my way as soon as he called last night. As far as the paperwork, there are fax machines." Yazzie turned to Toni. "Who asked for and paid you to set up the excursion?"

Toni frowned. "Mister Crawford knows that since he agreed to the meeting. The producer Tom Selkis. He wanted to pitch his latest project."

"Why wasn't Selkis on the boat?" Yazzie asked.

"I provided what was requested," Toni said. "The boat and security. I wasn't privy to the details of what the meeting would entail."

"Speaking of details," Yazzie said, "did Selkis specifically request Mister Kane or just someone to pilot the boat and provide security?"

Kane joined Yazzie in staring at Toni who was startled for the first time. "Selkis requested Will by name."

"Why would he do that?" Yazzie asked.

"Selkis was a client at my old firm," Toni said. "He came with me after I left. Will has a very good reputation."

"Convenient," Yazzie said.

"Let me ask you something," Kane said to Yazzie. "Crawford knew my background. How did he get that information?"

"We called and checked with Selkis about security arrangements," Yazzie said. "He gave us your name. I ran a background check. Your military service wasn't hard to uncover given it made national news in 1969, although your actual records seem to have disappeared. My deeper sources weren't as forthcoming. You have storm clouds in your past, Kane." He shifted to Toni. "When did you last speak with your father, Ms. Marcelle?"

"Hold on," Toni said. "What does that have to do with anything?"

"Please, bear with me," Yazzie said.

"Not since I left the firm," Toni said. "Almost a month."

"Was the parting amicable?" Yazzie asked.

"Why are you asking?" Toni said.

"I'm trying to get the lay of the land," Yazzie said. "Your father didn't ask you to arrange the meeting?"

"I told you I haven't had any contact with my father since I left his firm. It was Selkis."

"This conforms with the information I have," Yazzie said. "The only reason you are not under suspicion for arranging this attack is that lack of contact between you and your father."

"What information do you have to even consider such an accusation?" Kane asked.

"I was at Marcelle, van Dyck, Feinstein and Marcelle earlier this morning," Yazzie said.

"Did you talk to my father?" Toni asked.

"He wasn't there." Yazzie was focused on Toni. "Is there any reason your father would want to kill Kane?"

"You're forgetting the Captain or the Mister," Kane said, trying to give Toni some time to regroup.

"Are you implying he was the target?" Toni asked.

"The attackers knew where the boat would be. The only person, other than you, aware of who would be on board was Mister Selkis and he requested Kane by name. Selkis told this Truvey woman where to direct the boat. Selkis wasn't aboard the boat on which a bomb was planted. Rather convenient for him."

"You'd have to ask Selkis," Toni said.

"I did."

"You've been busy," Kane said.

"Selkis switched over to your firm, Toni, as a client at the specific request of your father three weeks ago, so this was not a matter of loyalty. At least not to you. It seems your father wanted to keep an eye on you. Selkis set up the meeting on the boat at the behest of your father. Your father told Selkis to ask for Kane by name. Your father told Selkis where the boat should go. Since there is no connection between my father and your father, that means that Kane was the target of the attack. Boss Crawford is not pleased that he almost became collateral damage in some sort of familial spat."

As Yazzie spoke, Kane looked out the window, watching an airplane curving over the Bronx to land at LaGuardia. He hoped his father was home watching TV and the descending jet drowned out the sound as one did every ninety seconds, but he knew, given it was a weekday, that his father was at work. He heard Yazzie's words distantly, not wanting to accept them.

Toni had put up a hand at the end of the second sentence and kept it up. "Wait. Wait. Why would my father do that?"

"That's what we'd like to know," Yazzie said, looking back and forth between her and Kane.

"This is bullshit," Toni snapped.

"You don't seem too surprised," Yazzie said to Kane who had turned back from the windows.

"My life is full of surprises," Kane said. "Takes a lot."

"Someone trying to kill you isn't a lot?" Yazzie asked.

"People have tried to kill me before," Kane said. "And I'm not buying your story. Makes no sense to go through all this just to get to me. Lots of easier ways. Selkis brought Crawford in from out of town to set me up? I live here."

"Deniability," Yazzie said. "Putting distance between the instigator and the act. Cloud the issue as to who the real target was. Use *my* father as a distraction as he has a much higher profile than you."

"Did you just insult me again?" Kane asked.

"I don't know what's going on here or between both of you and Mister Thomas Marcelle, but I can assure you that Boss Crawford is very, very irritated, to understate it, that he was involved." Yazzie stood, slinging the satchel over a shoulder and towering over both of them. "I'll take my leave."

"Sounds good," Kane said, also getting up.

Toni protested. "No! Wait. We need to—"

"Not right now, Toni," Kane said. "I'll walk you out," he said to Yazzie.

They left Toni behind with the cash on the table and shocked anger.

Mrs. Ruiz managed to smile at Yazzie and frown at Kane at the same time, which was an impressive contortion.

The two men walked to the elevator in silence. Took the local to the 78th Floor Skylobby. Rode it, then transferred to the one to ground level. They were the only occupants.

Kane broke the silence. "Who on *your* end knew that Crawford would be on the boat?"

"Me," Yazzie said.

The elevator dropped.

"That's it?"

"My brothers," Yazzie said. "There was no breach on our end."

"How many brothers you got?" Kane asked.

"Six."

"They also sons to Boss?"

"Yes."

"All adopted?"

Yazzie didn't answer. "It appears we received as much information as you, Kane. Be at that pier at a certain time. That was it. Boss was surprised when Mister Selkis didn't show and Miss Truvey did. But he assumed it was a rather obvious and crude attempt to sweeten the offer."

"He went below deck with her," Kane noted. "Seemed the crudeness appealed to him."

Yazzie stared straight ahead, face impassive.

"And there was the cocaine."

"That's a lie," Yazzie said, the first flash of anger.

"Why would I lie about that?"

"If there was, it came from Truvey."

Kane shrugged. "Right."

"Or perhaps you supplied it."

"Wrong."

The elevator reached ground level. The doors opened. They stepped into the lobby.

Kane spoke. "I figured Crawford would send the Marlboro man or someone like that. Why did he adopt you and your brothers?"

"That's none of your business."

"This still doesn't add up," Kane said.

Yazzie glanced at him, but didn't say anything.

"What will you do if I was the target of the bomb?" Kane asked.

"Boss doesn't take well to being attacked, whether intended or not," Yazzie said. "There must be a reckoning."

"That sounds ominous," Kane said. "If I was the target, you'd want to weigh in?"

"We'd like to be kept up to speed."

"Sounds vague," Kane said. "How come you or your brothers weren't providing security for Crawford?"

"I told you. We checked you out. You seemed adequate to the task and, as I noted, this is your stomping ground."

"Where were you?"

"I was otherwise occupied."

"What was more important than his safety?"

"I don't answer to you," Yazzie said.

"Did you confront Thomas Marcelle with your accusation?"

"I told you. He wasn't at the firm this morning when I went there." Yazzie faced Kane. "Who wants to kill you? Besides Mister Marcelle, obviously."

"I'm a friend to all mankind," Kane said.

"You've got scars on your wrists and neck. Recent ones."

"Got hurt remodeling my diner. Vic's in the meatpacking district across from the end of the High Line. You should stop by sometime. Good food. Even the sign says that."

Without another word, Yazzie walked away across the spacious and bright lobby and out of the World Trade Center.

Kane got back on the elevator and zoomed skyward.

Toni was in her office, behind the desk. An almost empty drink in one hand, the phone in the other. She slammed the receiver down as Kane entered.

"Father's disappeared. He's not at work. Mother says he never came home last night."

Kane went to the bar. "What are you having?"

"Fuck!" Toni threw the glass across the room. It bounced off the wall rather than shatter.

"Should I just bring the bottle?" Kane asked.

"He tried to kill you."

"He never liked me much," Kane said.

"There's nothing humorous about this at all," Toni said. "Not a fucking thing."

"Technically he tried to have me killed," Kane said. "But, yeah, the essence is the same." He left the bar and perched on the corner of her desk. "With such a great view, you should face the windows. I know you want to impress visitors, but you're in here more than they are."

"What do I do?" Toni asked. "Mother's losing her mind. He didn't say anything to her. No note. No message. No one at the firm knows anything. He's vanished."

"He didn't consider the possibility of his plan failing and is scrambling."

"What was the plan exactly? Why would he do this?" Toni demanded.

"To cut him some slack and I don't want to," Kane said, "the reality is that he pointed the people who wanted to kill me in the right direction. When I left his office the afternoon before the Blackout, he figured Damon and his Trinity would make short work of me. He must have been surprised it didn't turn out that way. When he didn't hear from Damon after the Blackout and learned I was alive, he had to assume the worst."

"Which was?"

"That Damon was gone, which meant divvying up Westway was screwed. Worse, in the more immediate sense, the IRA's connection with NORAID, the Irish Northern Aid Committee, for guns was gone. Along with a shipment of two-hundred-and-forty M-16s. And several million in cash."

"My father wasn't involved in that," Toni said. "You didn't say anything about several million to me or Yazzie."

"A man has to have a few secrets," Kane said.

"Stop that."

"One thing I learned when we were conducting cross-border ops was that a sense of humor gets more essential the grimmer it gets. We lost two teams before we realized Ngo was a double-agent. We didn't laugh about that."

"Father wasn't involved with the IRA," Toni insisted.

"Are you certain?" Kane asked. "Do you know what he was doing with Westway?"

"Not the particulars," Toni said. "When you found those maps on the back side of the boards, you had more than me."

"You never saw them?"

"Just a glimpse of the Westway plan."

"Who else would be pissed about Westway?" Kane asked. "The mob because Damon wouldn't be able to parcel out the contracts? Your friend Sofia Cappucci?"

Toni considered it, then shook her head. "No. Westway is years off. It's not a lock to happen and it depends on the election, which is up the air now. There's some buzz about Ed Koch, but it's still tight between Cuomo and Azbug. She wins, it's dead. Even if Cuomo wins and it's a go, by then someone will have replaced Damon to divvy out the contracts." Something occurred to her. "Unless Sofia knows about Quinn." As soon as she said it, she reconsidered. "No. She didn't care about Quinn except as a tool. She's all business."

"As you were with her?" Kane asked and immediately regretted.

Toni ignored the barb. "You said several million in cash. Whose?"

"I assume it was NORAID's," Kane said.

"They'll be wondering where the money went," Toni said.

"Your father was Damon's lawyer," Kane said. "He's the first person NORAID would come to when Damon disappeared along with their money and the guns. Once your father realized things had turned out differently then he'd hoped the night of the Blackout, he told NORAID I took out Damon. Then your father sent Selkis as your client to play you to get to me." Kane shook his head. "Your father is the key person who also knew I was meeting Damon the night of the Blackout. Before he died, Damon said he had insurance, that someone knew he was taking me there. Quinn thought he was full of shit."

"Slow down," Toni said. "Slow down."

"Your father must have been his insurance. Which meant your father knew that Damon was planning on killing me."

"No," Toni weakly protested.

"Your father gave me up to the Irish," Kane repeated. "It wasn't a hard decision for him since they probably couched it in terms of him or me. There's a likelihood it never got to the threaten stage."

"But—" Toni began. "The Blackout was three and a half weeks ago. What took so long?"

"People knew Damon was gone not long after the Blackout. The weapons didn't get to Ireland and the money was gone. That was definitely a blip on NORAID's radar. The IRA too when their guns didn't get delivered. So people start checking. Once they learned Damon was missing they went to your father. He gave me up, and it didn't take them very long to put together a plan and come after me. More likely, it's locals, probably guys from NORAID, doing the IRA's dirty work state side."

Toni was trying to catch up. "Why do it this way?"

"It sorta makes sense now," Kane said. "I'm sure Crawford has lots of enemies. Hell, Toni, even I didn't believe I was the target. No one else would think I was the intended since my connection to the NORAID angle died with Damon. Your father must have gone through his rolodex, looking for someone who would divert suspicion. He talked to Selkis, who told him about Crawford. It also means your father probably knew Damon was running guns for them. I hope he didn't—" Kane stopped.

"Hope what?" Toni was struggling to understand.

"Nothing," Kane said. "But I will say this: Yazzie is lying about something."

"About what?"

"I don't know," Kane admitted. "But something doesn't ring true."

"Is that why you kept baiting him with the Indian stuff? That's not who you are."

"When you take a deposition, don't you try to get the witness off balance? I poked Yazzie to get a reaction."

Toni stomped to the bar and poured herself another drink. "God-damn him. God-damn him."

"Yazzie?"

She gave Kane a withering look that wasn't intended for him, but he was in the blast radius. "My father. First, selling out to Damon when he was in the US Attorney's office. I finally wrapped my brain around that years ago. Managed to file off all the rough edges and put it in a box in my brain and seal it. But this?" She slammed back the drink and poured another. "Betrayal. He betrayed you. He betrayed me."

"It was him or me," Kane said. "He made the choice most would."

"Are you defending him?"

Kane went to the meeting table and sat down. He indicated for Toni to join him.

"No, I'm not. He gave in to Damon's blackmail and allowed that evil to exist."

Toni gave him a sharp glance. "What do you mean?"

"I watched one or two of Damon's films."

"Did you see—"

"I saw the case but I didn't watch it," Kane said, knowing she was referring to her own film. "The way it was set up, that place was a kill house. Damon called it a factory. They tortured and murdered people and then cremated the bodies in the ovens that used to make Oreo cookies." He sighed. "Your father hated me long before all this. Ever since Ted. He blamed me for it. He thought it should have been me."

"We've been over that," Toni said.

"You and I have. Your father has his own version, doesn't he?"

"He blamed both of us," Toni said. "Me for West Point. And for the company swap that happened when you both arrived at the 173rd. And you, because you were the one who was switched with Ted. He always felt you should have been killed at Dak To."

"I almost was, just five months later." Kane held up his right arm and peeled back the Velcro cover on the military issue watch that had once graced Ted's wrist. "This, and his dog tag, are all I have of Ted."

"Memories," Toni said. "We have our memories."

They both looked at the saber, the current storm forgotten in the sea of misery of the past.

Toni swam out of it first. "What do we do?"

"The immediate threat is the Irish. I'm going to check on the bomb and some other things."

"What should I do?" Toni asked.

"Try to find your dad. And talk to Selkis. Find out what Yazzie already knows."

"What about Crawford?"

"I'll check on him," Kane said. He took the two bundles of cash. "I might need this."

Friday Afternoon, 5 August 1977

GREENWICH VILLAGE, MANHATTAN

The battered pickup truck with Massachusetts plates had two tires on the sidewalk in front of the row of brownstones on Jane Street, blatantly ignoring the graffitied alternate side of the street parking signs indicating Friday was the day for Jane Street in Greenwich Village to be car free. A parking ticket was under one of the wipers. Kane pulled it off and stuck it in his pocket. Crime might be rampant in New York, but violating alternate parking was sacrosanct because eventually on some Friday, a street sweeper might actually come through and do what it was designed to.

One day, but not this day or any recent day given the amount of debris lining the curbs and sewer grates. The Sanitation Department, like the rest of the city, was still trying to catch up to the detritus of the Blackout. Kane imagined his father was logging plenty of overtime.

Trees grew on both sides of the cobblestone street, branches arcing over and meeting, giving welcome shade when the sun was out. Kane opened the gate to the steps leading to a small alcove in front of his basement apartment in the three-story brownstone.

The door was open, the matchstick he stuck in the doorjamb as a tell, on the small table inside.

"Making yourself at home?" Kane called out as he entered.

Master Sergeant Lewis Merrick reclined on the old couch, jungle boots propped on the coffee table, the bomb from the previous evening next to him and the detonating device in his lap. He wore OD green jungle fatigues, a faded and crumpled green beret stuffed in the cargo pocket. There was no insignia or patches on his uniform. An HK-94 submachinegun was on the couch next to his right hand.

"Want some coffee?" Kane asked.

Merrick indicated a mug. "Already made some."

"Why sterile?" Kane asked, referring to the lack of insignia or patches on the fatigues.

"We're supposed to wear Class-A's if we're in uniform off post and I only do that for payday inspection."

"You can wear civvies," Kane suggested as he sat in the drooping chair on the other side of the coffee table.

"You called a Prairie Fire." Merrick referred to the code word the team used for emergency exfiltration in Vietnam. "I came ready for whatever. Besides, lots of hippies wear old army stuff."

"I appreciate it." Kane didn't add that the grizzled master sergeant would never be mistaken for a hippy. Six-four, solidly built, his thinning red hair had a tint of gray. His face was lined with the stress of having gone to war at seventeen in Korea and then multiple tours in Vietnam

Merrick held up the C-4. "Military grade."

"You told me a guy in Third Battalion was nailed selling some in Boston," Kane said, referring to Merrick's unit, 10th Special Forces Group headquartered at Fort Devens, Massachusetts. "Could that be from the lot?"

Merrick tossed the explosives aside on the couch. "Possible."

"Who did he sell to?"

Merrick shrugged. "I'll ask around."

"You pick up anything about M-16s being stolen? Two hundred and forty?"

Merrick shook his head. "Nope. If I was going to steal some, I'd hit a National Guard armory. And there's a good chance whoever is in charge would want to cover it up for a while. Losing weapons is a career ender. Why? Did you find them?"

"I saw them. They're no longer functional. Tell me about the detonator?"

Merrick displayed the device. "Not bad. Radio controlled is interesting. Gives more operational flexibility than setting a timer. But it also requires the person initiating to be within FM range which means line of sight. And there's the off chance someone else transmits on the same freq before you're ready. That would cause an oops. That's why it wasn't hooked up before emplacement. You caught whoever made it just before they did that."

"Any idea who?"

Merrick shrugged. "I've played with radio detonation, along with some other demo guys on the teams, but they don't teach it at the Q-Course for the reasons I just mentioned. Too uncertain."

"Who does use radio detonation?" Kane asked.

"Either someone really stupid or really smart," Merrick said.

"That narrows it down to both ends of the bell curve."

"The Soviets on the smart end. They like to teach dangerous things to foreigners who come to their terrorist training camps and then go home and use it. Field-testing concepts via others as experimental dummies. Ditto for the Libyans who have their own camps cadred by people who were trained by the damn Russkies. And hadn't blown themselves up. Yet. The Jordanians run some camps."

"Who do the Libyans and Jordanians teach?"

"The Jordanians train Red Army Faction. Those people killed a banker in Germany last week. But they aren't into bombs. Or operating here in the U.S. The Libyans? They trained those Nation of Islam guys. Remember, those yahoos who took over those buildings in DC earlier this year? Again, though, not into bombing. Yet. They also train the IRA. They do like bombs, but haven't used radio detonated. That we know of, since the Brits keep intel close to the vest."

"Fuck," Kane muttered.

"You been to Ireland lately?" Merrick asked. "What do your folks call it? The Old Country?"

Kane leaned back in the chair. "Who else?"

"The Agency dabbles in it," Merrick said. "Which reminds me. Anything further from our friends at the CIA?"

"Not yet."

"What do you mean 'yet'?"

"I kinda told Trent I'd get back to him on something so I don't think they'd want to kill me."

"'Kinda'?"

"He bugged this place. And my landlord. I asked him not to any more. I didn't think he was going to take no for an answer."

"He's never going to stop."

"I know."

"I was thinking about it while driving down," Merrick said. "You and I know some shit that should never become public. Maybe someone was trying to permanently silence you?"

"Lots easier ways to do it than blow three people up."

"What couldn't you tell me on the phone?" Merrick indicated Kane's various wounds. "I'm willing to bet there's a connection. Debriefing time."

Kane quickly updated his former teammate on the events on the night of the Blackout, 13 July. It was like old times, a mission debriefing after being exfiltrated and back at the hooch in the A-Team basecamp in Vietnam, surrounded by sandbags and plywood and rebar and Marston mat. Succinct, just the facts. No interruptions.

When Kane finished, Merrick shook his head. "You were in a fucking war." Coming from one of a handful of soldiers who had a star on their combat infantry badge, indicating two wars— Korea and Vietnam-- that was saying a lot.

"But it's over."

"Apparently not." Merrick indicated the bomb.

"I doubt I was the target," Kane said, playing devil's advocate to see how Merrick would respond.

Merrick gave him a disbelieving look.

"No one is going to miss any of those people in the fire," Kane argued.

"Bullshit," Merrick said. "How much do you think was in those two duffle bags?"

Kane shrugged. "At least a couple million."

"And you just left it there to burn?"

"I wasn't thinking too straight after being drugged, burned and hung."

"Fucking pussy. Always letting the details distract you. Whose money was it? NORAID?"

"I assume so."

"They're not going to be happy. Nor the IRA about the M-16s."

"Fuck 'em," Kane said.

"You said Damon talked about some sort of insurance just before Quinn killed him," Merrick said. "What if he actually did have it? This Quinn guy was after his IRA info."

Kane shook his head. "Damon wouldn't have given up the location of that place to anyone other than his Trinity. He had to keep that close. Anything you can find out about who uses radio-controlled bombs and where the C-4 came from would be helpful."

"Will?" Merrick said, in a tone to get his attention. "The IRA? You took out their money to weapons connection. And the money. And the weapons. About the only thing you didn't do was piss on 'em."

"Let's not talk about getting pissed on."

"Oh yeah," Merrick said. "I kinda forgot that. That was a bad day."

"And technically, Quinn killed Damon."

"You're the only one who is aware of that. How many people know what happened?"

"You."

"Who else?" Merrick pressed.

"Thao."

"Who else?"

"Some people have an idea but nothing for certain," Kane said.

Merrick waited him out.

"I told Toni this morning," Kane admitted. "Sort of. A cop named Strong figured it out and said something. But he wouldn't tell anyone else. I trust him. Marine vet, Walking Dead. As I said, Damon didn't have friends. Nor Quinn. Except--"

"Who?"

"Sofia Cappucci," Kane said. "But she couldn't have known Quinn was at the factory or who he really was, given his cover. She just knows he's gone. And Toni says she isn't that upset about Damon being out of the picture or Quinn. I think Sofia gets over the men in her life pretty easily. She's not mourning her recently departed husband, that's for certain."

"Geez, you've got enemies in every direction. What do you think Damon's insurance was?"

"Told you, that was bullshit."

"What if it wasn't?" Merrick said. "Did you hear any of the names that he gave up to Quinn?"

Kane shook his head. "No. My ears were still ringing from the explosions. Woozy from the knock out drug on the dart. And I was too far away. And hanging. As you said: Always pre-occupied with the small shit."

"So those connections are still there," Merrick pointed out. "You're holding something back," Merrick added, having worked with Kane in life or death situations on multiple missions.

Kane sighed. "Crawford's man told us he believes Toni's father set me up with NORAID. Marcelle knew I was meeting Damon that night because I told him to arrange it."

"This is a clusterfuck," Merrick summarized.

Kane was still trying to untangle the knot. "It's a bit sophisticated and dangerous for NORAID to mount something like this. And if they were after me, why not just a bullet in the head on the street?"

Merrick held us his hands in surrender. "I got no clue. What about the IRA? Maybe they sent some people over?"

"It's possible." Kane saw his former teammate's eyes shift and he pulled the forty-five and spun about as the door slammed open. Merrick snatched the HK-sub, tucking the stock tight into his shoulder, finger on the trigger.

"Freeze!" someone yelled from the doorway. "Drop your weapons."

"Fuck you," Merrick responded. "Drop yours."

Two men crowded shoulder to shoulder in the doorway, revolvers at the ready. One was a tall, gangly black man and the other a short, stocky white guy with a pock-marked face.

Kane sidled right, eyes and muzzle on target, making sure he was out of Merrick's line of fire. "Who are you?"

"FBI," the white guy shouted. "Drop your weapons."

"I didn't hear a knock," Kane said. "Nor do I see a badge. You're outgunned. *You* drop your guns. You aren't dressed like Feds," he added.

The two exchanged a glance. They wore jeans, t-shirts, and unbuttoned denim jackets. The black guy sported an over-sized afro and the white guy had long, stringy hair, both trying too hard to look like anything but law enforcement which meant they probably were what they claimed.

Merrick didn't go for small talk when guns were drawn. He strode forward into their indecisiveness, submachinegun at the ready. Both men aimed at him, but he ignored their weapons. He went to the short white guy and pressed his forehead against the muzzle of the revolver while putting the tip of the HK under the man's chin.

"Wanna play?" Merrick asked. "Ever wonder if that firing on reflex when shot in the head thing works? I have. Wanna find out? I'm kinda curious."

"Back off," the agent said, with little conviction. He looked into Merrick's eyes and what he saw shook him. He lowered his weapon. "Take it easy."

His partner surprised everyone by pointing his revolver at his own head. "'Hold it! Next man makes a move, the nigger gets it!'"

Merrick burst out laughing and secured the HK. "Good one."

Kane was lost on the movie reference, which wasn't unusual for him.

The black guy holstered his gun and retrieved a thin leather wallet from inside his jacket. He flipped it open. "FBI. Agent Tucker and this is my partner, Agent Shaw."

Kane slid the forty-five into the holster.

While the two Feebs were gathering themselves from the unexpected confrontation, Merrick went to the couch and flipped a cushion over the detonator and C-4. The move, however, did not go unnoticed.

"We need to see that," Shaw said, pointing at the couch.

"See what?" Merrick asked.

"You got a warrant?" Kane asked as he moved between them and the couch.

"Are you William Kane?" Tucker asked.

"Do you have a warrant?" Kane repeated.

"We want you—" Tucker began, but Kane moved forward, indicating the door.

"You're on private property," Kane said, "and if you don't have a warrant, you need to step outside or I'll consider this breaking and entering."

"We were going to knock," Tucker said, "then saw the weapon and the explosives. You can't blame us for being a bit anxious. And that," he indicated the couch, "is probable cause."

"You just opened my door?" Kane had his arms spread, crowding them back, over the threshold. "Lucky we didn't shoot you."

"We had probable cause," Shaw echoed, but he was backing up.

"You're Kane," Tucker said, a statement, not a question. "We need to bring you in for a chat."

"I need to call my lawyer," Kane said, "and find out exactly what the term 'bring you in' means legally."

"Do you want my partner to sit on this address while I get a warrant?" Tucker asked. "And we tear the place apart? Put this, and you, into the system? NYPD queried you on our criminal database not long ago."

"What do you want to talk about?" Kane asked.

"We can discuss it at headquarters," Tucker said. "Do you need more shit in your life, Kane?"

"He's got a point, Will," Merrick said. "The *Blazing Saddles* bit was good, Tucker. I liked it."

Tucker leaned close to Kane, whispering so only he could hear. "How about murder, arson, and theft of government property? Given recent events, some people will be very interested in that last crime. We can do it easy and informal or messy and formal. Your call."

CIVIC CENTER, MANHATTAN

"Did you know this entire area used to be a big pond?" Kane asked as Shaw turned the unmarked Plymouth Fury onto Lafayette off of Canal Street. The Jacob Javits Building housing the New York City field office of the FBI was only two blocks from Toni's old law firm, run by her father on Broadway. Or formerly run by, depending on his current whereabouts and status. They were in the midst of the criminal justice center of Manhattan with various city, county, state and federal buildings all around.

"That so?" Tucker said from the front passenger seat.

"It was called Collect Pond," Kane said, "but was filled in after it got polluted and contributed to outbreaks of cholera and typhus. Then this became the Five Points neighborhood. Lots of gangs."

"Really?" Tucker turned to look over his shoulder. "Irish gangs, right?"

"All sorts of immigrants, not just Irish," Kane said. "As a matter of fact, up until 1792, the area just south of here was the burial ground for free blacks and African slaves."

"No mixing of the bodies back then? Even in death?" Tucker asked.

"Trinity Church passed an ordinance just before the turn of the 17th century prohibiting blacks from being buried in church graveyards," Kane said.

"Christian of them, wasn't it?" Tucker said.

"Actually," Kane said, "now that I think about it, I believe the ordinance prohibited blacks from being buried *anywhere* inside the city limits. This was north of Wall Street, which was the city boundary at the time. I doubt they exhumed all the bodies when they leveled the area so there's probably remains all around us." Kane was on a roll. "New York had the second highest number of Africans after Charleston at the time of the Revolution. Most were slaves."

They turned right on Duane Street and then an abrupt right on a drive that descended into the underground garage of the Federal Building.

"You're full of useless bullshit, aren't you?" Shaw asked as he rolled down his window and flashed his ID at a uniformed guard. A barrier was opened and they entered.

"Depends on your perspective," Kane said. He was in the back, having agreed to accompany Tucker and Shaw and saying his farewell to Merrick, who was headed back to Fort Devens with the detonator. He'd also managed to quickly ask his former teammate for a favor having nothing to do with the current situation using the Army's powerful NCO network.

The forty-five was in its holster and he wasn't cuffed so he viewed those as positive indicators that Tucker's threat had been only that: an inducement to get him here.

This was against Kane's better judgment, but too much was going on to take a chance on a search warrant. The fact they only wanted to talk meant the FBI was as clueless as Kane suspected.

Weak fluorescent lighting maintained a dismal glow in the garage as Shaw drove to the far end and parked among the other drab federal unmarked cars marked by their blackwalls and radio antennas.

"Come on." Shaw killed the engine and exited the car.

Kane got out and followed Shaw, noting that Tucker slid in behind him. Shaw opened a metal door and revealed a bleak grey corridor lined with similar doors. They walked in silence until Shaw stopped at one. He used a large key to unlock it.

"After you," he said to Kane.

The room held several filing cabinets, two desks with chairs, a single chair in front of them and little else. Grey government issue furniture. The charred remains of an M-16 was on one desk, the plastic stock and grip melted away, leaving the blackened receiver group and barrel.

"No windows?" Kane asked. "You guys don't rate a view?"

"Views are distracting," Tucker said.

"We like to stay focused," Shaw said as he sat behind the desk that held several file folders, while Tucker took the one with the weapon.

Tucker indicated the chair in front. "Sit."

Kane adjusted the seat so it was facing between the two agents.

"Sean Damon," Tucker said.

Kane didn't respond.

"Do you know him?" Tucker asked.

"No."

"You're full of shit," Shaw contributed. He wrote something on a legal pad.

"He's been missing for several weeks," Tucker said. "Ever since the Blackout."

Kane waited.

"I should have said he *was* missing," Tucker said. "He's been found."

"His remains," Shaw threw in. "Along with several others."

"Should we be in mourning?" Kane asked. He looked at Shaw. "Was he a friend of yours?"

Tucker spoke: "NYPD ran you through the database the week prior to the Blackout. In connection with the killing of a mobster named Leon Cibosky."

"Was that his first name?" Kane asked. "Leon? Seriously?"

"That murder is still unsolved," Shaw said.

"Nor has the murder weapon been found," Tucker said. "Twenty-two caliber."

"NYPD has cleared me of that," Kane said.

"No, they haven't," Shaw said. "No one is cleared until someone is convicted of the crime. No statute of limitations on murder. Do you know what unsolved means?"

"I didn't go to college," Kane said.

"You went to West Point." Tucker wasn't consulting notes, which Kane took as a bad sign.

"Not a college," Kane said. "More like a finishing school for wayward boys."

"You aren't funny," Shaw said.

"Many have accused me of that," Kane acknowledged.

"I tried to get a copy of your military records," Tucker said. "But was informed they were destroyed in the fire at the National Archives in St. Louis in '73."

Kane had not heard that cover story and wondered if Trent and the CIA had anything to do with it. "Shame." It also reminded him that Yazzie had mentioned not being able to access his records, which made him wonder what access Yazzie had.

"Which is bullshit," Shaw said, "since the records destroyed for the Army in that fire were for personnel discharged between 1 November 1912 and 1 January 1960." He was consulting notes, a file folder open on his desk next to the notepad.

"Before your time," Tucker said. "Weak cover at best."

"The Army and paperwork," Kane said. "You know how it goes. You guys are vets, right?"

Neither responded.

Shaw checked the folder. "But you were in the news, Kane. The Green Beret Affair in 1969." He held up *Life* magazine with the image of the Colonel on the cover. It had a label indicating it came from the New York Public Library. "You were one of them. That have anything to do with your file disappearing?"

"Did you steal that from the library?" Kane asked. "They don't lend periodicals. Stealing's a crime, you know? Librarians can be real bad-asses going after book thieves. I could turn you in."

Tucker didn't bite. "How do you feel about double-agents, Kane?"

Shaw didn't give him a chance. "He mustn't like them much, because he killed one."

"Interesting," Tucker said. "Why is the military hiding your file?"

"Ask the military," Kane said.

"Or perhaps it's the CIA?" Shaw said. "Clowns In Action."

"That's cute," Kane said. "They call you Boys in Suits."

"Yeah," Shaw said, "but ours actually matches the letters which means we can spell."

"And the N in Ranger stands for knowledge," Kane said. "We all have our cute sayings. Don't you guys work for the same government?"

"That's the theory," Tucker said. He indicated the charred metal in his desk. "Recognize this?"

"You don't?" Kane said.

Shaw spoke. "Damon's remains were found on the top floor of an abandoned building on the lower West Side. Along with four others. Three are tentatively identified as associates of Damon. There wasn't much left. No I.D. on the last one. Yet."

"You don't seem curious about any of this," Tucker pointed out. "Yet you were chatting about the history of this area on the way in."

"Current news isn't history yet. I prefer history." Kane glanced over his shoulder at the door.

"Nervous?" Shaw asked.

"Should I be?"

"You're acting weird," Shaw said. "Weird isn't good."

"Besides my lack of a sense of humor," Kane said, "I'm known for acting weird. I think I should call my lawyer."

"You are nervous," Shaw said.

"If you guys are doing good cop-bad cop," Kane said, "I can't tell who is who."

"Who are *you*?" Tucker asked.

"Why am I here?" Kane responded. "Told you I don't know this Damon guy. And what does that have to do with a melted M-16?"

"There's a report that you threatened Damon on the day of the Blackout," Tucker said. "And went to meet him."

Kane felt the familiar tingling, cold sensation. A distancing from the room, from Shaw and Tucker. "A 'report'? By who?"

"You didn't laugh when I did the *Blazing Saddles* bit," Tucker said. "Your friend did. The one who tried to hide the C-4 and was armed with an MP-5." It wasn't a question.

"I don't think your friend is all there," Shaw threw in. "Crazy eyes."

"I never saw *Blazing Saddles*," Kane said. "I like *Monty Python*, though. And it wasn't an MP-5. It was an HK-94. An MP-5 has automatic capability and *that* would be illegal." Kane suspected Merrick had modified the HK though and it probably *was* capable of automatic. Another reason a warrant would have been a problem.

"Good to know." Tucker sighed and leaned back in his chair, looking up at the ceiling. "Pieces and parts. So many pieces and parts. But the one constant is you."

"You lost me a long time ago," Kane said. "Pretty much when you busted into my apartment with guns drawn."

"Gotta admit I'm a little lost too," Tucker said. "Except for the fact you might have been the last person to see Damon alive."

"How do you figure that?"

Shaw was thumbing through papers in the folder. "A report."

"By who? About what?" Kane asked.

"A confidential source," Tucker said. "The explosives in your apartment. Where did they come from?"

Kane stood. "Time for me to talk to my lawyer."

Shaw stared at him. "You're acting awfully guilty. Isn't he, Tucker?"

"He is indeed."

"You haven't accused me of anything," Kane said.

"That's why you're acting guilty," Tucker said. "As if we had. The explosives?"

"Sergeant Merrick was on my team at Fort Devens years ago," Kane said. "He was showing me something he's working on. Demo guys like to show off their toys."

"You've never seen C-4 before?" Shaw asked. "Aren't explosives tightly controlled? Even among high speed units like Special Forces?" He pulled up another folder. "Interesting. A person from a Special Forces unit at Fort Devens was arrested earlier this year selling C-4 to some undesirables. You connected to that?"

"Okay." Kane held up his hands. "You guys are all over the place. If you have something you want to know, why not ask me?"

Tucker leaned forward, elbows on his desk. "We have been and you've been evading." He gestured to Shaw. "What hasn't he answered?"

Shaw read from his notes. "Do you know Sean Damon? Did you know the killing of Leon Cibosky is unsolved? Do you dislike double agents? Why is the military hiding your file? Or is it the CIA? Do you recognize the item on Agent Tucker's desk? Are you nervous? Where did the explosives in your apartment come from?"

"I answered some of them," Kane said.

"Evasively at best," Tucker said.

"You haven't answered any of my questions either," Kane pointed out.

Tucker laughed. "You are suffering from a serious misunderstanding of the current dynamics of the situation."

"What he means," Shaw said, "is we ask the questions."

"Why?" Kane asked. "You don't have a warrant. You haven't arrested me. I agreed to come here. What do you really want to know?"

"Let's start over," Tucker said. "Sean Damon. You were at the Marcelle Law Firm the same date and time Damon was on—" he paused and glanced at Shaw who had another folder open and supplied the answer.

"Eight July." Shaw smiled. "We have photos of him going in and then you."

"I didn't meet with him," Kane said. "He had business with Thomas Marcelle. I work with his daughter. Who is no longer with that firm. Nor am I."

"But you were then," Tucker said. "As was Ms. Antonia Marcelle."

"What's odd," Shaw said, "is that our surveillance didn't see you leave."

"I went out the back door," Kane said. "Why do you have Thomas Marcelle under surveillance?"

"We're like elephants," Tucker said. "We never forget. Thomas Marcelle cut a deal with Damon."

Kane raised an eyebrow. "That was 1967. You've had him under surveillance since then?"

"Elephants," Shaw said.

"You don't happen to have him under surveillance right now, do you?" Kane tried. "His daughter wants to talk to him."

"The surveillance is random and periodic," Shaw said.

Kane shook his head. "As I said, I didn't meet with Damon. I saw him in the hallway. He went into the conference room with Thomas Marcelle. I got no idea what they were up to."

"Really?" Tucker said. "Just an amazing coincidence?"

Shaw held up a piece of paper. "The following week, on thirteen July, you stood on the north corner of Jackson Square Park and were picked up by Damon. Hard to miss that big gold car."

Kane went still, waiting.

"Unfortunately," Tucker said, "the assigned agent lost the tail."

"Fortunately," Shaw said, "that car, a Mercedes 600 Pullman, was found in a loading dock underneath a building at 85 Tenth Avenue. The building whose top floor was incinerated the same night you took a ride in the car."

"The night of the Blackout," Tucker said. "And Damon's remains were just identified in what was left of that top floor. Which wasn't much. Except a number of these." He tapped the M-16 remnant. "Starting to see all the connections?"

Kane didn't answer.

Tucker picked up the M-16. "We ran the serial numbers. Stolen from a National Guard Armory in Vermont earlier this year." He tossed it on the desk with a thud. "What happened that night, Kane?"

"I've been falsely accused of things before," Kane said. He pointed at the magazine. "I know my rights."

"We haven't read them to you," Shaw said. "Unless I missed something. Did I miss something?" he asked his partner.

"Nope," Tucker said. "Do you know why we haven't told you your rights?" he said to Kane. "Because this is bigger than you. You're nothing. A nobody. Actually, you're worse than nothing, you're a walking disaster, Kane. You have no idea what you're involved in." He pointed at Kane. "But you're going to help make it right. Or you're going to go down. Hard. Because we think you're awfully guilty."

"Awfully guilty," Shaw echoed.

"Guilty of what?"

"Killing Damon, his three men and whoever else was there that night," Shaw said.

"If you had an ounce of evidence," Kane said, "you'd have arrested me, had a warrant, and torn my place apart. You got nothing."

Tucker sat back in his seat. "Do you know where these M-16s were going?"

"I'm not answering anything," Kane said.

"Ireland," Shaw said. "The IRA, Provos, whatever you want to call them. Damon was brokering their weapon purchases, using money collected by NORAID."

"If you knew that, why didn't you arrest him?" Kane asked.

Tucker gave a weird smile. "I did. Three years ago."

Shaw spoke. "That's why the question about double-agents was pertinent."

"You flipped Damon?" Kane asked.

"Surprised you were working for an informant?" Shaw asked.

"I never worked with or for Damon," Kane said. "Why did you flip him? Why not put him away?"

"Had no choice," Tucker said. "The government had an airtight case in 1967 and look what happened? I had a strong suspicion if I brought the case to the Southern District there'd be no rope or a very long one at best with which to hang Damon. Like the very loose rope Thomas Marcelle gave Damon when he should have gone away for the rest of his life. Damon boasted as much when I brought him in here. That he had connections in high places. We made a deal."

"Why would he make a deal if he knew you couldn't make a case?" Kane asked.

"We each had something the other wanted," Tucker said.

"And that was?"

"We're asking the questions," Tucker said.

Three years. Kane wondered how many people had died in Damon's 'factory' in those three years? How many films made and lives destroyed? Tammy, the girl Damon used in the films before Sarah, for certain. "To quote someone, *you* have no idea what you got involved in by doing that."

"That's not for you to question," Tucker said.

Kane stared hard at Tucker. "Why would you make a deal with Damon? He was a psychopathic killer."

"How do you know that if you never worked for him?" Tucker asked. "I don't have to defend or explain my actions to you. You're the one on the hot seat. A very hot seat. Here's what you need to know. Damon was giving us information. Some of it quite valuable. In the past three years we've made significant arrests around the country based on it. Took bad people off the streets. And when he departed the living, he was aware of something."

"Something big," Shaw added. "The question is whether you were involved in it."

Kane was getting tired of the Mutt and Jeff routine. "Fuck you guys. You made a deal with the devil. And if you made such significant arrests, why are you two idiots sitting in a room with no windows? Seems you should have an office with a view and your names on the door."

"Those guns were destined for the IRA," Tucker said. "Damon also had money from NORAID." He tapped the M-16. "We know what happened to these. What happened to the money? Whoever did the killings took it. Where's the money, Kane?"

"He had money there?" Kane asked. "How do you know that?"

"See," Shaw said. "That's an example of you not answering a question by asking a question."

"Hard to answer questions when I've got no clue what you're talking about. What money? How much?"

Tucker waved a hand. "Let's forget about the money for now. Here's the thing. From his contacts, Damon picked up rumors that the Provos were planning something big in the United States."

"What?"

"We don't know," Tucker said.

"That's why we're talking to you," Shaw added.

"This is the first I've heard of it," Kane said.

Tucker pushed forward. "His last report said that there was an IRA team in the U.S.. That they wanted weapons and explosives. Damon was trying to find out more before he so abruptly disappeared."

"If he was providing them with the weapons—" Kane began, but Tucker was shaking his head.

"He said he wouldn't help them," Tucker said.

"Why?" Kane asked.

Shaw answered. "He said they were crazy."

"That's a ringing endorsement from a psychopath," Kane said. "But otherwise he would have supplied them with weapons and explosives? And you'd have been okay with it? How many others has he supplied?"

"Nice try," Tucker said. "Here's the thing. In three years, I never saw Damon bothered. But whoever these people are, they bothered him."

"He actually used the word 'crazy'," Shaw added. "As you noted, that's a worrisome term for someone like Damon to use."

Tucker continued. "He said that when he refused to get them what they wanted, they were bypassing him and that there was nothing he could do to stop them. They would get the money, weapons and explosives elsewhere. Maybe you and your friend from Fort Devens are the elsewhere? Perhaps you supplied those M-16s?"

"Did your surveillance see me with them? Observe me putting them in the trunk of Damon's car?"

"Perhaps that C-4 your friend had was for them?" Tucker indicated the phone on his desk. "I could call the field office in Boston and have them take a trip to Fort Devens and talk to your friend. Search his quarters? His unit?"

"This doesn't look good," Shaw threw in.

Kane shook his head. "I'm going to talk slowly, since the two of you don't seem to be listening. If you seriously thought I was supplying C-4 and weapons to terrorists, you'd have cuffed me at the apartment and wouldn't have let Merrick drive off. Since you know so much about my past, you know that I was interrogated in Long Binh in Vietnam. The people doing that make you two look like Laurel and Hardy." When there was no response, Kane continued. "What's an IRA team doing here in the States? What did Damon say they were going to do with the equipment if they got it? Did he say exactly what they were looking for? What kind of guns? Explosives?"

Tucker and Shaw exchanged a glance. The latter fielded the answer. "We don't know."

"He didn't tell you," Kane said. "He could have been full of shit."

"Why would he lie about this?" Tucker asked and it sounded like a real question, which meant he was unsure.

"Do you know what Damon was doing in that building where he died?" Kane asked. "Either of you ever been there?"

"We didn't know he had a place in the old Nabisco Factory," Shaw said. "The car in the loading dock tipped us off and that's why we had the remains examined. We were never able to tail him there, the few times we were on him."

"In three years?" Kane was incredulous. "Your surveillance isn't very good."

"Our surveillance was on Thomas Marcelle," Tucker said. "Damon was our asset."

"This is very compartmentalized," Shaw added.

"Sounds like this is fucking blind," Kane said. "You never checked on your asset to see if you were getting double-crossed."

"That's your area of expertise, isn't it?" Tucker asked. "Double-agents?"

Shaw jumped in. "What you just asked means *you* know what he was doing there. You were up there, weren't you?"

"He threatened me," Kane backtracked. "Told me he killed people in that limo. Did you look at the back seat? The bullet holes and the blood stains? And the trunk? Steel-lined. That's where he threw people. He threatened to take me to what he called his 'factory'. Told me some of what he did to people to get them talking. I'm assuming that's where we're talking about."

"Why was he threatening you?" Tucker asked. "What did he want from you?"

"He was working with the Cappucci family on plans to divide up the contracts for Westway," Kane said. "I got wind of it because I was following Alfonso Delgado, married to Sofia Cappucci, over a divorce case. Damon wanted me to keep quiet. He is, was, good at threats. I said 'sure' and that was that."

"You know," Tucker said, "there is another possibility about what happened to Damon."

"There has to be," Kane said, "since I had nothing to do with it."

"Maybe," Tucker said, "this IRA team got pissed because Damon wouldn't work with them. Then they found out he was asking questions. And they took him out. That team has to be pretty good because they got him and his three top men."

Kane snorted. "The Unholy Trinity. That's what they were called. You had to know that. How many people you think they killed in the last three years while you've been playing your game with Damon? Actually, playing *his* game?"

Tucker ignored that. "Did the IRA kill him? There was the unidentified body. Who was that? One of the IRA team? Were they covering their tracks? You're the last person who saw him that we're certain of."

Shaw chimed in, and this time it seemed he was talking more to Tucker. "What doesn't make sense is them burning the place down with their guns in it. If they wanted weapons, why not take them? They wouldn't destroy guns that would be going to their cause. And the money."

"I got no clue what you guys are talking about," Kane said. "Damon wanted me to keep quiet. We chatted in his car, I agreed, then they dropped me off at my apartment. Whatever happened that night during the Blackout, I got no idea. I was busy defending the diner I own in the Village. Plenty of witnesses to that." He pointed at Tucker. "Maybe the IRA or NORAID found out Damon was a rat, working for you guys? Maybe you got a leak in your office?"

He went to the door, but Tucker's words paused him.

"Damon did give us something on this IRA team. Whatever they're planning to do, it will happen soon. It will be in the city. That was another reason he said no to them. He didn't like to shit where he ate."

Kane bit. "How soon?"

Shaw answered. "That was one thing he was specific about. Midnight, Wednesday next week. The 10th."

"That's very specific," Kane granted. "Why then?"

"He didn't know," Tucker said.

Kane looked over his shoulder. "Did Damon give you anything about this team beyond that? Composition? A target?"

Tucker and Shaw exchanged a glance once more. Tucker nodded and Shaw answered. "He said this team called themselves the Swords of Saint Patrick. We checked and there's no intel on that term. He said they would go around him since he said no. Go directly to NORAID for money. And arms merchants for the gear they wanted. He mentioned a place where they would probably make contact with NORAID."

Kane folded his arms, waiting for the reason he was here.

Tucker spoke. "A bar in the Bronx. Kelly's. On Broadway."

"Under the El," Kane said, referring to the elevated subway. "Across from Van Cortlandt."

"You know the place?" Tucker asked.

"Yeah. But I haven't been there since high school."

"They raise a lot of money for NORAID," Shaw said. "And Damon said it's *the* place in the city where one can make contact with the group."

"Other than him," Kane reminded them. "But he's past tense."

"We want you to—" Tucker began but Kane cut him off by opening the door.

"Since you studied my background you do know something about me. I did my duty for the country and got screwed. This is *your* job. Your problem. You made the devil's bargain with Damon. You better get to work." He left.

SOHO, MANHATTAN

"Hey, buddy! Got a cig?" The old man stepped in Kane's path, unusually aggressive for a panhandler, even in New York. Kane was twelve blocks and ten minutes from the Jacob Javits Federal Center, walking north along Hudson Street, having crossed Canal and passing over the eastern terminus of the Holland Tunnel.

"I don't—" Kane began, but as the old man's eyes shifted past him, Kane reached for the forty-five and was turning, but a tad late. Stars exploded as something hard slammed into the side of his head.

It wasn't a TKO, but close. Kane went to his knees, still trying to draw his pistol, vaguely aware that the old man was running away. Someone wrapped Kane in a bear, more a grizzly hug around the chest, powerful arms, one of them covered in a cast bent at the elbow, which explained the 'something hard'. Kane was dragged to the curb where a black limousine awaited. He was tossed inside and someone snatched the gun out of the holster. He got his first look at his attacker and understood who and what he'd been hit with: Matteo, Sofia Cappucci's enforcer, and the weapon was his right arm in a cast covering from above his elbow to the wrist. The result of his last run in with Kane. There was a sort of irony in that, which Kane didn't pursue at the moment.

Matteo pushed into the back seat, shoving Kane farther inside.

Kane shook his head and blinked, trying to focus. That wasn't helped by the dim interior, the result of heavily tinted windows. There were four people across from him, seated facing rearwards. Two had guns trained on him, so Kane didn't go for the knife in the small of his back. There was a powerful odor which Kane couldn't place, but made him slightly nauseous.

"Can you hear me?" Sofia Cappucci asked, her heavy Brooklyn accent a bit echoey. "I said I wanted to talk to him, Matteo."

"Sorry." Matteo didn't sound sorry at all. "He can hear you. He's still conscious."

"Kane?" Cappucci asked.

Kane focused and now there were only two facing him, her and a guy with a gun. He was smaller than Matteo's six and a half feet, but the only size that mattered was that of the bullet in the pistol.

"What?" Kane said. His eyes were adjusting and the stars fading away. He'd been hit worse sparring but that didn't make it hurt less.

Matteo jabbed his elbow, his good one, into Kane's right side. Hard. "Talk nice to the lady."

"Right," Kane said. "What Mrs. Delgado?"

Matteo repeated his nudge. "It's Ms. Cappucci, asshole."

"Right."

"Enough," the recently widowed Mrs. Alfonso Delgado said. "I've decided my maiden name is more appropriate. Don't you think?"

Despite the heat outside, she had a fur coat draped over her Rubenesque figure. Which explained the air conditioner running full blast. She had black hair, made up in what looked like a pile to Kane, but his women's hair fashion sense was on par with his knowledge of ancient Greek, although he did know a smattering of Latin from his altar boy days. Her face seemed to glow, the result of heavy make-up, covering the remnants of bruises from a beating her recently departed husband had inflicted, and her lips were bright red. The beating had brought about Alfonso's death sentence by Sofia's father, the Don of the Cappucci family.

Kane nodded. "Sure. Good idea. Sounds much nicer, Ms. Cappucci."

The limo was moving north, slowly negotiating the double-parked trucks in the rundown Soho neighborhood.

"You been on my mind lately," Cappucci said. "And I was in the neighborhood and then Matteo sees you walking and I thought, how fortunate. I figured we'd give you a lift. Isn't that nice of me?"

"Sure," Kane said. "Fortunate me." He figured she'd been at the Triangle Social Club on Sullivan Street, which was only six blocks north. "How is Vinny the Chin?"

Matteo's elbow indicated another social faux pas. "That's Mister Gigante to you."

Sofia Cappucci laughed. "Pretending to be crazy, as always. Crazy as a fox. He knows the FBI got eyes and ears all around him. Some people think he really is nuts. Who knows? He can act sharp when he needs and that's all that counts."

Vincent 'the Chin' Gigante, who had worked for Vito Genovese and was now boss in his own right, was well known in Manhattan for wandering the streets of Greenwich Village in his bathrobe and slippers. Preparation for a potential insanity defense in case he got pinched.

"Might be the wrong medication?" Kane suggested. "I've heard that—"

Matteo's elbow interrupted his medical advice.

"There you were," Sofia continued, "walking along and I took it as a sign."

"Like a biblical sign? I've never been accused of that." Kane leaned forward and looked past Matteo. "Kinda weird, though, that I was walking uptown and you were heading in the same direction when the Triangle is in that direction." He pointed the way they were going. "Were you lost?"

Matteo stuck out his good arm, heavily muscled, and pushed Kane back.

"Quinn said you were smart tactically and stupid strategically," Sofia Cappucci said. "Now, if I was around who I'm usually around, I'd have to pretend I don't understand those two terms." She dumped the Brooklyn accent. "But between you and me, I've got two undergraduate majors from Princeton; history and economics. I wanted to go to graduate school but my father needed me."

"It's good to be needed, Ms. Cappucci," Kane said.

She glanced to the side, then looked back at Kane. The Brooklyn was back. "Yeah. You've comprehended the tactical situation. This wasn't random. Now, tell me, what's the strategic?"

Kane shrugged, his ribs aching. "You're right. I don't know that. I assume it has something to do with Quinn?"

"You're still thinking tactical," Sofia said. "He was just a tool."

"I guess so," Kane said. "I've been hit in the head a lot, including recently, which doesn't help." He pointed at the tip of the scar extending out from under hair on the right side. "Even got shot in it. I think it affected me."

"Matteo wants to kill you," Sofia said. "Given that you hurt him, that should be his right. Why not apologize? I think he'll accept an apology."

Kane glanced to his right. "Sorry."

Sofia Cappucci gave a deep, disappointed sigh. "That was weak."

"Really sorry?" Kane tried. "Mea culpa, mea culpa, mea maxima culpa?"

The daughter of the Boss of the Cappucci crime family shook her head. "Quinn also said you were a smart ass." She waved a hand, dismissing that line of discussion. "By the way, do you know where Quinn is?"

"Last I saw him, you were there," Kane said, referring to the encounter at Mount Sinai Hospital, where she'd been brought after the beating. Alfonso Delgado had been found dead the next day, the result of a concrete enema. It was also where Kane had dislocated Matteo's elbow. "He informed me we had no more business between us and I was good with that. You remember."

"I wish I believed you," she said. She reached into her large purse and extracted a plastic bag containing a small gun with a bulky suppressor. "Recognize?"

"It's a pistol," Kane said. He'd assumed Quinn had some sort of backup plan because people trained like both of them, Special Forces and SAS, always had backup plans. Which reminded him he had no backup plan at the moment.

She tossed it on the seat between her and the guy with the gun. "Quinn told me it was yours."

"I used to own one like that," Kane admitted.

Sofia Cappucci looked over her shoulder. "Park," she ordered the driver.

The limo pulled over, cutting off drivers, earning horn blasts, and halted.

"Everyone out," Sofia ordered.

Matteo looked as if he were about to protest, but he joined the driver and gunman in exiting. As soon as all the doors were solidly shut, Sofia Cappucci pointed a finger tipped with a bright red nail at Kane, who wondered if she got her nails done at the same place as Toni.

"It's the gun that killed Cibosky." The accent was gone. "He wasn't a made-man, but he was part of our crew. I *could* have you tossed in the East River for that. And for what you did to Matteo, who *is* a made man I *should* have you tossed in."

"You could have me killed for whatever reason you want," Kane pointed out. "I didn't kill Cibosky. Quinn did."

"Why would he have done that?"

"So the cops would think it was me. Quinn stole that gun from my Jeep. My prints are on it and the shell casings."

"I give it to the cops, you're in trouble." It was not a question.

"It would cause some discomfort," Kane admitted, "but I don't think a solid case, especially given what happened to your late husband and the lack of chain of custody."

"You're full of shit. Where's Quinn? Last I saw him was the day of the Blackout. He said he had business with Sean Damon. Turns out Damon and those Irish pigs of his are dead. Burned up that night. There's another body found with them and hasn't been identified. Is that Quinn?"

"You're as up to speed on that as I am," Kane said. "Probably ahead of me, but I'm trying to catch up. I think you found me just now because you were at the Triangle and someone at the FBI called you. Although how some Fed has the number for the phone in there raises all sorts of interesting questions. They told you I was at FBI HQ and leaving, probably heading home. Was it Tucker or Shaw?"

"The old men in the club," Sofia said, referring to the Triangle social club, "think I only get in the door and am allowed to sit at the table because of my father and who my husband was. They thought he was an idiot, my ex, that is. And they were right. Thus, they don't think too much of me. I'm the only woman in there. They talk around me, over me, under me, to me, but never *with* me."

"Their mistake," Kane said.

"Yeah." She peered at him under thick lashes. "Quinn was very good at what he did. My grandfather appreciated him and then my father. As did I. But there was something off about him. What men fail to realize is that women see the world differently. We perceive another side of people and evaluate them with a different set of standards. And when you are, let us politely say, intimate with someone, you learn things about them."

Kane remained silent, waiting for the proverbial high heel to fall. Horns blared, trucks, busses and cars rumbled by outside the limo, but the two of them were in a bubble of Brooklyn mafia princess, red fingernails, a cloying perfume Kane was becoming more aware of, and possible execution at the order of the owner of all the above.

"Quinn had something going on," Sofia Cappucci said. "Something besides the family business. Is that true?"

"I don't know what the family business is specifically, nor do I know what he was up to."

"You're a bad liar," she said. "He'd disappear at night. Be gone for a while. Come back and I could tell he was—" Sofia searched her Princeton education for a term, then settled on— "aroused. The kind that comes from violence. It emanated off of him. His blood was up."

Kane knew what the violence was: prostitutes Quinn tortured brutally and then beheaded. And as a final sick touch, blowtorched their heads. Their pictures graced the wall at the Omega Task Force at the One-oh-Nine Precinct along with the other 'multiples' who weren't receiving anywhere near the attention the victims of Son of Sam were.

"He had crazy eyes," Kane said. "I could see that."

"Oh yes," Sofia said. "Picked up on that the moment I met him. Quite a few of my associates sport them." She leaned forward slightly. "Do I have them? What did you think when you saw me with Toni at Studio 54?"

"You're not crazy," Kane said, hoping his words were true. "You're angry."

Sofia Cappucci sat back and gave a very slight nod. "Interesting. Perhaps Quinn underestimated you."

"Do I have crazy eyes?" Kane asked.

Sofia cocked her head. "No."

"That's good to know."

But Sofia wasn't done. "You act crazy at times, Kane. But your eyes? You got sad eyes. About the saddest I've ever seen."

Kane didn't respond.

She shifted the topic. "How much do you make working for Toni?"

"I don't view it as work," Kane said. "I help her out when she needs it. We go back a long way."

"To West Point and her late brother, who was your best friend." Sofia nodded. "Loyalty is good. One cannot purchase loyalty. But one can purchase services."

"Can I ask you something?" Kane said.

She frowned but said: "Go ahead."

"How much did Toni tell you about me?"

"It would be impolite for me to betray a confidence," Sofia said.

"That's exactly why I'm asking."

"Not much, but enough," Sofia said. "She didn't mean to but she is a very lonely person. Champagne on top of coke is never good. I don't touch the stuff myself and I worry about Toni. She's got a problem, but otherwise she's sharp. She's been going through a hard time. She'll have to figure that problem out on her own."

"She has her reasons to be messed up," Kane said.

"Don't we all?" Sofia said, but she was on task. "I'd like to avail myself of your services occasionally."

"What services?"

"Negotiating. Investigating. The last time I talked to Quinn, he was approaching Damon about the Westway project and our share."

Kane shook his head. "I'm not getting involved in Westway."

Sofia waved a dismissive hand. "Since Damon is out of the picture, that's going to be a mess until we see who rises from the ashes. With Bella Azbug ahead in the polls, it might be a non-issue because if she's in City Hall it will never happen." She shook her head. "Westway? Too many were counting on it as a done deal. But another opportunity presents itself. Damon's people had been blocking Vito Genovese, and now Vinny the Chin and his crew, from getting a piece of the old Penn Central rail yard on the west side. The Irish claim it's their territory."

"I believe the gang Damon came from called themselves the Westies. And the rail yards are on the west side."

Sofia smiled. "They can call themselves 'fucked' now without Damon to protect them. The city's possibly going to put a convention center there. Lots of contracts will be forthcoming and the family will get our taste. But I've done some research and there's the issue of the ownership of the land."

"Who has it?" Kane asked, since it was better to keep her speaking about deals than contemplating reasons to kill him.

"Don't worry about that right now. I want a solid piece of the ground while everyone else is still figuring out what to do with Damon out of the picture."

"You personally?"

"Enough questions," Sofia said. Brooklyn was back. "You gonna do some work for me?"

"If I say no?"

She reached over and tapped the gun in the plastic bag. "Maybe you should think about it."

"You have a convincing argument," Kane said. He leaned forward. "I wouldn't trust Tucker or Shaw. Whichever one called you."

Sofia laughed. "I don't trust nobody. I didn't trust Quinn. He had secrets."

"Don't we all?" Kane asked. "You hear anything about IRA hitters in the city?"

Sofia answered with a question. "That what happened to Damon? He double-cross them on one of his weapons deals? Skim some of their money?"

"I don't know. I've heard rumors that they're in town and planning something."

"Irish and planning in the same sentence? That'll be the day. I haven't heard nothing. What kind of something? A heist?"

"No idea. But people might get hurt. Innocent people."

Sofia raised an eyebrow as if he'd said something puzzling. "What is an innocent person?"

Kane nodded his head toward the window, which he immediately regretted because it was still pulsing from Matteo's cast. "The average person out there. Who works a legit job. Pays taxes. Just wants to make it through the day."

"I should care about them?" Sofia said it like the shrug it was. "You gonna do some work for me?"

"Why not use Matteo?"

"Why not ask stupid questions?

"Can I think on it? I have something I'm working on right now that's got me real busy for the next few days."

Sofia chuckled. "Few people say no to me."

"It wasn't a no, it was—"

She waved a hand, red fingernails glinting. "You've got the weekend."

"How do I let you know?"

She reached into her purse and retrieved a black card with a phone number written in gold on it. "There's an answering machine. You can call and leave your yes on Monday. Then I'll tell you what I want done. I'll make it worth your time."

Kane took the card.

She reached over and powered down the window. Matteo was hovering. "Get in and him out." As the doors opened, she pointed at Kane. "I look forward to your yes."

"Ri—" Kane began but Matteo cut that off by grabbing him around the throat and pulling him out of the backseat. Kane allowed himself to be moved, but he grabbed the door frame. "My gun?"

Sofia Cappucci nodded and Matteo gave up the forty-five.

"Thanks for the lift," Kane said as the door slammed shut and the limo peeled away in the gathering dusk. He looked about. The ride had gotten him three blocks closer to home. It's the little things in life one had to be grateful for.

Friday Evening, 5 August 1977

MEATPACKING DISTRICT, MANHATTAN

Kane drew his forty-five when he saw the matchstick on top of the black iron gate. A note was taped to his door. He recognized his landlord's scrawl by the glow of the street light, but didn't holster the gun since he was having a bad twenty-four hours and didn't see any reason for it to get better.

SHE INSISTED.

Kane entered, expecting to see Toni in the small sitting room, but it was empty. Kane went to the doorway to the bedroom. It was dark, but someone was in the bed. He flipped the overhead fluorescent, gun at the ready.

Truvey was in Kane's bed, the sheet strategically layered along the upper curvature of her bosom. She lay on her side, head propped up with one hand held aloft by her elbow, a pose that was too perfect to be random. She looked pretty good despite the awful lighting.

"How come you didn't ask if anyone wanted to kill me last night?" Truvey asked.

"Are you alone?" Kane asked.

"Am I not enough?" Truvey pouted. "Are you going to shoot me?"

Kane holstered the pistol. "You broke the sheets."

"I what?"

"What are you doing here?" Kane asked.

Truvey raised an eyebrow. "Seriously?" She sat up, the sheet falling to her waist, revealing her prominent assets.

"Seriously," Kane said.

"I didn't 'break' your sheets," Truvey said. "I got between them. The idea is—"

Kane interrupted her. "By the way, there's a bomb under the bed."

Truvey blinked hard several times as if that helped process the words. "You're joking."

"I've been accused by a number of people of not having much of a sense of humor and at this moment, I would trust their opinion."

Truvey scooted out from between the sheets, revealing a pair of thong panties and a plethora of skin. Kane tossed her the sundress draped over the books on top of the dresser.

As she pulled it on, he told her: "Let me dispel with the possibility so we don't waste time. I'm not interested in having sex with you. I'm more concerned with who attacked us last night and why."

As the dress settled over her body, with some hard tugging, Truvey backed away from the bed. "The bomb?"

"It's under the bed," Kane said. "But it's not armed. Technically it's just the explosives. For it to go off it needs--"

"Why do you have a bomb?"

"It was on the boat last night."

Truvey's voice climbed a few octaves. "*What?*"

Kane indicated the sitting room. "Come on. I'll explain."

Truvey sat on the couch while Kane took the chair that allowed him to see the foyer and the couch.

"My apologies for my social faux pas last night," Kane said. "Do you know anyone who'd want to kill you?"

Truvey shook her head. "No."

"You sound pretty certain."

Truvey spread her hands in innocence. "I'm a B-level actress trying to make my break. Who'd want to kill me?"

"That's what I was asking," Kane pointed out. "Why are you here?"

"I liked the way you handled things," Truvey said. "I wanted to express my gratitude. I think it could have gotten bad if you hadn't stepped up."

"A thank you card would have worked."

Truvey frowned. "You're a weird man."

"I've been told that."

"You've a Vietnam Vet." She said it in a way that could it could taken as a question or statement. Kane chose to go the latter route and didn't respond. "A Green Beret. I deal with actors all the time. They pretend. You're the real deal."

"You also deal with people like Crawford," Kane said.

"The hardest part of show business is getting the money," Truvey said. "I'm surprised any movie is ever made given how difficult it is. Producers like to mix me in with their pitch to the money people."

"Right."

"The producer is a dear friend," Truvey said. "I believe in his vision."

"You're talking about Selkis, right?"

"Yes."

"How long have you known him?"

Truvey frowned and Kane thought he heard little clangs as numbers moved. "About three months."

"And he's a dear friend?"

"Oh! Not like *that.*"

Kane had his own little mental clangs as he processed what she meant by 'that' which wasn't what he had meant.

Truvey explained further. "He's, well, you know. Let's say he prefers different delights."

"Right. When did he ask you to meet Crawford?"

"Selkie, that's what I call him, phoned me yesterday morning and we had lunch. He explained that a big money man he'd worked with before was coming to town and he had a project he thought would interest him and that there was a role in it that I would be perfect in and that I'd definitely be cast if it got greenlit so of course I said yes."

Kane unpacked the run-on sentence and pronouns. "Why didn't Selkis come along?"

Truvey appeared shocked. "That would have been weird, wouldn't it?"

"I guess so," Kane said, having used his quota of 'right' in this conversation. "Did an Indian named Yazzie talk to you this morning."

"Oh, yes. Have you met him? So tall. His skin is so perfect. He could so be my leading man!"

Kane indicated the bedroom. "I thought I was going to be?"

She pouted. "I'm here, aren't I?"

"You are indeed. Did he give you money? Or did Crawford pay you in the limo?"

"I'm not a hooker."

"To not say anything about what happened," Kane clarified.

"Yeah. Crawford did. Did he give you some?"

"Yeah."

Truvey nodded. "Two thousand. Not bad for doing nothing."

"Except for the getting shot at and almost blown up."

Truvey frowned. "There is that." She frowned further. "How much did Crawford pay you?"

"Two thousand. What did Yazzie want to know?"

Truvey gave him what Yazzie had told them in the meeting. When she was done, she pouted slightly. "He's really handsome but there's something missing in him."

"He's crossed the river," Kane said.

"What?"

"Seen the elephant."

"Huh?"

Kane moved on from the combat references. "Can I ask you something else?"

Truvey became wary. "What?"

"Did you bring the cocaine or did Crawford?"

"You won't rat on me will you?"

"Scout's honor."

"Selkie supplied it. I don't use myself. I tried it a few times but I've seen what can happen. I want to have a career, you know? Not be here today, gone tomorrow."

"Good plan," Kane said.

Truvey changed the subject. "What's with all the pictures?" She indicated the framed prints leaning against the wall, everywhere there wasn't cinderblocks holding makeshift bookshelves.

"I like maps. They're mostly of New York City and show the evolution and history of the city."

"See? That's part of what the movie is about. New York City. I think. At least Selkie said it was. He never really gave me the script. He said it was about the dark underbelly of the Big Apple. Did you see *Taxi Driver*? DeNiro? Wasn't that some acting? Selkie said it was like that, thematically."

"I haven't seen the movie. But I think I've experienced that part of the city."

"Anyways, it opens with a scene like that one in *Godfather*. Or was it *Two*? Kid on the boat seeing the Statue?"

"Haven't seen either of them either." He pointed at a book. "There's *The Godfather*."

"What?"

"The book the movie was based on," Kane said.

"There was a book?" Truvey leaned forward, her sun dress looser at the top. She suddenly spoke as if they were being listened in on. "You know there weren't any storyboards, don't you?"

"I kind of guessed."

Truvey sighed, having exhausted small talk. "You obviously like to read," she said. "What else do you like?" She walked over, settling on the arm of the chair.

Kane forced himself to remain in the seat. "Run. Go to the gym and workout and spar. Work the heavy and light bag."

"You look like you're in good shape."

"I try."

"I gotta do two hours every morning," Truvey complained. "And I can't eat much of nothing. People think it's easy to look like this."

Kane didn't know what to say to that.

"I appreciate a man who takes care of himself," Truvey said.

"Right."

Truvey became inspired. "I've never done it with a bomb under the bed."

"I doubt that's an exclusive club many have aspirations to," Kane said.

Truvey frowned. "What-da-ya mean by that?"

"I mean not many people have done it with a bomb under the bed. That they knew about."

"Oh." She reached for him and he flinched. "What's wrong with you?"

"I got shot in the head," Kane said. "Kind of messed me up. Plus, I've had a bad day."

"We can work on that. And really, the head's over-rated."

"That's an interesting take," Kane said.

Truvey got off the chair and went to the light switch for the sitting room. Turned it off. Her body was silhouetted inside the sundress in the doorway to the bedroom, which strangely was more enticing than almost completely naked in the bed. "You know where I'll be. Above the bomb."

She turned the bedroom light off.

Saturday Morning, 6 August 1977

MEATPACKING DISTRICT, MANHATTAN

"You forgot the fiver," Morticia remarked as she placed coffee and water/two cubes in front of Kane.

Kane pulled the bill off his money clip and put it on the edge of the table. "Thanks."

But Morticia had already slid away to take an order from another booth, leaving behind a folded meal ticket.

Kane blinked because he'd missed her doing that. He unfolded the ticket and sighed. Another encrypted message. Sometimes he wished Thao would just come out of the kitchen and tell him who had called and what the message was. Kane transcribed and decrypted the groupings. He smiled when he read what Merrick had told Thao regarding the personal matter. Crumpled the ticket and torched it.

Kane spooned the cubes into the coffee. He wrapped his hands around the mug, letting the warmth sink into the scars on his palms. Closed his eyes.

Morticia interrupted his reverie. "What fresh hell is this?" She put a plate in front of him, several peppers on top.

"Say again?" Kane reflexively drew the forty-five with his left hand, resting it on his thigh.

Morticia didn't leave the edge of the booth. "I think Dorothy Parker was channeling some Shakespeare with that line because—"

"Move to your left, please," Kane said.

She shifted out of his line of fire, but continued her literary train of thought. "Because in *Henry VIII* Abergavenny is talking about Cardinal Wolsey and says '*and he begins a new hell in himself*' which is kind of close. Parker was the best with turning a phrase."

"Right," Kane said. He recognized the man coming in the Washington Street door. "Fuck."

"Is that a bullets are going to fly 'fuck' and hit the floor?" Morticia asked.

Kane reholstered and flipped a small switch underneath the table top. "It's a *he's an asshole* fuck."

"You'll be right at home then." Morticia hovered away, having done her duty delivering Thao's pepper warning.

Trent had cigarette in hand, ash precariously long. He strolled to Kane's booth, some of the ash drifting to the previously spotless black and white tile floor.

"Told you I'd be seeing you," the CIA man said as he took court directly across from Kane. Pulled the ashtray close, lit another cigarette from the remnants, which he dropped into the tray without stubbing out. A forlorn tendril of smoke drifted up from it, much like Kane's hopes for a peaceful morning.

"You've been known to lie," Kane said.

"Still sore over that?" Trent said. "Come on. It's been years. And you said you'd work for me."

"I said I'd consider it."

"Hmm. No. No. Not the way I remember it. The deal was I back off surveillance on your apartment and you'd get me information." Trent was a portly man with thinning dark hair. Black framed glasses with thick lens fronted a red face that appeared permanently flushed. He wore a tacky sports jacket, slacks and rumpled white shirt. A thin wire crept from inside his jacket to a small speaker in his left ear. He affected a slight New England accent that sounded practiced rather than native and Kane hadn't heard in Long Binh Jail when they first met eight years ago under trying circumstances. Trying for Kane that is.

"You have security outside?" Kane asked, indicating the wire.

"Sure. We discussed that. This city sucks."

"See? You're already changing your story," Kane said. "You said you liked New York."

"I said I relished the potential for intelligence work in New York," Trent clarified. "It's as dangerous as Vietnam was."

"How was Vietnam dangerous for you?" Kane asked. "Did you ever leave your desk?"

"Sure, I—" he startled as Morticia appeared next to him. "You're quiet," he said to her. "Sneaking up on people isn't nice."

"I don't like to disturb folks engaged in conversation," Morticia said, "but my boss wants me to do my job. He's a hard ass that way. Can I get you something?"

Trent turned to Kane. "What's good here?"

Kane pushed the plate across the table. "Get him some cold coffee and he can have my peppers."

Trent looked at the plate. "Thao in the kitchen?"

"That's his job," Kane said. He addressed Morticia. "He doesn't need anything to drink."

"Fine. Whatever." Morticia left.

"What's she all about?" Trent asked, watching her glide away. "Morticia?"

"It's a persona," Kane said. "Didn't know you could read."

"You're not being hospitable," Trent said. "You weren't last month when I visited your apartment."

"Broke in to my apartment," Kane corrected. "What do you want?"

"Westway?"

"What about it?"

"You were supposed to give me information on where the money would go if it's approved. Who'd be skimming what."

"The information I managed to uncover is no longer viable intelligence which is why I didn't get back to you."

Trent chuckled. "Really? Is that because it involved Sean Damon?"

Kane didn't respond.

"Mister Damon had been missing for a while," Trent said. "Certain parties have taken notice."

"Anyone I know?"

"I don't know who you know," Trent said. "The FBI for one. And there's some Injun going around town, asking questions. Some about you. Wanting to know if anyone disliked you enough to want to kill you. Too bad he didn't ask me."

"Did Robert Redford tell you that?" Kane asked, referring to Trent's earlier explanation about how the CIA gathered information by using the example of *Three Days of the Condor*, six days in book form.

"Remember the important things," Trent chided him, "not the trivia."

"I've been told details are important."

"Anyway," Trent said, "that jogged my memory. Reminded me you owed some information. Also, I was wondering why the FBI and this Injun are asking questions about my asset."

"Not your asset," Kane said. "As you pointed out, I haven't given you anything. Is your memory tired?"

"What?"

"From the jogging."

"That was bad," Trent said.

"I've been saving it for a special person."

"Keep saving it," Trent said. "I was discussing you with Phil King a week or so ago. We both still wonder if you were the trigger man in Cambodia."

"Elephants," Kane said.

Trent frowned. "What?"

"Someone said elephants have long memories. I wonder if that's an urban legend, or more accurately, a jungle legend."

Trent took a deep drag on the cigarette, the end burning bright red. Expelled the smoke. "Damon isn't the only one who went missing. There's a fellow who worked for the Cappucci clan. A chap named Quinn."

"Since when do you care about the mafia?" Kane asked, but he knew what was coming based on what Quinn had revealed before departing the mortal coil at the other end of the rope that had been around Kane's neck.

"We keep tabs on organized crime," Trent said, "but that's not who is asking about Quinn. Our friends across the pond are making discrete inquiries reference his whereabouts. Very hush-hush, top secret stuff."

"Then why are you telling me? Lost my clearance a long time ago, about the time I got a dishonorable discharge. By the way, what's the progress on that?"

Trent tsk-tsked. "Why do I have to remind you to keep the conversation mature? Did you know Quinn was working deep cover for MI-6?"

Kane indicated the wire. "Why not pull the microphone out so I can speak into it directly and avoid any possible distortion? And really, you want to keep this mature? Don't ask stupid questions when the answer will be recorded."

Trent nodded as he fired up another cigarette. A small cloud was beginning to hover over the booth and Kane was regretting not taking Morticia's suggestion about upgrading the heating and cooling.

Trent pulled a small radio out of his jacket pocket and switched transmit off. Put it back. "Her Majesty isn't pleased. Actually, let's be real, Her Majesty has no fucking clue who Quinn was or what he was doing. The Brits like talking that way. As if they still answer to royalty. But like us, MI-6 is a world unto itself. They are not pleased. And their displeasure can have consequences."

"I heard a rumor that Quinn was trying to infiltrate the IRA's gun buying operation here in the States," Kane said.

"Which is why he was after Sean Damon," Trent said. "Fucking Micks are a pain in the ass. They've been fighting the Brits so long, most of 'em have no clue what they're fighting about."

"Isn't it about freedom?"

Trent made a sound of disgust. "What does that really mean? Are any of us free? We just trade the yoke from one self-centered group of pricks to another."

"Never took you for a philosopher," Kane said.

"I worship at the altar of pragmatism."

"Which self-centered group of pricks are you working for?" Kane asked.

Trent reached across the table and took Kane's water. Drank. "Damon is missing. Quinn is missing."

"Perhaps they committed suicide together?"

"That would have been fortunate but it's not what happened, is it?"

"No idea."

"That's not the only thing you have no idea about," Trent said. "The key fact in front of me is *you're* not missing." He waited on the response.

Kane took a sip of coffee.

"Well," Trent finally said, "what's done is done. Blood over the dam." He chained another cigarette. Morticia glided by, shooting him a dirty look, a thimbleful of water splashed unnoticed into a waterfall of sewage. "Five bodies were found on the top floor of a building not far from here. Damon, three of his guys and one unknown. I don't suppose you know what happened to them?"

"Ask your buddies at the FBI," Kane said. "They took over the scene from NYPD."

"I did. Got nothing from them. Boys in Suits. Think they can run counter-intel when they can barely tie their shoes."

"Sometimes I wonder how this country functions at all," Kane said. "Between the various alphabet soups, I don't think anyone knows what they're doing."

"And you know what you're doing?" Trent asked. "That was, by the way, rhetorical, because we both know you're clueless."

"There's an inherent logic flaw somewhere in there. Then why ask me anything?"

"Quinn's missed three contacts with his handler at MI-6," Trent said. "That means he's either dead or gone rogue."

"I think he was always rogue," Kane said.

"You used the past tense," Trent observed. "Thus, he's the fifth body." It wasn't a question. "Phil King wants to mollify our British cousins. Quinn was working on a long-term deep cover op. Damon was just one part of it and—"

"Then he wanted to become head of the Five Families," Kane said. "Or married to the head. Seems Sofia Cappucci has aspirations."

"That may be," Trent said. "MI-6 hasn't exactly filled us in on their plans."

"What do you know about Sofia Cappucci?" Kane asked. "I hear she has a degree from Princeton."

"Thinking of switching one lady boss for another?" Trent asked.

Kane didn't take the bait. "Quinn was involved with her. She's on the periphery of this discussion."

"Let's leave her there," Trent said.

"Operation Underworld," Kane said. "Before your time. Before the CIA's time. During World War II, Naval intelligence, an oxymoron, recruited Lucky Luciano to influence the mafia to ensure the New York docks were safe from saboteurs and squash any strike by the unions that could affect the shipment of war supplies."

"Ancient history," Trent said.

"I was wondering why you, the CIA that is, cared so much about how Damon was going to parcel out bids to the various families here in New York given you have no jurisdiction over them. I'm thinking leverage against future possibilities. Get some chips you can cash later with the mob?"

"*'You just keep thinkin' Butch. That's what you're good at'.*"

"You must have a thing for Robert Redford," Kane said. "Damon was point of contact for NORAID and buying guns for the IRA. Your cousins across the pond or lake or ocean, should be happy that he's no longer acting in that capacity."

"But someone will take his place," Trent pointed out. "Quinn's goal wasn't to take out Damon. If that had been it, he could have done it relatively easily as you've shown." Trent made a point of looking at Kane's wrists and neck. "Probably more efficiently than you."

"Doubtful," Kane said, "as he's also among the missing."

Trent gave a slight nod. "That is a point of consideration." He chained another cigarette. "Irregardless, one of the goals was uncovering the IRA infrastructure in the US along with contacts in what the Irish like to refer to as the 'old country'. The Brits have troops in harm's way in Ireland. Names, Kane. They wanted names, not a massacre."

"They wanted an infiltration and for Quinn to stay in place," Kane said. "Be a mole. No matter what he was doing outside the mission tasking. No matter how many people he killed or hurt."

"Let's stay mature," Trent said. "The machine will always be grinding away. People are replaceable. The goal is to get the right people in the right places and control the machine. Not throw wrenches in it. You seem to have a limitless supply of wrenches."

"You're assuming the machine is inevitable," Kane said.

Trent shook his head. "You know--" He reached up and put a hand to the earpiece. Glanced over his shoulder as the Washington Street door opened.

The Kid approached the table, missed a step seeing Trent, but continued. Tossed the *Times* on the table and snatched the five-dollar bill. Kane gave him a forced smile and a slight shake of his head. The Kid departed without a word.

"Keeping up on the news?" Trent asked.

"Did MI-6 know what Quinn was up to off the clock?"

Trent shrugged. "Who cares? The problem is *you* went rogue and fucked up their op."

"You don't know that," Kane said. "And there is nothing for me to go rogue from."

"Phil King believes you owe. Thus, you owe."

"Let me repeat: how can I go rogue when I don't work for anyone?"

"You still do jobs for your girlfriend lawyer. I notice her father wasn't part of your Blackout—well, what do we want to call it? You were there. Fiasco? Clusterfuck?"

"I got nothing for you."

"Bullshit," Trent said. "You got between Damon and Quinn and walked away with nothing? I got a bridge on the other side of the island to sell you. There's some buzz that there was a lot of money besides the weapons."

"Twenty-seven men died building the Brooklyn Bridge," Kane said. "And six days after it opened in 1883, a woman fell on a staircase and caused a panic, killing twelve more people. Sometimes the building of something has unintended deadly consequences as well as the completion."

Trent stubbed out a cigarette, rattling the ashtray. "I don't have the patience for your bullshit."

"Yet, here you are."

"What's with Thomas Marcelle?" Trent asked. "He was involved, wasn't he?"

"That's a question I'm currently pondering," Kane said.

Trent was reaching for the pack in his jacket pocket when his hand shifted and went to the earpiece. He turned and got up, rattled. "What the fuck, Kane?" He headed for the door on Gansevoort.

Kane followed. They exited into the middle of a burgeoning standoff. Two men, Trent's security, stood next to the big Lincoln, mini-Uzi's in hand, but not raised.

Ting Van and Tong Van faced them. The twins had *their* hands hovering near their waist, ready to draw and pull whatever firepower they were packing under their silk suit jackets, which last Kane had seen, the night of the Blackout when they helped protect the Diner, were Mac-10s. Van Van were identical twins, Chinese, with dark hair and sporting black silk suits with white shirts and thin black ties. They were solidly built, five and a half feet tall.

"Easy," Kane said to Van Van. He pointed at the guards and then indicated Trent. "They are here with him, to talk to me."

The Van on the right glanced at Trent, while the other Van kept his focus on the two security guards.

"They are not here for you," Kane added to Trent.

"Nungs?" Trent laughed, trying to recover his composure. "What kind of place you running here, Kane? You got mercenaries working for you?"

"They don't work for me."

"You never cease to amaze me," Trent said.

Kane spoke to Van Van. "Talk to Thao in the kitchen."

They bowed slightly at the waist and went into the diner. One looking forward, the other walking backward, keeping watch.

Trent gave a signal and his security retreated to the air-conditioned comfort of the Lincoln.

Kane and Trent returned to the booth.

"Did they help you with Damon and his Trinity?" Trent asked. "And Quinn? That would explain a lot."

"Do you think I would have needed help? Hypothetically speaking, of course."

"I think you need help right now," Trent said. "Take that kid who just delivered the paper, like he does every day."

Kane tensed, waiting for the hammer.

"I'm disappointed in the details you've let slip your mind," Trent said, "given you were just lecturing me on that matter. You've forgotten that our surveillance picked up your kerfuffle with those two Delgado musclemen who broke into your place. That was before you finally realized we had the bugs. The night you were crying? Did you spill some milk? I still wonder about that. Anyway, that caught our attention. Remember asking them for the keys to their Cadillac? We have that on tape. Surprised you let those guys go still breathing. We put surveillance on the car.

"Seems that young friend of yours has some dubious acquaintances; besides you, of course. Somehow, he ended up with the keys and sold the car to what is called in the vernacular, a chop shop. That's a felony. We've got photos. I suspect the young fellow would be very popular among the inmates on Rikers."

"Were you born this way?" Kane asked.

"Smart? My parents told me I was a genius from a very young age. If I'd studied the violin, I'd have been a virtuoso."

"They lied."

Trent waited.

"I might have something about Westway," Kane finally said.

"Yes?"

"What Damon was planning on doing with the contracts. But as I said, with him gone, it's out of date."

"The people on the other end aren't," Trent noted. "It's all data. The stuff we feed into that computer. Never know what turns out to be important."

"The computer Robert Redford runs?"

"Bring me what you have."

"It's about money, isn't it?" Kane asked. "That's what you told me last time we met. That money is the fuel for everything."

"Glad to know you listened."

"Where did you hear there was money in Damon's place?"

Trent reached into his coat and pulled out a crumpled pack. Fired one up. Took a deep drag. Gave Kane an appraising look. "That's the FBI's case."

"You called them 'boys in suit'," Kane pointed out. "You know anything about who uses radio-controlled detonators?"

Trent ignored the question. "When can you get what I want?"

"It will take me a day to produce," Kane said. "That should give you time to get me some answers."

"You work for me," Trent said.

"No. We're dealing with each other as mature, responsible assholes."

Trent snorted. "All right. Live your fantasy."

"And something else," Kane said. "Do you know anything about an IRA team here in the States planning something?"

Trent's eyes narrowed behind the tinted lenses. "What have you heard?"

"Ask the FBI," Kane said. "They queried me. I'm clueless, as you've pointed out."

"When did they ask you this?"

"Yesterday."

Trent inhaled deeply on the cigarette dangling from his lips. Let out a cloud of smoke. He lit another one from the remains, even though he was barely a third through. "Why are they talking to you?"

"Ask them."

"Fucking Irish," Trent muttered. "Tilting at windmills while drunk and singing heroic ballads. Do they have windmills in Ireland? What did the Feebs say?"

"They said that an Irish squad of what they called the Swords of Saint Patrick is in the States trying to procure weapons and explosives for a mission and that it would occur next week."

Trent blinked. "You're shitting me. How do they know that?"

"From Damon."

Trent processed that one for a few seconds and then delivered his summation. "Fuck me to tears."

"Yeah," Kane said. "Left hand, right hand, no brain controlling either one and certainly no coordination."

"You took out the Brits' guy *and* the Feeb's guy in the same evening?" Trent shook his head. "Un-fucking-believable. But I should expect you to do epic things, Kane. Your little escapade in Cambodia almost ended the war."

"As I said last time you mentioned that," Kane said, "would that have been a bad thing given subsequent history? Also, I didn't say I took anyone out."

"Yeah, yeah," Trent said but his mind was elsewhere. "The IRA has never done direct action on U.S. soil. It would fuck with their base here. They need the money. It's not adding up. It might be something Damon fed the Feebs to keep them happy and confused."

"That might be," Kane agreed. "But I think the team is real."

"Why?"

Kane checked to make sure Morticia wasn't within range. "They tried to kill me the night before last."

"You're just full of surprises," Trent said. "What happened?"

"What do you know about a guy named Crawford? Rich oilman from Texas."

"Never heard of him."

"Might want to check him out, because it was either him or me as the target."

The ash was almost an inch long on Trent's neglected cigarette. With his free hand he rubbed his forehead. "What happened?"

"Someone tried to blow up a boat we—Crawford and I-- were on in the harbor Thursday night. Radio controlled timer to C-4. I was lucky and interrupted them before they finished the connection. Wounded one of them in the shoulder."

"And the cops don't know," Trent said.

"If the cops knew, you'd have known."

"True." The cigarette was so far gone the red glowing edge reached his fingers. He looked at it for several moments as it reached flesh, then put it out in the ashtray. Pulled the pack out, fumbled for a lighter, checking one pocket, then found it in another. Fired up. "Who from the FBI told you this?"

"Two agents. Tucker and Shaw."

"Never heard of 'em."

"They said they've been running Damon for three years."

Trent snorted. "Or he was running them. He was a wily old bastard who outlived a lot of people."

"I'd agree that's more likely. They said he was close to giving them more information. But I doubt *that* was going to happen. Anyone with any sense of covert ops would never let that kind of info out."

"The IRA isn't that professional," Trent said.

"A small cell could be. If they sent someone over here, they'd send their best."

"Yeah, but what would that be, given it's the Irish? Hell, they skipped out on World War II. They spend more time fighting each other than the Brits." Trent shook his head. "Damon was stringing them along."

"Yeah, except someone tried to blow up the boat I was on the other night," Kane reminded him. "It wasn't the CIA, was it?"

"If it had been, we wouldn't be having this conversation."

"Really?" Kane asked. "Did *you* know about Quinn beforehand? That he was a foreign agent operating on *your* turf, Trent, here in the city."

Trent took a deep drag on the cigarette. "Who is that?" He indicated Riley, who was bussing a table.

"My cousin."

"You have a weird family tree," Trent noted. "He sure isn't pure Mick like the rest of 'em. Not that you married inside the immediate gene pool. Iranian? Really?"

Kane knew Trent was poking him which meant the CIA agent was off kilter by the new information. "You didn't know about Quinn, did you?" Kane pressed, ignoring the feeble attempt at diversion by bringing up Taryn.

Trent didn't answer.

"Yeah," Kane said. "Thought so." He held up his forefinger. "Even in your own organization you didn't know what the other was doing." As he said that he lowered the first finger and raised the middle to Trent.

"Compartmentalization," Trent said. "Need to know and all that."

"Right." Kane shook his head. "I'm fifty-fifty on whether the target was me or this oil man, Crawford. That Indian asking around is his guy. We want the same answers."

Trent tossed the newly lit cigarette into Kane's coffee. "Monday morning. I'll come here and enjoy the fine atmosphere and excellent service. Bring what you have on Westway."

He departed, leaving a cloud hovering over Kane's booth.

"You were right." Morticia appeared in the midst of the smoke, waving her hand. "He's an asshole. I saw those Yungs give Thao an envelope in the kitchen. I thought businesses paid off mobsters, not get money from them."

"Sometimes it's better to mind one's own business," Kane said.

"You're off this morning," Morticia said. "What gives? Rough night?"

"Strange night," Kane said.

"Care to share?"

"No. And remember, Van Van helped us during the Blackout."

"Speaking of which," Morticia said, "what happened with you that night?"

"You're the literary expert. Is irregardless a word?"

"It's a nonstandard synonym for regardless. The first two letters are redundant."

"Hmm. Thought so." Kane exited the booth. "I've got to make some calls. Be better if you don't listen in."

"Don't let me hear then, but can I say something?"

Kane waited.

"Actually," Morticia said, "it's attributed to Sherlock Holmes."

Kane fidgeted, glanced at the payphone.

"In one of the books, Holmes tells Watson that *'there is nothing more deceptive than an obvious fact'*."

"Right," Kane said. "You probably shouldn't listen when I talk to the CIA. You might hear something you can't unhear."

"CIA?" Morticia rolled her eyes. "You have a lot of strange friends, Kane. *His* friends had guns out there. I thought we were going to have a massacre between them and the Yungs."

"He's not my friend. And they're Nungs."

"Sorry. Your associate? And Nungs."

"Hey, can you help Thao with something after your shift?"

"With what?" Morticia asked.

"You'll see," Kane said.

"Such an enticing offer." Morticia moved off with coffee pot in hand.

When her back was turned, Kane knelt, reached under the front edge of the bench and popped out a microcassette and put it in his pocket. He went to the phone and deposited several dimes for the long-distance call to an area code fifty miles north on the Hudson River. He rolled the dial and it was answered on the second ring.

"Archives. Plaikos."

"I require a withdrawal." Kane told his cut out what he needed and when he would be at West Point.

Plaikos ended the call as abruptly with one word. "Putnam." The phone clicked off.

Kane called his landlord next. It was answered on the fourth ring. The old man sounded hungover. "Pope."

"It's Will. I need information on a Texas oilman named Crawford. And anything about the IRA in New York City. Contacts, addresses, anything."

Pope became alert. "What's going on?"

"I'll tell you later today. But there's a clock on this."

"I'm on it," the former newspaperman for the *NY Post* said. "About the woman yesterday—"

"Don't worry about it. Talk to you later."

Kane deposited a single dime. A man answered, the sound of phones ringing and many voices resonating in the background. "Task Force Omega."

"I need to talk to Detective Riley," Kane said.

"What-da-ya-got?" All one word as only a NYer could do. "I can help you."

"Nathan's my uncle," Kane said. "It's personal."

"Hold on."

Kane waited. Morticia cleaned off his table, giving him a look he wasn't sure how to decipher but that was nothing new.

"Riley."

"Nathan, it's Will."

"How you doing, William? Haven't heard from you in a while. Nor has your mom."

Kane didn't waste time on a preamble or lingering family matters. "What do you know about the IRA?"

There were a few seconds of silence. "That's a pretty broad question. Can you tell me why you're asking and that would narrow things down?"

"If some IRA soldiers were to come here, is there a point of contact in the city they'd hook up with?"

"The Organized Crime Task Force never had much to do with the Irish," Nathan said, "mainly because their gangs weren't very organized. And nothing on the IRA. They don't operate here. Nothing off the top of my head. Ask Conner," he added, referring to his younger brother, also a police officer. "He's more into that 'old country' malarkey."

"All right. Let me ask you something else. If a body went into the harbor near the Statue of Liberty and the tide was going out, would it get taken out to sea?"

"Oh, Christ, William. What did you do?"

"I didn't do nothing," Kane said, feeling like the kid he used to be, scolded by his uncle. "It's a hypothetical."

"Weird hypothetical," Nathan responded. "Why do you want to know?"

"Forget it," Kane said.

"Hold on," Nathan replied. "I'd have to check. Ask a buddy in harbor patrol. Want me to?"

"If it's no trouble."

"Will do."

"Thanks."

"Hey. You all right? You were acting pretty weird last time I saw you."

That was three and a half weeks ago, the afternoon before the Blackout. "I'm fine."

"I hear you have Liam's son working there," Nathan said. "Your mother would—" Nathan began but Kane terminated the conversation.

"Gotta go." He hung up. Dialed Conner's home and found out from his wife, Aileen, that he was at work. Called the precinct in the Bronx and discovered Conner was out.

Kane hung up. He went into the kitchen. Thao was just over five feet tall, wiry, with short dark hair and brown skin.

"Dai Yu," Thao said with a nod. He had several meals going and a medical text propped next to the grill. Along with a wood crossbow.

"Sergeant."

"What did the CIA want?" Thao asked.

Kane indicated the weapon. "Were you going to shoot him?"

"You would have no problem dealing with Trent on your own." Thao nodded at the mirror tilted toward the small window in the kitchen's exterior door. "When his guards exited the car and faced Van Van I was concerned. Van Van never had much patience. Or common sense. I am glad you were able to keep the situation from escalating but I was prepared."

"I appreciate it," Kane said. "I need a new tape in the device."

"I will do that," Thao said.

"Can you handle the delivery Merrick called about?"

"Certainly," Thao said.

"You know where to bring it?"

"Yes, you told me."

"Take Morticia," Kane said. "She'll enjoy it. I gave her a heads up."

Thao nodded. "May I ask you something?"

"Sure."

"Why did you not want my help?"

Kane knew what he was referring to: the Blackout. "You've done enough. You're building a new life."

"And what are you doing?" Thao slid an omelet off the grill onto a plate and to the counter top, all without looking away from Kane.

"There's a little less evil in the world," Kane said. He'd confided in Thao the events of the evening as soon as he'd regained consciousness after Thao, the Kid and Wile-E brought him back from outside the Nabisco building.

Thao nodded. "Understandable. But you know you can always count on my assistance."

"I do," Kane said. "You saved me that night."

"Next time please let me know where you're going and what you're doing. Even if you do not want me along. It will make saving you easier."

"I'm sorry, Thao. You're right." He paused as Riley came in with a load of dishes.

"Hey," Riley said.

"You enjoying the job?" Kane asked.

"Sure. And I appreciate the work," Riley replied as he unloaded the dishes into the sink.

"I'm heading uptown to the Bronx," Kane said. "You want a lift?"

"I have to finish my shift," Riley said.

"Right. Well, tell your dad hello from me.

"Will do." Riley headed out of the kitchen with the empty tub.

Thao turned to the grill and the next orders. "What did Trent want?"

"Information."

"Will you give it to him?"

"I'll give him what he wants. The pictures I took reference Westway."

Thao nodded. "Appeasement."

"It's more than that," Kane said. He filled Thao in on recent events, making sure Morticia wasn't on the other side of the serving counter listening in.

"This is not good," Thao said when Kane was done.

"No, it's not. I agree with Trent that the IRA would be foolish to do something violent in the United States, but who knows? We've both seen people do dumber things."

"You are involved once more," Thao said.

"I was never uninvolved," Kane said. "I tried to get away but I don't think there's any escaping the past." He realized the implications. "I'm talking about me, not you. That's why I didn't involve you the other night."

"That is thoughtful of you," Thao acknowledged, "but we were and always will be teammates."

Kane pulled the original banded five thousand Crawford had given him out of his map case. Put it next to the book. "Send it to North Carolina. For the others."

Thao nodded. "I will take care of it. I spoke with Tam and she says the girl, Sarah, is doing well."

"Ask Tam to give her some of the money."

"How much?" Thao asked.

"Tam will know best."

Thao smiled. "She will. She is very wise. That was a good thing you did, helping Sarah."

"Are you all right with what I did?" Kane asked, knowing that Thao would understand the question was about more than the young prostitute Kane had rescued from Damon's clutches.

Thao put down the spatula and gave Kane his full attention. "I have reflected on it. We fought in a war together and we were uncertain of the larger reasons. We fought for each other. But we lost that war. Perhaps it is not wrong to fight for people you know and care about without there being a larger reason? Especially if those you fight against are evil."

Kane nodded. "Kind of the way I look at it."

"The problem," Thao said, "is that there will never be an end to the evil people."

"But there will be less."

THE BRONX

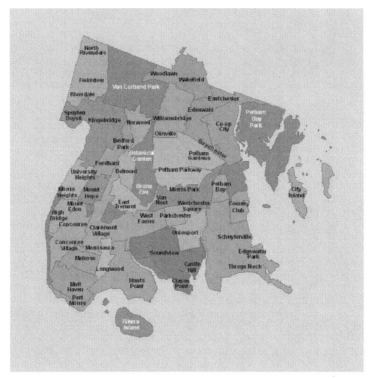

Saturday Mid-Morning, 6 August 1977

BAYCHESTER, THE BRONX

Kane ignored the no parking signs on Eastchester Road and pulled the Jeep on the sidewalk next to the playground between East Gun Hill Road and Arnow Avenue. He checked his watch. Slightly after ten in the morning. His Jeep was old, vintage 1965, and stripped down with no top, basic canvas seats, a footlocker in the back. The windshield was up, a concession to the drive to the Bronx from Manhattan.

Small playgrounds populated three of the four corners of the intersection. Holy Rosary Church was to the northeast and the elementary school that had consumed eight years of Kane's childhood to the southeast.

An unmarked police car approached from across Gun Hill and stopped at the light. Kane recognized the driver. The cop car cut across the double lines, earning an irritated horn blast, and rolled onto the sidewalk facing the Jeep. Conner Riley got out. The youngest of Kane's mother's three brothers, he was a once solidly built man gone to not quite complete seed. He possessed an Irish face, papered with broken blood vessels. Some vestiges of hair covered his scalp. His suit was rumpled and cheap, his tie, as usual, undone, top button the shirt open. A .38 snub nose was tucked under his gut along with a silver shield.

"We got to stop meeting like this," Conner said. "Heard you called the house."

"It's Saturday," Kane said. "Thought you'd be home."

"My schedule's all fucked up," Conner said. "We got so many guys pulling weird shifts because of Son of Sam. But no fucking overtime, except for Omega. And when I said we got to stop meeting like this, I meant you need to stop coming here every Saturday."

"It's my way."

"Way of what?" Conner asked. "Seriously, Will. What are you accomplishing by being here?"

"I remember," Kane said. "And sometimes . . ."

"Sometimes what?"

Kane pointed at his head. "My mind does weird things. Thinks crazy stuff."

"Everyone thinks crazy stuff," Conner said. "As long as you don't act on it."

"I can't act on it," Kane said. "It's not about the future. It's the past. I wonder what if. What if that trial in Vietnam had never happened? I'd have been home a month earlier at the regular end of my tour. Taryn and Lil' Joe would never have been in this intersection. And if Ngo's disappearance hadn't happened there never would have been a trial. If I hadn't joined Special Forces. If I hadn't been in the Army or gone to West Point. If Maria hadn't introduced me to Taryn. All these things and—" he pointed to the intersection—"that wouldn't have happened."

"You're right," Conner said. "I'm not the brightest guy in the family, as I'm constantly reminded, but that crap is silly and stupid. You need to get your shit together and think about the future."

"Right," Kane said.

"I fucking hate when you say that," Conner said. "I heard you stopped by your parent's place a few weeks ago and said a bunch of crap."

"Nathan tell you that?"

"No. My sister. I actually talk to her. Unlike some people I know. She was upset. Said you was acting crazy."

"I'm not sure if I'm going crazy or getting saner," Kane said.

"Your sister said you was asking about Taryn. You've never heard from her?"

"No."

"Any idea where she is?" Conner asked.

"No."

"What about her parents? They lived here in the city, didn't they?"

"Why all this interest in people no one gave a shit about when it mattered?" Kane shot back.

Conner held a hand up, defensively. "Hey. Just asking."

"Her father worked for the Iranian government," Kane said. "They went back home after Joseph died. Might have been because of that or his tour of duty was up. I've got no way to contact them there. Taryn probably went back with them."

Conner changed the subject. "What happened to you? Your neck?"

"Nothing." Kane glanced at his watch. Ten-ten.

"I don't think this is mourning," Conner said. "I think it's like your mom says: nuts. Seems you're starting to agree."

Kane turned away from him and stared at the intersection where his son was killed at 10:12 on a Saturday morning in 1969 as Kane was flying back from Vietnam. "Because I feel it."

Conner followed his gaze and his shoulders slumped, giving up on the futile and trying to understand something too horrific for him to contemplate for his own children. "Okay."

They remained still, both ignoring the cars, trucks and buses passing through the busy intersection.

After a couple of minutes, Kane finally faced his uncle. "No one has ever been with me here before. Thanks."

"Welcome, I guess," Conner conceded. "You know . . . " he began but trailed off.

"What?"

"You weren't the only one to take Joseph's death hard. He was my sister's only grandson. You skipped out of town so fast afterward you didn't—" Conner abruptly stopped and shook his head. "Forget it. Now, what did you call about?"

"The IRA. If some of Provos came over here and needed weapons and explosives, who would they hook up with?"

"Sean Damon," Conner promptly answered. "Speaking of which—"

"Besides Damon?"

"Shit, Will. What's going on?" Conner wiped sweat off his forehead with a stained handkerchief which he stuffed back into the suit pocket.

"I got wind that the IRA is planning something in the city."

"They wouldn't do that."

"If they were?"

"Planning what?"

"No idea. But it might involve a bomb."

A city bus chugged by, bathing them in diesel fumes. The windows were obscured by graffiti.

"Who told you this?" Conner asked. "I gotta run this up the chain of command."

"The FBI, so the powers that be already know. I assume they've informed NYPD."

"How are you involved?"

"I'm a concerned citizen," Kane said.

"You're a pain in the ass." Conner shook his head and looked at the traffic going by. "I haven't heard anything."

"I doubt many people have," Kane said. "Might not even be true. I'm just checking. If these people are here, they'd need someone local to help. Maybe if I did some digging . . ." He waited for Conner to step in.

"How are you gonna dig into that mess?" Conner asked.

"That's what I was going to ask you. Supposing Damon is out of the picture, where would they go in the city if they wanted to talk to somebody from NORAID?"

"Why are we supposing Damon is out of the picture?"

"Keep your eye on the ball, Uncle Conner. NORAID?"

"Not to the offices," Conner said. "It would have to be unofficial."

Kane waited.

"Kelly's Bar," Conner finally said. "As close as we got to an IRA headquarters in the city, but they aren't doing anything illegal. They take collections, have singers from the old country come in, that sort of stuff. You go in there asking the wrong questions, it's gonna piss some people off."

"Are there right questions?"

Conner laughed. "You always were a smart-ass."

"How about you go with me? After you get off?"

"That might piss someone in there off even more," Conner said.

"How so?"

Conner was staring intently at the church, as if there were answers in the stone and brick. "I owe a guy some money."

"How much?" Kane asked.

"Six large."

"All right," Kane said. "What time you get off?"

Conner told him. He ended by shifting the discussion back to family. "I heard Liam's kid is working for you down in the Village."

"He's at the diner," Kane said. "I'm not his boss or anything. I just got him a job until he goes to Basic."

Conner nodded. "That's good. Maybe you should stop by and say hi to your mom? Since you're only a few blocks away?"

"Yeah, all right."

"Don't sound too fucking enthused," Conner said. "And like I said before. Go to the fucking cemetery like a normal person."

Conner went to the unmarked and pulled out into traffic to look for bad guys.

Kane started the Jeep and drove onto Gun Hill Road, then left onto Arnow. He paused at the Post Office and dropped off the same envelope with a check and one with cash he did every week. He'd changed the return address on the check from *Marcelle, Van Dyck, Feinstein & Marcelle* to Toni's new firm, which meant he'd been aware the Towers had their own zip code. Since he'd come back to the States this last time in '75 he'd sent the agreed upon check to his ex, Taryn, via her family's lawyer. None had been returned and none had been cashed. The lawyer's office refused to take his calls or allow him in.

The cash didn't have a return address and he knew it was used by the widow of the machinegunner who'd held the line on

Hill 875. His family had been given the Medal of Honor from a grateful nation but Kane knew medals didn't pay the rent.

Kane drove along Arnow Avenue, down the hill he'd trudged up to school for twelve years, eight in Holy Rosary Elementary, then four more years to go to Mount St. Michael's High School. However, he didn't turn right onto Bruner Avenue where his parents and elder sister still lived. Pulled a U-Turn in the garbage strewn dead end on Arnow and found his way to I-95 and Manhattan.

Saturday Afternoon, 6 August 1977

GREENWICH VILLAGE, MANHATTAN

Kane knocked on the door to the main floor of the brownstone, tested to see if it was unlocked, then opened.

"In the kitchen," Pope called out.

Kane followed the aroma of pipe smoke down the hall to the rearmost room, overlooking the small garden the owner tended with a varying degree of diligence, lately more lack. The recently laid-off reporter for the *NY Post* was ensconced in his usual spot, seated in a comfortable armchair pulled up to a round, wood table. A scattering of newspapers and books covered the surface. A teacup that might, or more likely not, hold tea was in front of him.

"William. I missed you this morning."

Kane had noted Pope getting up later and later, lost without the call of the story. "I was out early."

Pope wore his usual: khaki shorts and loud Hawaiian shirt. His straw hat with black band was on a hook next to the back door. A pair of reading glasses rested on the tip of his red nose.

"I apologize if I misinterpreted by letting the young woman into your apartment last night," Pope said. "She said you'd been together the previous evening and, to be honest, I was at a bit of a loss to deny her request. I've always had a problem saying no to a pretty woman. In retrospect it was a betrayal of—"

Kane waved a hand. "She said we'd been together? As in the biblical sense?"

Pope frowned. "Now that I think of it, no. I might have made an error of assumption."

"I was driving a boat she was on while she was pitching a movie to a producer. That was the together part."

"Apologies," Pope said. "In my defense, I *had* seen Ms. Truvey before last night so it wasn't like I was letting a complete stranger in. She is not easy to forget."

"Seen her where?"

"An off-Broadway production." Pope frowned. "Unfortunately, I can't quite recall what the name of the play was."

"Was she any good?"

"To be frank, I only remember her because of her, shall we say, charms? Please tell me if I misjudged by allowing her in?"

"Don't worry about it," Kane said. "I needed to talk to her. The name I gave you, Crawford. He was on the boat. And she was trying to use her charms on him to get funds for a movie."

"The pernicious life of the ingenue," Pope said. He picked up a thin stack of Xeroxed pages. "This was messengered over from my friend at the *Post*. Anything particular you're interested in?"

"Who would want to kill him?"

Pope raised an almost hairless eyebrow. "Was your boating expedition challenging?"

"Someone planted a bomb on the boat."

"A bomb? Who?"

"That's what I'm trying to figure out," Kane said. "Give me the quick version." Kane sat down in the chair, half facing the back door and half the hallway.

Pope looked at his notepad. "Born in Escalante, Utah in 1922 to a poor family. Father was a minister on an Indian reservation. Mother died when he was four. A tough depression era childhood as many endured in the thirties. Joined the Marines at nineteen the day after Pearl Harbor." Pope pulled a sheet out. "This is interesting. He was—"

"A Marine Raider," Kane said.

Pope frowned. "He took part in the Makin Island Raid but it doesn't say he was a Raider, although that would seem likely. The information I've gathered on that event is sketchy and contradictory. Regardless, he was wounded and eventually evacuated to Hawaii. Honorably discharged from the Marines." Pope flipped to the next page. "There's nothing on him until 1947. I imagine he was recovering from his wounds."

Kane knew what that could be like.

"He was involved in starting a program that's very much a controversy but was popular for decades; LDS—Mormon--families adopting Indian children."

"How many did he grab?" Kane asked.

"Seven."

"What about family outside of the Indian orphans? Wife? Kids of his own?"

Pope checked the sheet. "His wife passed ten years ago. Breast cancer." Pope raised an eyebrow. "No children of their own. Then he went to Texas and started working in the oilfields. Bought his way into a fledgling company, eventually taking it over. His worth is estimated to be over fifty million."

"Enemies who might want to kill him?"

"Nothing specific. But to rise from nobody to those heights meant stepping on some toes. It's said that behind great fortunes are great crimes although that is ascribed to Honore Balzac and what he originally wrote was—" Pope halted his digression, sensing Kane's mood.

"Why does he mess with financing movies and plays?" Kane asked.

"I imagine taxes," Pope said. "Using them as write-offs since most lose money. I don't know how it works as I've never been flush enough to avail myself of that part of the tax code. That's what lawyers are for."

"Who is his lawyer?"

"A firm in Amarillo." Pope began to dig through the Xeroxed pages, but Kane stopped him.

"Don't worry about that. Any connections between Crawford and the IRA?"

"The Provos?" Pope shook his head. "Not that I read."

"Ever hear of Provos called the Swords of Saint Patrick?"

"They all consider themselves some sort of holy warriors," Pope said. "Fighting for freedom and to expel the heathen Brits. Do you mean formally?"

"Yeah."

"Not off the top of my head, but I'll check. Why do you ask?"

"Do you think the IRA would conduct an attack on U.S. soil?" Kane asked. "Perhaps a bombing?"

Pope frowned. "It would seem to their disadvantage as they generally have a misguided groundswell of support in the States that is quite lucrative." Pope's alcohol-fogged brain finally made the connection. "You think the Provos planted the bomb on the boat?"

"Appears likely," Kane said. "I think I was the target, not Crawford. I was kind of hoping it might be him."

"You were targeted because of Damon?" Pope asked.

"Yeah. But more so, because of Marcelle."

"You never filled me in on what happened to Damon," Pope said, almost a question.

"Let's just say I interrupted an arms shipment to the IRA."

Pope made a tsk-tsk sound as if scolding Kane. "They are relentless in the pursuit of revenge."

"Trying to cheer me up?"

"Just the sad reality," Pope said. "They put more effort into tracking down those who've betrayed them than anything else."

"You're making me feel so much better," Kane leaned back in the chair, thinking. "Ever hear of Kelly's Tavern?"

"In the Bronx?" Pope said. "NORAID central."

"That seems to be the consensus."

Pope dug in his papers. "My friend, Maggie, was intrigued by the properties Damon and Marcelle were purchasing. She checked the tax records, deeds, and other paperwork. Someone went through a lot of trouble shielding ownership in shell corporations that are headquartered overseas."

"Owned by Marcelle and Damon, right?" Speaking of Maggie, Kane noticed two theater tickets stuck to the door of the fridge with a magnet: the tickets he'd paid Pope for to take her out with to thank her for the information on the Marcelle/Damon properties. They were among a number of other papers magneted to the door, but if Kane remembered rightly, the date for the play was past.

Pope shook his head. "Hard to tell who truly owns them beneath all the paperwork. The bottom line is who holds the deeds and she wasn't able to dig that deep. Between fifteen and twenty million is invested in this. I doubt they had that much money between them."

"Does Marcelle get Damon's portion now that he's gone?"

"Financial law isn't Maggie's expertise. But it would seem logical."

"And Marcelle is in hiding," Kane said.

"The—" Pope paused as his phone rang. He picked it up. "Pope." He listened for a second, then held it out. "You should consider getting your own line downstairs with an answering machine, not that I'm complaining, but I'm sure it would be easier for you."

"Then it would make this like a permanent move," Kane said as he took the receiver. "Yes?"

Toni's voice echoed through the line. "Will, I've tried talking to Selkis. He's blowing me off. Whatever Yazzie said to him weighs on him more heavily than anything I say."

"You want me to put some weight on him?"

"I want to get to the bottom of this. I did some checking. My father still hasn't surfaced. He was gone from the firm beginning at noon on Thursday. No one has heard from him since."

"Are you with Selkis now?"

"I'm outside his office."

"Where?"

Toni gave him the address. "Not exactly the nicest part of town," she added.

"Where is the nice part?" Kane asked.

"Don't be a smart ass. Get over here. And hurry please. He was acting squirrelly."

"I'll be there in fifteen minutes. If he leaves, try to follow."

"That's your expertise."

"I'm not there."

"No shit. See you in fifteen."

Kane handed the receiver back to Pope. "Duty calls."

"We're missing something in all of this," Pope said, papers spread out on his table.

"As Toni just told me, 'no shit'."

TIMES SQUARE, MANHATTAN

Kane took the Kawasaki dirt bike, which was parked with his jeep in an old garage on West 4th, off Seventh Avenue. He wove through traffic, avoiding bike messengers and pedestrians. He made it in twelve minutes, including the time to run to the garage, open it, and unlock the chain from the bike.

Kane jumped the curb and stopped in front of Toni. Even though she was a native New Yorker, Toni was out of place standing in the doorway to a small tourist shop selling New York themed trinkets. It was next to the Big Apple Movie Theater whose marquee was promoting four hits in continuous showing: ORAL ANNIE, SEX SCHOOL, INSIDE JOY and WET RGY.

"What's a wet rgy?" Kane asked.

"Not funny," Toni said. "Some guy offered my twenty dollars to—" she waved it off. "Let's get this over with."

"Where's his office?"

Toni indicated the adult theater. "In the back of that place. Door's in the alley."

"What kind of producer is this guy? And how did he become your client?"

"I don't need any shit right now," Toni said. "He has a legit office over on 52nd. That's the one in the phone book. But he wasn't there. I know about this place from his files."

"What does he use this one for?" Kane asked. "His not legit stuff?"

"I don't know," Toni said. "It never came up."

"He's hiding from Yazzie." Kane released the clutch and rolled the dirt bike into the alley, off the sidewalk. He killed the engine and put the kickstand down. "Let's go."

They moved along the alley, stepping carefully. A body lay to the right, a homeless person, curled up and hopefully alive, but neither stopped to check. Toni indicated a metal door. Kane pulled it open on hinges that needed some WD-40. A dimly lit hallway threatened.

"Left at the end of the corridor," Toni said, "then first door on the right."

Kane led the way, Toni following close behind. He paused before the end of the hall. Took a step back. "Something's off. He alone in there?"

"He was," Toni said. "I didn't see anyone go in the alley but it opens on the next street."

"Is there a back way out of his office?"

"There was a door."

Kane edged around the corner, muzzle of the gun leading on an angle where he could see the shot. It was dark in the next hall. "Were the lights off or on in the hallway?"

"On."

Lions and tigers and bears, oh my.

Kane moved into the hall; his eyes having adjusted. There were several wooden doors, all closed. With his right hand he reached up to the bulb. Still warm. He twisted it, illumination, and as quickly he untwisted. "Someone was here after you."

Kane stopped at the first door on the right. Checked the door jam. Wood and needing a coat of paint. It hadn't been kicked in. There was no sign to indicate whose office it was.

"Get out of here," he whispered to Toni. "Do *not* come in."

Kane tried the handle. It turned easily and he pushed. The only light in the dingy, windowless office was a feeble desk lamp.

Selkis was seated behind a grey metal desk. His head was lolled back. The walls were covered with posters, surprisingly not skin flicks, but nothing Kane had ever heard of, which actually didn't mean that much as the only movie he'd seen since coming back to the States was *Star Wars* with Toni and the Kid and Thao a few weeks ago. There was the desk and a filing cabinet and an empty chair in front of the desk.

Kane noted that the door to the right rear of the desk was cracked open and he went to that, gently opening with his right hand, gun ready in the left. He spotted a figure silhouetted against a single bulb forty feet down a corridor walking away, not running but moving with purpose.

Kane spun around as Toni came in.

"What's—" she began, but Kane put his finger to his lips and cut her off.

"Take a cab back to your office," he hissed. "Now!"

"What's going on?"

Blood was still dripping from Selkis' slit throat. Kane gave her a shove out the door. "Go!" He shut the door and went to the back one. He ran into the corridor, focused on where the man had exited. Stopped at it, took a deep breath, shoved it open, crouching low, gun at the ready.

A dimly lit area. A maze of booths, each door just a few feet apart. No windows. Low ceiling.

Kane entered and it took him a few moments to get oriented: an adult bookstore and these were peepshow booths. Dirty, sticky floor. It was difficult to locate the entrance in the dark maze. He turned a corner and an old man stared at him and the gun without much concern. Kane pushed past. He reached an intersection and saw a flicker of movement to his right that was gone as quickly as he'd spotted it. He went that way. Reached the corner, came around gun at the ready.

A man wearing jeans, work boots, and a black leather jacket over a white t-shirt was trapped in a dead end. He had a leather satchel similar to Yazzie's over one shoulder. He about-faced. His skin was toned bronze like Yazzie's. His hair was cut short on top, white walls on the side, screaming ex-Marine.

"Disgusting place," the guy said. "This city is a sewer."

"There are plenty of folks who would agree with you," Kane said.

"Walk away," the guy advised Kane.

"You're not from around here," Kane centered the gun on him. "Texas?"

"I'm from a much nicer place." The man smiled. "You going to shoot me? Bring the cops here?" He held his hands wide. The movement opened his jacket and revealed a very large knife in a sheath underneath his right shoulder, a gun under the left. "Your call. I'd recommend the walking away."

Kane holstered the forty-five. And held his ground. "You're one of Yazzie's brothers?"

The man straightened with pride. "We are the *Beesh Ashiike*."

"That doesn't translate well here."

"The Hard Flint Boys," he said. "You wouldn't understand. You are Kane?"

"Yeah. You?"

"Johnson."

"Seriously?" Kane said.

In reply, Johnson pulled his knife and came forward with it at the ready, blade down in his right hand. The knife was impressive, a Bowie, the blade ten inches long. It had a thick heft on the spine, razor sharp edge on the business side.

Kane drew his Fairbairn commando knife from the small of his back. His blade was less than half of the other guy's, narrower, and double edged.

"Blade on blade," Johnson said. "The old way."

Johnson slashed, a feint to get a feel for his opponent. Kane easily dodged. The space they were dueling in was narrow, five feet wide, with booth doors on either side. Not much room to maneuver.

Another angled slash, from Johnson's upper right down low left. This was closer, the tip of the big knife barely missing Kane's chest as he spread his arms wide to avoid getting cut. Echoes of bayonet training at West Point floated in a part of Kane's brain that was detached from what was happening in real time: *there are only two types of bayonet fighters: the quick and the dead.*

Kane took a step back.

"You can still run," Johnson suggested as he spun the knife in his hand, reversing it to blade up in his fist. He came at Kane with a low strike, upward, aiming to gut Kane.

Kane dropped to the floor as he spun his body, left leg lashing out as the tip of the Bowie nipped the hair on the top of his forehead. His boot hit Johnson on the side of his right knee, toe sliding behind it. Kane slammed into the floor, continuing in a roll and hooking Johnson's leg, pulling the knee forward, causing him to lose his stance.

As Johnson struggled to regain balance with his arms, Kane jabbed upward with the Fairbairn, point driving into the thigh on the interior, severing the femoral. Kane pulled the blade back as fast as he'd struck. Warm blood surged forth, soaking Kane's arm. Kane rolled to the left, hitting the wall, then scrambling backward with his feet, knife raised in a defensive posture.

It wasn't needed as Johnson was momentarily stunned. He stared at the blood pulsing out of his leg in disbelief. Kane got to his feet.

Johnson wasn't stupid. He dropped the Bowie and clamped both hands over the wound attempting to stop the bleeding. Went to his knees as thick red flowed around his hands. Johnson stared at him, the realization of impending death subsuming all other thoughts and emotions.

"Why did you kill Selkis?" Kane asked.

All wasn't totally subsumed though as Johnson let go of the wound with his right hand and grabbed the Bowie. He slashed at Kane's legs, the effort causing more blood to pump and quicken the inevitable.

"Why kill Selkis?" Kane repeated.

Still on his knees, Johnson dropped the knife. He raised both bloody hands in supplication. He whispered something in Navajo. Kane, the former altar boy, recognized a prayer when he heard it.

Then he died, arms dropping, still on his knees, his head slumping forward onto his chest, then the upper body teetering until his forehead was on the stained floor. A profane position to end in.

Kane knelt next to him, avoiding the spreading pool of blood. He used the point of the Fairbairn to push open one side of the jacket, exposing the pistol in a holster, then the other side, revealing the leather shoulder sheath for the Bowie. And a Motorola Pageboy II pager clipped on the left side of his belt.

Kane snatched it off. Searched for a wallet but came up empty other than several crisp hundred-dollar bills which he left. He grabbed the satchel and tossed it over his shoulder. Kane stood, then paused. He reached down and tipped the body over, rolling Johnson onto his back, his dead eyes staring upward.

Kane retraced his steps, out of the peep show room. Into the corridor and back to Selkis' office. The producer's skin was pale, bled out; head lolled back, his shirt soaked with blood. He was sitting in a pool of it and there was a steady drip-drip-drip as it soaked through the leather and onto the floor.

Kane checked the desktop but it was clear. The deep drawer on the right side was open and empty, the lock broken. Kane took a moment to look in the satchel: a half-dozen film cases, the same design as the ones that had been in Damon's factory.

He looked about the dingy office, briefly wondered if Selkis had ever imagined this would be the place where he died. Kane shut down the extraneous mental meandering and left.

Saturday Late Afternoon, 6 August 1977

TOWER ONE, WORLD TRADE CENTER, MANHATTAN

"What happened to Selkis?" Toni asked as Kane walked into her office. She had a glass in hand and was standing next to a narrow window, Manhattan spread out behind her, the late afternoon sun casting long skyscraper shadows west to east across the island.

"He's dead." Kane sat at the table. He wore the grey t-shirt, having tossed the blood-stained denim shirt in a dumpster. There was dried blood underneath his fingernails, the quick scrub in a restroom inadequate. He put the satchel with the film canisters on the seat next to him.

"Where did you catch the cab?" Kane asked. "Right in front of the place?"

"No. I had to go to Forty-Fifth. Dead how?"

"He got his throat slit," Kane said.

"Who killed him? Why?" Toni walked over, putting the empty hand out to steady herself, the other still holding the drink as she sat.

Kane placed the pager on the desk.

"Yazzie?" Toni asked. "What happened? Why would he kill Selkis? Where is he? What's going on, Will?"

"It wasn't Yazzie," Kane said. "But one of his people. I got that off him."

Toni was still for a moment. "Where is the guy?"

"We fought and he ran off," Kane said. "But not before I got that."

"Did he hurt you? Are you okay?"

"I'm fine."

Toni downed the rest of the glass, went over the bar and filled it. She glanced at Kane; eyebrow raised in question.

"No, thanks. I don't suppose Yazzie left a way to get hold of him with Mrs. Ruiz? His pager number?"

Toni shook her head. "No." She went to her desk and sat down. "Why?" It was obvious her question wasn't connected to Kane's.

"Why what?"

"Why kill Selkis?"

"Because he knew something," Kane said. "I will give Yazzie that. These things," he indicated the pager, "allow them to respond fast."

"What could Selkis have known?"

The motorcycle ride from Times Square had given Kane time to grasp this twist. "Selkis knew about the connection between your father and Crawford."

Toni stared at him. "What?"

"*There is nothing more deceptive than an obvious fact*," Kane quoted Morticia quoting Sherlock Holmes. "We've been wondering why the bomb on the boat and not something simpler? To kill me. *And* kill Crawford."

"How is Crawford connected to my father?"

"That I don't know yet, but the obvious fact is the bomb was planted to kill both of us. It's the only thing that makes sense."

"How is Crawford involved with the IRA?" Toni asked.

"He's probably not," Kane said. "The attack was set up by your father. Crawford is tied to *him*. Your father is a smart man. He saw a way to take care of two problems at the same time."

"I'm not tracking," Toni said.

"You don't *want* to track, Toni," Kane said. He walked to the front of her desk, put both hands on it and leaned forward, meeting her eyes. "Betrayal, Toni. It's the worst thing someone can do. Your father did it in '67 when he made the deal with Damon. Betrayed his oath of office. Once you do something like that, it becomes easier and easier. How many crooks has he gotten off since then? People he knew were guilty?"

Toni couldn't meet his gaze. Nor did she say anything.

Kane lifted his hands and went to his usual chair. Sat down, rubbed his eyes. "Did you know your father was buying up property on the west side? Land that Westway would need? And adjacent property? So was Damon. The map was on the back of one of the boards in the conference room."

"No."

"That property cost a lot of money. The estimate I've gotten is fifteen to twenty million. Did they get the money from your mother?"

"I don't know." Toni's voice was barely audible. "No. She wouldn't have given it to him. She's not worth anywhere near that much."

"You think he had that lying around at the firm?"

"No."

"Perhaps Damon had it in his back pocket?"

"No."

"Right," Kane said. "Even if your mother could have, Damon and your father wouldn't do that. Because then it could be tracked. Accounted for. Taxed. You're the lawyer. Figure it out. You told me that's what Selkis did with his films. Ran Crawford's money through them. A tax break. But what about money laundering?"

Toni put a hand up, as if to get Kane to stop, but she didn't say anything.

"Crawford was your father's money man. Probably Damon's, too."

"You don't know that for certain."

"Come on, Toni." Kane indicated the pager. "Do you know how this works?"

Toni didn't look at it. She was staring out over Manhattan, but not really seeing anything. Kane examined the Pageboy II. At the top on the right was a jack for headphones and a scroll on the left labeled volume. Below the hole of the headphone jack was a button. He pressed it and a double tone sounded, then Crawford's voice.

That drew Toni back to the room. "What was that?"

"Navajo," Kane said. "That was Crawford ordering Johnson to kill Selkis.

"'Navajo'?"

"Code talkers," Kane clipped the pager on his belt on the right side.

"What's in the bag?" Toni asked.

"Films the guy took from Selkis' office," Kane said. He'd checked the labels. "They're from Damon. I recognize one. Tammy. She was the girl Damon used in the apartment on Gramercy before Sarah."

"Who?"

Kane remembered that Toni didn't know her real name. "Farrah. The girl you hooked me up with. Remember her? The girl before her was Tammy. Damon told Farrah that he'd let her go in another six months. Just like he had Tammy. Except the only place Tammy went to was the factory on the top floor of the Nabisco building." Kane tapped the bag. "I've seen part of it. Damon's Trinity took her. Tied her to a table. Tortured her. Raped her. And eventually, killed her. I'm assuming the other films are of the same vein."

"He showed me one." Toni admitted what she knew Kane already knew. "To threaten me."

"Yeah," Kane said. "There's six films." Kane gave it a few seconds but Toni didn't reply. "The question is, how did Johnson know the films were there? And why did he take them?" He didn't add that Toni had been followed to Selkis' secondary office. He answered his questions. "They're all connected. Crawford. Damon. Your father."

"Father—" Toni began but nothing further was said.

"Did Ted ever talk to you about the honor code?"

Toni blinked at the abrupt shift in topic. "What?"

"Did he ever talk to you about the honor code at West Point?" Kane asked. When she didn't reply, he continued. "We spent a lot of time discussing it. Arguing about it, actually because it was one area where Ted and I disagreed. '*A cadet will not lie, cheat, steal or tolerate those who do.*' Seems pretty basic. Ted thought it was a good thing, but I wasn't a big fan. I didn't understand why we needed one. I figured a person was either honorable or not long before they came to West Point. All the code did was make the liars and cheaters and thieves hide what they're doing or place it on hold for four years." Kane put a hand on his chest. "It's either in here or it isn't. I don't know if someone is born with honor or grows up to learn it. Maybe a bit of both. My dad's a shit in many ways, but I always knew I could count on him in the crunch. All of us kids did. His anger would make us pay, but he always anted up via actions when it was needed."

Toni turned her seat once more to face the window as if that would hide her from Kane's words.

"I went to West Point to get away from my dad's anger," Kane said. "Ted went there because he wanted to get away from something else in your father. I never truly understood what it was until today. Ted couldn't trust him. On some gut, instinctual level, Ted sensed that. It's why he rebelled against your father's plan for him. It's why he clung to the honor code. To the sense of duty, we were shaped with at the Academy. Far more than I ever could, Ted embodied the best of Duty, Honor and Country."

Toni gave a deep gasp and her shoulders shook as she sobbed.

Kane remained in the chair. "When the Civil War was starting, Ulysses Grant said something that has always stuck with me, especially given how many West Pointers who'd sworn an oath to the United States went to fight for the Confederacy: '*There are but two parties now: traitors and patriots. And I want hereafter to be ranked with the latter and, I trust, the stronger party*'." Kane stood. He picked up the paper bag. "I know where I'm ranked. If Yazzie contacts you, tell him he can page me. If you hear from your father, tell him I'm coming for him. "

He left.

Saturday Evening, 6 August 1977

RIVERDALE, THE BRONX

"This might not be such a good idea," Conner said to Kane.

They were on the Van Cortlandt Park side of Broadway in the northwest Bronx. Conner had been waiting next to his car for Kane to come down from the elevated subway. Behind them in the darkness, amongst the trees at the south end of the park, was a dilapidated stadium and abandoned swimming pool, victims of city cutbacks. The large open plain called the Flats was a couple hundred yards to the north. Conner's personal vehicle, a red 1970 Chevy Nova that had seen better days, was illegally parked in front of a fire hydrant. Conner wore his cheap suit, no tie, a ring of sweat around the collar.

"I'm sure it's not." Kane could smell the booze wafting off his uncle.

"Yeah," Conner said. "I think—"

Kane pulled an envelope out of the cargo pocket of his pants. Held it out to his uncle. "Six thousand."

Conner instinctively reached for it, but stopped short. "I can't take that, Will. I mean—"

"Don't worry," Kane said. "It's not my money. It's a bad guy's money and he's not going to miss it."

Conner took the envelope and slid it inside his jacket. "Thanks." But he hesitated, looking under the elevated tracks, across the street, with trepidation.

"Come on," Kane said. He led the way, crossing Broadway. Just above was the rattle of the #1 train Kane had been on, pulling out of the northern terminus at 242nd Street and returning south toward Manhattan. The elevated subway was a contradiction in terms but a reality of the train system in the outer boroughs. The #1 tracks centipeded from here, south through the Bronx, on a bridge across the Harlem River into Manhattan and only descended below ground after the Dyckman Street Exit in the Fort George neighborhood, above Harlem.

"I never found the rubber el you told me about," Kane said as they passed one of the stanchions holding up the tracks, trying to get Conner to wind it down a notch.

"I thought it might make you calmer for your driver's test," Conner said as they stepped over trash lying in the gutter and passed between two parked cars, NO RADIO cardboard signs displayed in the windshields. The rubber el was an urban legend told to many an anxious beginning driver negotiating a street like Broadway straddled by the elevated subway that one of the stanchions wasn't iron but rubber.

"It was nice of you to help me learn to drive," Kane acknowledged.

"All I did was sit there," Conner said. "Your dad was a little nuts about you riding the clutch so your mom asked me."

Kelly's was dimly lit. The windows were tinted green and covered with posters advertising singers, bands and rallies, many featuring the Irish national flag. The sound of voices raised in drunken revelry and loud music echoed out of the brick walled tavern. It used to be a garage for horses and carriages and been converted to a tavern early in the century. The name, Kelly's Tavern, was painted on a large board extending on a pole over the door with a shamrock between the words.

Conner paused before the door, on the edge of the sidewalk. "Nathan called me this afternoon."

Kane waited.

Conner turned to face his nephew. "Why do you want to know about bodies getting swept out to sea?"

"Research," Kane said. "That's part of my job. Find out things for people. I've learned it's best sometimes not to ask why."

"Toni wants to know?" Conner asked, assuming he was on a job from her.

Kane took his uncle's arm and pulled him away from the door, farther down the sidewalk to the pool of light underneath one of the few functioning street lights, adjacent to a dark alley on the north side of the tavern. "The reason we're here is I'm trying to figure this IRA thing out. I'm involved because someone put a bomb on a boat I was on the other night. I asked Nathan because I was wondering if the boat had blown up, whether my corpse would have been swept out to sea. Okay?"

"Geez, Will. Coulda told me that up front."

"I just did."

"Hold on," Conner said as it sunk home. "Someone tried to blow you up? Nathan didn't say nothing about that."

"I didn't tell Nathan or it would have involved a long conversation I didn't have the time for. What did Nathan tell you?"

"He talked to a guy he knows in harbor patrol and the guy said it's a possibility, but odds are the body or debris wouldn't make it through the Narrows. Probably get washed up on Staten Island or Brooklyn before the Bridge. Not many bodies from Upper Bay make it to Lower. But Lower, if the tide is going out, they're gone."

"Thanks," Kane said.

Conner sighed and nodded toward the bar. "We gotta be careful. Lots of hot-heads in there. What do you expect to find out?"

"I don't know," Kane said. "But in all my ops, we never infiltrated anywhere without the locals eventually discovering we were there. Even in the deepest jungle where we didn't think anyone was within miles." He indicated the tavern. "This is the locals. If the IRA is in town, someone knows. We listen, see what's going on."

"Don't seem like much of a plan," Conner complained.

"As you noted," Kane said, "just walking in is going to upset someone. We'll see what happens."

"All right, but let's be careful." Conner opened the door to the sound of a man accompanied by several others on instruments singing an Irish ballad about long lost unrequited love in the green, green hills of the Old Country. A simpler fantasy time if one ignored little bumps in the road like famine. The kind of song Kane's dad would sing around the house every so often, especially on the rare occasions he had a drink or two. Not that Kane's dad had ever been to the 'Old Country', having been born in Manhattan, but both his father's and mother's parents had been immigrants.

The bar was crowded and Conner had to push his way through to find a spot that had arm's access to the bar between a couple of stool squatters. He waved to catch the bartender's attention and indicated he wanted two of something.

Kane didn't bother to tell his uncle he didn't want to drink. He was scanning the crowd, mostly older, white men in various stages of inebriation. There were NORAID jars for *Widows and Orphans* on the bar and scattered on tables. All had small bills and change in them. Kane imagined a fiver would be a massive donation for these people. At one table were a couple of out of place college students, probably from Manhattan College which was just to the west, uphill from the tavern, a location in the Bronx which didn't match the name of the school, a contradiction most never questioned.

Conner managed to retrieve two mugs. Kane shouldn't have worried as his uncle shot-gunned the first, fortifying himself. Kane spotted a table open up in the corner near the front window and made for it, assuming Conner would follow. He claimed the real estate, sitting with his back to the wall, the dark window to his left.

A long bar dominated the side of the tavern opposite the door. Over thirty tables were jammed in the open space. The lighting was hodgepodge with several spotlights focused on the stage and a scattering of cheap semi-chandeliers hanging from the twenty-foot ceiling. The walls were brick with faded painting on the exposed portions. Some were old advertisements for horse feed. The band was directly to Kane's front, on the other side of the door. The stage consisted of a plywood platform built up five inches from the floor. There was no space for dancing as tables crowded right to the edge. Dancing wasn't the point of the music.

There were some women in the place, a few wives with husbands, but not many. Several older ladies, most likely widowed as divorce wasn't in the Catholic lexicon, trolling for replacements for the lost paycheck. There were several bar flies who'd given up caring what others thought of them years ago, and were at that next to last stage before drinking alone in their one room apartment.

Conner hadn't followed. He was talking to a white-haired gentleman sporting a cap. There was a fancy cane lying across the top of the table the man commanded in the opposite corner.

The ballad was picking up pace and some of the crowd joined in, stomping their feet and singing the refrain.

"You a copper?" A middle-aged man, broad-faced, widely built, and wearing jeans and a white button-down shirt leaned over the table, crossing the invisible line into Kane's personal space which caused him to lean back. The interloper spoke with a slight brogue, but mostly New Yorker, which was the predominant dialect in here. He had a mug of beer in his hand, half empty, or, Kane mused, half full depending on the mood.

"No."

"You're with Conner," the guy said. "He's one."

"He's my uncle."

"Shit for family then," the man said, grinning as if he didn't mean it but not pulling off the negation.

"We don't choose them," Kane said.

"No, we don't, but we're stuck with 'em." The man grabbed a seat, but it hit the back of another chair at the next table. "Move the fuck outta the way," the man snarled at the occupant.

The chair's owner complied with alacrity, not just shifting the chair, but vacating it and heading across the tavern with his three comrades.

"I'm Patrick," the man said as he sat down, thumping the mug a bit too hard and not offering his hand.

"Kane."

"Haven't seen you in here before, Kane," Patrick said.

"We'd stop in after races across the way in Van Cortlandt when I was in high school."

"That's a while ago for you, weren't it?" Patrick noted.

"It was."

"But you haven't been recently."

"Nope."

"You're not drinking."

"I usually don't."

"Then why are you here?"

"I'm imbibing the ambiance."

Patrick pressed. "You look like a copper. And not a copper like your uncle. You look like a serious man. Your uncle is more of a joke in these parts given his various vices." Patrick gave the same non-smile. "Are you a serious man?"

"When the situation warrants."

The ballad came to an end with a rousing chorus and many mugs and shot glasses lifted, but Patrick wasn't participating. He was focused on Kane. The band took a break, which lowered the volume a bit. A woman claimed the vacated table, sitting in the chair away from Patrick, and turning toward the stage.

"If you're not a cop, why are you carrying a gun?" Patrick demanded.

"I'm wearing one. If it was in my hand, I'd be carrying it."

"You're a serious man yet a smart-ass," Patrick said. "Not an engaging combination."

Kane saw Conner glance this way, get nervous and start to get up, but the white-haired man put a hand out, tapping Conner on the forearm and shaking his head. Conner obediently sat.

Patrick also saw the exchange. "You gonna try to muscle me for your Uncle? The fucking degenerate gambler? That why he brought you?"

"He has the money. Six thousand."

Patrick laughed and shook his head. "That's what it was yesterday. Today it's seven large."

"I never understood how that works," Kane said. "What's it called? The vig? Seems odd it would go up that much in one day."

"'Vig'? That's what the wops and the Jews call it. For us good folk, it's interest, pure and simple and fair, for a loan. Your uncle's not keeping you up to speed. He bet on today's Yankees game in Seattle. Know who won?"

"Not a baseball fan."

"Lots of non-fans gamble," Patrick said. "It's not about the game. It's about the betting. There're folks who will bet on whether it's going to rain tomorrow. Catfish Hunter got bombed in Seattle and they lost by seven. So that's another five hundred. And it went up another five hundred since I sat at this table and decided I didn't like you."

"Bad first impression, eh? I get that sometimes. Not Conner's fault."

"You came with him. You're not drinking, you're not mixing with people, just sitting here giving everyone the cold eye," Patrick said. "If you aren't a copper, then you're something else, but whatever it is, I don't like it."

"Then it's six thousand, five hundred," Kane said.

"Seven."

"Bad business model. Take the six point five and don't accept his bets anymore."

Patrick poked a finger toward Kane, stopping six inches short of his face. "See? That's what I don't like. Being told what to do."

"Did Conner tell you he'd be here this evening to pay?"

"Only reason I took today's bet," Patrick said. His eyes shifted.

Kane had spotted Patrick's associate, a hulking young redhead with a smashed nose edging toward them, twenty seconds ago. "He a boxer?" Kane asked, keeping his attention on Patrick.

Patrick nodded. "Aye. His ring name is Magnus. Means great in battle."

"Optimistic," Kane said. "He any good?"

"The lad's good enough to get seven large off ya." Patrick laughed. "Not like you're gonna pull that gun, are you? Your uncle isn't the only cop in here and most of them are my friends."

"'Friends'?" Kane said. "But you're right. Gun play is not likely. And not necessary."

Magnus was to Kane's right, looking down at him and looming over the woman at the next table. She scooted the chair away from his presence.

"Is that his mean look or his ugly look?" Kane asked Patrick. He looked up at the boxer. "How you doing, Magnus?"

Magnus glanced at Patrick, searching for direction. "Okay," he said for lack of any witty repartee.

Kane forced a smile, doing his best at appearing reasonable but it was lacking in his own repertoire. "I've reconsidered, Patrick, since you've made this a negotiation rather than a simple business transaction. Let's make it five large. A little something taken off for your rudeness. We can all go home happy."

Patrick got up, his chair bumping hard against the empty chair behind him. It hit the table and slopped beer out of the woman's mug. Kane had already figured out his angles of attack and was tensed to move, but the situation paused when a life-weary waitress in black slacks and a stained white blouse and apron, her age somewhere between a bitter twenty-five or a hanging on forty, tapped Patrick on the shoulder. "Not in here, will ya, Patty? Walsh has told you how many times? Take your nonsense outside, the lot of you."

"Sure thing, my dear," Patrick said, keeping his eyes on Kane.

"Ma'am," Kane said, nodding at the waitress. He pulled out his money clip and peeled off a twenty. "For the lady's beer." He looked at the woman. "Apologies."

The woman twitched a narrow smile in appreciation.

Patrick indicated the door. Kane got up, Magnus shadowing him as they made their way out. Conner was watching and the white-haired man gave a slight point, releasing him. Conner joined the procession. They exited the front door onto Broadway.

"Keep going," Patrick said. "The alley to the left."

"I've got the money," Conner said. "No need for—"

"Shut up," Patrick said. They moved into the alley, out of sight of the street. The odor of rotting garbage, spoiled milk, vomit and urine filled the air.

"I've got the money," Conner repeated, stepping between the bookie and Kane.

Patrick put a hand on Conner's chest and pushed him out of the way. "You're late to the negotiations."

"He wants seven thousand," Kane informed his uncle. "I think that's unreasonable." He faced Patrick, the boxer hovering to the left. "But I'll offer you a better deal. Let's make it ten thousand."

Patrick frowned. "How so?"

"Throw in some information."

Patrick folded his arms, waiting.

"There's a story floating about that some fellows from the old country are in the city," Kane said. "Calling themselves the Swords of Saint Patrick? I'm trying to track them down. Heard a rumor they're looking for certain equipment. I can make the right connections for them with some of my old army buddies. Everyone will be happy."

Patrick spit, hitting the toe of Kane's boot. "You're a lousy liar, you fucking eejit. You're a rat Fed. You smell of it. We've had your kind 'round here before. Sent 'em running with their tail between their legs."

"My grandfather used to yell that at me when he watched us as kids," Kane said. "Never liked the term. Eejit." He glanced at Conner. "Did he call you that too, when you were growing up?"

"Yeah, he called everyone that," Conner said. "Listen, Patrick. I've got the six thousand. I don't see what the problem is."

Patrick poked Kane in the chest. "The problem is this piece of shite you brung around, Conner. And the Yanks lost today so that's another five hundred."

"He's my nephew," Conner tried to explain. "A veteran. He's not a cop. We're just here to pay what I owe. You know I always pay up."

"No," Patrick disagreed, "you don't always pay up, Conner Riley. Mostly I let you skate, because you eventually pay what you can but you're always behind. And I give you rope because you're a cop. But don't lie to me and say you've paid up all. You'll never pay all. That's what makes you degenerate. You're always chasing the action."

"Ten thousand," Kane said.

"Paying is what I've got in mind for both of you," Patrick said. He stuck out his hand toward Conner. "The money."

"Don't give it to him," Kane said, but his uncle ignored him and passed over the envelope.

"Now," Patrick said as he slid it into his pocket, "another grand."

"Got the math wrong," Kane said. "By the way, were the names of the FBI guys Tucker and Shaw? Tall black guy and short white guy with bad skin? Trying to dress like they weren't Feds?"

"I knew you were another one of them," Patrick said.

"My government days are long past," Kane said. "I imagine Tucker didn't fit in at all. Surprised he could even get in the door."

"We run 'em off easy enough," Patrick boasted.

"I've told you why I'm here," Kane said. "I've made a reasonable business proposition."

"An extra thousand for my troubles," Patrick said. "Perhaps I'll let both of you walk away and not get hauled off in an ambulance."

"There's two ways this is going now," Kane said. "Either I give you another four for the information I requested or you give us a grand back and call it even with my uncle and we all go on our merry way."

Patrick nodded toward the boxer, which Kane had been patiently waiting for. Magnus launched a sucker punch aimed for the side of Kane's head.

He struck air because he was big, but not fast, which the smashed nose was prime evidence. He had all the marks of a brawler, not a true boxer, one who traded punishment and counted on his size and stamina to be the last one standing, but that required some degree of rules of the ring, and this wasn't a ring.

Kane ducked, ignored the boxer and hit Patrick just under the right ribcage with a savage uppercut jab, angling it, driving the fist with not just his arm but his legs like a steel coil exploding, knocking the air out of the lung on that side and cracking the lowest rib.

Flowing, Kane wheeled, right arm folded, and slammed the elbow into Magnus' solar plexus as the boxer was rearing back to punch again. That had minimal effect, the young man was used to absorbing blows, but did delay the punch long enough for Kane to bring his own hands up in a defensive posture. He used a right arm high-block to deflect the punch aimed for his face and jabbed three times with his left, hard, directly into the crumpled nose. There wasn't much left to break, but what little cartilage remained gave way and blood started flowing.

Magnus took two steps back, re-assessing the fight and shaking his head, snot and blood flying.

Kane used the opportunity to turn back to Patrick who was reaching under his shirt. Kane lifted his left leg up, knee high, then snapped it parallel to the ground with a side kick, just above the spot he'd punched, breaking the already cracked rib. Patrick screamed in agony and staggered several steps back.

Conner, meanwhile, was fumbling for his gun, so Kane accelerated to prevent this from escalating to deadly force. He half-curled the fingers on his left hand into a modified crane beak, used his right forearm to hook Magnus' punch as it went by, pulling the large man toward him, and struck the 'beak' of fingers into Magnus right eye, not hard enough to rip it out, but enough to elicit a yelp of pain from the attack on a part of his body that could never be reached in the ring by a gloved hand. Kane continued into Magnus, close to him, jerking his knee up into the boxer's groin, then stepped back. Basic, retro move, but always effective.

Magnus went to his knees, one hand on his bruised eye, the other covering his smashed testicles, moaning in pain.

"Easy," Kane said to his uncle as Conner finally cleared his revolver from the holster.

Kane went to Patrick, who was hunched over. "Your rib's broken, but it'll heal. My offer is still good. Ten thousand?"

"Fuck you," Patrick gasped.

Kane pressed the wounded side, eliciting a yelp of pain. "Really?" He slid his hand across Patrick's body, found the gun, a cheap .38 revolver and tossed it into the darker end of the alley.

"Fuck off." Patrick stepped away from Kane. The bookie stood hunched, pain rippling across his face. "You made a big fucking mistake. I got connections."

"Damon?" Kane asked. "Heard from him lately?"

Patrick didn't reply. Magnus slowly got up but the fight was gone.

"I'm going to ask one last time," Kane said. "Anyone come around looking for weapons? Explosives?"

"I'm going to kill the both of you," Patrick threatened.

"I despise empty threats." Kane pushed his right hand into the bookie's busted side, eliciting a squeal of pain.

Despite the pain, the bookie was paying attention to Kane, his eyes wide.

Kane shook his head. "You've never killed anyone, have you, Patrick? I can tell. There's a big difference between those who have and those who haven't. And you haven't. It's the River Styx. The living on one side and those who've danced with death on the other. And you've never taken a whirl. All you do is bets. And you have this fool," he nodded at Magnus, "threaten people, but that's as far as you extend into the darkness. Listen very carefully, because you won't hear these words again. If you come for me or for my uncle, you better be prepared to go all the way. Complete black. Not just dance with the devil but become intimate." Kane put his face close to Patrick's, looking him in the eyes. "But you're not going to. Are you?"

Patrick shifted his eyes and hung his head.

"Are you?" Kane pushed his hand into the broken bone.

"No," Patrick gasped.

Kane withdrew the hand. "Anyone come here asking about weapons? Explosives?"

Patrick shook his head. "Not that I've heard."

"Who would have heard?" Kane asked.

"Maybe Walsh," Patrick said.

Kane glanced at Conner. "Know him?"

"He's in there," Conner said. "I was with him earlier. Feeling him out."

"Get anything?" Kane asked.

"Not yet," Conner admitted.

Kane turned back to Patrick. "Could have made four thousand. Instead, you played it wrong. Now. One thousand back. For our trouble."

Patrick fumbled with the envelope, withdrew the money. Handed it to Kane.

"My uncle clear with you?"

Patrick nodded. "Yeah."

"You can leave now," Kane said. "Both of you."

Patrick shuffled off, Magnus at his side. They turned left on Broadway, away from Kelly's.

"I don't think you can place any more bets with him," Kane said to his uncle.

"Jesus, Will." Conner's hand held the revolver limp at his side. "Jesus," he repeated.

"You look like you need a drink," Kane said. He took his uncle by the arm and led him clear of the alley.

"We need to get out of here," Conner said as they walked onto the sidewalk bordering Broadway, Kane guiding them toward the door to the tavern.

"Why?" Kane asked. "Not likely either of them are returning this evening. I still need to get some info. And your debt is paid off."

"Patrick won't let this go," Conner said.

"He will." Kane stopped in front of the door. "He won't come after you, Uncle Conner. Especially since this is the last time you're going in here. Right? And the last time you're placing a bet with him. Correct?"

"Fuck," Conner muttered. "Yeah. All right."

"Plus, what I said is true. He's a lot of bluster but in the end, that's as far as he goes. That's the way it is with most people." He paused at the door. Indicated the small revolver still in his uncle's hand. "Might want to holster that."

Conner belatedly put it away.

"Who is this Walsh?" Kane asked.

"He's president of the Emerald Society," Conner said, referring to an organization of cops and firemen with Irish heritage. "Head of the board of NORAID."

"Is Patrick connected to him?"

Conner frowned. "He pays a slice to Walsh so he can take book in the tavern."

"Family connection?"

"Huh?"

"Is Patrick married to Walsh's daughter or his nephew or something personal?"

"No."

Kane nodded. "Just business then. All right. Tell him I'd like to talk to him. I'll give you a couple of minutes."

They went inside. Conner headed straight to the bar. Kane noted that someone was sitting at his former table: the woman whose beer had been spilled. She was in her thirties, red, curly, shoulder-length hair, a narrow, drawn face, edging her appearance from attractive to ascetic. Her eyes were green. She wore a short coat over a knee length dress as if the air-conditioning was too much, which Kane agreed with. A full mug of beer. She acknowledged his return with a nod at the beer. "Thank you."

"Do you mind?" Kane asked, indicating the chair he'd previously occupied.

"Be my guest." Her brogue was stronger than her New York. "The other table was sticky."

Kane sat.

"You have blood on you," the woman noted, pointing at Kane's hand.

Kane took a paper napkin from the dispenser next to the full ashtray and wiped Magnus' blood off his left hand.

"You left with three, came back with one," the woman said.

"I helped them get a taxi," Kane said. "They'd had too much to drink."

"One way of lying about it."

Kane laughed, her comment a nice release from recent events. "It is, isn't it?"

She nodded toward the dark glass. "I saw them limp off." The woman stuck out her hand. "Caitlyn. Not Kate. Not Katey. Caitlyn. With a C."

Kane shook it, noting her firm, callused grip. "Kane. With a K."

She let go and turned her attention to the stage. "This ancient fellow oughta be interesting."

An old man teetered up to the mike, one hand with a death grip on a cane. Someone ran up, placing a high, padded stool in the center of the stage. The white-haired man gratefully sat down. The microphone was positioned in front of him and the height adjusted. The crowd was quieting on its own, a respectful ripple from those closest to the stage outward, until even the most boisterous drunks at the farthest tables hushed.

The old man spoke with a deep brogue. "I came over on the *S.S. Marine Flasher* in '45." Another old man in the crowd howled. The singer smiled. "Some of you know what that means. Four hundred war brides from the Old Country, and just me brothers, meself and the sailors. And don't be asking how we boys wrangled our way on board. It was an uneventful journey; I assure you as they were good Catholic women." He smiled. "Almost all."

There were laughs. Kane glanced at Caitlyn, who hadn't. She had a wedding band on her left hand but there was no man hovering nearby which tagged her most likely a widow, since no self-respecting married woman would be in this crowd alone.

"This is an old song about a young man," the singer announced. "His name was Jack Duggan. And the tale is how he left his home in Ireland and traveled to Australia where he took up a career of brigandry, but always with a good heart, taking from the rich and bestowing to the poor."

The name sounded familiar to Kane, another doggerel his father had warbled on occasion.

The old man began singing, without any instruments backing him up, his voice deep, melancholy and echoing inside the brick walls.

"There was a wild colonial boy,
Jack Duggan was his name."

"Cac tarbh," Kaitlyn muttered.

"Excuse me?" Kane said, recognizing the harsh language from his mother's father: Gaelic.

"Bullshit," she said. "Trying to make a bad man into a good man. Robbed the rich. Helped the poor? You don't think he took a hefty piece for himself?"

"He was his father's only son,
his mother's pride and joy
And dearly did his parents love
the wild colonial boy."

Kane focused on her. "Robin Hood from Ireland to Australia. What's not to like?"

"It's a fantasy," Caitlyn said. "And ballads like that encourage young boys to indulge thoughts of heroism that get them in trouble. Gets them killed."

"Is that what happened?" Kane asked.

She shot him a sharp look. "Aye, I lost my husband. But he was no boy."

"Sorry," Kane said.

"He robbed the rich, he helped the poor,
he shot James MacEvoy."

Caitlyn twitched a smile. "What a refreshing response. I'm usually told he's in a better place. I cannot tell you how infuriating that is. He's no place. He's nothing."

"Not the way the priests see it," Kane noted, edging back in his seat a bit.

"More bullshit they peddle for their own aims." She glanced at his hand. "No ring. Married?"

"I was."

"Did you lose her?"

"She left me." Kane expected some comment about divorce but Caitlyn simply nodded.

"Children?"

"We had a boy.

"A terror to Australia was
The wild colonial boy."

"'Had'?"

"He died. Car accident. It was my fault."

"You were driving?"

"No. But it was my fault."

"I'm sorry to hear about your loss," Caitlyn said, not questioning the guilt, the most Irish of traits.

"Up stepped a band of troopers:
Kelly, Davis and Fitzroy
They all set out to capture him,
the wild colonial boy."

Kane noticed that Conner was moving away from the bar with a cup of coffee. His uncle went over to Walsh's table.

"The men you left with," Caitlyn said. "I feel sorry for the strapping, young lad. He's under the thrall of a scared, angry man."

"Aren't those two emotions always together?" Kane said. "Anger comes out of the fear?"

Caitlyn nodded. "True enough."

"A bullet pierced his proud young heart,
from the pistol of Fitzroy
And that was how they captured him,
the wild colonial boy."

The crowd applauded loudly as the old man's voice trailed off.

"Is the blood his?" Caitlyn asked.

"Who?"

"The lad."

"Nothing serious."

"I hate that," she said with surprising venom.

Kane misunderstood. "I didn't really hurt him—"

She cut him off. "The old making the young do the fighting for them. That's every war, isn't it? Every bully. Every so-called leader. They get others to shed their blood. The worst of 'em don't even give it a second thought. The deaths mean nothing to them." She reached out and tapped the NORAID jar. "American fools put money in here so Irish fools can kill British fools. It's the innocents who get caught between that they don't think of."

"It's every war," Kane agreed. He was beginning to regret stepping out of his no-small-talk persona. He pushed his chair back. "It was nice to meet you."

She looked at him and nodded. "The same. Be safe, Kane with a K."

"Right."

Kane walked over to his uncle. Conner indicated an empty seat at the table.

"Mister Walsh," Conner introduced, "this is my nephew that I was telling you about."

Walsh didn't extend a hand. "You left with Patrick, but came back without him."

"He had other business to attend to," Kane said.

"Did he now?" Walsh said. "I saw you were chatting with the widow." Walsh inclined his head toward the woman.

"You know her?" Kane asked.

"Spoke to her briefly a few nights ago," Walsh said. "Didn't get far. She's a bit skinny and hard for my tastes. Perhaps you had better luck?"

"We chatted briefly about death," Kane said.

"Geez," Conner muttered.

Walsh stared at him. "I suspect you didn't have better luck, then. She seems a bitter sort."

"I'm not here for luck," Kane said.

"What are you here for?" Walsh asked. "Running off the local bookie?"

Kane indicated the NORAID jar on the table. "Widows and orphans?"

Walsh frowned. "Yes? And?"

"How about guns?"

"I'm not following, lad."

"The money buys guns here in the States that get smuggled to Ireland," Kane said.

"That's a terrible, malicious lie," Walsh said, without much passion. "Spread by enemies of the Cause. If we were doing that people like Conner here would have shut us down long ago. We're a relief organization." He tapped the table. "If the man of the house is illegally detained by the enemy, and you know, of course, the Brits throw anyone they desire in prison without due process or a trial, we help the poor family. We give them food, money, put clothes on their back. Or would you rather wee lads and lasses go to school naked with empty bellies, Mister Kane?"

"The last line was quite stirring," Kane said, not stirred at all. "You know anything about Provos, so-called Swords of Saint Patrick, here in the city looking for weapons and explosives?"

Walsh arched an eyebrow. "You go right to it, don't you? With your uncle sitting right here? Did you hear him, Conner? Going to arrest the young fellow? Something like that would be illegal."

Conner stared at Kane in disbelief.

"I don't have the energy to play word games," Kane said.

Before he could continue, Walsh pointed at the door. "Conner, I suggest you depart now before you hear things you can't unhear. I assume you settled up with Patrick one way or the other, eh?"

"Yeah," Conner said, "but—"

"Time to be going, Detective Riley," Walsh said.

"It's okay," Kane said to his uncle. "Drive safe."

Conner tried not to show his relief as he quickly departed.

There was a break in the music and the sound of drunken arguing, a staple of an Irish bar, and dinner table, filled the air. But no one approached the table where Kane sat with Walsh.

"Your uncle is in over his head," Walsh said.

"He's not in anything," Kane said. "This is me."

"What did you do to Patrick and his young bull, Magnus?"

"We paid them," Kane said.

"And?"

"They had pressing business elsewhere." Kane leaned toward the old man. "You've been financing weapons that are shipped to Ireland. Maybe the people whom those weapons kill seem like some sort of distant drama for you. But if there are IRA operatives here, in New York City, how do you think that's going to turn out if they get their hands on guns? On explosives? Cutting close to home."

Walsh glared. "Who do you think you are, lad, coming in here speaking to me like this in my own place?"

"Talk to Sean Damon?" Kane asked.

Walsh's eyes narrowed. "His name has been bandied about lately. Seems he's a popular man."

"You give him the money for the guns," Kane said.

Walsh sat back and reverted to his rote defense. "Last year we donated half a million dollars from sympathetic Americans to over a thousand families. Money that kept food on the table."

"Two hundred and forty M-16s burned up the night of the Blackout," Kane said. "Along with Damon. And his Unholy Trinity."

"And what do *you* know about that?" Walsh demanded of Kane.

"I know those guns were bought with your money," Kane said.

"We send money, not weapons," Walsh said. He shrugged. "Between you and me, if the Provos use the spare cash in other ways, there's nothing we can do about it. The brave men fighting the oppression have to get them somehow. We support the Provisional IRA one hundred percent, with no ifs, ands, or buts. Armed struggle is the only recourse against British Army violence. Do you remember Bloody Sunday? Innocent people, peacefully protesting in Derry, gunned down by the Paras?"

"I wasn't there," Kane said.

Walsh tapped the tabletop. "Were you there when Sean Damon died?" He asked. "And the guns burned up? What about the money?"

"'Money'?" Kane said. "What money?"

"I know your father, William Kane," Walsh said. "I used to be an attorney for the Sanitation Department. He's a proud member of the Emerald Society, to boot. Small world, eh? He's a good man. I'm sure he'd be upset if something happened to his son or vice versa."

Kane put his hands flat on the table. "The problem with threats is they telegraph possible action or inaction. Patrick threatened me just a few minutes ago. As I pointed out to Conner, they were empty."

"Mine aren't," Walsh said. "The IRA doesn't take well to betrayal. Nor does NORAID."

"You're not talking about me then," Kane said. "Because betrayal means someone was loyal."

"Cross us and it's betrayal," Walsh said.

"That's a pretty broad definition," Kane said. "How do you know Damon had money the night of the Blackout?"

The band was back, playing something fast-paced with tambourines and foot stomping and incoherent lyrics. Kane tuned it out.

When Walsh didn't answer, Kane backtracked. "If the IRA sets off a bomb in the city, you're going to lose a lot of your backing."

Walsh replied. "Which is why I don't know a thing about anybody from the old country being in the city doing what you say they're planning. And if they were, I'd certainly be opposed to it."

"Right." Kane stood. "Then we have nothing further to discuss."

Kane didn't look back as he went to the door. He exited into the normal sounds of New York: train brakes squealing as a #1 pulled into station, cars driving on Broadway, a ship's horn blast from the Hudson, a siren in the near distance.

Conner's Nova was still illegally parked on the far side of Broadway. Kane's hand floated over the butt of the forty-five as he scanned the area for his uncle.

"You're a rather stupid man," Walsh said from behind him.

"Everyone is so judgmental," Kane said.

Walsh pointed with his walking stick past Conner's Nova, toward the park. "Let's take a walk and have a chat, lad."

"Where's my uncle?"

"He's fine for the moment," Walsh said. "Whether that remains so depends on the outcome of our chat."

They walked past the car, out of the struggling light of the streetlamps and under the trees. Walsh turned right on the path toward the stadium and the concrete bleachers facing the track and field.

"You waltz right in to my place asking questions," Walsh said, "with your sorry ass uncle at your side. I made some calls after he contacted Patrick this afternoon. Learned some things about you." He jerked a thumb back the way they'd come. "In there was not the place to talk."

"Is that what we're going to do?" Kane asked as he spotted two strangers in the stands, halfway up, Conner between them. "Talk?"

"The FBI was here the other night," Walsh said. "Asking the same questions. Your name was mentioned as having something to do with Sean Damon's demise."

"Odd that the FBI would be dropping names," Kane said. "Seems it should be the other way about."

Walsh halted at the base of the stands, thirty feet short of Conner and the two men out of earshot. Both were large and looked like they worked construction. Dirty, concrete dust smeared pants, black t-shirts, heavy boots. One was in his twenties, long blond hair, the other older, with a high and tight. Conner's arms were behind his back, cuffed.

"Where's the money?" Walsh asked.

"What money?" Kane asked, more as a delay while he assessed the tactical situation.

"The money Damon had."

"What do you know of that?" Kane asked.

"Don't get cute with me, boyo. Damon had a good chunk of my money."

"'My money'?" Kane repeated. "You mean NORAID's money, right? How much?"

"Five hundred thousand." Walsh said. "For a while I wondered if he'd run off with it, but that seemed unlikely after all the years we've been working together. I know Damon's heart wasn't in the Cause, but his greed certainly was. It's been a very profitable arrangement for him for a number of years now. Then we learn yesterday that he's deceased. Along with his lads. Along with a consignment of relief supplies that was to be shipped. All burned up."

"It would be my guess then, that your money is in the same condition," Kane said.

"No one burns money," Walsh said. "They take it. The FBI told me that you were spotted with Damon that evening. Getting in his car. Then he's never seen alive again and you are. Thus, I will ask once more, and for the last time without rancor, where is the money?"

"Why would the FBI tell you that?" Kane asked.

"I find it mightily irritating to get a question in response to a query of me own," Walsh said. He stepped closer to Kane, white hair glinting in the few working lights of the stadium and the faint moonlight that managed to penetrate the layer of smog lying over the city. "But your question is the same I had when they told me this. They said they were trading, telling me where my money is, or rather who would have it, in exchange for information on the Provos. They were under the same delusion you are: that a group is here in the city bent on mischief."

"They were under that delusion because Damon told them," Kane said.

Walsh arced an eyebrow. "Is that so? And why would he have done that?"

"He was a rat."

"I didna hear you clearly," Walsh said.

"Damon was an FBI informant," Kane said. "Been one since '75."

"Malarkey." A short pause. "How do you know that?"

"Those same loose-lipped FBI agents."

"Did you believe them?"

"Did you believe them about me?"

Walsh muttered something under his breath.

"I think my uncle needs to go home, if you don't mind," Kane suggested.

"You have to answer some questions first," Walsh said.

Kane waited.

"Were you with Damon that night?"

"Yes. He picked me up. We talked. Said he was meeting someone and then he dropped me off near my apartment."

"Who did he say he was meeting?" Walsh asked.

"A man named Quinn. Worked as an enforcer for the Cappucci family."

"'Worked'?"

"They found five bodies in Damon's place in the old Nabisco building," Kane said. "They've identified four. Damon and his three men, whom I'm sure you've met. The fifth was probably Quinn."

"A mobster?"

"An assassin," Kane said. "And, who, like Damon, was not what he appeared. He was actually a deep cover agent for MI-6."

"Bullshit."

"Just telling you what I know."

"How do you know *that*?" Walsh asked.

"Because a man I know in the CIA told me," Kane said.

"You make the rounds," Walsh said.

"My curse," Kane replied. "Quinn was trying to infiltrate your organization."

"Jesus, Mary and Joseph," Walsh muttered, looking past Kane as he tried to process these revelations.

"From the results," Kane said, "it appears that Quinn and Damon had an altercation. Seems it turned out poorly for everyone. I would assume if there was money involved, it burned up with the guns."

"You're saying no one walked away?"

Kane spread his hands. "I'm telling you as much as I know which is more than you knew. In the long run, this is a positive for you. Damon was an informant and Quinn was working for the Brits. You're rid of two problems that would have taken you down."

"If it's true."

"Why do you think the FBI was here last night?"

"They were asking about the money. They don't seem to think it burned up."

"Did the two of them seem like the sharpest knives in the drawer?" Kane asked. "Money can be replaced. Damon was the one who told the FBI about these Provos here in the States. Said they came to him for weapons and explosives and he said no. I think he was telling the truth about that."

"Why?"

"Because someone tried to kill me night before last thinking the same as you: that I was responsible for the loss of the weapons and the money and Damon. I suspect that would be the Provos."

Walsh muttered a curse.

"You know something, don't you?" Kane said. "They came to you."

"How do I know you didn't take the money?" Walsh's tone indicated his confusion.

"If I had the money," Kane said, "I sure wouldn't be standing here. Nor would I be asking stupid questions, as you've noted. I'm just trying to stay alive. Find out who is after me and get them to stop."

Walsh shook his head. "I've not heard a thing about any Provos coming over and they'd tell me about something like that."

"Not if they wanted to be secure," Kane said. "But you're lying. You didn't know they were coming. They just showed up, didn't they?"

"They wouldn't try anything here without clearing it by us first," Walsh insisted, but there was an undercurrent of something.

"Is there anyone in the city they could go to directly to get weapons and explosives?" Kane asked, trying to get through the denials.

Walsh shook his head. "Damon had the city wrapped up tight. If he said no, they had no options here."

"What about Boston?"

"That's a different beast," Walsh admitted. "Can't help you with that."

"Someone pointed those Provos at me," Kane said. "Might have been you."

"It wasn't me."

"What about Theodore Marcelle?"

Walsh's eyes narrowed. "What about him?"

"He's Damon's lawyer. He's involved in all this, isn't he? I think he sent the Provos after me."

"Why would he do that?"

"A lot of reasons," Kane said. "If you hear anything about the Provos, will you let me know?"

"Why would I help you?"

"Maybe we can find who took your money? If it didn't burn up," Kane added.

"How would I get hold of you?" Walsh finally asked.

"Call Conner."

Walsh looked over at Kane's uncle, sandwiched by muscle.

"Are we good?" Kane asked Walsh.

Walsh waved his cane at the two men. One of them uncuffed Conner and handed him his own cuffs, gun and key back.

"Don't come back to the tavern," Walsh said to Kane as Conner came down, the two men following.

The shot hit Walsh in the side of the chest, sending him sprawling. The sound of the gun was muted, suppressed and barely audible.

Kane drew and dropped to one knee as he wheeled in the direction of the shooter in the trees at the south end of the stadium. One of the guards had a revolver drawn, the other was next to Walsh, checking him. Conner was at Kane's side, gun in hand.

"Where are they?" Conner asked.

"Already running," Kane said. He glanced at Walsh. The old man was alive. "Stay with him," Kane ordered his uncle.

He didn't wait for an answer, sprinting for the tree line.

Lions and tigers and bears, oh my.

The refrain echoed in a distant part of Kane's brain as he ran along the cinder track toward the tree line under the assumption the shooter wasn't hanging around given there hadn't been a second shot. It was darker under the trees and he stopped, pressing against a trunk and peered about, gun aimed, but no target. Broadway was to the right, Van Cortlandt Park South directly ahead. He couldn't see anyone.

Kane sniffed. The smell of gunfire. He took a step left, then to the right. Found a tree where it was strongest. Checked the ground for a shell casing. Nothing, which meant it had been collected or was a revolver.

Reluctantly Kane backtracked, but at the edge of the open ground of the stadium he paused and slowly turned, bringing the forty-five up. Peered into the darkness under the trees. Waited;

the hardest thing to do under stress. Scanned with the off-center of his vision, section, by section, searching for movement.

He heard yelling behind him; Conner's voice and one of Walsh's men.

Reluctantly Kane ran back to the stadium. Conner was making a ruckus about calling in his fellow police, but he quieted as Kane ran up.

"You get 'em?" Conner asked.

"No."

One of Walsh's men was gone, the other was using his shirt in an attempt to bandage the chest wound.

"I gotta call this in," Conner said.

"No police," Walsh hissed, barely audible.

"No police," Kane echoed to his uncle. He knelt on the other side of the old man, running his hands underneath the body, checking for an exit wound. Nothing. "Hold on," he said to the guard, stopping his crude attempt to stop the bleeding from the wound, which was a dark, black hole with red bubbly froth.

Walsh was having trouble breathing.

"Sucking chest wound," Kane said. "And the bullet is still in him. You need to get to a hospital."

"There's a—" Walsh had to pause to get air—"a doctor in the tavern." A gasp. "My man's getting him. No police."

Kane went to an overflowing trash bin and grabbed a plastic bag. He leaned close, putting his mouth next to Walsh's ear. "It was the Provos who shot you. Where are they? How can I find them?"

"Fuck you," Walsh managed to get out.

Kane put a hand on the other side of the chest. He whispered: "I push here, on your good lung, you won't be able to get much air. You'll suffocate, slow and hard. Did these Sword fellows come to you?"

Walsh's eyes flared anger and fear, a look Kane had seen before. "Yes," he hissed.

Kane removed his hand from the side and placed the bag over the wound, sealing it.

"Take a breath," Kane advised. "What happened?"

The old man took a deep inhale, wincing in pain. He exhaled. "Ah. Better."

Walsh checked to make sure his guard couldn't hear. "Wouldn't tell me why they were here. They wanted weapons and explosive but I figured it was about the missing guns and money. They didn't seem to know about that until I mentioned something. Told them that the man to talk to was Damon but he was gone. Marcelle was next best thing. They're crazy. They'd have killed me."

"Did you tell them where to get weapons?"

Walsh shook his head. "They seemed to know. That's all I can say. There was something off about them . . ."

"What was off about them?" Kane cinched the field-expedient bandage tight, sealing off the hole.

Walsh didn't answer.

"They're going to kill you," Kane said.

Walsh shook his head. "No, lad. This was a warning. You have no idea what you've stepped into."

"You don't either," Kane said.

Headlights flashed through the night as a big, black Lincoln Continental bumped over the uneven ground and rolled to a stop next to them. Two men got out, one the missing guard, the other a bespectacled, old man.

"What have you gone and done now, Walsh, me boy?" the old man asked.

"One round in the side." Kane pointed. "No exit wound. Sucking chest. It's sealed for the moment."

"I've seen worse," the doctor said as he inspected the old man.

"That makes me feel so much better, you old devil," Walsh replied.

"Okay, lads, let's get him in the car and to my office."

Walsh reached out as his two guards lifted him and grabbed Conner's arm. "Don't you call this in, you bastard. This is our internal business." He let go.

Kane walked alongside as they carried him to the back seat. "This is going to turn out bad," he said to Walsh.

"It's already past bad," Walsh said.

The doors slammed shut and the big car threw gravel as it sped away.

"What am I going to do?" Conner asked.

"Nothing," Kane said.

"It was a shooting," Conner said.

"The shooter's gone and the victim just drove away and isn't going to say anything."

"Damn it, Will," Conner said. "This is crazy."

"Come on. Let's get out of here."

They headed toward Broadway.

"They jumped me," Conner said. "Walsh's guys. I didn't have a chance."

"It happens," Kane said. "You won't be going back to Kelly's, will you?"

They reached the battered red Nova.

"Hell, no," Conner said.

Kane faced him. "You called and told Patrick you were coming to pay him off."

"You knew I'd call," Conner said. "It was a set up on your part. Kick the hornet's nest and use me to start it. Was it worth it?"

"The hornet stung," Kane said. "The Provos are here. And they're watching. They approached Damon and he turned them down. Walsh couldn't help them."

"Why did they shoot him?" Conner asked.

"To send a message," Kane said, although that didn't click solidly into place. "No one is going to talk now. They're watching their back trail."

"What did you do the night of the Blackout?" Conner asked. "Did you kill Damon?"

"No." Kane held up a hand. "I swear, Uncle, on my mother, your sister, I did not kill Damon."

"Then what happened to Damon? And his guys? And the guns?"

"You don't want to get involved in that," Kane said.

"A bit late for that, isn't it? Did you learn anything else?"

"I wanted to see if Walsh knew who I was beyond what the FBI told him," Kane said. "He didn't. Which means Damon didn't tell him."

"Tell him what? What did you do, Will?"

"The other thing I learned? The Irish are as crazy as they always were. Drive safe, Uncle."

Conner looked at Kane. "You know, Will, you always were an odd boy. Different."

"I'm my parent's son."

Conner shook his head. "No. You've got a brother and two sisters and you were different than any of them." He turned away and got in his car.

He watched Conner drive off. Then he faced to the south, looking down Broadway, trying to make sense of what he'd felt in the trees that had caused him to pause. It finally came to home: what he'd experienced that night on Hill 1338 in the Central Highlands, during his first combat, waiting for dawn, expecting an overwhelming assault to come. Death. There'd been death there under those trees.

GREENWICH VILLAGE, MANHATTAN

When Kane checked the door to his apartment, he was surprised that he was vaguely disappointed that the matchstick was in place and the door locked. He entered, securing the door behind him.

He wasn't overly surprised, though, to see Yazzie sitting in the chair facing the door, the butt of his gun resting on one thigh, pointed in Kane's direction.

"Come in the back?" Kane asked.

"I suspected a man trained as you are would be prepared," Yazzie said.

"Not well enough, apparently."

Yazzie indicated the sofa. "Have a seat."

"Kind of you considering this is my place."

"I do not like this city," Yazzie said, adjusting the chair and his aim, as Kane sank into the broken springs of the couch. "Too many people. Too dirty. The air reeks of garbage."

"That's my father's job," Kane said. "Garbage. Probably the most secure civil service job in the city. Cops and fire can strike, but garbagemen? People get upset."

"You validate my point," Yazzie said. "People aren't very friendly either. No one will look you in the eye."

"That's viewed as a challenge here. Could get you hurt."

"Have you found Thomas Marcelle?" Yazzie asked.

"Nope. Since you asked, I assume you haven't either."

Yazzie had his finger on the trigger. His leather satchel was on the floor next to him. "You have some things that don't belong to you. Put them on the table. Off hand."

Kane unclipped the pager with his right hand and did as ordered.

"His bag?" Yazzie asked.

Kane reached toward the cushion next to him.

"Right hand," Yazzie warned.

Kane retrieved Johnson's satchel from underneath with his off-hand and put it on top of the cushion.

"His blade was too big," Kane said.

Yazzie nodded. "Bowie. But it has a certain panache. Scares people."

"Scaring only goes so far."

"Obviously," Yazzie agreed.

"You don't seem upset about Johnson," Kane noted.

"He told you his name?"

"We exchanged a few pleasantries before getting down to business."

"He bled out from a knife wound," Yazzie said. "Blade on blade. That means it was a fair fight and he lost. He died with honor."

"That's it?" Kane asked.

"The police do not seem concerned given the location of his death and it appears he had just murdered someone. They're closing the books on it. It seems killings in that part of town don't rate much interest, plus they seem preoccupied with that Son of Sam fellow. Another reason not to like New York. A certain callousness toward the sanctity of life."

Lawyers, Guns and Money 171

Kane didn't point out the obvious disconnect. "You talked to the police?"

"No," Yazzie said. "One of our associates who is a former U.S. Attorney, and has the proper connections, made some calls. A further reason the incident is closed."

Kane indicated the pager. "Your father sent Johnson to silence Selkis. Why?"

"You should be content you are still among the living," Yazzie said.

"What shouldn't he have told us?" Kane asked.

The look Yazzie gave him indicated what he thought of the question.

"Killing me isn't going to clean things up," Kane said.

"I told you," Yazzie said. "That's already been taken care of. Regarding today's incident, at least."

"That's it?" Kane said. "One of your men gets killed and you just move on?"

"For now."

"Your stepfather was laundering money through Selkis."

"No," Yazzie said. "He was doing legitimate investments." He indicated with a nod of his head. "The satchel. Off hand on the table."

Kane did as ordered. "You know what's in here?"

Yazzie didn't respond.

Kane took a chance. "You *don't* know what's in here. Crawford sent Johnson to kill Selkis without informing you."

Yazzie's face displayed no emotion. "Marcelle has some deeds that belong to Boss Crawford. We want them back."

"He was the money behind Damon and Marcelle," Kane said.

"Legitimate real estate investments. Who else knows about the property?"

"Toni. There was nothing legitimate about Damon and I'm beginning to think the same about Marcelle."

"Who else knows?"

Kane was on a roll with honesty, at least a degree of honesty. "That's it right now."

Yazzie holstered the pistol. "We have the same objective. Find Thomas Marcelle."

"I've got a more immediate problem," Kane said. "The IRA gunmen Marcelle sent after me."

"Marcelle also sent them after my father. Our interests coincide since they crossed that line. What do you know of them?"

"One just shot a point of contact I was trying to get information from up in the Bronx. Dried that well up rather effectively. That will keep anyone else from talking."

"They got away?"

"Shooter from the woods," Kane said. "He was gone before I could get there."

"Hmm," Yazzie said, which irritated Kane as much as the drawn gun had.

"The FBI is interested in discovering what the Irish are up to," Kane said. "The Feds heard that they're planning some sort of operation in the city."

"Beyond trying to kill my father?"

"And me," Kane reminded him. "Yes." He told Yazzie what Tucker and Shaw had said. And gave a brief summary of what had just occurred in the Bronx.

"What kind of weapon?" Yazzie asked.

"Suppressed," Kane said. "I know that sound. The entry wound was clean, but the round didn't go through. A pistol. Good shot though, at about forty yards and subsonic round and only trying to wound."

Yazzie leaned back in the seat. "We have to find Marcelle and the deeds."

"You still haven't explained Johnson killing Selkis," Kane pointed out. He indicated the satchel. "Take a look. Selkis was killed for what's in there."

Yazzie didn't reach for the satchel. "Selkis betrayed my father and was a disgusting human being who won't be missed."

"Didn't know the man," Kane said, "but what little I saw there jives with that assessment. You didn't talk to him face to face, did you?"

"We spoke on the phone."

"You couldn't find him. My guess is that he was feeling the heat. He knew you and your brothers were looking for him. After Toni talked to him and revealed that we knew about the connection with her father, he called Crawford and tried to negotiate. Maybe even threaten him with that." He pointed at the case on the table. "From what little I know of your step-father, he's a hard man to negotiate with and dangerous when threatened. He had Johnson trailing Toni. Or you did. That would be the smart move in case she was lying about not knowing where her father was. Johnson paged Crawford when he realized she'd found Selkis. So Crawford paged Johnson back to take out Selkis and recover the films. Wrap up a loose end."

"You tell a good story."

"It was a dumb move by Selkis, but he didn't have many options since Marcelle had disappeared. His time for regrets was brief." Kane pointed once more at the leather bag. "The snuff films?"

"No clue what you're talking about." Yazzie sat up straighter in the chair.

"Right."

"Do you believe Toni Marcelle when she says she doesn't know where her father is? And that she hasn't spoken to him since she left the firm?"

Kane nodded. "Yes."

"Are you two involved?"

Kane launched himself from the couch so quickly Yazzie didn't attempt to draw his gun. He put his arms in defense, taking the brunt of Kane's charge and the two toppled with the chair onto the floor.

Kane jabbed hard at Yazzie's head, but they were tangled together and the punch was relatively ineffective. Yazzie wrapped his arms around Kane, squeezing tight and trapping Kane's right arm inside the embrace. Kane hit Yazzie's right ear with a left-hand open palm strike and rolled away as the blow stunned the Navajo.

Kane drew his gun as he came to his knees. To face Yazzie's Browning Hi-Power which he'd pulled despite the ear blow.

"Touchy about that?" Yazzie asked. He slid his finger outside of the guard. "Truce?"

Kane stood, aiming at Yazzie, then holstered the forty-five.

Yazzie did the same with his gun, then straightened the chair. He rubbed his ear as he sat down. "I don't know whether to take that as a yes or no."

"She's my best friend's sister," Kane said.

"He's been dead a while," Yazzie pointed out. "I'm trying to ascertain whether your judgment is clouded by an emotional attachment. It appears it is regardless of the existence of a physical relationship."

Kane took a step toward Yazzie but he held up his hand. "Hold your horses. I've got a right to question this. She worked with her father for many years. To pretend she had no idea what he was up to is naïve."

"Do you know everything your father is up to?"

"Yes."

"How can you be certain about that?" Kane challenged.

"That's personal."

"Right. Because he's your foster dad. Some families are different. My dad could have had a heart attack last night and died and I doubt anyone would call me. You didn't know he ordered Johnson to kill Selkis. So that's one. Did Crawford finance *all* of Selkis's films?"

"No, just the ones he approved."

"You're full of shit," Kane said. "Look inside the bag that Johnson killed Selkis for."

"I want Marcelle," Yazzie said. "As do you. Or did something change?"

"What if Marcelle gave you the deeds?" Kane asked. "Would you let him walk?"

"No. He crossed a line. He can't go back."

"What line?"

"Same one he crossed with you," Yazzie said.

"But killing one of your people isn't a line?"

Yazzie didn't respond.

"You weren't on the boat that night because you were looking for Marcelle," Kane said, not a question. "Were your brothers already in town or did they fly in? The Hard Flint Boys? What's that mean? Johnson said something in Navajo but I won't disrespect the language by repeating it."

"*Beesh Ashiike*," Yazzie said. "He was a talker. Too much of a talker."

"He thought I'd be dead."

Kane was a bit surprised at the change that passed over Yazzie as some of his hardness faded. "The Hard Flint Boys are the seven stars in the Pleiades Constellation. Among my people when they disappear from the sky, it is time to begin planting."

"What's the connection to you guys, other than the number?"

Yazzie was back. "It's what Boss Crawford calls us."

Kane spread his hands. "Why are you here?"

"Because I didn't want you to get off track and come after me after today's regrettable incident. Marcelle is the target. Nothing has changed."

"Things have changed," Kane said. "Marcelle isn't *my* priority. I think you need to re-evaluate your position."

Yazzie didn't say anything.

"What unit were you in?" Kane asked.

"Trying to bond with me?" Yazzie said. "I freelanced."

"No one freelanced in 'Nam."

"When you have certain specialties, you do. I was a code talker."

"We didn't use those in Vietnam," Kane said.

"Don't tell me I didn't do what I did," Yazzie said. "I also spent some time as a tunnel rat."

"You're a bit tall for that," Kane pointed out.

"I bend."

"Like a snake." Kane pushed. "You're a crook working for a crook."

"I could have killed you when you walked in," Yazzie said. "Boss Crawford is a legitimate businessman who invested money to purchase properties via a prestigious New York law firm run by a former Federal prosecutor. There is nothing criminal about that."

" *'You just keep thinkin' that Butch. That's what you're good at'.*"

Yazzie stood. "Don't get in my way, Kane. You've gotten your only pass."

"How do I get hold of you?" Kane said. "To avoid a collision in case our paths coincide?"

Yazzie thought for a second, then tossed a card on the table. "Page me." He looked at the pager and satchel on the table. Picked up the pager.

"Take the films," Kane said.

Yazzie grabbed the leather bag and slung it, along with his own, over his shoulder. He walked out the front door leaving Kane alone in his small apartment.

Thursday,
21 February 1957

BAYCHESTER, BRONX

Thirteen-year-old altar boy William Kane spins the combination to the last number, hears the click, and turns the handle on the vault door. The heavy bolts retract and he swings it open. The interior is lined with shelves full of gold and silver and other precious metals and stones in the form of chalices, crosses, plates; the objects the Catholic Church considers an integral part of their ceremonies.

There are four cases of wine stacked inside. The wine used to be in the closet on the other side of the sacristy, where the altar boys don their cassock and surplice. However, the supply has been dwindling at a much quicker rate than can be accounted for by the sips at mass by the priests. Thus, the move to the vault and the combination is entrusted to a handful. Kane removes an already open bottle from the top box, fills the cruet for the morning service, and returns the bottle.

Before he can shut the heavy door, the priest walks in.

"Good morning," Father Mukami says in his Kenyan accent. He's on temporary assignment from Africa to Holy Rosary Church in the Bronx, an anomaly the parishioners have grudgingly accepted only because of the white collar.

"Good morning, Father."

Father Mukami stares at the contents of the safe. "I find this most curious. Such riches locked in a church."

"Yes, Father," Kane says automatically, as taught by the nuns' rulers.

"Yes to which part?" Father Mukami asks.

Kane is stumped by a question that surpasses a yes. "It is curious, Father?"

Father Mukami smiles. "And why do you find it curious, my son?"

"I don't think anyone would break into a church, Father."

"Ah! Of course, someone would if they were desperate enough. I've seen people force themselves into a church. But not to steal. For safety. For sanctuary. And then I have seen worse people come into a church for a different reason."

It's 5:50 in the morning. A cold and grey February day. Ten minutes until Thursday daily mass. Father Mukami isn't putting on his vestments. He wears a simple black cassock with the white band in high contrast to the garments and the skin of his throat. He walks away from the vestments Kane has laid out on the wide table on the priest side of the sacristy. To the double doors leading into the church and peers out the window.

"See them?" Father Mukami indicates a cluster of old women, along with a scattering of others among the pews, awaiting their daily deliverance. Kane's mother is there.

"Yes, Father."

"Do you think they believe?"

"Yes, Father."

"I wonder. They make mass a routine, a habit. Every morning."

Kane shifts his feet nervously. He should put on his altar boy costume but Father Mukami isn't moving. This is unfamiliar, a break in ritual.

"It was my flock that broke in initially," Father Mukami says, more to himself. "Seeking refuge. Mostly my flock. Others came with them. It is strange how in times of peril, those who don't believe suddenly want to believe. I let them all in. That, of course, is the Christian thing. And, naturally, it was a mistake. Because wolves hide among the sheep."

He falls silent.

Kane glances nervously at the clock. His father, even more than the nuns, has taught him punctuality. Things happen on time and for a reason. It is five minutes to the hour.

Is it a sin to start mass late?

The nuns haven't covered that one.

Kane thinks George Carlin might have but the thought immediately fills him with shame for having listened to the record.

Is it a sin to start mass late if it's the priest's fault? That gave Kane some solace, as the responsibility is not his. The nuns would agree. Naturally, his father wouldn't.

Father Mukami shivers. "And now I am here for the time being as the flames burn in my homeland. They made me leave when I should have stayed." He looks down at Kane. "Do not be afraid of me, son. I am not the wolf in this parish. But I fear some of my brethren are."

Kane stares out at the congregation.

Father Mukami puts his hand lightly on Kane's shoulder. "There are wolves in many guises in every place, even the most sacred. Often, they are whom we least suspect. I fear for the sheep. I wonder often, who protects the sheep?" He removes his hand. "I will do the mass alone, my son. Go home. Do not come back."

Sunday Morning, 7 August 1977

MEATPACKING DISTRICT, MANHATTAN

"We'll be closing early today," Kane informed Thao. "I've already informed Lynn and Riley." He was referring to the waitress who worked Sunday mornings, Morticia's day off, and his cousin.

Thao had food going on the stove for the light crowd already in the diner. He noted the external frame rucksack on Kane's shoulder. "How early, Dai Yu?"

"As soon as I get transportation arranged," Kane said.

"What should I bring?"

Kane smiled. "You didn't ask where."

"Where?"

"And I didn't ask you to go."

"You said *we're* closing early," Thao noted.

"Yeah, that I did. But it might involve contact."

Thao nodded. "I am honored that this time you are including me. Where?"

"First to West Point to visit Mister Plaikos. Then Fort Devens. After that, I'm not sure. Depends what we learn. Probably Boston, where we might have a conversation that isn't friendly."

"Will we visit Bahn?" Thao asked, referring to Merrick's Montagnard wife, and his sister.

"I called and they're home."

"The goal of the trip?"

Kane quickly laid out recent events. "I need to get the pictures of Westway for Trent. Check Damon's book. His weapons suppliers should be in it, and we see who he has in Boston. If we can find out what these Swords are after in terms of gear, we might get an idea what they're planning."

Thao nodded. "I will be ready." He turned to the stove.

Kane went to his booth, putting the ruck on the other side.

When the Kid came in with the thick Sunday *New York Times*, he was surprised to see Kane sitting there, since this was normally run in Van Cortlandt Park day for the ex-Green Beret.

"What's up?" the Kid asked as Kane peeled off ten twenties and gave them to him.

"I need a car," Kane said.

"Fast?"

"That would be nice," Kane said.

"Back in fifteen," the Kid said.

A few minutes after he departed, the pay phone on the wall across from the booth rang. Kane grimaced, waited for Thao to get it. Riley was clearing tables and apparently payphone answering wasn't in the job description Thao had given him. It kept ringing and Kane reluctantly answered after the seventh disturbance.

"Vic's Diner."

"Ah, the prodigal himself," Kane's older sister, Maria said. "To what do I owe the honor of you answering? It's been Thao for the past several months. I'm sure he's passed on my messages."

"How's the weather?" Kane asked.

"Unless I dialed the wrong number, look out the window and you tell me, Willy. Not like the Bronx is that far away. I'm fine, by the way, but your mother wouldn't mind seeing you. We're going to the ten o'clock. Holy Rosary. You know where that is, right?"

"I've got to work today," Kane said. He forced a smile at Riley as he came by with a load of dirty plates.

"Of course. Work. What exactly is that, anyway?" Several seconds of silence ticked by. "Last time you were here," Maria finally said, "you wanted me to tell Taryn you were sorry. About what?"

Kane gripped the receiver. "Have you seen her? Talked to her?"

"No. I'm just wondering what's going on, Will. You seemed pretty agitated. Then we didn't hear nothing from you. Not that that's unusual. In '69, after the accident, you went into a black hole for five years and we didn't know if you were alive or dead or what the weather was like wherever it was you was."

Kane was tempted to hang up. "Last time I was at the house, I was agitated because everyone had lied to me about Taryn being there before the accident. I still don't know what happened that day. Did dad have one of his rages? In front of his grandkid? Run them off? Is that why Taryn wasn't paying attention when she was driving?"

"You know younger brother, perhaps you should look in the mirror."

"Meaning?"

"Perhaps you're not that much different than dad. A chip off the old block." The phone went dead. Kane leaned his head against the wall, that familiar crushing of his heart as he thought of Lil' Joe.

At the Washington Street door, a trio of weary prostitutes tried the door, found it locked. Lynn pointed at the closed sign. As Kane hung up, Thao hustled past with several containers of take-out. He unlocked the door and handed the grub to the women, waving off payment. He also let Lynn out and locked the door behind her since the diner was empty except for the sound of Riley cleaning dishes in the kitchen. On the way back he removed his apron.

"I am ready whenever you are, Dai Yu. How is your sister?"

"The same," Kane said. "They're all the same there."

"And you?" Thao asked as he went into the kitchen, propping open the swinging door.

Kane leaned against the doorframe. "Apparently I'm the same."

"Change is difficult," Thao said as he retrieved an OD green kit bag from a cabinet. He placed his machete in it, then the crossbow the Montagnards were renowned for. It was a simple device, made of wood, stained dark brown. The bow string was composed of bamboo fibers woven together. He put a quiver containing extra bolts in the bag.

"What's going on?" Dave Riley asked, elbows deep in suds, but watching the weapons.

Kane pulled a key out of his pocket and put it on the counter. "You're locking up."

Riley eyed the crossbow, then Kane, but nodded. "Yes, sir."

"Say hey to your dad for me."

"Will do."

Kane led Thao out of the kitchen and grabbed his ruck. "I've got a Swedish K in here," Kane said, an offer and upgrade of firepower. "Also, a spare forty-five."

Thao nodded. "The K is a good weapon, but I like the bow. I will carry the pistol, though. Are you anticipating battle?"

"No idea," Kane said. "Best to be prepared."

Thao looked past Kane and smiled. "I have not told you about the good news from yesterday afternoon. But now you can see for yourself."

Kane turned. Standing outside the glass door was Morticia, tall and slender, wearing jeans and a blue t-shirt, and without her wig, revealing short red hair. Next to her was Wile-E. The latter had a leash in hand. There was also an old man with silver hair and beard.

"Three legs?" Kane asked Thao when he saw the dog. It was a German Shepherd and the right front leg was gone.

"She is a good animal," Thao said as he opened the door.

Wile-E unleashed the dog, then said something to it in a low voice. Surprisingly, instead of charging forward and inspecting its new surroundings and Kane and Thao, the dog sat.

Wile-E smiled, looking much better than last time Kane had seen him, wearing clean clothes and his hair was pulled back by a tied-dye headband. "This is Lucky. Lucky, meet Mister Kane and Mister Thao."

The dog walked forward with a smooth but strange gait on the three legs. First to Kane, who started to reach out, then looked at Wile-E questionably.

"Go ahead," Wile-E said. "Lucky is safe. Unless I tell her not to be."

"Let's not do that," Kane said, as he ran his hand through the thick black hair on the top of her head. Now that the dog was closer, he could see grey in her snout. When Kane removed his hand, Lucky went to Thao, who knelt and met the dog's gaze.

"Hello, Lucky," Thao said. Lucky canted her head as Thao scratched her ear. The dog happily whined.

Riley came out of the kitchen and also met Lucky.

Kane looked at the old man who seemed vaguely familiar. Wile-E sensed his confusion. "Kane, this is MacQuinn."

"Mac?" Kane asked, stunned at the difference a shower and clean clothes had wrought.

"Didn't recognize me without my coffee?" Mac asked. He had on a short-sleeve khaki shirt and pants along with a pair of sneakers.

Done with the introductions, Wile-E called to the dog and she promptly returned to his side. His hand was shaking as he clipped the leash. "I gotta thank you, man," he said to Kane. "No shit. I couldn't believe it when Morticia and Thao showed up yesterday afternoon with Lucky. And she's a working dog. Military trained. Just like, well, you know. How'd you pull that off?"

"Thank Master Sergeant Merrick when you meet him," Kane said. "I made a phone call to him and he used his old boy network. He called Fort Dix where they train the dogs. I guess they could part with Lucky."

Thao nodded. "The Staff Sergeant who brought her to us said she was retired. She was wounded in 1975 in 'Nam, just before the final pull out of the Americans. There is an interesting story behind her wound and her return to the States. It seems—" He abruptly stopped himself. "The story must wait."

"She's a great dog," Wile-E said. "You can always tell the good ones."

A black car with gold accents and a ram air intake on the hood rumbled up to the diner on Gansevoort. The engine cut and the Kid stepped out.

"Cool dog!" he exclaimed when he saw Lucky. He didn't ask permission but ran over and knelt next to her, giving her a big hug.

"That's an attack dog," Kane admonished him. "Could've bit you."

"Nah," Wile-E said. "She can attack on command but she's a scout dog." He tapped the side of his nose. "I'm going to have to practice with her. I think we're both out of shape, training-wise."

"Is that your car?" Riley asked the Kid.

"Nah," the Kid replied. "Got it for the man for the day."

Riley approved. "It's far out." The two went over to it, Riley asking the questions that never occurred to Kane about the car and the Kid answering.

Kane grabbed his rucksack. "We gotta get going."

"You're closing?" Morticia asked, making a show of looking at her wrist, which was unadorned with a watch.

"There's something Thao and I have to do," Kane told her.

"You're going to pay Lynn and Dave for their full shift?" Morticia asked as Wile-E, and Mac went outside, chatting excitedly about Lucky while Riley came back in and returned to the kitchen.

Kane couldn't determine the right answer to that question based on her tone. "Should we?"

"Yes."

"Okay. Full day."

Morticia smiled. "That was awfully nice of you."

Kane was confused for a moment. "Like I said, I just made a phone call. No big deal."

"But you thought of it. You're a piece of work, Kane, a good one." She leaned forward and gave him a light kiss on the cheek, then joined the others.

Thao had the kit bag in hand. "Wile-E is very happy. He says he will be back tomorrow. But he wanted to know what to do with the dog while he is working. I said Lucky can join me in the kitchen."

"What about the health—" Kane began, but Thao cut him off.

"We pay them off, Dai Yu. I have been slipping an envelope every time our inspector comes around."

"I didn't know that," Kane said as he opened the door and they went outside.

"It is the way it works. I will add a little to the envelope for Lucky."

Wile-E, Morticia, Mac and Lucky were strolling down Washington. The Kid was waiting by the car with the keys, anxious to follow them.

"You're really lucky," the Kid said as they joined him. "This here's a fiftieth anniversary package Trans-Am. They only made like fifty of 'em. Eight-cylinder, 455 cubic inch, four speed."

"A bit conspicuous," Kane said.

"It is very pretty," Thao said.

The Kid sighed. "It's wasted on you guys. Riley gets it."

"Listen," Kane said, "can you lay low for a while?"

The Kid handed over the keys, which were attached to a pair of fuzzy dice. "What do you mean lay low?"

"Be careful," Kane said. "That chop shop you took the caddy to?"

"What about it?"

"Don't go there again. And try not to—" Kane realized he didn't know exactly what he was trying to say. "Forget it."

"Something I should know?" the Kid asked.

"Nah," Kane said. "Just be careful."

"I always am," the Kid said.

"You got a roof over your head?" Kane asked.

The Kid nodded. "In Tribeca. With the money you gave me from—"

Kane cut him off. "Yeah, good. And the job is still open."

"I know."

Kane indicated the car. "Bring it back to the concierge at the Washington Square Hotel?"

"Yep. Or if it's late the doorman."

"Thanks," Kane said.

The Kid smiled. "May the Force be with you."

Thao replied. "And you also."

The Kid hurried after the others.

Kane tossed the ruck in the back and got in. Thao put the kit bag on the narrow rear seat and assumed the passenger's seat.

"I don't understand why he won't take the job," Kane complained to Thao as he looked over the instrument panel and controls, a bit more modern than his Jeep.

"There could be many reasons," Thao said. "Perhaps he enjoys his freedom and does not relish the idea of a schedule? Perhaps he does not want to work for someone else? Perhaps—"

"I get it," Kane said. "He has a reason. At least Wile-E will be back."

He cranked the engine and music blasted out of the speakers. Kane dialed it off.

"We can listen to the music," Thao said, "or we can talk."

Kane turned the music back on, just above audible, put the car in gear and pulled away to head north next to the Hudson.

UNITED STATES MILITARY ACADEMY, WEST POINT, NEW YORK

Plaikos greeted Thao in a dialect of his people's language. They bowed slightly to each other. Then he addressed Kane: "Welcome back, Mister Kane."

"Sir," Kane acknowledged. He shook hands with the older man and two Montagnard bracelets jangled on Plaikos' wrist.

It was mid-morning and they were on the casement of Fort Putnam, five hundred feet above the Hudson River which was a half mile away to the north and east. The fort had a commanding view of the Military Academy. Michie Stadium, where Army played home football games, was to the south. It was named for a graduate of the class of 1892 who organized the first football team at West Point, but was subsequently killed in action in Cuba in 1898 during the Spanish-American War, one of those wars lost in the murky mists of history. Next to the stadium, the almost noon sun was reflected by the smooth surface of Lusk Reservoir. The terrain to the west dropped off abruptly, leading to more hills.

"The fort's in a lot better shape than I remember," Kane said.

"They cleaned it up for the bicentennial last year," Plaikos explained. "Entire Academy went through a pine cone patrol." The latter was an inside reference to the time most of the troops stationed at Fort Bragg were ordered to police up pine cones prior to President Kennedy's visit; the infamous one where the green beret was introduced to the President and he endorsed it as official headgear for Special Forces.

"It is nice to be among mountains and green," Thao said, looking about.

West Point was fortified during the Revolution because it commanded a sharp bend and narrowing in the Hudson River. Sailing ships heading north or south had to slow to negotiate the narrow turn. The Americans stretched a Great Chain across the river as an impediment. Given that the British had made their North American headquarters in New York City, keeping them from being able to freely travel north on the Hudson was essential to the war effort. It is the oldest, continuously occupied military post in the United States. It had been Kane's abode for four years from summer 1962 through graduation in 1966 and he couldn't say he missed it. His stomach still churned, as it began to do every time he drove north along the Hudson.

"Do you miss your home?" Plaikos asked the Montagnard.

Thao pondered the question. "It is not my home any more. The news we receive from the highlands is sparse but always very bad. The communists are worse than the South Vietnamese. Many of my people have been killed. Most of the rest have been rounded up and sent to re-education camps. Only a few are still living free."

"I'm saddened to tell you it will not get better in the foreseeable future," Plaikos said. "There will be open war soon between Kampuchea and the Vietnamese." He was referring to what had formerly been called Cambodia, but had been retitled since communists took over in 1975, another domino to fall after South Vietnam. "Seems even the communists disagree among themselves."

Thao shook his head. "There has always been war in my homeland. I don't remember a time when there wasn't. My father fought the Japanese and then with FULRO for many years until he was killed."

"War is mankind's burden and I don't foresee it being relieved any time soon," Plaikos said. "FULRO is still in the mountains fighting the communists. The CIA promised them arms, but, of course, did not follow through." To get off that dark topic, Plaikos pointed at the reservoir. "How many gallons, Mister Kane?"

The automatic reply was imprinted in Kane's brain. "Seventy-eight million U.S. gallons when the water is flowing over the spillway, sir."

"Have you found that information useful over the years?" Plaikos asked as he led them to the rampart facing east. Plaikos made a distinct thump each time his mahogany peg leg struck the stones. The archaic artificial limb was attached just below the functioning knee joint. He was a graduate of the Academy; his class having earned the moniker Black '41 for its escapades as cadets. He was dressed in khakis with no insignia, but carried himself in a way that left no doubt about his martial background. His GS level was the equivalent to a one star general but few cadets knew that. He was short, silver-haired and trim, weighing the same he had as a cadet thirty-six years earlier when he graduated into the prelude of World War II.

"Absolutely, sir. Right up there with the grazing fire for the M-60 machinegun. Actually, I found that more useful."

"But your head was full of all sorts of interesting facts when you arrived, wasn't it, William?" Plaikos put his hands on the old stone rampart. "Brother Benedict and his historical odes to your city? And once you arrived, did you ever wonder if being forced to memorize the arcane helped you with the essentials later?"

"Is that the purpose of Plebe poop, sir?" Kane asked, standing to his left as Thao went to the right. "Improve our memory?"

"Performance under stress," Plaikos said. "That is one of the main goals of Beast Barracks and Plebe year. And improving memory isn't a bad thing."

"Pretty much every Army school I went to, sir," Kane said, "focused on performance under stress."

"It's the best one can do short of war," Plaikos said. "But, as we three know, nothing can truly prepare you."

"Charlie Beckwith would certainly agree with you," Kane said.

"Still nursing that grudge?" Plaikos asked, with a slight smile.

Kane shook his head. "It's not a grudge. What he taught us in Ranger School probably saved my life once or twice."

"Ah yes," Plaikos said, recalling. "What happened to your classmate there. Beckwith is doing interesting things at Bragg."

"I heard," Kane said. "Delta Force. I doubt it will be better than what Fifth Group put together."

"Doesn't matter if it is," Plaikos said. "The decision will be made by the Pentagon. 'Better' will have little to do with it. It's all politics." He stared out over the Academy. "The Chapel is higher than all the academic buildings and the barracks. But here, we are higher, which I believe is appropriate. This was the linchpin to defending Fort Clinton, which defended the Great Chain, which denied the Hudson to the British during the Revolution. All the pieces were necessary for the whole to work.

"Speaking of the British," Plaikos continued, getting on topic in his usual roundabout way, "I understand they are perturbed over the loss of a deep cover asset in New York City. They've always looked down on us Americans as newcomers to the world of covert operations and intelligence. The OSS was the SOE's little bastard brother during the war. World War II, that is. I find it odd to have to clarify that since Korea and Vietnam were not, technically, wars. But the British tend to forget that when we went head to head in the Revolution, they lost."

Kane was glad Plaikos and Toni had never met since she thought his own historical meanderings were too much.

"Of course," Plaikos continued, "the British almost pulled off quite the coup right here during the Revolution by turning Benedict Arnold. This redoubt was among the plans he intended to sell to the British. I think some of their resentment comes from the fact that we managed to defeat them in that war and have outpaced them ever since, our own empire growing while the sun descended on theirs. However, in the Far East, I had nothing but excellent relationships with my English counterparts."

"That asset," Kane began, trying to focus the dialogue on the more immediate issues, "was—"

Plaikos held up a hand. "In the country without authorization or knowledge of our government. Thus, the case for reparations is weak."

"He was a multiple killer off the clock," Kane said.

Plaikos turned toward him. "Explain."

"The New York City police have at least five unsolved homicides of prostitutes killed and mutilated in the same manner. That was the work of the Brit's man, Quinn. He was ex-New Zealand SAS. He also killed a number of people while working as an enforcer for the mafia. He was an out of control psychopath. Beyond that, I had no choice. He tried to kill me to keep his cover."

"Interesting," Plaikos said. He faced the Academy, but his eyes were unfocused. "There is a very thin line in the covert world. We used to joke that the Army wanted us to kill, but only when, where and whom it authorized. Do it outside those parameters and one is a criminal. Do it inside and one is a hero and awarded a medal. It was even murkier in the Agency."

Kane patiently waited for Plaikos to work his way out of his musings.

"I assume it was Trent who approached you about this latest matter representing King?" Plaikos finally asked.

"Yes."

"What do they desire as reparations?"

"What he originally wanted," Kane said. "The plan for Westway and how Damon anticipated parceling it out among the various mafia families."

Plaikos frowned. "But Mister Damon is no longer with us. The information has been superseded by events."

"I mentioned that, sir," Kane said. "He said it could still be useful."

"Probably," Plaikos allowed. "Also, when you turn it over to him, you will have, in effect, become his asset. That might be more his point."

"I don't have much choice," Kane said.

"Why is that?" Given that Plaikos had joined the fledgling CIA out of the OSS, Office of Strategic Services, at the end of World War II and served up until 1961 when he was shot down over Vietnam and lost his leg, he was still tuned in to the Agency and the covert world.

Kane explained the threat Trent had made about the Kid.

Plaikos listened, then asked: "Did Trent ever give you the 'being part of the machine' speech?"

"Yeah, when he showed up at my place several weeks ago."

"What he fails to completely understand," Plaikos said, "is that this concept includes himself. He is part *of* the Agency, but he is not *the* Agency. Sometimes people like him get a little full of themselves. The CIA will chug along fine without him as will his boss, Phil King. Ask yourself this, my young friend: if Trent follows through on his threat to your young friend, what will happen?"

"He'll have me on his ass," Kane said.

"Not an upside, is it?" Plaikos didn't wait for an answer. "It's a hollow threat. He might even do it, but I doubt it. People like Trent never do anything that could harm themselves. And every move must have a positive gain."

"I can't ignore him," Kane said.

Plaikos shrugged. "Give him the information he wants, then. It's not important, is it?"

"Not to me," Kane said.

"But do not accept any quid-pro-quo. That keeps the relationship at arm's length. Not following through on a threat is not a payment, per se. Technically, you won't be his asset."

Kane nodded. "Getting my discharge changed won't make much difference anyway." Which reminded Kane of Mutt and Jeff. "There's something else. It could be more important." He explained the meeting with Trent and Shaw, the information about Damon, NORAID, the IRA et al. This took a while longer. While he was updating his mentor, Thao wandered off, examining the ruins of the fort.

When Kane was done, even though he tried being succinct as in a debriefing, it had taken ten minutes. Plaikos never interrupted or asked for any clarification. Nor did Kane introduce his own conjectures about possibilities.

"I'm glad you survived," was the first thing Plaikos said, when he was sure Kane was finished. "I've heard nothing about the IRA sending people here. Seems like neither had Trent. But the bomb and what happened in the Bronx indicates they very much are. Do you have any idea what they could be planning?"

"No, sir," Kane said. "That's why I want to check Damon's ledger. See who the IRA contacts for weapons in Boston are since Damon blocked them in New York."

"Let's look," Plaikos said. He led the way down from the rampart. Thao joined them.

They went to the gravel parking lot off Delafield Road.

"I would say something about being conspicuous," Plaikos said, indicating the Trans Am, "but I do not travel incognito, either." His car was a rare MGA Mark II Roadster. He opened the trunk, or as he called it, the boot. He passed a manila envelope to Kane. "The photos and information for Trent." Then a leather ledger.

Kane took the ledger and opened it, paging through. While he did this, Plaikos and Thao walked a short distance away, speaking in the Montagnard dialect. Kane found what he was looking for and wrote the information in his notebook.

"Got it," he told Plaikos. He gave the older man the book. "The film?"

Plaikos handed over the canister labeled *Thomas Marcelle, 1966.* "You know something isn't right about this. Why would the Provos try to blow you up before questioning you about the missing money?"

"I don't know," Kane said. "That bothers me too. Walsh also said something was off about them."

"Tread carefully," Plaikos advised. "There are always wheels moving within wheels."

"Story of my life," Kane said.

"Where now?" Plaikos asked. "Boston?"

Kane nodded. "By way of Devens."

"Give my regards to Sergeant Merrick," Plaikos said. And he said something to Thao, probably for his sister.

As the three walked to the Trans Am, Plaikos held up a finger. "You forget something, Mister Kane. If your records truly are lost or most likely removed from circulation by the Agency with a cover story so bad even the FBI could see through it, so is the dishonorable discharge."

"But I still have a copy," Kane said. "What if someone asks to see my discharge? Or DD-214?"

Plaikos shook his head. "Have I taught you nothing? Find a forger. Those documents are easily mimicked."

"Wouldn't that be dishonorable, sir?" Kane asked.

"I will take that in the spirit of irony," Plaikos said.

"Thanks, sir."

The three men shook hands.

As Kane drove away, he glanced in the rearview mirror. Plaikos was standing next to his vintage car, watching. He disappeared as they went around a bend.

"He is an interesting man," Thao said. "He is very sad about my people. When I was a boy, the people in my village spoke of him as a legend. They say he tried to keep his word, a rarity among the CIA people who used us."

But Kane was already sinking into his own melancholy as he drove Delafield north, past the pond of the same name, eventually ending up on Washington Road and turning into the cemetery. He parked, reached behind, and retrieved the four pack of Harp beer he'd picked up on the drive from the city.

"I will wait," Thao said.

Kane nodded his thanks. He didn't meander, because there was much to do this day. He swiftly walked to Section XXXIV, where Theodore Joseph Marcelle was buried. Along with a number of their classmates. Thirty had given all, making '66 the class most blooded by Vietnam. They'd graduated as junior officers as the war rose to a fever pitch. Bad timing, much as Plaikos's class in 1941 where the plum assignment in June 1941 had been the Philippines under MacArthur. In six months, that turned into a death warrant for many.

Kane opened one of the beers and poured it in front of Ted's government issue marker. "Cheers," he said, even though he didn't partake. As the beer oozed into the sparse grass, Kane opened a second, but paused before pouring.

"Your father is what you always knew he was, Ted. I'm sorry to tell you that. I wish I could say something else. Something positive. Toni is hanging in there. Got her business set up and running, but your dad's fucking things up for her. She can't let go of him." Kane poured the second beer. He frowned as he opened the third. "I thought I'd let go of my old man. We both tried to do that by coming to the Point. But I guess it isn't that easy, my friend." He tipped the bottle.

An MP patrol pulled into the cemetery, attracted by the flashy car parked near the admin building. Thao talked briefly to the military cop and it did a U-turn.

Kane opened the last bottle. "Hate to say this, Ted, but I got to take him out. There's no other way around this. It's all too deep. He's tied in with evil people who've done really nasty things. And whatever is coming, I've got a bad feeling about it."

Sunday Afternoon, 7 August 1977

FORT DEVENS, MASSACHUSETTS

Thao wrapped his sister, Bahn, in a warm embrace while Merrick held out a cold beer to Kane. The master sergeant was grilling in front of his quarters on Fort Devens, in a section where senior enlisted lived in brick duplexes. Merrick's rank and name were written in removable black letters on a placard in front of their one step stoop. A half dozen soldiers, their spouses and assorted children were gathered, members of Merrick's team. They were all younger and Kane didn't recognize any of them.

"No thanks," Kane said to the beer. "Thao and I have to go into Boston soon."

"For?" Merrick asked. He looked at his wife, chattering away. "Thanks for bringing Thao. She's been bitching at me ever since I made the mistake of telling her I saw you. She wanted to know why I didn't take her down to New York. As if it were a pleasure trip."

"I'm afraid this is also some work stuff," Kane said.

"Does it have anything to do with the detonator?" Merrick asked, making sure no one was within earshot.

Kane nodded. "Learn anything about it?"

"Nobody I talked to recognized the configuration but I did find something odd on the fuse. It had been inserted into explosive before. Probably for training purposes. There was a trace of the explosive on it."

Kane wasn't following. "And? C-4 is C-4."

"It wasn't C-4," Merrick said. "C-4 is white. This was orange. Semtex."

"Who uses that?"

"Libyans," Merrick said. "And they train the IRA with it and send it to them in covert arms shipments."

"That confirms what I was pretty much sure of," Kane said. He briefly told Merrick about the FBI interview and the shooting at Van Cortlandt Park.

The master sergeant flipped a couple of burgers while he listened. He called out and a short line formed. He doled out burgers and hot dogs, but the team members recognized that something was up, and after grabbing their food, backed off to lawn chairs and a picnic table, giving their senior NCO his privacy. While Merrick, with his two stars on his CIB was a semi-legend in Special Forces, Kane was more of an enigma, a name rarely brought up and then with uncertain stories. The Green Beret Affair was still a raw wound among the older members in the tight knit Special Forces community and a topic rarely discussed among the younger who had not experienced Vietnam.

"You're lucky," Merrick said. "I tested the detonator. If they'd armed the bomb, it would've gone off. I figured out the frequency." He chuckled. "Actually, I had my junior demo guy figure it out with my commo guy by trial and error. They kept trying FM freq's until they got a spike on the meter."

With the top of the grill clear of food, Merrick shut the top. He nodded for Kane to come with him as their small bubble of conversation was becoming uncomfortable amongst the others. They walked down the street.

"What do you think the micks got planned?" Merrick asked.

"No clue," Kane said. "We know they can use explosives and remote detonators. So that's not good. The question is how much more demo do they have?"

"I made some calls," Merrick said. "Talked to a guy at Bragg who's done some work with the SAS. Even did a short tour in Northern Ireland with them. They don't publicize it, but the SAS does dark work there. He told me the IRA is pretty good with bombs. It took them a while to get proficient and they had a lot of what they call 'own goals' which I call fucking up and blowing themselves to little bits. But those guys are in it for life, not a tour of duty. And those who survive pass on the knowledge they acquire."

"What do they look for in terms of targeting?" Kane asked.

"They started out going for damage to personnel; to kill and maim," Merrick said. "But they've backed off that because of the negative press. Now they focus on symbolic targets and minimal causalities, especially to what they consider non-combatives. British troops, opposing countrymen and politicians are fair game. Fucked up."

"It's always fucked up," Kane agreed.

Merrick paused in the street. "Something else, Will. After I talked to my guy he went to his commander and—"

"Oh, fuck—" Kane began, but Merrick waved that away.

"No, no. Not like that. He didn't tell him anything about what we talked about. He told him about me. They want me in the unit."

"What unit?" Kane knew as soon as he asked. "Beckwith? Delta?"

Merrick nodded. "Yeah."

"Why would—"

"Promotion to E-9," Merrick short-circuited Kane's objections with pure practicality. "My oldest, Frank, is in college and the other one will be starting. Not that I think they need to go; what the fuck, I did pretty well without it. Still, maybe they can do something that doesn't beat the shit out of their body and get them shot at. Doctor or lawyer or something. Plus, my ex is up my ass for money. And thanks for asking how they're doing, by the way."

Kane felt the weight of the notebook in his pocket and Merrick's 'particulars' that he hadn't bothered to check on the drive up.

Merrick was past that, knowing Kane as he did. "Plus, Bahn will be among her people at Bragg." He turned back toward his place. His wife and Thao were sitting side by side in lawn chairs, deeply engaged in conversation. "I owe her."

"Yeah," Kane said. "It makes sense."

They began walking back to the cookout.

"What's in Boston?" Merrick asked. "I checked on the guy that got busted in Third Battalion but couldn't find out anything. He's in Leavenworth, making little rocks out of big rocks. Nobody's talking about it."

"I've got intel on an arms dealer in Boston," Kane said. "Someone Damon worked with. There wasn't much detail in his ledger. Just an address and a name."

"Shit," Merrick said. "You got no clue what you could be walking into."

"I've got Thao with me."

"You've got me with you."

BOSTON, MASSACHUSETTS

Kane and Merrick peered at the dark alley through the windshield. There was no movement, nor had there been any for the past forty minutes. The alley cut behind a row of warehouses near the waterfront in South Boston. Merrick had been working with some demo for the past twenty minutes on what he called a special, then they'd taken five minutes to rig it on Kane.

Merrick started as Thao suddenly appeared at his open window, a wraith in the night.

"I forgot how quiet you were," Merrick said.

"How's it look?" Kane asked.

Thao leaned in the passenger window. "Two men inside the front room with lights on. There is a larger section in the rear, the storage area, which is dark. I did not see any weapons, but I assume the men are armed. I sense they are waiting for someone."

"Not us," Merrick said.

"Him." Kane pointed.

A man strolled into the far end of the alley and stopped at the door. He rapped once and then opened it and disappeared inside.

"Three," Merrick said, pulling the bolt back on the Swedish K, seating a round in the chamber.

"We're here to get information," Kane reminded him.

"Yep," Merrick said. "Information."

"The rooftop is clear," Thao added. "Warehouses on either side unoccupied. How will we approach this?" Thao asked as Merrick leaned forward. Thao slid into the back seat, the kit bag on the seat next to him along with Kane's ruck.

"*Magnificent Seven* style," Merrick suggested.

"It is a fine movie," Thao agreed, "but do you think that is appropriate for the circumstances?"

"We don't know what the circumstances are," Merrick said. "This is like doing a blind insertion into bad guy country. We got no idea how those guys are going to react. We go in all together it could provoke a response we don't want. Because we're after information, right?" He pointedly asked Kane.

"Right," Kane said. "I'll go first. Give me two minutes or the sound of firing."

"Does that make you Yul Brynner?" Merrick asked. "'Cause I want to be James Coburn. He was the one with the knife?"

"At the end of the movie," Thao pointed out, "only three lived. Coburn's character was not one. But, yes, he was the one with the knife."

"Then Steve McQueen," Merrick said. "Does he live?"

"Yes," Thao affirmed.

"Good," Merrick said. "McQueen."

"Two minutes for me to make my pitch," Kane said, checking that the .45 was clear in the holster, then he looped the map case over his shoulder, the silenced High Standard .22 ready. He adjusted the wiring of Merrick's special rig. He walked down the alley, shoulders tightening.

Lions and tigers and bears, oh my!

He stopped at the personnel door set in the larger truck doors. He knocked once, hard, then pushed it open. Despite what Thao had said, the interior wasn't that much better lit than the night outside so his eyes were adjusted.

There were three men seated at a wood table and they all turned toward him. Kane took two steps in, letting the door swing shut behind him. Ceiling fans were pushing cigarette and cigar smoke about. A beer keg was set on cinder blocks and a cluster of bottles on another table. There were boxes stacked everywhere, not just booze but VHS and Beta recorders, stereos and more. The loot from various truck hijackings.

"Get the fuck out," one of the men snarled. He was closest to the door, half-turned in his chair. He wore a black leather jacket despite the heat, had a long scar on his left cheek, was mostly bald and looked like the proverbial trouble.

"I'm here for Joe Mac," Kane said.

Scar turned to the man to his left, which was a sort of an introduction. Joe Mac was a short fireplug, thick black hair, and darker skinned; Black Irish, Conner would have called him.

"Who are you?" Joe Mac asked. The third at the table was a balding man with piercing eyes. He was the one who had recently entered.

"Name's Brynner," Kane said. "I'm from Fort Devens."

"So? I should give a flying fuck?" Joe Mac said. "What do you want?"

"I don't want anything. I have some things you might want." He reached toward the map case.

"Whoa!" Scar said. "What are you going for?"

"Show you what I got," Kane said. He pulled out a block of C-4 they'd borrowed from the hidden stash above Merrick's team room. He held it up. "Government grade."

"You one of those fucking girl scouts?" Joe Mac asked. "Wears a green beanie."

"Yeah."

"Bullshit," Scar said. "Your hair is too long."

"It's called relaxed grooming standards so we fit in," Kane said. "I just got back from a six-month TDY tour overseas in a place we weren't supposed to be. Had to look like the locals. Brought some goodies back with me in the team box. We don't go through customs when we return to the States so I packed as much as I could in the box. Got some weapons too. AKs."

Joe Mac stood. "How do you know my name? Where'd you hear about this place?"

"Sean Damon," Kane said. "One of my uncles is a cop in New York. I asked him and he checked around and then I got contacted by Damon a few weeks ago."

The third man spoke for the first time. "Why'd you wait?"

"I wasn't in a rush," Kane said, wondering how much of his two minutes he'd used. It wasn't like he could do one-Mississippi-two-Mississippi like they used to as kids and carry on a conversation with a trio of psychos. "I got a friend with me. Also a Green Beret. He'll be coming in shortly."

Scar stood, reached inside his jacket and produced a very large revolver. "Why?"

"I wasn't sure of the reception," Kane said.

"Are you sure now?" Joe Mac asked.

"No," Kane said. "That's why he's coming in. Just don't want anybody to get twitchy when he does."

Joe Mac went to the keg, reached behind, and retrieved a pump action shot gun. "I'm feeling kind of twitchy. How about you Seamus? Whitey?"

Scar appeared to be Seamus as he lifted the revolver and aimed at Kane. "I'm twitchy but my hand's not shaking."

Whitey kept his hands on the table. "I think we should talk to the gentleman," he said. "Hear his offer out."

"What do you mean 'we'?" Seamus asked. "Since when you working with us? This is our gig. We'll finish our business with you after this guy."

"You always want to talk, Whitey," Joe Mac said. "Then when you're done talking you get all twitchy. I like things the other way ar—" he paused as the door opened and he brought the shotgun to the ready.

"Easy," Kane said to Merrick as his former team sergeant slid in the door, the Swedish K submachinegun wire stock tight to his shoulder, finger on the trigger. Kane held his hands up. "Now everyone but Whitey and me are twitchy. We all need to calm down."

Merrick moved to the right, getting separation from Kane, forcing the two bad guys with guns to make a decision. They both tracked Merrick, which was bad teamwork. Whitey still had his hands on the table.

Kane waggled the C-4. "Hey. I've got a bomb here."

"Not without a fuse you don't," Joe Mac said.

Kane reversed the block, showing the fuse and the wire running into the sleeve of his denim shirt. It went across his back under the shirt and down the other arm. He held up his other hand, with the detonator that had literally, been up his sleeve. "It's a bomb."

"You fucking nuts?" Seamus said, glancing at Joe Mac.

But Kane was watching Whitey. His eyes were dead and he wasn't afraid. The other two were trouble, but he was the danger in the room.

"Can we talk?" Kane said.

"Or what?" Joe Mac said. "You gonna blow yourself up?"

"No," Kane said. "*You're* gonna blow all of us up if you shoot me, because I'm holding a dead man's switch. I let go, we got a big boom. I don't plan on blowing us up and would prefer not to."

"Fuck," Joe Mac muttered, lowering the shotgun. "You girl scouts are crazy. Seamus, keep an eye the other guy." He went to the table and sat down, indicating Seamus's empty seat for Kane.

Kane sat, placing the C-4 on the table, shaking out a little extra length of det cord so he could put that hand on his lap, close to the map case with the High Standard.

"You're saying Sean Damon sent you?" Whitey asked.

"No," Kane said, "I'm saying Sean Damon told my uncle the address of this place and the name Joe Mac."

"Why would he tell a cop that?" Joe Mac asked.

"My uncle is a degenerate gambler and he does jobs for Damon." Kane had been taught to stick as close to the truth as possible in this kind of situation. Lies were harder to keep track of. "I can give my uncle a slice if we make a deal and he can pay off his debt to a friend of Damon's. Everyone makes out."

"Damon doesn't make book," Whitey said.

"No, but a friend of his does," Kane said. He was beginning to see the flaw in Merrick's plan, because Thao's entrance was going to be one too many. His back itched, since the door was behind him. But two of the potential problems were in front of him and Merrick was focused on the third.

"How many AKs?" Joe Mac asked, which earned a frown from Whitey.

"Twelve," Kane said. "And the C-4."

"Ammunition?" Joe Mac asked. "They fire a weird round."

"Seven-point-six-two by thirty-nine," Kane said. "I don't have any, but it can be found on the open market. Nothing illegal about bullets."

Joe Mac laughed. "Depends who they end up in."

"They have full automatic capability," Kane threw in.

"Damon hasn't been heard of for a while," Whitey interjected.

"Who am I making the deal with?" Kane asked, focusing on Joe Mac, worried the door was going to open any second and Thao was going to set off a bloodbath. Out of the corner of his eye he could see Whitey's face go cold.

"What do ya think?" Joe Mac asked Whitey, but he was buying time as he struggled to come to a decision.

"I think this guy is full of shit and working for the cops," Whitey said, giving the extra push the situation didn't need.

Kane recognized the decision in Joe Mac's eyes as he started to bring up the shotgun. Kane shot him in the elbow with the High Standard. There was a quick pop-pop-pop behind him: the Swedish K, followed by a grunting sound.

Kane shifted his aim under the table, but Whitey had his hands in the air, wanting no part of the battle he'd instigated. "I'm covered. I got insurance."

"Motherfucker!" Joe Mac screamed; a pistol Kane hadn't spotted in his off hand.

A crossbow bolt pierced his neck from left to right, punching through, the barbed head dripping blood. Joe Mac dropped the gun and reached up, feeling it, first on the feathered side, then the point end, disbelief mixing with the death shading his face. His mouth moved as he tried to say something, but his vocal cords had been severed along with one of the carotid arteries which was spraying blood.

Joe Mac keeled over, hitting the floor the hard way dead men do: Solidly.

"Everyone okay?" Kane called out.

"Never better," Merrick said.

"Thao?"

The Montagnard appeared out of the shadows near the back door, a bolt loaded in the crossbow. "Sorry, Dai Yu. I did not know if you saw the pistol."

"I didn't," Kane said. "Thanks."

Whitey still had his hands in the air. "A fucking bow and arrow?"

Merrick stepped past Kane, staying out of his line of fire and frisked Whitey, removing a semi-automatic pistol from his belt. Merrick tossed Whitey's wallet on the table. Then stepped back, Swedish K covering him.

Kane glanced over his shoulder. Seamus, Scar, whoever, had bullet holes in his face. Two in the forehead, the third in the center. "Three?" Kane asked. He inserted a pin in the clacker, then carefully removed the fuse from the C-4 and then the det cord from the detonator. He slid the det cord through his sleeves, putting all in the map case, relieved he was no longer a walking bomb.

"My fingers slipped a little on the first two and they kinda came together," Merrick said. "Been a while since I've used a K."

Kane picked up the wallet and checked the driver's license. "James Joseph Bulger, Junior. Why do they call you Whitey?"

"People started calling me that a long time ago when my hair was blond," Whitey Bulger said with a shrug. "It kinda stuck. I'm not particular to it myself, but Joe Mac was an asshole and didn't care if I was particular to it."

"Sit down," Kane said. "Thao, check the front door."

"Yes, Dai Yu."

"Who are you guys?" Whitey asked. "You're not here to sell guns or demo. Damon is dead. He died the night of the Blackout. You with the FBI? Or the military? CID?"

"How do you know Damon is dead?" Kane asked, resting the High Standard on the table, aimed at Bulger's ample stomach.

"That's the word floating about." Whitey didn't seem upset about the two bodies.

"The alley is empty," Thao reported. He moved past, going through the door he'd entered, to the back of the warehouse.

"You said you had 'insurance'," Kane said. "I've heard someone use that term before. That person was an FBI informant."

"That so?" Bulger said. "I think you and your buddies got a big problem. These guys are hooked up. Their people are gonna hunt you down and make you bleed and hurt a long time before they kill you."

"You're not 'their' people?" Merrick asked.

"I'm an acquaintance," Bulger said. "We do business sometimes. But I don't do weapons and I'm not related to either of them."

"They can't hunt us down if they don't know who we are," Kane said.

"Which they won't, if we kill you," Merrick added.

Whitey Bulger believed Merrick. "What do you guys want?" he asked. "I'm sure we can make a deal?"

"Some Provos went to Damon to buy weapons and explosives," Kane said. "He refused. He told his weapons people in the New York area not to deal with them. So the Provos came here, didn't they?"

Bulger stared into Kane's eyes. His lacked any sense of humanity, a psychopath evaluating how to play this to his own benefit, not overly concerned about the death threat. "Told you, guns ain't my gig. Gets too much heat from the Feds." He nodded at the cooling body next to him. "Joe Mac dealt with the Irish."

"What did he sell them?" Kane asked.

"Some guns. Some explosives."

Kane sensed the lack in the answer. "What else?"

"We all walk out of here and go our merry ways?" Bulger asked. "Nobody saw nothing? Nobody said nothing? Nobody heard nothing."

"Right," Kane said. "Three fucking monkeys."

"A machinegun of some sort. Some M-16s. Some explosives. Three rockets. The army kind."

"Be more specific," Kane prompted. "What kind of rockets?"

"Is there a toe rocket? Why would the army name a missile after a toe?"

"Fuck," Merrick muttered.

"TOW missile," Kane said. "T. O. W."

"Still don't make sense," Bulger said.

"What kind of machinegun?" Merrick asked.

Before Whitey could answer, Thao called out from the open back door. "Dai Yu."

Leaving Merrick covering Whitey, Kane joined the Montagnard in the door. The lights were now on in the main part of the warehouse. There was a row of high-end cars, most likely stolen. But Thao was pointing at several wooden boxes. A long one was stenciled **M-2**. A cluster of smaller wooden boxes were next to it.

"You gotta be kidding me," Kane muttered. He put a hand under the edge of the box and tried to lift it. The weight confirmed what the stenciling suggested. The smaller boxes were labeled **.50 CARTRIDGES**.

"He said the Irish got three TOW missiles, explosives, some small arms and a machinegun. If they got a Ma-Duece, that's some heavy firepower."

"Indeed," Thao agreed.

"Come on," Kane said, leading Thao back to the room where Merrick looked ready to practice his trigger control on Whitey.

"Did the Provos get a machinegun like the one in the warehouse?" Kane asked.

"I don't know what kinda gun they got," Whitey said. "Joe Mac just boasted he sold them the stuff. He was always trying to act like he was more than he was." He got up. "Time for me to be going before someone breaks up the party." He walked over to the keg and kicked the back of it. A trap door popped open, prompting Merrick and Kane to bring their weapons to the ready. "Easy," Bulger said. "Just getting my due." He pulled out a burlap sack. "No point leaving this here for the cops to find. I say fifty-fifty split?"

"How much is in there?" Merrick asked.

"Should be one hundred thousand." Bulger upended the sack on the table. "It's what the crazies paid for the toes and the machinegun and the rifles."

"How many trackers were with the missiles?" Kane asked.

"Huh?" Bulger was splitting the money into two piles. "'Trackers'? Told you, I wasn't there for the deal. Joe Mac was dumb but not that dumb. I just know Joe Mac was saying he'd made a hundred grand for three rockets and some guns he bought off some National Guard loser for twenty-five g's."

"When did this deal happen?" Kane asked. "The Provos buying the stuff?"

"Last week," Bulger said. "Tuesday, I think." He frowned. There was one bundle of money left between two even piles. "Guess they spent some. Tell you what? For my troubles." He put it in the pile closest to him.

"We're the ones with the guns," Merrick said.

"Ah," Bulger groused. He tossed the bundle into the other pile. He put his into the sack. "I don't know who you guys are and I don't ever want to see you again here in Boston. Because next time it aint gonna be this easy. These two idiots were easy."

Merrick stepped in front of Bulger, inches away. "They come for us, they better bring a lot of body bags. Because there are a lot more of us than there are of you scumbags."

Whitey Bulger stared into Merrick's eye, recognizing a kindred darkness. "I'm outta here." He left them with two bodies, fifty thousand dollars and really bad news.

*****

"Are we covered on this?" Merrick asked. "Does the Agency or the FBI or someone got our backs?"

"You were never with us," Kane said to his former team sergeant as he glanced in the rear-view mirror, trying to see out the narrow, slanted back window. He checked the side mirror.

"Are *you* covered on this?" Merrick asked, handing the Swedish K to Thao in the back seat after clearing it.

"Yeah," Kane said. "This is bigger than us. I'm meeting the CIA tomorrow. It will be their problem. The FBI's too."

Merrick didn't pursue it, but he didn't look happy with the answer.

"You okay?" Kane asked Thao.

Before they'd exfiltrated the bar, after locking the door and with Merrick guarding it, the Montagnard had pulled his crossbow bolt through Joe Mac's neck, cleaned it, and put it back in the quiver. Then he'd opened up his small med kit and gone to work on Joe Mac's elbow. He'd retrieved as many of the fragments of the .22 bullet, working quickly while Kane shined a flashlight for him. It took a little longer to get the one 9mm out of the chest and the two slugs out of Seamus's head. And it was a bit messier, involving a bone saw, a small hammer and a chisel.

"TOWs," Merrick said in a voice Kane recognized. His former team sergeant was mulling over the situation. Analyzing. It was what Special Forces engineers, Merrick's original specialty before he made rank and became team sergeant, did. They were more commonly known as demo sergeants. Good ones looked at everything around them differently than normal people: *'how can I blow that up?'*

Kane glanced over at him. "And?"

"They got TOWs because they're gonna hit a target they either can't plant demo on without getting caught or can't get to."

"Targets," Kane corrected. "Three missiles. They could fire all three at the same thing, but I think they'd spread the impact. Make more of a splash."

"CARVER," Merrick said. He was referring to the matrix Special Forces used to assess targets. Criticality, Accessibility, Recuperability, Vulnerability, Effect and Recognizability.

"New York City is a big place," Kane said.

Thao spoke up from the back seat. "Are we certain they're attacking the city? They could strike somewhere else. Washington D.C., perhaps?"

"It's New York," Kane said.

"Target rich environment," Merrick noted, which was a way Kane had never looked at his home town before.

They rode the rest of the way on Route 2 to Fort Devens in silence. Kane drove Merrick to his quarters.

"Here." Kane held out the bag with the money. "College fund for the kids."

Merrick didn't argue. Kane noted that the lights were on in Merrick's side of the duplex as they pulled up, even though it was well after midnight. Kane remained in the car while Merrick decamped and Thao ran up to say goodbye to his sister. Bahn opened the door before Merrick and Thao reached it. She wrapped her arms around Merrick and then her brother. She abruptly stepped back and in the glow of the porch light, looked her brother up and down, taking in his blood-spattered clothes from his post-mortems. Her voice went up, speaking in their native tongue. Thao dropped his head and meekly received the tongue lashing, then was dismissed as Bahn led her husband inside, slamming the door.

Thao returned and claimed the roomier passenger seat. Kane stayed at the speed limit, given the kit bag and rucksack full of weapons on the back seat. Thao was silent.

"I'm sorry," Kane finally said as they roared along in the dark.

"I came along willingly," Thao bowed his head for a moment, the glow of the dash reflected off his smooth skin. He looked ahead. "I thought I was done when we left Vietnam. I never wanted to kill again. I believed, and still believe, my life path is the opposite. To help people. To save lives."

"That's why I'm sorry," Kane said. "It's why I didn't want to—"

Thao interrupted him. "After what you did the night of the Blackout, I had to reflect on many things. What we did in the war. During the escape. There are actions I've ignored, because it is easier to do so. One is the fact that Van Van bring us tribute that is tainted with blood and pain. It reminds me of the war. For you, it was clear-cut. You wore a uniform and fought for your country. My people have never had a country."

"I don't wear a uniform anymore," Kane said.

"I know." Thao fell silent.

Kane didn't know what to say because he rarely did when things took an emotional turn; something Taryn has accused him of more than once.

He tried. "What's Morticia's real name?"

"That is not mine to disclose."

Miles rolled by.

Thao spoke. "Dai Yu, you do know there are other things that are important about a person besides their name?"

"Sure," Kane said. He waited a moment. "Are we talking about Morticia?"

Thao sighed. "There are times you frustrate me very much. Does it bother you that she wears a wig and disguises herself at the diner?"

"Her choice," Kane said. He glanced over as something finally occurred to him. "Does it bother you?"

"I saw through it from the first," Thao said. "It did disturb me. I wondered why? I granted her that she had reasons but it was troublesome that someone would pretend to not be who they really are."

"Does it still bother you?"

"No. I asked her why she did it."

"I did too. She told me it was a persona," Kane said.

"And what does that mean to you?"

"I figured she wanted to separate her work from her life outside the diner. I don't know. I didn't think much about it." Kane watched a pair of headlights in the side view mirror rapidly approach. A car zoomed by, red taillights disappearing ahead in the dark. He knew the Kid would be unhappy he was driving so slowly.

"Why didn't you ask her why she does it?" Thao asked.

"I thought that was kind of personal."

"She is an aspiring singer and actress," Thao said. "I believe she works in the diner not just for the money, but as training."

"A persona, yeah," Kane said. "Makes sense, sorta. She certainly deals with all sorts of characters in there."

"She often comes to work directly from her performances," Thao said. "There are times she changes into her 'persona' in the bathroom."

"Right," Kane said. A couple of miles of darkness passed by. "Is there a problem?"

"There are many problems," Thao said. "Are you referring to our most recent topic? Morticia?"

"Yeah. Morticia. Something I should know?"

"Not that I am aware of," Thao said. "I like her but I do not want you to be confused by her. Because of her training, or perhaps because she's drawn to being an actress, she can be different people. She asked you one time to help a friend, did she not?"

Given all that had happened this evening, Kane thought this topic was not exactly focused, but he'd been the one to bring it up. So much for his attempts at small talk. "Yeah. I referred her to Toni. She said she had a friend who needed a lawyer."

"Do you know any more than that?"

"Nope."

"You didn't follow up?"

"Not my business."

"Do you know who the friend was?"

"Nope."

"Her lover. A woman. She has talked to me about her. They live together."

Kane glanced over at Thao. "Really?"

"Yes. The issue had something to do with their cohabitating in a rent-controlled apartment."

"I hope Toni was able to help her," Kane said.

"Good."

Kane shrugged. "I thought she'd hooked up with Omar Strong."

"They are friends," Thao said. "They share some common interests, such as literature. She is well read and full of knowledge, both pertinent and esoteric." Thao flashed a smile. "Like you, my friend.

Kane waited for more but the miles rolled by.

"I'm glad you thought ahead about recovering the bullets," Kane said, trying safer, more practical ground.

"Something we never worried about in combat," Thao said.

"Why did you think of it?"

"Do you not watch *Quincy*?" Thao asked.

"Who?"

"A television show about a medical examiner. Jack Klugman is an excellent actor. It is on Sunday nights."

"I don't own a television," Kane admitted, which made him realize Thao had never seen his apartment. Morticia would give him shit about that. "I've got lots of books. You need to stop by sometime and check them out."

"*Quincy* is my Sunday night indulgence." Thao sounded apologetic, as if working seven mornings a week in the diner and then going to med school in the late afternoon didn't allow him an evening of television. "When he examines homicide victims by firearm, he recovers the bullets. They are tested to determine if they came from a particular gun."

"I appreciate it," Kane said.

"You are welcome."

They drove through the rest of the length of Connecticut in silence. Kane felt a twinge of something, not exactly nostalgia, when they passed the sign indicating they were entering the Bronx. This early on a Monday, the traffic was light. He took the Cross-Bronx, his father's most hated road, into Manhattan and immediately looped off just before crossing the George Washington Bridge, onto the Henry Hudson Parkway South, which turned into the West Side Highway, cause of much recent grief for Kane. He took the last southbound exit and wove his way to Gansevoort and Washington. Kane dropped Thao off at the diner with the kit bag.

"Do you know what the last line of the *Magnificent Seven* is, William?"

The fact he used his name caught Kane's undivided attention. "No."

"The two main characters, Yul Brynner and Steve McQueen, are riding past the graves of their fallen comrades, heading north.

The Brynner character, I am sorry, I forget what he was called in the film, says to the other: *'The old man was right. Only the farmers won. We lost. We'll always lose'.*"

"Trying to cheer me up?" Kane said.

"No. Trying to let you know that please do not listen to Sergeant Merrick if he has a plan next time. Your plans are usually better."

"Thanks."

"There is something else," Thao said.

"Yeah?"

"We cannot involve Sergeant Merrick in any more dangerous activities that might cause him to be hurt or end up in jail."

Kane waited for further explanation.

"Bahn asked me."

"All right," Kane said. "She seemed a bit upset."

"She is pregnant."

"Oh." Kane didn't know how to respond. "Yeah. That makes sense. No more involving Lew."

Thao smiled. "I will be an uncle. I will see you in the morning. Sleep well, my friend."

The door shut and Thao locked it, disappearing inside.

"*'Usually'*?" Kane wondered out loud.

*****

Kane walked home from the Washington Square Hotel after tipping the doorman to pay off the day time concierge a little extra for the trouble. This was on top of the original money he'd given to the Kid. A former fixer at Toni's old firm had impressed on him that tipping was an investment in the future and paid dividends. He trudged back to his apartment, the rucksack with the Swedish K in it heavy on his back. A murder weapon. He considered whether he needed to get rid of it. He was in uncharted territory as a criminal. Even with Thao's impromptu post-mortem surgery it could be a problem. It was bad enough that Sofia Cappucci had the High Standard that had killed Cibosky.

By the time he made it to Jane Street he decided not to. The bullets had been recovered and it was a special weapon, one he might need again. Kane had a feeling that in any confrontation with the Swords of Saint Patrick he was going to be out gunned and out manned, especially since he had promised not to involved Merrick in any more escapades, which he found a bit ironic considering the man was going to the newly formed Delta Force.

Ruminating on the lack of firepower, Kane wasn't in a good mood when he saw the tell was lying in front of his door. No note from Pope. He drew his .45. Checked the knob. Locked.

Lions and tigers and bears, oh my.

Kane backed up, went around the brownstone to the left, through the narrow alley and to the fence separating that yard from Pope's. He peered over the wood barrier. There was a light on in his apartment; from the dimness and shadows, he could tell it was the bathroom. No sign of Yazzie lying in ambush in the backyard. Kane slid over the fence and dropped the ruck. Pulled out the K, unfolded the stock and pulled back the bolt, loading a round in the chamber. He moved to the door. That tell, which he'd emplaced since Yazzie's uninvited visit, was present.

Stock tight to his shoulder, left hand holding the weapon, he tried the knob. Locked.

Kane gently slid the key in the lock. Turned it.

He entered fast and low, shoulders tensed, the barrel of the K tracking with his eyes. He was through the kitchen into the narrow hallway between bedroom and bath, stopping short of being silhouetted by the light.

Someone was in his bed.

"Fuck," Kane muttered, relief, and something more, flooding through his body. He flipped on the light as he said: "Truvey? Listen—" he stopped before the figure in bed became aware, because he recognized the scent.

"What?" Toni murmured. "Will?" A hand brushed thick dark curls out her face and she blinked in the sudden light. She sat up. "Will? I'm sorry. I had nowhere else to go. You gave me the key a long time ago. Please don't point that at me."

Kane had forgotten about the K in his hands. He lowered it. "Sorry, sorry. I didn't know who was in here. Last visitor wasn't so friendly." Although the one before . . . Kane chopped the stream. "What do you mean you had nowhere else to go? What's going on?"

Toni was wearing loose jeans and a t-shirt. She slid out of the bed, barefoot. She was a woman who could climb startled out of a bed looking gorgeous. "Where have you been, Will? Why do you have a machinegun?"

Kane nodded toward the kitchen. "Let's talk. I gotta eat something." A sudden feeling of starving had punched up from his stomach; something he recalled from his combat tours. It happened after getting back from a mission, once the combat high wore off. As he passed through the bedroom, he was glad he'd remade the bed after Truvey's visit.

He put the K on the counter and opened the cupboard. "I'm gonna make some soup. Want some?"

"No, thanks." Toni sat at the tiny table, facing Kane, lines pressed into her face. "My office was raided today by the FBI."

"Were there two idiots named Tucker and Shaw in the raid?"

"That was the entire raiding party," Toni said. "A couple of assholes, but they had a legit warrant. I called and checked on it before I let them do anything."

Kane used a P-38 to open a can of soup without checking the label to see what it was. Plopped it in a pan and used a match to light one of the ancient gas burners. He added some water to the can to make sure he got every bit of the soup and added that to the pan, then tossed the can in the trash.

"They make better openers," Toni noted, indicating the small hinged metal opener that came with every C-ration.

"What was the warrant for?" Kane asked.

"Anything to do with my father. They'd already hit his offices so I had a feeling they were on the way."

"That made you afraid to go home?" Kane asked as he used a spoon to stir the soup.

"Yazzie made me afraid to go home," Toni said. "I got a call from my mother that he showed up at her penthouse looking for father."

"Is she okay?"

"She's on her way out of the country as we speak," Toni said. "She was furious. She said Yazzie threatened her. Given father's disappearance, she might not ever come back."

"Why didn't she call the cops?"

"Because she's scared," Toni said. "Afraid of what father might have been involved in. I didn't tell her, but she's no idiot. Other than the cops my father had on the take, they don't like him given his history and clients."

"Why didn't you go with her?" Kane asked.

"I've got a business here," Toni said. "But I didn't want to run into Yazzie showing up at my place. Plus, I brought my cache with me."

"Your 'cache'?"

"Remember? You told me to keep my most important stuff in a single briefcase? I grabbed it before the FBI showed up and sent Mrs. Ruiz out with it. Picked it up on the way here. There're things in there I don't want the FBI looking at."

"What things?"

"Nothing illegal," Toni tried.

"Right." Kane poured the soup into a bowl that had seen better cleanings. He took the same spoon he'd used to stir and sat across from her.

"Hungry a little?" Toni asked as Kane tore into the soup.

"Busy day," Kane said, between shovels of soup. "Did your mother give Yazzie anything?"

"He's lucky she didn't shoot him with her derringer," Toni said. "Have you found out anything about father?"

Kane shook his head as he swallowed. "I've been on something connected. But nothing about your father's current location." He remembered the film in his backpack, but now wasn't the time. Pope's struggling garden in the back was visible in the glow that always hovered over the city and was reflected back by the clouds and smog.

"It was a mirage," Toni said.

The spoon paused on the way to Kane's mouth. "What? What was?"

"My family. My father. My mother. Ted got away from a mirage. I never saw it for what it really was. Even when I left the firm."

Kane shrugged. "Most families are."

"Bullshit," Toni said. "Don't give me that. There's got to be some normal people."

"Not in my social circles," Kane said, which caused Toni to laugh.

"That's a circle that could hold a get-together on the top of a pin."

"Hey." Kane mimicked being hurt. "I saw Lew Merrick and his wife today. Thao and I visited."

Toni raised one eyebrow. "Really? Just to visit? In the midst of this shit-storm?"

Kane took the empty bowl to the sink, ran some water in it. Sat back down. "There's a more immediate problem than your father and Yazzie."

"And that is?"

Kane got her up to speed on the IRA and the Boston visit, leaving out the fatal by-products of the encounter.

"What are these TOWs?" Toni asked when he was done. "How dangerous are they?"

"They're anti-tank missiles," Kane said. "TOW stands for Tube-launched-Optically-tracked-Wire-guided. Which means you fire, track a target and hit it."

Toni let out a deep breath. "What do you think they're going to do, Will?"

"No idea," Kane said. He stood. "We'll talk in the morning. Get some sleep. I'll be on the couch in the front room."

Toni didn't argue. She climbed into the bed, between already broken sheets. Kane shut the door between the bedroom and sitting room. He looked out the blinds in the street level, narrow window. Nothing suspicious from this perch.

Kane sat in the chair, facing the front door. He drew the .45 and rested it on his lap.

Monday Morning, 8 August 1977

GREENWICH VILLAGE, MANHATTAN

Kane closed his eyes and feigned sleep as he heard Toni get out of bed. The first glow of dawn had crept in the street level window a half hour ago. He waited, hearing her move about before she finally opened the door.

"Will?" she whispered.

Kane opened his eyes and stretched. "Morning."

"I thought you would at least be on the couch," Toni said. "You could have slept with me; I mean in the bed."

"Springs are shot on the couch," Kane said. He stood, holstering the .45. "The chair is better."

"What now?" Toni asked.

"Go to work," Kane said. "Yazzie won't come after you like your mother. He thought she might have known something about your father's location that you didn't. He understnds you want to find your father as much as he does." He didn't add that Yazzie, or one of his men, had probably followed her here.

"And the FBI?"

"I'll be talking to them today," Kane said, as much a prediction as a possibility. "Let me get changed and I'll walk you to the corner to catch a cab."

Toni didn't look positive about his outlook, but she nodded. "All right."

Kane replaced his clothes with similar, black jungle fatigue pants, grey t-shirt, blue denim shirt. The most time intensive part was threading the knife scabbard and holster on the A-7 strap belt.

Toni shook her head when he came out of the bedroom. "You really need to let me take you shopping."

"That would be a waste of time," Kane assured her. "Where's your cache?"

Toni went to one of the prints leaning against the wall and retrieved a locked metal briefcase from behind it.

"Do you want me to take it?" Kane asked.

"The FBI won't come back," Toni said. "I'll put it in the safe."

"Anything in there that might help us find your father?"

Toni sighed. "It's *my* clients, Will. Things they want kept buried, but also be prepared for in case they became public. That's a big part of the job. And why I need *you* to work with me. It's more about PR than the law. Even the *Post* is turning into a scandal rag. Lots of money being paid to keep certain things quiet."

"Otherwise known as blackmail," Kane said. He wanted to add *just like Damon* but he preferred not getting his eyes ripped out of his skull this early in the day.

"Protecting people from blackmail," Toni clarified.

"Where's your father's?" Kane wondered out loud.

Toni didn't follow his wondering. "What?"

"Your father had to have his own form of cache, right? Sensitive information on people. Where is it? I doubt it was at the firm. Where did he keep it, Toni?"

"I've considered that. The FBI went through the firm. Frankly, Father never trusted his partners enough to let them know his secrets. He didn't trust *me* enough."

"Robert?" Kane asked, referring to her ex-husband and an ex-partner at the firm.

"Definitely not," Toni said.

"Who then? Where? He couldn't have counted on Damon. In fact, he probably had some leverage over Damon in his cache. Yazzie went to your mother thinking your father trusted her, right?"

"That was a mistake," Toni said. "I'm not sure father trusted anyone, Will."

"He went to ground somewhere," Kane said. "His ERP."

"His what?"

"Emergency rally point," Kane said. "It's where someone goes after they've been ambushed. The question is, where is your father's? And where's *his* cache? He had to have one."

Toni looked as tired as Kane. "I always felt like father had a secret life. A lot of men in his position do. A mistress stashed in an apartment. But it seemed normal in an abnormal way. It just was. I've got no clue what that was though. Maybe he just went to Central Park and fed the pigeons."

"I doubt that," Kane said. "Thomas Marcelle would as soon stomp the pigeons as feed them."

It was a sign of how far Toni had separated that she didn't disagree.

Kane went on. "Your father has the paperwork, the deeds, that Yazzie wants somewhere and it's not at the firm."

"I've got no idea, Will."

"Did Yazzie search your mother's penthouse?"

"She didn't let him in, but she said enough that he accepted father wasn't there and that he wouldn't leave valuable documents at home." Toni hefted the briefcase, indicating the conversation was over.

Kane grabbed his map case and opened the door. He replaced the tell. And speaking of the *NY Post*, he heard Toni greet his landlord and upstairs neighbor after she went out the door.

"Good morning, Mister Pope."

"Morning, young lady." Pope was on the front steps, a stack of newspaper next to him on the left, a tea cup to his right. "And I told you before. Just Pope. No Mister." He peered at Toni and Kane over reading glasses perched on his nose.

"Morning," Kane called out. He noted that the paper in Pope's hand was the *Post*, which the old man still read despite his firing and the new owner, Rupert Murdoch, an Australian, doing exactly what Toni had complained about: shifting from serious news to sensationalism. The front page screamed:

NO ONE IS SAFE FROM SON OF SAM

"You two look bright and chipper this morning," Pope said. Kane didn't know what to make of that, but Toni was in a different league.

"I was out late," Toni said, "and I've had a stalker hanging around my apartment. I preferred coming here. Will kindly lent me his bed while he guarded my honor in the chair."

"Yes, of course," Pope said. "I didn't mean to suggest, well, let us say, oh, hell, I didn't mean anything."

He was saved by a rare cab rattling along the cobblestone street. Kane waved it down. "I'll talk to you later," he said to Toni as she got in.

"An interesting woman," Pope said. "I'm glad she left that firm. She should do well on her own."

Kane checked his watch. It was early for diner time. He sat on the stoop, one step down from Pope. "How are you doing?"

"Fair to middling," Pope said. He looked like hell, his eyes blood shot with dark pouches underneath them. Skinny to start with, he seemed to have lost weight. "How goes your investigation?"

"Fair to middling," Kane lied.

"I did more digging since last we spoke," Pope said. "Trying to figure out why the IRA would consider violent action here in the States given their financial base is reliant on good will."

Kane waited.

"The IRA isn't a monolithic organization," Pope said. "They've had schisms over the years, usually over policy, but one is significant. The vast majority of the time when referring to the IRA, we're talking about the Provos or Provisional Irish Republican Army. Their main goal is to end British rule in Northern Ireland. But in 1969 a handful of members split away and formed the Official Irish Republican Army, also called the NLF—National Liberation Front."

"Communist?" Kane asked.

"Marxist, so yes," Pope said. "In Ireland they're called the Red IRA. Same goal, kick the Brits out, but what they want after that is more of a people's utopia."

"Right," Kane said. "Like that's going to happen. And?"

"NORAID is Provo," Pope said. "The Red IRA is grassroots and has no support here in the States. In '74 the Reds moved away even further, with the most radical forming the Irish National Liberation Army."

"We'll need a scorecard to keep track of these people," Kane said.

"Indeed. The NLA are led by a fellow named Kevin Flanagan. Under his leadership, they tried to assassinate the leader of the Provos not long ago but only succeeded in wounding him."

"No wonder the British still rule Northern Ireland," Kane noted. "The Irish spend more time fighting each other."

"What I'm getting to," Pope said, "is that if the Reds, Flanagan's group, wanted to hurt the Provos, a bombing in the States that was blamed on the IRA would do the trick. Most Americans wouldn't understand the difference between the two groups."

"Most Americans don't know the difference between a hand grenade and a door knob," Kane said.

"A bit cruel, but true," Pope said. "I love my adopted country but the ethnocentrism is a bit much."

"Watch the big words this early in the morning," Kane said. "Hold on. There's a disconnect. Why would this NLA try to kill me for breaking up the Provos arm shipment?"

"If they're pretending to be Provos, they might. They need money and arms here and the best way to do it is pretend to be IRA," Pope said. "I imagine the communication lines are a bit sketchy between the States and Ireland, given that US and UK intelligence are watching."

A rough piece of the puzzle that had been grating Kane's mind clicked in place. "They went to Damon, but he saw through them. Refused to deal. Wouldn't put them onto any of his arms dealers in New York. Then Damon disappears. They go to next in line: Walsh. He tells them about Marcelle. That's who paid them the hundred grand with the proviso they take out me and Crawford. Jesus," Kane muttered, surprised at the depth of Marcelle's betrayal. "Marcelle didn't even care what the Irish were here for. He just seized the opportunity and funded a terrorist operation."

"It does line up," Pope agreed.

"Can you get a projector?" Kane asked.

Pope raised an eyebrow. "What size?"

Kane pulled the film canister out of his ruck and gave it to Pope.

"I can indeed," Pope said. "When do you want to schedule the showing?"

"Later this morning," Kane said. "I've got to meet someone first. And whatever is on this, it aint gonna be pretty or entertaining."

"But informative?"

"That's what I'm hoping."

MEATPACKING DISTRICT, MANHATTAN

"Get on the other side," Kane told Trent when he got to his booth. He'd spotted the big Town Car outside the diner, engine idling, tinted glass hiding Trent's security as he approached Vic's.

"Good morning to you too," Trent said. He didn't move. He met Kane's eyes, waited a few heartbeats, took a deep drag on his cigarette, stubbed it out in the ashtray, then slid out and sat on the other side. He left the ashtray with several smoldering butts where it was. "Didn't they teach you at that boy's school at Bragg that routine is bad?"

"You're routinely an asshole," Kane said, "so they don't teach it at Langley, do they?" He pushed the ashtray across the table while he activated the tape recorder under the table top with his other hand.

Trent sighed. "Let's do without our usual witty repartee, shall we?"

Morticia slid over, depositing Kane's coffee and water, two cubes. She didn't look at Trent.

"Get me . . ." Trent began but his request faded as she glided away. "What did I do to her?" he wondered.

"Start with breathing," Kane said.

Trent fired up another cigarette and then waved away any further small talk. "What do you have for me?"

Kane retrieved the manila envelope containing images of the Westway map in Marcelle's boardroom and passed it across.

Trent opened it and thumbed through without removing the photos. "Good."

Wile-E passed by with a plastic tub to clear a table. He nodded at Kane and gave a questioning look at Trent. Kane kept his focus on the CIA man.

"See?" Trent said. "That wasn't hard."

"Transmitter off," Kane said.

"Are we going to share intimacies now?" Trent asked, but he pulled the radio out of his coat pocket and turned off the transmit, leaving the receiver leading to the plug in his ear live so he could hear his security.

"Crawford?" Kane asked.

"Leave him alone," Trent said.

"Why?"

"He's oil and gas from Texas," Trent said. "My titular boss at the Agency is oil and gas from Texas. Do I have to draw it with crayons?"

"Bush knows Crawford?"

"I don't travel in those circles," Trent said. "Leave Crawford alone. He's got connections and is not to be trifled with."

Kane moved on. "Radio-controlled bombs?"

"I'm sure you know more about that than I do," Trent said.

"You're just a wealth of information," Kane said.

"I do my best."

"What about Tucker and Shaw?"

"The boys in suits? They work out of the New York field office. Nothing special about them. Minor schmucks."

"Then why are they getting warrants going after Thomas Marcelle?"

"Ask them," Trent said. "The FBI's had a hard on for Marcelle ever since he let Damon off the hook in '67. I bet they have a stack of warrants for Marcelle already signed by a judge that just require the date and reason filled in." He looked around the diner, at the early crowd. "You need to get better clientele here, Kane, if you want to make a go of it. Perhaps a new waitress with a better attitude."

"I like her attitude," Kane said. "It's a persona."

"A what?"

"What do you have on IRA soldiers here in the city?"

"'Soldiers'?" Trent chuckled. "I wouldn't call anything the IRA has soldiers. Speaking of which, are your Nung mercenaries anywhere around? I brought a couple of extra guys in the car just in case they want to have a go around."

Kane waited.

Trent finally shook his head. "Nothing on the IRA stateside."

"What about the Brits? Did you ask them?"

"That's a touchy area, given your recent actions," Trent said. "But the word from our friends across the water is nil. You might be chasing a ghost that doesn't exist."

"They exist," Kane said.

"Because of your boat excursion and the bomb that luckily, or unluckily, depending on perspective, didn't go off?" Trent asked.

Kane watched Thao pass a small paper bag of meds to a hooker who started to cry. Thao patted her on the shoulder and leaned across the counter, as much as his short stature would allow, whispering words of reassurance. Kane focused back on Trent. "Because they recently bought three TOW missiles in Boston for a hundred thousand dollars. I think they also scored a fifty-caliber machinegun with ammo. And small arms. And some demo."

Trent had been in the process of chain-lighting another cigarette from the half remaining of his latest one, but his hands froze. "What?"

"You heard me," Kane said.

Trent finished lighting the cigarette. Tossed the remains of the old one in the ashtray. "When did this transaction go down?"

"Last week. Tuesday. In Boston."

"Who sold it to them?"

"The seller won't be able to answer questions," Kane said.

"Fuck, Kane. You ever hear of questioning someone before killing them?"

"Circumstances often dictate precipitous action," Kane said. "And I didn't say I killed anyone."

"Yeah," Trent muttered. There was a deep furrow on his brow, which Kane guessed was his worried and thinking look. "What the hell are they going to do with TOWs? How many trackers?"

"Don't know." Thao walked the hooker to the Washington street door. They hugged and she wandered into the sunshine of a new day without bursting into flame.

"They could have just wanted the warheads," Trent supposed.

"A hundred grand is a bit much for eight-point-six pounds of explosive times three," Kane pointed out. "Plus, they bought some C-4. Perhaps you can check with the Pentagon and see if they're missing any?"

"Right, like they'll 'fess up to that," Trent said. "What the hell are these Irish idiots going to shoot a TOW at?"

"No idea," Kane said. "Sounds like you have a problem."

"Fuck you," Trent automatically responded. "This is the boys in suits' problem. The Agency doesn't operate domestically. But thanks for giving me a heads up so I can duck my head when the shit hits the fan. Now take it to those whose jurisdiction this falls under. Didn't you recently have a chat with our friends at the Bureau?"

"You can call them," Kane said. "I've done my duty."

"No," Trent disagreed, standing up and snuffing out his cigarette. "I didn't hear anything. Thanks for the photos." He left quickly, brushing past the Kid and ignoring the young man's smile and greeting.

"Who was that jerk?" the Kid asked as he tossed the paper on the table. He noted there was no money waiting, so he sat down. "You okay?"

"That was your government in action," Kane said. "Or rather inaction."

"Looked like a shithead. He's queer, but won't admit it."

"You can tell just by walking past?"

"Sure." The Kid shrugged. "It's a thing. He's giving off the repressed vibe."

"I thought it was just his asshole vibe," Kane said.

"There's that too," the Kid agreed.

Morticia glided up. "Hey, sweetie. Can I get you something?"

"No, thanks," the Kid said. "How'd you like the car?" he asked Kane.

"It was nice," Kane said. Morticia rolled her eyes and moved off to serve some new customers, tourists who'd taken the wrong turn somewhere.

Kane tried to be social and he'd checked the particulars on the walk from Jane Street to the diner this morning. "I met a friend who has a classic. An MGA Mark II Roadster."

The Kid frowned. Apparently, his automotive expertise was limited to domestic and muscle cars. "What kind of engine? Horsepower? Torque?"

"No idea," Kane said, his mind grappling with the tactical employment of TOW missiles in a murky strategic scenario. He belatedly pulled out his clip and peeled off a five. "Thanks."

"Take care of yourself," the Kid said as he got up and left.

Kane was not completely immune to self-preservation. He went to the pay phone on the wall across from the booth. Dropped a dime as he pulled his notepad out. Sofia Cappucci's black card was sticking out. He dialed the number, rehearsing the message he'd leave on her machine.

It rang. And rang. And rang. After six rings, Kane wondered if—

The receiver clicked as it was picked up. "Who the fuck died?" Sofia Cappucci did not sound pleased.

Kane was tempted to tell her, even though he wasn't sure of the real names of the two victims.

"It's William Kane."

"'William Kane'," she repeated as if searching her memory, but more screwing with him. A few seconds passed. "You're in your diner, aren't you?"

Kane frowned. "Right."

"And?"

"I'm still caught up in a case," Kane started, "and I won't be able to get to—"

"Wrong." The word was a whip.

Kane waited.

"I told you what your answer would be," Sofia said. "This is not it. What are you doing when you leave the diner?"

"Going to the FBI and—"

"Wrong."

Kane gave it a few moments. "There is—"

"Wrong. You do not go to the fucking FBI, Kane. They come to you if you want to talk to them. Never go to their turf unless you have no other choice. That's a rule of negotiating. Jesus, I'm beginning to wonder if I made the right decision about you."

"I agree," Kane managed to get out. "I don't think you did. There is—"

"Shut up. You still live in that dump on Jane Street?"

"Yes." He tensed as Truvey entered the Washington Street door. Danger of a different sort.

"Be waiting out front of it at—" the phone was muffled and Sofia spoke to someone in the background—"eleven. Don't make me send Matteo in to get you. I know he'd love to, but you wouldn't love him to. Capisce?"

"Right."

The phone clicked off.

Truvey and Morticia were having a discussion, the possibilities of which immediately gave Kane a headache. Morticia led the aspiring actress to Kane's booth as he hung up. Truvey was wearing white bell bottoms, a red, white and blue blouse tied just underneath her breasts, which left her midriff bare. She was the focus of the meat truck drivers at the counter and Riley almost tripped carrying some dishes to the kitchen. She was holding a large brown purse made of leather with strands hanging from it. Kane thought it looked like it had been made at the Wild West arcade in the old Freedomland amusement park in the Bronx.

"Look who's here to see you," Morticia said, overly brightly. "She says her name is Truvey. Isn't that neat?"

"Yeah," Kane said, "I know."

"I'll be right back with your coffee, honey." Morticia flashed a smile at Truvey and glided away.

Kane sat down, exhausted from the long night, Trent and Sofia Cappucci.

"I was worried about you," Truvey said as soon as he settled in. "I mean, you aint like any guy I've ever met."

Morticia slid up, cup and pot in hand as Truvey continued. "And when I left your place Saturday morning, we didn't get much of a chance to talk."

Morticia gave Kane the eye, which one he wasn't sure of translation, and moved off. Not very far.

"Right," Kane said, unable to devote many brain cells to this conversation and hoping that would suffice.

Truvey reached across the table to take Kane's hand but his instinct was to jerk it back, given he wasn't focused.

"Whoa!" Truvey said.

"Sorry," Kane said. "Bad morning."

Truvey smiled. "It's okay. You weren't much into getting touched the other night, either. So. You doing okay?"

Kane thought the bad morning comment had covered that, but apparently not. "I've got a couple of meetings I've got to get to this morning."

"Oh." Truvey was chewing on her bottom lip.

"Something wrong?"

Tears actually appeared at the edges of Truvey's eyes. "Selkie is *dead!*"

"No!" Kane tried to put some oomph in his reaction, but he fell far short, not that Truvey noticed. Belatedly, he grabbed a paper napkin out of the dispenser and held it out for her.

She took it and dabbed her eyes. "I went by his office yesterday and they had that yellow tape all around, just like in the cop shows. His door was locked, but someone from the theater told me he'd been murdered! And that another guy had been killed inside the theater; they think it was the guy who murdered Selkie. It's just terrible."

"It is," Kane agreed.

"I mean we all know the city is tough," Truvey said. "But getting killed? That's too much, isn't it?"

Kane was uncertain whether that was an actual question, because the answer seemed obvious. "It is."

"I don't know what I'm gonna do," Truvey said.

"Do you need money?" Kane regretted as soon as he asked.

"I got the money from the other night," Truvey said, not offended, but the comment captured Morticia's attention. "Selkie was also my agent. Sort of. I mean he put in a good word and I got some off-Broadway gigs. Small parts, but it was work. I got to work if I want to make it."

"True." Kane was tempted to check his watch but forced himself not to.

She blinked the last of the sort-of tears out of her eyes. "I can sense things about people. You seem like a good guy. Odd, but good."

"Right," Kane said.

"Crawford said you work for an entertainment lawyer," Truvey said. "Does she like, get gigs for people or what?"

"I don't actually work for her."

"Weren't you working for her that night on the boat?"

"Yeah," Kane said, "but it was more a favor."

"But she has connections, right?"

"I guess," Kane said. He mustered some energy. "I'm sure she does. You want I should talk to her?" He frowned as he uttered the last sentence, realizing he was channeling Sofia Cappucci's Brooklyn.

Truvey shifted from sad to glad in a New York second. "Would you? I'd be forever grateful."

"Do you have a card or something?" Kane asked.

Truvey reached into her bag, rummaging through, dumping a couple of combs, lipstick cases, other stuff Kane had no clue as to their purpose, and produced a couple of wrinkled pink cards with her nom-de-plume on it and a 212 number. "It's a service, but they get me messages."

"Right." Kane retrieved his notebook and put Truvey's pink cards in there, next to Sofia Cappucci's black one, which pretty much summed up his relationship with the female persuasion, with Morticia hovering in the background. "Can I ask you something?"

"Sure."

"You said Selkis gave you the cocaine and that Crawford didn't use any?"

Truvey pulled back slightly. "Uh, yeah."

"Was Crawford upset when you took it out and showed it to him?"

Truvey sighed. "I guess since Selkie's dead, it doesn't matter. Crawford told me to tell anyone who asked that he had nothing to do with the cocaine. But Selkie told me that Crawford had asked for it. I wouldn't just put coke on the night table in front of some stranger. I mean. That would be stupid, right?" She raised her hand, sharp fingernails pointing skyward. "But I didn't use any. I swear. Scout's honor. Crawford asked me for it, like he was expecting me to have it, when we went below and he took a bump before, well, you know."

"Thanks," Kane said. "Why were we looking at the Statue of Liberty anyway? I know you didn't have the storyboards, but was there really a movie?"

The cocaine and dead Selkie were forgotten. "Oh yeah!" She frowned. "Well. I guess there was. Selkie said it was sort of a *Godfather* rip-off. Or he might have said it might be like the second movie, but that's still a *Godfather* movie, right? But you know, I looked and the book don't start that way, you know. Like the movie. Or the second one. Mobster comes to America from Italy as a child years ago. He did say the opening shot is the lead as a kid looking at the Statue of Liberty as he sails into the harbor from wherever those people came from. You remember that shot from the *Godfather*, right? Selkie wanted me to get Crawford inspired by that. The American dream and all that. Except the weather was so crappy. And Crawford wasn't enthused about the movie." She pouted. "All he wanted was the coke and, well, you know."

"Right." Kane wondered if she remembered already telling him most of this. "Was he expecting to meet someone, other than you I mean?"

Truvey frowned. "Yeah. It was like he didn't expect Selkie. But someone else. But who would he be meeting?"

Kane stood. "I'm sorry, really, I've got to get going."

Truvey bounced up and gave him a big hug, the envy of every male in the place with a pulse. "Thank you so much!"

"You're welcome," Kane said.

He was surprised when Truvey sat back down. "What's good here?"

"Uh. Everything," Kane said. "I know the cook," he added.

"Great," Truvey said. "I'm starving. Since I've got nothing lined up, I can eat. Today at least."

"Enjoy," Kane said. He headed for the kitchen door and Morticia did a flyby on her way to take the order.

She whispered. "Rhymes with groovy? Really?"

"It's a persona," Kane said. "Be kind." He pushed open the door, grateful when it whooshed shut behind him. Thao was at his post, manning the grill.

"Morning, Dai Yu."

"Morning, Thao." Lucky was lying in the corner, out of the way, in a bed consisting of a pile of old tablecloths, looking content. "Morning, Lucky."

The dog watched him, withholding judgment.

"Where's Riley?" Kane asked.

"Day off," Thao replied.

Wile-E came bustling in with a load of dirty dishes and glasses. "Hey, cap'n. Who's the lady?"

"A friend," Kane said.

"Nice," Wile-E said with a grin. "The guy earlier looked like trouble," he added as he unloaded into the deep sink.

"CIA," Kane said, but he was staring at Lucky. "You said she's a tracking dog?"

Wile-E paused in his work. "Yeah."

"How old of a scent can she pick up?" Kane asked.

"Depends," Wile-E said. "Weather conditions and—"

"Two days ago, in the Bronx," Kane said.

"No problem," Wile-E assured.

"Wait here after the diner closes," Kane said. "We've got a job to do with Lucky."

"Sure thing, cap'n."

Kane pushed open the door to the diner to grab his map case which he'd forgotten in the fluster of Truvey's presence. Just in time to see Morticia putting a cup of coffee in front of Truvey. He paused in the doorway.

"Here you go, sweetie," Morticia said.

"Thanks," Truvey replied. "Hey, I saw you talking to Kane and the way you were close to him. Is he your guy? Because, you know nothing happened the other night. I mean, I slept there, but he stayed outside the door. It's weird, because it's the best night of sleep I've gotten in the city since I got here. He's like a big old watchdog."

"'Old watchdog'?" Morticia repeated, but she couldn't help smile. "I like that."

"But he did seem kinda of upset 'cause he said I broke his sheets, and I don't get that, because all I did was sleep."

Kane retreated through the kitchen and asked Thao to grab the map case later.

GREENWICH VILLAGE, MANHATTAN

Kane was grateful that Pope was set up, ready to roll in his upstairs bedroom. The blinds were closed, the projector was pointed at a sheet hung on one wall, and the film was loaded.

"You look like shit," Pope greeted him, as Kane took one of the two chairs facing the sheet. The card table with the typewriter was pushed over to a corner of the room. Kane noted a sheet of paper was in it, the page blank.

"I feel like it," Kane said. "It's been a bad twenty-four hours and doesn't look to get better any time soon." He peeled back the Velcro and checked the time. "Sofia Cappucci is going to be outside for a date at eleven. She said she doesn't want to come up the stairs."

Pope stared at Kane for several seconds, trying to ascertain whether he was serious. "All right then. Let's get on with it." He turned the lights off and started the projector.

The image was grainy, black and white. The first thing Kane noted was that it was not filmed in the apartment at 7 Gramercy

Park, where Damon had kept his hookers over the years to entrap people.

"Where is this?" Kane asked. It was a bedroom with a large, ornate four poster bed. The lighting was dim, the curtains drawn. Bookshelves stuffed with leather-bound titles lined the room. The camera was set somewhere high in the room.

"No idea," Pope said. "Upscale. A lot of money in the furniture."

Two men entered the room, one of them Thomas Marcelle from eleven years ago. The other was older than Marcelle, silver-haired with a broad white mustache. They wore suits which they quickly dispensed with.

"I imagine this would have hurt Marcelle if it got out," Kane said.

"It's not just Marcelle," Pope noted. "Do you recognize the other gentleman?"

"Nope."

"He's a judge. Second Circuit."

"A prosecutor and a Federal judge," Kane said. "Damon scored big time. Wait a second. You said 'is' a judge? He's still on the bench?"

Pope nodded. "Not just on the bench. He's Chief Judge now. Second Federal Circuit. The Honorable Charles Edward Clark."

"Can you go faster?" Kane asked. "We don't need the gritty details. See if there's anything else on the reel."

"The details are important," Pope said. He pointed. "That's not sex."

"Looks like sex to me," Kane said.

"No," Pope insisted. "Look. They're making love."

"Whatever you want to call it," Kane said. "I got nothing against two guys or two women or whatever. But—"

"You're not following me," Pope said. "They're making *love*."

Kane tried to clue in. "It's not a set up with a prostitute."

"We know that by who they are." Pope sounded disappointed that Kane wasn't following. "This isn't two guys hooking up at the piers."

Kane remembered Quinn and his whip and Alfonso Delgado in the corner in the Christopher Street Pier, which had started him down the path that led to him sitting here watching this. "What are you talking about?"

"These are two guys who know each other," Pope said. "The way they're treating each other indicates it's not a one-time thing. I'd say this is a private residence, not a place of Damon's. Someone had to break in, set the camera up. Then go back and retrieve it."

"Unless one of them filmed it to blackmail the other," Kane said.

"You found it in Damon's stash," Pope said. "Damon had this done."

The last clues clicked. "They were in a relationship. Marcelle and Clark. They could *still* be in one."

"I'll make an investigative reporter out of you yet," Pope said. He hit the forward, spinning the reel for several seconds then played it. More of the same. He did this several times, then stopped. "This isn't the same encounter. Look at the top of the curtains. This is night time." The reel came to the end. Pope was already putting together his article on what they'd witnessed and the ramifications. "I think Marcelle made the deal with Damon as much to cover for Clark as himself. His career as a prosecutor was over. But Clark continued on."

"Damon would have wanted Clark to stay on the bench," Kane said.

"Exactly."

"And Marcelle certainly had a soft landing," Kane pointed out. "His firm hit the ground running."

"This explains a lot," Pope said. "A lot," he murmured, more to himself than Kane.

Kane checked the time. "What are you talking about?"

"Marcelle's law firm was a set up from the start."

Kane was behind again. "By Damon?"

"No. The firm was financed by Clark and others like him. They also steered clients his way."

"I'm not tracking," Kane said. "Clark can't have been happy about the film."

"It's not about the film," Pope said. "This is bigger than Damon."

Kane held up his arm and indicated the green watch band.

"I've heard rumors," Pope said. With a shaking hand he poured more 'tea'. "There was talk, whispers really, that there was a club. Of the elite of the city. The untouchables. Who shared a certain predilection that is not socially acceptable and would destroy them if it became public. Judges, clergy, politicians, media. Top law enforcement people."

"Homosexuals," Kane said.

Pope nodded. "But so far in the closet they were in a tornado shelter." He waved that bad analogy away. "More like a steel penthouse overlooking the city. They protected each other."

"This judge is still around," Kane said. "I wonder if he's where Marcelle went to ground?"

"Either the judge or this group . . ." Pope paused in thought. "There was a name for it. I can't quite recall. Anyway, I'm sure this group has a way to hide someone if they want to. They've hidden a part of their lives while they're in plain sight every day. On the front pages of the paper and the evening news." Pope held up a finger. "Ah, yes. The Gentleman Bankers. That's it."

"Does it have a headquarters or something?" Kane asked.

Pope looked at him as if he were nuts. "It's supposed to be secret, William."

"You've heard of it," Kane pointed out.

"I've covered the city for decades and all I've heard is rumors," Pope said. "Nothing concrete. They'd crush any attempt at investigating, never mind publishing a story."

"As you noted," Kane said, "I'm not the best at being an investigative reporter, but I've got other skills." He stood up. "But first, I have to chat with my new best friend. I appreciate your help."

"Stay safe," Pope advised.

Kane paused. "By the way, the telephone people will be here sometime today to install a line for me downstairs. Will you be around to let them in?"

Pope looked at him and nodded.

"Thanks."

WEST SIDE, MANHATTAN

"Are we going any place in particular?" Kane asked. He was crunched between Matteo and some other no-neck big guy in a dark suit. It was freezing in the car and Sofia Cappucci's perfume was so thick and cloying, Kane had concerns he'd ever be able to free himself of it.

"I didn't meet," Sofia said, "for you to ask me questions. I met for you to tell me yes, you will do as I say, and then I will say what you will do." She was in Brooklyn, not Princeton, mode.

"Yes, ma'am."

"Do I look like I run a whorehouse?" Sofia asked. "Don't call me ma'am." Then she laughed. "But, actually, some people I know do run whorehouses. So, one for you. But don't call me ma'am."

"Yes, Ms. Cappucci."

"Since we'll be working together, Kane, you can call me Sofia."

The rumble of disapproval from Matteo was palpable. Kane had a sense that Matteo didn't get to call her by her first name. Then again, Kane wasn't sure it was an honor.

The car was negotiating south Manhattan traffic on a Monday morning to the accompaniment of a nonstop symphony of horn blasts, brakes squealing, sirens, and intermittent jackhammers. As best Kane could tell they were crawling north on 8th Avenue, past Jackson Square Park. A historical tidbit from Brother Benedict about the park flickered through his mind, but reading his audience for once, he fought back the urge to pass it on.

"You don't look too good, Kane." Sofia was peering at him under extraordinarily long eye lashes. She was lounging in the seat facing Kane, ensconced in her fur coat. This time she didn't have a man with a gun sitting next to her.

"I had a busy weekend," Kane said.

"Oh, yeah," Sofia said. "The stuff you blew me off over. Don't do that again."

"I'm sorry, Sofia," Kane said, "but we seem to have gotten off on the wrong foot."

"I was just telling you that."

"No," Kane said. "I'm telling you that." He felt Matteo tense and shift in his seat, which was what Kane anticipated because he was already moving, twisting, as Matteo had given him the better angle to strike. Kane hit Matteo's thick neck at a seventy-degree angle, avoiding the built-up muscles on either side, with a savage and abrupt punch led by the extended knuckle of his middle finger striking Matteo's vagus nerve on that side.

Kane didn't bother to see the result, turning in the other direction. The goon's hands were scrambling for the gun in his shoulder holster which was stupid because Kane was too close. Kane did the same to him with his other knuckled fist.

Both men were out for the moment.

Kane sat back and folded his hands in his lap. "Are we communicating on the same wave length, Sofia?"

"How long are they unconscious?" Sofia asked in her Princeton voice, as if inquiring about the weather outside.

"Not long. Their necks will be sore."

"Their pride will be sore," Sofia said. "But we are now communicating. What Matteo has always failed to understand is that by subjugating himself to my command, he became less effective."

"Some guys don't understand power," Kane said.

"I thought you were going to say don't understand women," Sofia said.

"That is not something I would pretend to have achieved," Kane said.

"But you understand what I need you to understand," Sofia said as Matteo began to stir. "Get over here so I can talk to him. You pulled the pin, I want to keep it from going off, to use an analogy *you* understand. What was that you just did? Some sort of James Bond karate chop thing?"

Kane moved to the other side of the back of the limo, claiming the corner away from Sofia. "It took me over two years to become proficient with that strike under the tutelage of one of the best masters in the Orient. Master Pak would have approved."

Brooklyn was back. "Yeah, whatever." She held up a hand. "Easy, Matteo, easy."

The big man glared at Kane but remained in the seat. The other guy took a few more seconds to rejoin them. The limo took a left on 15th. Matteo's face flushed red with anger but he didn't attack.

Sofia glanced at Kane, arcing a thick eyebrow as if to say 'you see'?

The limo turned right onto 10ᵗʰ and paused at an angle. Sofia flicked a finger and the guy on the left side of the limo powered down the window. The old Nabisco factory where Kane had had his showdown with Damon and Quinn was outside. The top floor was blackened, the roof burned through. Scorch marks were etched through the bars covering every window on that floor.

"They don't build 'em like that anymore," Sofia said approvingly of the building. "It's still standing."

She gestured and the window powered up. She rapped on the divider and they headed north along 10ᵗʰ, through Chelsea. Sofia's driver was heavy on the horn, which didn't add pleasantry to the ride. The High Line rail line was paralleling their route, crossing the side streets and going through or alongside the various businesses it served, or mostly used to serve, given trains rarely ran on it any more.

The limo took a left on West 35ᵗʰ and came to a stop overlooking a desolate rail yard bounded by the West Side Highway and the Hudson River on the far side.

Sofia Cappucci opened her door. "Come with me, Kane." She put her palm out to Matteo and the other guy, much like one would signal a dog to stay.

Kane walked next to Sofia, who still wore the mink coat, despite the sunshine and humid eighty-five degrees. He wasn't sure to be more impressed by that or the six-inch stilettos she was balanced upon.

"They teach you to walk like that, between a lady and the street, at West Point?" Sofia noted.

"They did. We had classes on what they called Cadetiquette taught by the Cadet Hostess."

"Chivalry. A lost fucking art."

They came to a fence overlooking the sprawling yard. Broken-down warehouses surrounded the tracks.

"Pretty, isn't it?"

Kane wasn't sure what she was using as her reference. The place was abandoned and strewn with garbage and the occasional derelict freight car.

"One owner," Sofia said. "Prior owner I should say. Penn Central Railroad. Went bankrupt last year."

"Right."

Sofia glanced at him and went Princeton voice. "Don't be a smart ass, Kane. Here's the situation. The city wants to build a convention center. They got three potential sites. The Times Square area somewhere between Sixth and Eighth, Battery Park, or here. What do you think?"

Given his recent experience, he rejected one outright. "Forget Time Square. It's a cesspool. People don't want to come to the city to begin with. What tourist wants to go to Times Square?"

"Some want to, but you're right. Not much appeal. And it would be tough to clear out the space for the building. Lots of legal wrangling. And the others?"

"I guess either will do."

"No." She sounded quite adamant. "Battery Park is too far from Midtown. Times Square may be decadent, but in Midtown we've got the theater district and the restaurants and, most importantly, we've got hotels. Not many hotels by the Battery." She pointed. "This will be it. I want in on the ground floor. A slice of the buy-in, a slice of the construction, a slice of the operation. Lots of unions involved in the last two which the family already has a piece of. But the first one? Not something my profession has tapped into. Real Estate. We squeeze the builders and the occupiers, but I want to be a buyer."

Kane waited.

"A company has been appointed to dispose of Penn Central's assets, including these rail yards. That company is experienced at balance sheets, not real estate. The convention thing is going to be very political. Thus, they tapped some young schmuck wanna-be developer from Queens who they think is connected to the political big-wigs. Donald Trump. His father *is* a developer who we've done work with over the years."

"Go to the father, then," Kane suggested.

"I wouldn't be talking to you if I'd decided to do that," Sofia said. "The father is connected to all the old goombahs. He wouldn't give me the time of day. Plus, he's not the one they appointed. His son is."

"You're doing this on the sly," Kane said.

"Gee, what gave you that idea?" When she was sarcastic, the Brooklyn was back.

Kane cut to the chase. "You want me to talk to this Trump guy and do what?"

"I don't want you to talk to him. He wouldn't give you the time of day. To do business, the guy you need to talk to is his lawyer. Roy Cohn."

"That name sounds familiar," Kane said.

"He was McCarthy's lawyer," Sofia said. "Now he's Trump's lawyer."

"Talking to lawyers is Toni's thing," Kane said.

"Cohn's a criminal lawyer."

"Yeah, but I'm not a lawyer and—"

"No," Sofia cut him off. "I mean he's a *criminal* lawyer."

"Doesn't that mean he'd be mobbed up, too?"

"Yeah, he's connected," Sofia admitted.

"That's why you want me to talk to him, not one of your people."

"I knew you'd figure it out eventually," Sofia said, giving him a little gold star on his homework. "I'm doing this off the family ledger." Sofia sighed. "Cohn is tied in to this thing called the Favor Bank. It's how hoity-toity people with influence get things done without contracts or the law or paperwork. You scratch my back, I scratch yours. Sometimes its money. Usually its trading favors or future favors. Cohn got fingers in everything in the city, even the church."

"What's his mob link?"

"The Genovese family has connections with Cohn which is another reason I have to stay in the shadows. But he's got no loyalty to the Genovese or anyone else for that matter. A lot of them are finocchi, like Cohn. He was tight with Cardinal Spellman for many years before that bastard died. Another finocchi."

"'Finocchi'? I was an altar boy. Took Latin in high school." Kane waited for clarification.

"They like men," Sofia said. "Not that I am in any position to pass judgment, am I?"

"I didn't say anything. Would that mean he's a member of the Gentleman Bankers?"

"Who is that?"

"A powerful group of what you call finocchi."

Sofia shrugged. "If there's a group like that, he'd be with him. I never heard of them but I don't traffic in high society, in case you haven't noticed."

"Who would I say I'm representing?"

"An un-named wealthy entity," Sofia said. "Guys like Cohn eat that shit up. And when he tries to figure out who *you* are, he won't find much will he? And what he does learn should scare him a little bit, not that he scares easy. You're starting to get a bit of a street rep, Kane."

"Is that a good thing?"

"It could save your life."

Kane faced her. "Since we're on a last name-first name basis, Sofia, let me be frank. I've got something very important going down right now."

"Thomas Marcelle's disappearance?"

"That's part of it. But not the most important part."

"Enlighten me."

Kane noticed that despite the heat and her fur coat, the heavy make-up on her face wasn't streaking. Either she had no sweat glands or it was absorbed by the layer closest to the skin. "The IRA has a hit team in town." He thought it was easier to stick with the IRA angle rather than explain the internal schism. "They tried to kill me the other night because I interrupted one of their weapons purchases a few weeks ago."

"The old Nabisco place and Damon," Sofia said. "Go on."

"Did you know Quinn was working for the British government?" Kane asked.

Sofia didn't blink. "Working what for them?"

"Working you, to begin with. But he was also gathering intelligence on the IRA's connections here in the States. The money. The weapons."

"I knew he had some weird angle," Sofia said. "Go on."

"Two hundred and forty M-16s destined for Ireland burned up with Damon. Along with money. Over two million."

"That's a lot of cash." Sofia nodded. "I can see why they'd try to whack you. And Quinn? Did he burn up?"

"He killed Damon," Kane said. "Then he tried to kill me."

"Sounds like there's a whole fucking saga to this, Kane, but the bottom line is you're the one breathing and Quinn isn't, right?"

"This IRA team tried to kill me but it's not their main objective. They're here for something else. Bigger. They bought explosives and guns and missiles in Boston off some Irish mobsters last week. The missiles can do a lot of damage at a distance. By the way, Damon was an FBI informant as a side job. He told the FBI that whatever the Irish were planning was happening Wednesday night."

Sofia turned away from Kane and stared at the rail yard. A Circle Line cruise ship was chugging by on the Hudson River, showing tourists the island from the relative safety of the water.

When Sofia spoke, it was almost a normal voice, somewhere between the girl who'd grown up in Brooklyn in a mob family and the woman who'd come back from Princeton with two majors. "I like this city, Kane. I don't want see it get hurt. Especially by some crazy micks. What do you need?"

"The mobster in Boston who sold the stuff was a guy named Joe Mac. He had a partner named Seamus. They won't be selling any more missiles. There was a third guy, Whitey Bulger, present at our discussion. I don't know anything about him and he says he wasn't involved in the arms deal. He walked away with some cash and didn't seem to give a shit about the two dead guys. But he said there would be people from Boston coming for me and a couple of my friends. I've got enough to do without having Boston Irish gangsters on my ass."

Brooklyn was back full force. "Fuck them. They've killed a lot of my compatriots in Boston. Animals." She shifted to Princeton. "The Irish in Boston have a penchant for violence. They'll kill on the slightest provocation, justified of not. They are not, however, renowned for their ability to run things once they take them over. They've grabbed most of the numbers rackets from my compatriots via bloodshed, but the businesses have fallen into disarray from mismanagement and frankly, neglect. They're too busy drinking and fucking to run things. But there is a line of communication established out of necessity. Quinn had something to do with that as he came to us via Boston and was caught up in some of the blood-letting. I'll make some calls. Don't worry about the Boston Irish."

"Thank you. I'll check this Cohn out. But I've got stuff to do today to track down these Irish guys. I've got to talk to the FBI and—"

"Why?"

"It's their job," Kane said. "They came to me with this. I've got to tell them what I found out."

"I wouldn't trust the FBI, Kane. Or the cops. They will fuck you over, either because they want to or because they can't find their ass when they're shitting. By the time they do anything, it will be over."

"I know," Kane said. "It's the reason I'm staying on this. Besides the fact they tried to kill me. But I got to let the Feds know."

"Kane. Listen to me." Princeton, full force. "If I'm reading you correctly, you're involved in multiple homicides. Here. And in Boston. The less you mingle with law enforcement, the less you tell them, the better. You can't do the things you need to do from the inside of a jail cell."

Kane reached up and put his fingers in the fencing but didn't reply.

"You know," Sofia continued, her voice lower, "this isn't your job. Why are you doing it?" She didn't wait for an answer. "Because those same people you want to go tell either aren't doing their job, are corrupt, or are incompetent. Or all of the above. Right?"

Kane nodded.

"Bullshit," Sofia said. "You got some sort of code, don't you? White hat kind of guy?"

"I'm just trying to do the right thing."

"Who appointed you?" She didn't wait for an answer. Brooklyn began returning. "You're gonna have to make a choice, Kane. Either stop what you're doing and walk away. Or do it all the way. Which means you are, in legal terms, a criminal. Capisce?"

Kane let out a deep breath.

"All right," Sofia said. "Time for you to chat with Mister Cohn."

"Now?"

"Aren't you one of those go-getter types?" Sofia led him back to the car. "Don't put off for tomorrow sort? Besides, my *criminal* lawyer tells me Cohn's doing some sort of preliminary backdoor thing today with some city schmucks about the rail yards, so the clock is ticking."

*****

"That's his car," Sofia said as the limo drove past a Rolls Royce with personalized New Jersey license plates: ROY C. It was illegally parked in front of a hydrant on East 68th Street in the Lenox Hill neighborhood between Central Park and the East River. "That's his home and place of business," she added.

A town house sheathed in limestone glitzed above the sidewalk, standing out from its staid neighbors not just by the rock but also jutting forward slightly.

"I'm not an appreciator of architecture," Kane said, "but isn't that a bit tacky?"

"Supposed to be imposing," Sofia said. "Different tastes."

"Right."

The limo stopped at the corner.

"I'm not sure exactly what you want me to achieve with this guy," Kane said.

"We're just sticking our beak in," Sofia said. "Play it by ear."

"That doesn't turn out well with me sometimes," Kane said.

"I believe in you," Sofia said with little conviction, more like encouraging a dog to go outside and take a pee on the hydrant. "Use the words three hundred thousand cash as a buy in." She leaned forward. "Maybe ask him about Marcelle? The two of them got to have crossed paths a number of times as they're both the same kind of lawyers."

Matteo threw the door open, eager for Kane to get out.

Kane walked up the steps to the imposing building. He rapped on the door and after a few moments it was answered by a barefoot young man dressed in jeans and a t-shirt.

"What?" the guy asked.

"I need to speak to Mister Cohn," Kane said.

"You have an appointment?"

"It's about the rail yards," Kane said.

"What about 'em?"

Kane had a moment of inspiration. "Tell him it's also about the Gentleman Bankers."

The young man frowned. "The what?"

"Just tell him rail yards, convention center and Gentleman Bankers," Kane summarized, getting more confident the more irritated he grew at this guy.

The door opened a little wider. "Wait here." He let Kane in and then went up the stairs, taking them two at a time.

Kane was surprised at the interior. The air was musty with a tinge of foul. A stack of old newspapers was toppled over near the door, barely allowing space to open it. Legal boxes lined the ground floor hallway. The sitting room to the right had curtains drawn and was so dark he couldn't make out the interior.

Another young man, dressed the same, came down the stairs and pivoted on the landing toward the rear, completely ignoring Kane.

"Hey!" The first guy was at the top of the landing. "Come on up."

Kane took the stairs and was ushered into a room that was combination bedroom and office. A large bed, sheets not just broken but exploded and not remade, and a desk covered with papers behind which Cohn sat. A couch covered with stuffed frogs was the only place to sit beside the bed.

Kane stood.

"Who the fuck are you?" Cohn was a small man, with a face that looked like it had been smashed in and reconstructed, although the nose was overly large. He was unnaturally tan and his voice was angry New Yorker. He was dressed in a bathrobe.

"Will Kane."

"That supposed to mean something to me?" Cohn asked.

"No. You asked me who I am. I represent someone who would like to invest in the rail yards and participate in the construction and running of the convention center."

"Did you hear me the first time? Who. The. Fuck. Are. You?" The phone rang but he ignored it.

"My client has three hundred thousand to start," Kane said.

Cohn's tongue kept darting out of his mouth as if he were a snake seeking something to bite and devour. "Who is your client?"

"They prefer to remain anonymous. That's three hundred thousand in cash," Kane added, exhausting his negotiating arsenal.

Cohn twirled a packed rolodex, then leaned back in his chair, the bathrobe opening partially and revealing a scrawny chest with grey hair. "What about the third thing you dropped on my boy at the door?"

"'Gentleman Bankers'?"

Cohn looked at Kane under droopy eyelids, pure hatred pulsing. He could give Matteo lessons. "Well?" He didn't wait for answer. "Get the fuck out of here. I don't know anything about you yet, but I will. And then I will crush you. I'll bury you. I'll take every dime you have. Everything you own will be mine."

"Don't you think that's a bit of an over-reaction?" Kane said. "Besides, I don't own shit," he semi-lied, but the diner was actually entirely in Thao's name. "There's nothing for you to come after. I learned a long time ago that those who threaten when they're ignorant of the parameters of the situation are bluffing. It might work with the people you hang with. I rent the basement of a dump in the Village. I don't have shit for you to come after except me. And you won't find that easy."

"Everyone has something or someone they care about," Cohn said.

"Mine died years ago," Kane said. "And yeah, I've heard you're mobbed up. I don't give a shit. If you have any connections to the Gentleman Bankers, I need to find Thomas Marcelle. ASAP. Or else there's going to be hell to pay. And, I gave you a good faith offer from my client which is a win-win for both of us. You either want to talk or you want to have two different conversations, one on your frequency which is a bunch of bullshit lawyer threats or one on my frequency which is business."

"Marcelle?" Cohn's snake eyes narrowed ever further. "He's disappeared."

"I think the Gentleman Bankers know where," Kane said.

"Why do you think I know anything about these Gentleman Bankers? You want to know the truth, I've never heard of them. You want to talk about the convention site, go to someone else."

"Trump's got the inside track," Kane said. He shrugged. "I'm making an offer. Maybe I am in the wrong place."

"I got friends who will make you hurt," Cohn said.

"The Genovese? They've tried and failed," Kane lied, but not completely since the mob had attacked him several times recently. "The offer is good. And giving me Marcelle's location is in everyone's interests because he's associated with people who are going to do some bad shit in the city. Something that will hurt everyone who has anything to do with them. I just put you in the blast radius."

"I'll need to see the cash," Cohn said in the same angry tone. "Not negotiable. I take a fifteen percent fee up front."

"Ten."

"Get the fuck out."

"All right," Kane said, not his money. "Fifteen. Marcelle?"

Cohn nodded at the rolodex. "I'll ask around."

Kane stared into those snake eyes and felt nothing coming from them but cold contempt. "Right."

"You'll owe me."

"The money——" Kane began, but Cohn was shaking his head.

"Money is easy. *You're* asking me for a favor which means a favor will be due one day."

*****

"He wants to see the cash and he takes fifteen percent."

"You negotiated?" Sofia asked as Kane settled into the back seat, feeling Matteo's elbow in his side.

"I said ten. He insisted on fifteen. He doesn't negotiate." Kane passed across the phone number Cohn's assistant had given him on the way out. "We call that and arrange the drop off."

"Think we can trust him?" Sofia asked.

"I wouldn't trust him," Kane said, "but it's not my money or my deal." He checked his watch.

Sofia amended the question. "Think he'll give me the slice?"

"Sure," Kane said, "as long as he gets his. He says I owe him a favor. I don't like that."

"It's the way the world works," Sofia said. "Where can I drop you off?"

Monday Afternoon, 8 August 1977

BUILDING ONE, WORLD TRADE CENTER
MANHATTAN

Tucker and Shaw were sitting in the reception area as Kane entered. Mrs. Ruiz wasn't making small talk with them, which Kane appreciated since she never made small talk with him and he'd hate to think that FBI received better treatment. Then again, she'd been awfully chummy with Yazzie.

Both popped to their feet. Tucker spoke for them: "Kane, we don't like—"

"Shut up," Kane said. He didn't slow, entering Toni's office and trusting Mrs. Ruiz to keep them out until they were summoned.

"Why did you have them come here?" Toni demanded as soon as the door shut behind him. "Last thing I need is the FBI around the office." She was wearing a grey business suit and looking considerably more professional than when he'd put her in the cab this morning.

"Calm down," Kane said. "I thought I needed to tell them about the missiles and someone smart suggested I have them come to me rather than me go to them. It might be good to have my lawyer at my side."

"Who told you that?"

"Sofia Cappucci."

Toni blinked. "When did you see her?"

"Just now. But she told me that on the phone. Just now, in person, she recommended I tell them nothing. That it won't do me any good. What do *you* think?"

Toni shifted gears, becoming the person who could bill high three figures an hour. "I agree with her recommendation. Technically, if you're not under a Miranda warning they can act on what you tell them but not use it against you. However, anything you say will give them more angles they can come at you from. They start digging and we both know they'll find something. You haven't been an angel lately, Will."

"But they're the ones who came to me with the information about this Swords of Saint Patrick thing. They involved me." Kane walked to the window. "I tried warning the CIA this morning and got blown off."

Toni was startled. "What did you tell the CIA?"

"The threat," Kane said. "He said it was the FBI's problem."

"That's correct."

"I *know* that," Kane snapped, harsher than he intended. "But aren't we all on the same side?" He turned to face her. "I fucked up, didn't I? Getting involved. Going after Damon. I should have walked away."

Toni walked up to him, slightly inside his personal space armor. "Then Damon would still be doing what he did. And this thing these guys are planning would still be happening."

"Your father wouldn't be on the run," Kane said.

"That's his fault," Toni said. She put a hand on Kane's forearm and he fought not to flinch. "Do what you think is right, Will. I'll do everything I can to protect you, legally and otherwise."

Kane wasn't so sure once he told her about other matters. "I got some things we need to talk about reference your father, but let's deal with these two idiots first."

Toni nodded toward the door. "We'll do it in the conference room. I don't want them in here again."

Kane paused. "I assume you can record what goes on in your conference room?"

"I can."

"We need this on tape."

"Remember something," Toni said. "The fact they came here so quickly means they don't feel very secure in their position."

"I think their position is made of toilet paper," Kane said. He opened the door and let her lead. They trooped into the conference room, Toni taking possession of the head of the table, Tucker and Walsh sitting on one side, Kane on the other.

"This better be worth us coming—" Tucker began.

"You going to talk or you going to listen?" Kane asked. He didn't wait for an answer. "I've got my lawyer as witness. I went to Kelly's Bar as you suggested, Agent Tucker."

Tucker opened his mouth to speak, but Kane shushed him. "No speak. Here's the bottom line. That Sword team you told me about got its hands on three TOW missiles, explosives, small arms and a fifty-caliber heavy machinegun. I don't know how many tracking systems for the TOWs, but all they need is one."

Kane sat back.

"How do you know that?" Tucker asked.

"I talked to Walsh. You met him, didn't you, when you went to Kelly's the other night? White-haired fellow? Runs the place and everyone in it."

"We tried to talk to him," Tucker said. "He didn't say anything to us."

"I've got a friendlier face," Kane said.

"What else did he tell you?" Shaw asked.

"Nothing, Agent Shaw," Kane said. "You now know what I know. Go do your duty."

"Bullshit, Kane," Tucker said. "You want us to take your word on this?"

Kane shrugged. "I've done my civic duty warning you of a grave threat to the city. I've got a witness to that. What you do with this information is up to you. You two are the ones who involved me in this."

Toni stood. "You may leave now."

"Bullshit," Tucker said. "You just can't dump this on us and kick us out."

"Why not?" Toni asked. "You dumped it on my client, who, by the way, went with you willingly when he didn't have to. I understand you also entered his premises without a warrant, weapons drawn?"

"We had probably cause," Tucker said, but Shaw was shaking his head.

"Where is this probable cause?" Toni asked. "Was it logged in at headquarters as evidence?"

Kane walked to the conference room door and opened it. "You guys better hurry. You've got a lot to do."

"You taped this," Shaw said. "Didn't you?"

"It's my office," Toni said.

The two FBI agents exchanged glances. Shaw walked out. Tucker reluctantly followed. Once they were gone, Kane and Toni returned to her office.

"What do you think they're going to do?" Toni asked as she went to the wet bar. She didn't bother to ask Kane if he wanted any. She brought the glass to the four-person table.

"I have no idea," Kane said. "They thought they were running Damon but he was actually running them. I don't think Damon was a true asset in that they never built an official file or else the CIA would have known about it, especially after I told Trent. They wanted people to think they were coming up with whatever Damon gave them on their own. The fact they didn't get promoted says he fed them shit. Even if they do send what I just told them up the chain of command, I know how that kind of bureaucracy works. I don't expect much by Wednesday night. The FBI is built to go after bank robbers, not terrorists."

"What are you going to do?" Toni asked.

"I've got a couple of leads I'm following," Kane vagued.

"Anything on my father?"

"Charles Edward Clark."

Toni frowned. "What about him? He's an old family friend."

Kane thought her reaction could give Truvey and Morticia a lesson or two in acting. "It's strange the things we don't focus on at the time." Kane put his hands flat on the table. "I missed it when it happened, but afterwards I was running it through my mind. As you've pointed out, Toni, I'm a little slow, but I get there eventually."

"What are you talking about?" Toni asked.

"When Yazzie was in here the other morning and asking about the trip, you said you had no idea who was going to be on the boat. Just that Selkis had arranged it. But just before that, when you and I were sitting at the bar in Windows on the World, and I was telling you what happened, I said the 'Actress' and you told me her name, Truvey. How did you know her name if you didn't know who was going to be on the boat?"

Toni's face was still and she didn't respond.

Kane pressed on. "Your film. The one Damon made."

"You told me you didn't watch that," Toni said.

"I watched the beginning," Kane said. "Enough to get an idea what happened. You had to know I did that. You'd told Damon to back off. To leave you and your father alone. You went to meet him at the Gramercy Park apartment."

As Kane spoke, Toni turned her head, no longer looking at him, staring at the vista of Manhattan spread out on this sunny, afternoon. The city was shimmering in the August heat.

"In your recording, Damon asked if you'd seen the films he sent," Kane said. "Of your father and your husband. There was only one film case for your father. From 1966. I've got it. I watched it this morning. Which brings me back to the Honorable Charles Edward Clark, Chief Judge for the Second United States District. You know Clark is more than just a family friend with your father because you saw the same film."

Kane gave it a few seconds but there was no response.

"That's two lies. Truvey and Clark," he pressed.

Toni was still staring out the tall windows. She lifted the glass to her lips and took a sip. Put it on the table. Let go of it and placed her folded hands in her lap, as if sitting in mass.

Kane waited.

"How far into my film did you watch?" Toni finally asked.

"Until the Unholy Trinity came in and you got sucker-punched by Haggerty. Your nose busted. That was it. You might feel better knowing that Haggerty died hard. I broke his knee first, then I destroyed his eye with the toe of my boot. I finished him with a shot through the head with his own gun."

Toni held up her hand, as if to silence Kane. "You assumed the rest of what happened to me?"

"Yes."

"It was worse than you assumed. I can assure you that. Do you still have my film? You told me it was destroyed in the fire."

"It was. I was out of it when I left that place the night of the Blackout. I grabbed what I thought might be important in my fucked-up state. Your film was not part of that."

"You thought my father's film was important?"

"Apparently I did. You don't?"

She didn't immediately answer.

Toni shifted in her seat and looked Kane in the eye. One hand was on the table and her forefinger began to tap, very lightly. "Do you think what happened to me that day ended when the film ended? Is that what you also assumed? That, like all the men, it was just what was on the film that was the key?"

"Tell me."

"I was pregnant when I went in there," Toni said.

Kane sagged back in the seat as if punched in the chest.

Toni continued. "No one knew except my doctor. It was early and I wasn't showing. I hadn't told Robert yet. Hadn't told anyone. Not my father. Not my mother. I had my reasons. *You* weren't around to tell. And before you ask, yes, I wanted that baby. More than anything. I was surprised by the feeling. I'd been pretty ambivalent about kids to that point. I think that's part of the reason I made a mistake and called Damon, asking him to back off. I wanted a clean life, or some sort of one. Whatever. I certainly wasn't thinking straight. It was a stupid move."

Toni closed her eyes. The sounds of the city were distant this high.

Toni continued in a low voice. "After what they did to me, after they threw me in the trunk of Damon's car and then dumped me, like so much trash, underneath the Brooklyn Bridge, I had a miscarriage. At first, I thought the blood was from the rape, because they were anything but gentle. I managed to get to my doctor that night. He confirmed I'd lost the baby lying there in the gutter.

"He took care of me as best he could, but given the circumstances, late at night, the rush, the secrecy, and the fact he'd already had a few drinks in him when I called, he made a mistake. After that, not only had I lost my baby, I could never have any more. *Can* never." Her finger was doing a steady, slow beat. "I've never told anyone that either. Not Robert, for certain. Not my mother. Not my father. Not my priest. No one. Ever."

"I'm sorry to hear that, Toni." Kane felt the futility. "That's fucked up and horrible. It was the only thing someone said to me after Lil' Joe died that made any sense at all. There's nothing that can change it and it's fucked."

Toni gave a brief nod of acknowledgement at the shared grief. "I think about it," she said. "Sometimes, after talking to you or seeing you, I wonder if losing that baby compared in any way to what happened with Taryn and you and Joseph. You had the joy of him for the time he was alive, then the tragedy of his death. Was the joy worth it? Or would it have been better if he'd never existed, like the child I didn't give birth to?" She looked at him. "So yeah, it's fucked up."

"Since I've been back, I go to the Bronx every Saturday," Kane said. "Stand at the intersection of Gun Hill and Eastchester at the exact time Joseph died. Conner was there this last Saturday. I told him I 'what if it' a lot. The accident, all of it. He told me I was being silly and stupid. He told me I have to think about the future. Normally, advice from Conner is easily ignored. But he's right on that topic." He gave it four taps of her finger before following up. "It was terrible, but that doesn't excuse you lying to me about Truvey being on the boat. Where is your father?"

Toni's eyes were hard; they reminded Kane of her father's in that moment and caused his heart to ache. "Fuck you, Will."

The look was gone and the Toni he knew was back, but he had to wonder if he knew Toni. "Is he with Clark?"

"I've got no idea," Toni said. Her shoulders drooped. "I never thought of Clark as someone father would run to. Then again, I never thought father would run." She stopped tapping and reached out for Kane's closest hand. He forced it to remain there as she put hers on top. "Tell me something, Will. Be honest. As honest as *you* can be. What happened in Boston?

What happened the night of the Blackout? You just told me you killed Haggerty."

Kane was shaking his head, but she lifted her hand and placed a finger lightly on his lips. "Hush. Hush. Listen. Listen. I'm not asking you to tell me. I'm asking because I want us to understand something. I know you lied to me about Selkis. I can read the papers, even the stuff buried in the city section. You killed the guy who cut Selkis's throat, didn't you? Took the pager off him. He was the John Doe found in the peepshow next door. Crawford must have a long arm, because the entire thing is wrapped up as far as the cops are concerned according to my contacts."

Kane didn't respond.

"Yeah," Toni said. "We all got secrets, Will. But here's the one thing at the heart of what's between us. Long before all this." She glanced at the saber hanging on the wall, then at the lone picture on her desk taken on Trophy Point during graduation in 1966. "You, me, Ted. We had something. A special friendship. It didn't end when Ted died. I think it still exists. But it was damaged badly long before this. When you wrote to father and me about what happened to Ted in Vietnam. Can you honestly tell me there are no lies or withholding of information about how Ted died?"

It was Kane's turn to not be able to meet her gaze.

"You did what you thought was right about that," Toni said. "Didn't you?"

Kane nodded.

Toni walked to the bar, poured herself a drink and then filled another glass. Came back, put it in front of Kane. "We're a pair, aren't we, Will? Broken. Shattered."

Kane reached out to the glass. Ran his finger around the rim. "You're right. We are." He pushed the glass aside and reached across. He took her wrist. "I hate that I have to ask this. The fact I have to means something is broken between us, Toni, and I'm not sure we can ever get it back. Did you know the boat was a set up?"

"No."

"How did you know Truvey would be on the boat?"

"Selkis told me. I kept it from you, because as you said, you'd have felt like a pimp and probably said no to the gig."

Kane stared at her and her eyes blazed back at him. They remained like for several seconds before she spoke. "You're hurting my wrist, William."

"I believe you." Kane let go. "The actress? Truvey. She needs some gigs. I told her you might be able to help her given you have all these show biz connections. It's the least we can do since she almost got killed over bullshit she had no clue about." He put one of Truvey's card on the table. Then he put Thomas Marcelle's film next to it. He placed the card Yazzie had given him next on the other side from Truvey's. He got up. "Page Yazzie. Tell him to be at the diner at three."

As he walked out, Kane expected to hear Toni ask him what he planned to do. The door swung shut on her silence and he took that as her assent.

GREENWICH VILLAGE, MANHATTAN

In combat, ambushes are usually cleverly disguised. At the very least, even if it's a hasty ambush, it's camouflaged. The one coming toward Kane on Washington, two blocks from his home, was neither, which gave him the option of avoiding it.

Kane was tired, upset and had a lot to do this afternoon. He didn't have time to avoid it nor was he so inclined. The two men looked like construction workers, with heavy, beat up boots, jeans stained by concrete dust and once-white t-shirts. More details came into focus as they got closer and he recognized them. They were the two who'd held Conner in the stands at Van Cortlandt. An older man, hair and beard prematurely grey, his arms scrolled with tattoos, including one of the Screaming Eagle of the 101st Airborne. The younger guy was bigger and walked with more swagger, the way the immature often do.

They halted fifteen feet away, blocking the sidewalk.

Kane didn't stop until he was just outside of arms reach.

The older one updated Kane on the purpose of their visit. "Mister Walsh said you need to be taught a lesson."

"I'm a fast learner," Kane said. "Can you give me the Reader's Digest version?"

"It ain't a speaking we'll be giving you," Airborne said.

"To be fair," Kane said, "I've spent a lot of time learning lessons in the vein you seem to be indicating. But really, if your goal is to beat me up, how will that teach me anything? What will it change?"

Airborne shrugged. "Won't change you, most likely, but it will make others think twice about betraying the Cause."

"Do you know how I supposedly did this?" Kane asked.

"No," Airborne said. "Don't need to."

"How is Mister Walsh doing?" Kane asked. "Last time I saw him, he was bleeding. I bandaged his sucking chest wound. You were there," he said to the older guy. He had to assume Sofia Cappucci's phone call might have reached the Boston Irish, but the New York Irish were a different story. Given how rarely his siblings talked to each other, Kane imagined Boston and New York Irish mobsters were worse.

"That's why you're just gonna get a beating." Airborne glanced at his partner. "Chris?"

The youngster responded by reaching behind him and retrieving a set of nunchuka, two wooden sticks attached by a six-inch length of chain.

"You gotta be kidding me," Kane muttered.

Chris stretched the nunchucka and moved his feet into an approximation of a fighting stance, doing his best to imitate Bruce Lee. Airborne was more traditional, balling his hands into fists. Chris whirled the nunchucka in a blur of movement in front of him, indicating he'd done more than just watch the movie, finishing with one in his left armpit. Airborne's stance was on the balls of his feet telegraphing he wasn't an amateur or a brawler like Magnus. The two spread apart, indicating they'd done this before. Chris readied the nunchuka, one in each hand, held out in front of him.

"I see your tattoo," Kane said to the older man. "Screaming Eagle or puking chicken?"

"Fuck you," Airborne said as he charged forward, Chris belatedly following suit.

Kane helped Airborne's momentum and weight on its vector by stepping to the side, letting the fist whiff by and punching him hard on the side of his head with his right hand while drawing the forty-five with his left. He lifted the gun, not to shoot, but slashed it toward the approaching nunchucka as Chris whirled them, holding one stick, aiming the other at Kane's head. The barrel of the forty-five hit the chain, abbreviating the strike and the closest piece of wood, rather than strike Kane, wrapped the chain around the gun.

Kane jerked the gun, pulling Chris toward him and used his other hand to clamp down on Chris's hand. Squeezed hard. Chris gasped and let go and Kane claimed the weapon with his right hand, left hand still holding the gun. Kane's internal clock was ringing; it was taking too long.

A punch hit Kane in the lower back, just missing his kidney. He staggered forward several steps, going with the force of Airborne's punch, pain radiating.

Kane spun about, holstering the pistol and stretching the nunchucka in front of him. Airborne and Chris faced him. Airborne didn't appear bothered by Kane's punch and Kane pretended the same.

"Want to call it a day?" Kane asked. "We didn't spend much time on the nunchucka, since Master Pak considered them frivolous, but he felt it appropriate we train on all possible weapons an opponent might possess."

Airborne's eyes narrowed, appraising Kane, but Chris came at him, fists swinging. Kane used the ends of the batons to block each blow, the attacker's flesh and bones the worse for the encounter with the hard wood.

After five swings and wooden hits, Chris backed up, cursing, knuckles bleeding, fingers bruised.

"How about you just tell Walsh you beat me up?" Kane suggested. He whirled the nunchucka in a blur, advancing on Chris, who stumble-retreated as they flashed within inches of his face. Then Kane dropped them and stepped back. They clattered at Chris's feet. Keeping a suspicious eye on Kane, Chris picked them up, wincing in pain.

"I've got a lot to do this afternoon," Kane said. "I played your game." He nodded at Airborne. "You got a good punch in. I'll be sore tomorrow." He shifted to Chris. "Nothing broken in your hands. They'll be okay. Even-steven?"

"What unit and when?" Airborne asked.

"173rd in '67 and then 5th Group in '69."

"101st in '69." Airborne nodded. "Fuck it. You don't tell nothing to nobody, we won't either." He walked away. Chris looked at Kane, at the nunchucka, then followed Airborne, tucking them in the back of his pants.

*****

It was two-twenty when Kane sat down at Pope's kitchen table.

"You're sweating," Pope noticed.

"It's hot out," Kane said. He drank a glass of tepid water from the tap while Pope sipped his likely not tea. The table was covered with papers and books and maps.

"I'm a bit scattered," Pope admitted, indicating the material, but his words were slightly slurred. "I can usually focus, but I start working on one thing, then it occurs to me that it's possibly connected to something else, but behind it all, I feel the ticking clock to Wednesday night. Crawford and Marcelle seem relatively insignificant compared to that."

"But connected," Kane said. "As you noted, Marcelle met or at least talked to someone from these Swords in order to set Crawford and me up. He also paid them at least one hundred grand. Right now, that's our best line on finding who they are and where they're hiding. I also have a feeling Crawford is in deeper than the building deeds. Too many lies around him to just be about money. He's a man with secrets."

Kane wanted to add that those secrets were worth the death of at least one of Crawford's other adopted sons, but Pope didn't need to be burdened by that. He relayed what Truvey had said about the cocaine and added his own information about the snuff films he'd found in Selkie's office from Damon's factory. "Crawford was funding more than B-films," he concluded. "I believe he was laundering money through Crawford and there's a lot of money around those films in the underground. Cash. Untraceable."

"It's likely," Pope agreed. "But the CIA said Crawford is untouchable."

"Someone told me Damon was bulletproof," Kane pointed out. "I believe that was you."

"Valid point." Pope picked up a piece of paper. "You wanted to find Judge Clark." He passed it to Kane. "That's his home address. Clark has always been single. Always listed as one of the most eligible bachelors in the city."

"I doubt he'd stash Marcelle in his own place, but people have done dumber things." Kane folded it without looking and put it in his shirt pocket, behind the notebook. "Something came up since we talked this morning. At first, I thought it was a completely different thing, but it occurred to me there might be a connection." He relayed Sofia Cappucci's request regarding the rail yards. He noted that Pope eyes lit up when he mentioned Roy Cohn. He concluded with: "If this Cohn guy is gay and, in the closet, wouldn't it make sense he knows about this Gentleman's Club?"

Pope was nodding. "Definitely. Cohn is a snake. Eisenhower sent the Department of Defense lawyers after Cohn during the McCarthy hearings trying to leverage his homosexuality."

"Okay. If Clark doesn't work out, Cohn will have to be second choice. I put a bug in his ear." Kane checked his watch. "What about the Swords of Saint Patrick? Anything?"

"Not specifically," Pope said. "Lots of babble about religion but nothing I'd feel comfortable saying is applicable. If they're NLA, they're not religious. I think they picked that moniker to point the blame at the IRA." Pope indicated the maps. "I've been racking my brain trying to figure out what they'd target. But it's overwhelming. I try to think like them. A target that won't cause much, if any, loss of life, but will be significant, and I come up with dozens, if not hundreds."

"We're looking at it wrong," Kane said.

"What do you mean?"

Kane indicated the maps. "We've been focused on what the target or targets could be. Given the TOWs have a range of three k's, even if we know the target, they could be firing from a lot of places. That's the key. Not what they're shooting at. Where they're firing from."

"Ah!" Pope got it right away. "A tall building would be the first thing I'd think of."

Kane nodded. "Or the top of the suspension towers of one of the bridges. GW. Brooklyn Bridge. Any of them. They'd have a great field of fire. Can I borrow your phone?"

"Ah, yes, a phone," Pope remembered. He passed a couple of papers to Kane. "The phone guy came by. He hooked a line up in the basement and put a phone there. The number is on the top piece of paper, but the line won't be activated until this evening."

Kane took the papers, copied his new number into his notebook, then indicated Pope's phone. "Mind? Until mine works?"

"Go ahead."

Kane called Merrick's team room. The soldier who answered fetched the team sergeant. Kane relayed his sudden insight.

"Really?" Merrick said. "No shit. We figured out firing position was key in about forty seconds. I got the team working it as a theoretical right now. We're wargaming a lot of different scenarios. Empire State Building. Either of the World Trade Center towers. Of course, the guys are going to look at me a little funny if this does go down. You need to get me something more to work with."

"I'm trying," Kane said.

"Okay. I mean, from what you said, they want to make a splash and if they're doing this at midnight, odds are whatever they're targeting could be vacant, right?"

"Most likely," Kane said.

"I'll call the diner and tell Thao if we come up with anything," Merrick said.

"I appreciate it," Kane said.

"You want me to come down? Help out if you've got to take action?"

"We've got it covered here."

There were several seconds of silence. Finally, Merrick spoke: "*Lions and tigers and bears, oh my.*"

Kane gave the correct reply. "*Yea, though I walk through the valley in the shadow of death I will fear no evil, for I am the meanest motherfucker in here.*"

"But watch out for the flying monkeys," Merrick warned. "They show up when you least expect them." The line went dead.

Kane put the receiver back on the hook and sat down with a sigh. The clock was ticking on his next action and on whatever the Swords had planned. "I've got experts going over the targeting," he told Pope.

"I heard," Pope said. "To be honest, I'm a bit surprised at how much I care about this city. I was a lad in London during the Blitz and . . ." His voice trailed off.

"Hey," Kane said. "Your friend, Maggie?"

Pope frowned. "Yes?"

"When's the last time you met her?"

"A week or so," Pope said. "Why?"

Kane was uncertain how to proceed. "Maybe you should invite her over or something." He glanced at the trash bin overflowing with bottles.

Pope's eyes narrowed. "You fathering me?" Before Kane could reply, he spoke harshly. "I've been drinking scotch since before you were sucking out of your mother's teat."

"Yes, sir. Sorry." Kane checked the time. "Got to go."

Pope didn't respond.

MEATPACKING DISTRICT, MANHATTAN

"Your cook is a dangerous man," Yazzie said as Kane approached his usual spot in the diner.

Yazzie was seated in the adjacent booth, back against the wall, one leg cocked up on the seat, allowing him a vantage of the diner and both doors. The booth was next to where Kane usually perched, which made him wonder if he was missing something.

"He is," Kane agreed. The place was empty except for the sound of dishes and pans clattering in the kitchen as Wile-E and Thao closed out. Kane went to his normal spot.

Yazzie twisted on the seat, vinyl squeaking, to look at him. "Really?"

"Really."

Yazzie switched seats so that he was facing Kane in the same booth. "Happy?"

"You don't know Boss Crawford as well as you think you do," Kane said.

"I don't believe you're in a position to say that."

"Did you look at the films I gave you?"

"No."

"Have you found Thomas Marcelle?" Kane asked.

"If I had, I wouldn't be here," Yazzie said.

"What happened to your offer regarding the people who planted the bomb?" Kane asked.

"Have *you* found *them?*"

"No. But I did discover they've acquired three TOW missiles."

"That sucks for somebody," Yazzie said. "Why am I here?"

Kane reached into his pocket and passed Judge Clark's address across the table.

The Native American unfolded it. "Who is this?"

"Thomas Marcelle's lover."

"Charles Edward Clark. *Charles?*"

"It's likely they've been in a long-term relationship," Kane said. "At least since 1966."

Yazzie folded it and put it in the inner pocket of his leather jacket. He was still for several moments. "A secret life for Marcelle. Which means he might have gone to ground with his lover. Or at his lover's place, since I'm assuming this isn't widely known."

"Toni suspected something, but had no idea who it was," Kane lied.

"Why are you passing this to me?" Yazzie asked. "Why aren't you and her following up?"

"I'm more concerned about the TOW missiles," Kane said.

"And Toni?"

"I think she's done with her father."

"You think? I was under the impression she was done with him when we met."

"Emotional matters take time to settle in. I assume you know that there is some sort of connection between your adopted father and George Bush, head of the CIA?"

"They're acquainted with each other. Don't tell me you tried running it up the Agency flagpole?"

"I haven't run anything up any flagpoles," Kane said. "I made inquiries."

"Do you have anything else for me?"

"No."

Yazzie tapped his pocket. "If this is a set-up, it will not go well for you. There will be a long line of people coming for you."

"Be still my beating heart. You mean your five adopted brothers?"

Yazzie stood. "You can tell the cook to put away the crossbow." He walked out.

Kane turned off the tape recorder as Thao came out of the kitchen, along with Wile-E and Lucky.

"Are you gentlemen ready for a trip to the Bronx?" Kane asked.

Monday Evening, 8 August 1977

RIVERDALE, THE BRONX

The Conrail train rattled south ten feet away from Kane, Wile-E, Thao and Lucky as they stood on the garbage-strewn, rocky, east bank of the Hudson River. Turgid water lapped over the rocks. Looking west, the setting sun was in their eyes, murky behind clouds and smog. The air was tainted with salt and a mixture of industrial waste.

Wile-E tilted a canteen for Lucky, the dog's tongue lapping. The dog wanted nothing to do with the polluted water, even after the journey from the south end of Van Cortlandt Park, pulling at the leash. Kane and Thao had been surprised that it wasn't a case of Lucky putting nose to ground; at least for most of the journey.

Wile-E had started him at the tree where Kane had smelled the gun smoke. Lucky had picked up a scent and they were off, ending here, a half mile west of where they'd started. Most of the way, Lucky had three-legged unerringly, head held high. Through alleys, along streets, crossing the Henry Hudson Parkway on the 232nd Street bridge, and then through Seton Park until they scrambled down to river level and across the Conrail commuter rail lines.

The train disappeared around a bend, heading into the city.

"They had a boat the night they came after me," Kane said to Thao as Wile-E walked Lucky along the shoreline, mission accomplished. "This confirms they still have it." He looked across the Hudson at the Palisades looming over the New Jersey

Shoreline. "They could be camped in the woods on top of the Palisades."

"The boat would have to be at the bottom, though," Thao pointed out.

Kane looked to the left, down river. The George Washington Bridge arched from Manhattan to New Jersey. "That's about three klicks."

"A little farther," Thao said. "And the missiles would have negligible effect on such a structure given the warheads."

"What if they fired from the top of the Palisades?" Kane said, but he was grasping, frustrated that the dog hadn't led them to the Swords of Saint Patrick's lair. He had the rucksack on his back, the K inside, along with Thao's crossbow and quiver.

"They could be anywhere along the river," Thao said. "Less people to the north. More opportunities to hide."

"They fled toward the Jersey shoreline," Kane said, remembering the brief encounter. "Of course, they could have turned north or south once they were out of sight." He shook his head in frustration. "Lots of refineries in that area. Blowing up some tanks would cause quite the blast."

"This does help, though," Thao tried. "I would suspect they are hiding close to the water and their firing position would also be on or close to the water. They will not want to travel very far on land with the missiles and launcher."

Kane shook his head. "Staten Island. Brooklyn. Queens. Hell, all of the city except the Bronx is an island."

"Do you remember Cambodia?" Thao asked.

"Of course."

"How hard it was to hide from the locals?"

"We always got discovered," Kane said. "Eventually."

Thao indicated the river. "There is much shoreline, but there are also many people. It is very hard for them to hide and not be spotted."

"Unless they have an isolated spot," Kane said.

"What do you suggest, Dai Yu?" Thao asked as Wile-E joined them, Lucky panting at his side.

"We've got forty-eight hours," Kane said. "We have to shake something loose." He pulled out his key ring and handed it to

Thao. "You and Wile-E and Lucky take the jeep back to Manhattan. I'll catch the subway later. We'll meet in the diner in the morning."

"What are you going to do?" Thao asked. "In case I must take action later tonight?"

"I'm just going to the local bar."

*****

It was dark by the time Kane entered Kelly's. There was relative quiet on Monday evening compared to Saturday. No singers, no juke box, just a low hum of conversation and the mutter of a black and white TV above the bar tuned to a baseball game. There was a decent sized crowd, but several tables were open. Walsh wasn't holding court at his table, which was to be expected. Kane spotted a face he recognized, hesitated, then resigned that it would be impolite not to at least say hello.

"Good evening, Caitlyn," he said as he stood across the table. There was a mug in front of her, a quarter down.

"Good evening, Mister Kane, with a K." She indicated the empty seat he stood behind. "Join me?"

Kane glanced over his shoulder, then indicated the seat to the side. "Do you mind?"

"Not at all," Caitlyn said.

Kane descended through the light haze of cigarette, pipe and cigar smoke. He angled the chair so he could watch the front door and the bar, Caitlyn to his left, the brick wall behind.

"A cautious man, I see."

"Old habit," Kane said.

"Not one many pick up, willy-nilly."

"Army training," Kane explained.

"You have that soldier look about you," she said. "Noticed it right away. Hard to extract that life from a man once he's absorbed it. Seeps into his spine, makes him stand a little taller."

No Walsh. No Patrick or Magnus. No one else he recognized. No one singing for which Kane was grateful.

"Expecting someone?" Caitlyn asked.

"Just seeing who is who and what is what," Kane said.

The same hard waitress from the other night cruised up. "What can I get you?"

Kane debated. "Tap." It was the kind of bar where that was a sufficient answer.

Kane waited in uncomfortable silence, aware of Caitlyn's presence, but at a loss for small talk. He gave it a shot. "Do you come here often?"

Caitlyn stared at him. "Do you?"

"My second time," Kane said.

"Seventh," she said.

The waitress returned. "Thanks for the other night," she said as she put a chilled mug in front of Kane. "Mister Walsh doesn't like trouble inside."

"But outside is all right?" Kane asked.

The waitress laughed. "Outside is other people's business, but I've not seen Patrick or his strapping young man since you went through the door with them. Nor your uncle. You might be bad for business."

"I'll try not to be," Kane said. "If you don't mind, have there been any visitors in here lately?"

"Besides you?" the waitress asked. "What-da-ya-mean 'visitors'?"

"From the old country," Kane said.

"Every night," the waitress replied as she swept a hand to indicate the other patrons. "Pick one. You be sitting next to one, as a matter of fact." She leaned toward the table and lowered her voice. "I'd not be asking too many such questions if I was you. People like their privacy."

She walked away.

"You are not a subtle man, are you?" Caitlyn asked. "Seems you didn't get the information you were seeking the other night?"

"Not exactly," Kane said. He focused on her. "When did you come over?"

She feigned surprise. "Does my accent give me away?" She smiled. "I listen to the voices here and I discern more New York than I do Ireland, even among those who arrived just a few years ago. I imagine it will be the same for me eventually. Three months, this past Tuesday, I've been in these fair United States."

"Did your husband come with you?" Kane asked, tensing as he saw Airborne enter the front door, and realizing his oversight as soon as he said it.

"He passed in Ireland and that is why I came," Caitlyn said. "My future prospects were not bright back there." She took a sip from her mug.

"Sorry to hear that."

"Do you know the man with the tattoos?" Caitlyn asked, pulling his attention back to her. "Or is that where your desires lie since you watch him so closely? I'm not one of those judgmental sorts. It seems a truth that the priests who rail against the flesh the loudest are often most deeply involved in it on the sly and often with those with the same set of equipment the Lord blessed them with."

"I met that fellow earlier today and we had a chat," Kane said.

Airborne was at the bar before he spotted Kane. He frowned and looked about to see who else was inside. He glared at Kane, shook his head, but that was the extent of it as he grabbed a full mug and a shot glass and went to the far side of the tavern.

"Neither of you look the worse for the chat," Caitlyn noted. "I come here to watch. One can learn a lot about people just by watching."

"Such as?"

"You haven't touched your beer."

Kane nodded. "I'm not much of a drinker."

"An odd thing for a man in a tavern to say. Did you feel obligated to order it because I have one, because you're sitting here and the waitress asked, or you felt like drinking a few moments ago and that ship has sailed since speaking with me?"

"Is the 10th of August a significant date in Irish history?"

Caitlyn was still on the beer. "Not partaking of spirits is considered unmanly in some quarters, but I'm in favor of it in some men. My departed had too much of a taste for the devil's brew. To answer my own question, since you did not, I have this--" she tapped the mug with a finger whose nail was gnarled down to the quick—"because I am occupying this seat and it seems fair price for passage."

Kane was regretting his decision to try and stir things up in Kelly's and he was recognizing it for what it was: desperation.

"Ten August," Caitlyn said. "Off the top of my head I'd say there must have been some battle in olden days or some great political argument made. Seems there's one of each for every day of the calendar spread out over the years. We Irish love to argue and fight. Fair sir!" she called out, gesturing to the old man who'd sung unaccompanied the other night about the Wild Colonial Boy.

"Aye, lass?" he said, from his table, where he was nursing a mug.

"Ten August, sir. Does it portend something important in Irish history?" Caitlyn asked.

He answered right away, albeit indirectly. "Today, the eighth, was the sinking of the mighty Armada off our lovely shore in the year of our Lord fifteen hundred and eighty-eight and the polluting of that black blood amongst some of our people. The tenth?" The old man frowned. "Ah. The Second Battle of Athenry!" He rose to his feet with some difficulty and leaned heavily on the cane as he made his way over.

Kane pulled out a seat for him and signaled to the waitress to bring him a drink.

"The 'Second' Battle?" Caitlyn said.

"Aye. I don't quite recall when the first was. But the second is recorded in the Annals of Lock Ce. An uprising arm-in-arm with the Scots under Edward Bruce against the heathen English."

The waitress put a shot glass and a mug in front of the old man and Kane slipped her a twenty.

The old man downed the shot, then began drinking the beer. And drinking. Kane and Caitlyn watched as he gulped the contents, then slammed the empty on the table. This was obviously not unusual, because the waitress had waited and scooped up both empties, taking them with her.

"What happened in the battle?" Kane asked. "Why was it important?"

The old man shrugged. "I just know it was fought on that date. lass. Don't know what year or who won."

Caitlyn contributed. "I suspect, given subsequent history, the Bruce side, with which our forefathers allied, were not the victors."

"Aye," the old man said, "but it must have been a valiant fight as they all were." He rose and caned his way back to his table.

"That was enlightening," Kane said.

"What are you seeking?" Caitlyn asked.

Kane almost told her, but caught himself. "Nothing."

"Rather specific questions for nothing," Caitlyn said and continued to speak in the same calm, tone. "Your friend is coming over."

"You don't look beat up," Airborne said. "What if Mister Walsh hears?"

"Will he?" Kane slid his untouched beer across the table. "On me."

Airborne considered it, then sat down. "Where'd you learn those moves?" he asked. He picked up the mug and drained half of it.

"Various places," Kane said. "Thailand. Japan. Korea. The pits at Camp Mackall. Fort Benning."

"Vietnam?" Airborne asked.

"Not much time to train there," Kane said.

"True." Airborne held out a callused hand. "Danny."

Kane shook it. "Will."

"How touching," Caitlyn said. "Men bonding over their shared experiences in killing. Tell me. Who won the war?"

Danny's face flushed red, but he didn't say anything.

Kane answered. "No one won. Some lost more than others."

Caitlyn raised a hand for the waitress as she spoke. "My apologies, Danny and Will. That was uncouth and unkind of me." When the waitress arrived, Caitlyn ordered a round.

"How is Mister Walsh doing?" Kane asked Danny.

"He's on the mend," Danny said. He glanced at Caitlyn. "What's your story?"

"It's a long, sad tale," Caitlyn said, "and I doubt you'd have the patience for even a quarter of it, lad."

Danny laughed. "Gotta agree with you on that."

"I wouldn't ask," Kane began, "but it's important. Have you seen anybody recently from Ireland in here? Present company excepted."

"What do you mean?" Danny asked.

Caitlyn laughed. "He's talking about the two Provos who came in last week, for fuck sake." She shook her head at Kane. "You going to ask everyone but me?"

"You keep your mouth shut," Danny hissed at her, as the waitress approached and deposited three mugs.

Kane ignored the veteran. "When? How many?" he asked Caitlyn.

She shrugged. "I believe it was Monday, week past. Easy to pick out, not just because of their brogue but they have that look in their eye. Sort of like the both of you. Men who've killed. Except they had no military in their spine, one can see that. Not much of a spine at all in the likes of them. Just the violence and that makes them snakes. I know their sort from home."

As Kane opened his mouth to speak, Caitlyn silenced him with a lift of her hand. "All I saw was two men. They spoke to Mister Walsh briefly. It was odd to see such here in the United States."

"How do you know they were Provos?" Kane asked.

"Told you. I've seen the sort often enough." Caitlyn indicated the mugs. "Drink up, lads." She took a deep draught. "They haven't been back since then." She looked at Danny. "That's what happened, is it not?"

"I got nothing to say on the matter." Danny drank half his mug. "Shouldn't even be sitting here," he added, making no move to depart. He looked at Kane. "Walsh said you might be a Fed. But you aint, are you?"

"No."

"Didn't think so. Not a cop either, like your uncle."

Kane focused on Caitlyn. "Can you tell me *anything* about the two men? I need to find them."

"Why?" she asked.

"I think they're planning to do something bad," Kane said.

"And what might that be?"

"I'm not sure," Kane said.

Danny was pushing his chair back, bit by bit, looking more uncomfortable with each word spoken in front of him. "I want no part of this." He walked away, leaving Kane alone with Caitlyn.

"Whatever you can tell me about those two men would be useful," Kane said. "Did they come from the subway? Or a car?"

"Why do you care?" Caitlyn asked. She indicated the tavern. "The people here live in a reality of their own choosing, but it doesn't seem to be yours. 'The old country'." She almost spit the last three words. "What do they know of the bombings and the shootings and the kneecappings? The innocents caught in the crossfire, as if it matters from which side the bullet came? The bombings are worse. Just chance who is standing by. But it does matter who pays for the bullet and the bomb, doesn't it?"

"I agree," Kane said. "That's why I care. They call themselves the Swords of Saint Patrick."

"Oh, fuck me to tears," Caitlyn said. "Saint Patrick never had a sword. If I still believed in the divinity of that poor bastard who got himself nailed to the cross, I'd called that blasphemous at best."

Kane flinched as Caitlyn reached out, but she persisted and lightly touched the scar on the side of his head with her nail-worn forefinger. "A little the other way and you wouldn't be sitting here, would you, Kane with a K?"

Kane didn't respond to the obvious.

"Not much I can tell you," Caitlyn said, her fingers still touching the scar, "to help about those two men other than they were average size, one a shaggy redhead and the other dark-haired, fair skinned, a strange combination. That's it, I'm afraid. They came in the front door and left by it. No idea what their mode of conveyance was."

"More than I had before," Kane said. "Was one of them wounded?"

"'Wounded'?"

"Nose broken? Arm in a sling?"

"No." She leaned forward, spreading the rest of her fingers on the side of his head, into his thick hair, her face just a few inches from his.

Kane remained still, feeling her rough, strong fingers holding his head, her green eyes staring into his.

"Are you trying to be a real Jack Duggan?" Caitlyn quietly asked. She removed her hand, slowly, fingers sliding over skin, through hair. "Now, if you're not going to drink, be off with you. You're ruining whatever reputation I might possibly have left."

*****

Kane took the stairs to the elevated subway platform slowly, his hand on the railing. Upon arrival, he glanced in both directions. The platform was dimly lit and held a scattering of people, not unusual for a Monday evening at the end of the line. He was on the center platform, tracks to either side. They both terminated at the northern end of the station as this was the terminus of the #1 subway line. Kane walked to the southern end and away from the other waiting passengers.

In his memory floated a tidbit Brother Benedict had distilled about Jack Kerouac and this station and *On The Road*, which he thought even Morticia would find interesting, but he didn't have the energy or focus to write it down in his notebook. In the distance echoed the approaching clatter of steel on steel that New Yorkers were attuned to, but the train wasn't in sight yet.

The lack of focus allowed the barrel of a gun to be pressed into the base of Kane's skull.

"Keep your hands away from your sides," Tucker hissed.

"Where's Shaw?" Kane asked, doing as ordered, his hands extended away from his body at the elbows.

"Shaw's got nothing to do with this," Tucker said.

"Did Damon have something on you?" Kane belatedly realized his oversight at West Point. He should have checked the pictures to see if Tucker's name was on one of the film cases.

"Fuck you," Tucker said. "Where's the money?"

"Burned up."

The headlights of the inbound train rose above the tracks in the distance.

"You were Damon's insurance, weren't you?" Kane asked but he already knew the answer. "The person who knew he was taking me there." Another piece clicked into place. "Which means you knew about his factory. The fifth chair. There were five chairs in the film room in Damon's factory. You sat in that fifth chair when he played his films, didn't you?"

The barrel pressed harder into his skin. "I never sat in there. I never watched any of his films except the one he showed me that he'd made of me. He didn't offer a seat when he did that."

Kane's focus was now razor sharp, not just because of the gun, but the realization of Tucker's complicity. "You're a piece of shit, you know that?" The train was rattling closer and Tucker grabbed the back of Kane's collar with his free hand, pulling him into the darkness of an advertisement stanchion so the motorman in the lead car wouldn't see them.

"Who the fuck are you?" Tucker demanded. "Some has-been ex-Green Beret working divorce cases. Why did you get involved and fuck everything up? You know too much, Kane. You—"

Kane whirled, ducking, left hand grabbing the gun before Tucker could react. Tucker fired, belatedly, as the train reached the end of the platform, the round ripping harmlessly into the dark night inches above Kane's head. Kane kept his momentum on the spin, pulling Tucker by the gun hand forward, toward the edge of the platform, before he let go.

The front of the train flashed by, brakes squealing for its final stop.

Tucker turned and swung the gun toward Kane, but the ex-Green Beret's foot was faster. Kane snap kicked into Tucker's chest, sending him flying backward. Tucker hit the moving train, bounced off, spinning from the train's speed, dropping the gun, arms wind milling, trying to regain his balance.

Kane timed his next kick accurately, boot into Tucker's stomach, doubling him over and sending him exactly into the gap between the second and third cars of the ten-car train as they went by.

Tucker disappeared into the darkness of the tracks, his scream barely audible above the sound of the train coming to a halt and cut off in less than a second. Kane picked up the gun and put it in his pocket.

The doors slid open and a handful of passengers disembarked, emptying the train. Kane stepped inside and sat down, facing the open door. He was the only one in his car. He waited, anxiety building whether anyone had noticed Tucker going onto the tracks. Should he just exit and hit the streets instead of being trapped inside here and—

The door at the end of the car rattled open and the motorman entered, his large key in hand as he switched ends of the train. He didn't spare Kane a glance as he inserted the key in the cubicle in the front right of the car and disappeared inside.

The doors slid shut. With a lurch, the train reversed direction.

Underneath the elevated subway, a steady drip of blood splatted onto Broadway un-noticed. Just before the train cleared the station, the steel wheels finished slicing through flesh and bone and Tucker's right hand dropped between crossties and landed on Broadway.

It too was unnoticed in the dark.

******

Kane relaxed as they cleared the platform. The train didn't accelerate much, rolling the four blocks to the next station at 238th Street. No one got on Kane's car. The doors shut and the train picked up speed for the next stop in the Bronx at 231st Street.

Kane glanced right as the door at the end of the car opened.

Caitlyn entered and strode unerringly to Kane, sitting next to him. "Exciting evening, it's turned out to be, eh?"

Kane couldn't conjure up a response.

"It seems you still possess your martial skills, Will Kane," Caitlyn said. "Taking down a man holding a gun on you is no mean feat."

"He was too close," Kane said. "Never get within arm's reach when holding a firearm. Negates the advantage."

"I'll keep that in mind if I'm ever unfortunate enough to be in that situation," Caitlyn said.

An inarticulate, static filled gargle came over the intercom as the conductor taunted the name of the next station as they arrived. The doors opened. No one came in. Doors closed. The train rattled south,

"I lied to you," Caitlyn said. "It was born of necessity as many lies are."

"You know more about the Provos than you told me in the bar," Kane said.

Caitlyn shook her head. "Oh, my friend, they're not Provos."

"National Liberation Army," Kane said.

Caitlyn nodded. "You've done your homework. The Provos would be insane to do anything in the United States to generate ill will. But ill will is the goal of these gentlemen."

Kane waited for Caitlyn to enlighten him.

"I watched the man you helped commit suicide and his partner with Walsh the other night. They had badges. A brief confrontation before they were escorted from the premises. Why was he after you?"

"He was corrupt," Kane said. "I discovered that among other things."

"Ah. That makes sense. Many who swear to uphold the law sometimes become seduced by that which they aim to stop. One has to wonder who polices the police?"

The doors opened at 225th Street. They remained the car's only occupants besides the motorman ensconced in his compartment. The train pulled out and crossed over the Harlem River which separates the Bronx from Manhattan.

"The lie?" Kane prompted.

Caitlyn looked at him. "Your blood is up, is it not?"

Kane frowned.

"After a killing, my husband's blood would always be boiling. He'd want to have relations which I found disgusting. It's something primal in our species. When a man faces death, he wants to revel in life and what is more basic than carnal relations?"

"Your late husband," Kane reminded her.

"That was the lie," Caitlyn admitted. "He is very much alive. Unfortunately. His name is Kevin Flanagan."

They approached the last station above ground, Dyckman Street.

Kane turned on the hard plastic toward her. "He's here in the United States. How many are with him?"

"Five."

"Where are they?"

"I've been trying to ascertain that," Caitlyn said. "Which is why I've been in that tavern."

"Why are you telling me this?" Kane asked.

"You seem like a man of serious intent," Caitlyn said. "As you noted, law enforcement is of questionable integrity, but I sense you are a man who possesses it. You seek to stop this attack. As do I, but you have more resources and skills as you recently demonstrated." She glanced up as the train slowed for a stop, but the windows were covered with graffiti and it was impossible to see what the station was or understand the conductor. When the doors opened, Kane managed to read 168th Street on the tiled wall.

"How long until you get off?" Caitlyn asked.

Kane told her.

She leaned close, resting her head on his shoulder. She smelled of soap and something else that stirred memories. "I will tell you what you need to know, as much as I know, before you depart. Several months ago, Kevin and his boys, men, attempted to kill the head of the Provos. They made a mess of it. An eleven-year-old girl was caught in the crossfire. I'd been done with the Cause a long time before, but being done wasn't enough after that. I had to stop them. I continued to play the good wife, cooking his meals, washing his dirty, bloody clothes, allowing him his way with me whenever he wanted. I was so quiet and meek I was part of the walls. They forgot I was there."

Another stop and she paused, then continued as the train moved on. "They're here to make the Provos look bad and cut off their funding from the States. They'd rather fight fellow Irish than the Brits, and fighting the Brits is futile. However, there would be a secondary gain to pressure your current administration to pressure the Brits to pursue a peace with more alacrity."

"What's their plan?" Kane asked, unable to turn his head or his chin would be touching her forehead.

"Kevin isn't foolish. He kept the details to himself. All I, and the five who signed on, knew was that it was to be in New York City. The day after they left for the States, I followed."

"To do what?"

"Stop them."

"How are you going to do that?" Kane asked as the train rattled into another station.

"I'm doing it right now, aren't I?" She lifted her head slightly. "I knew someone would step up."

Kane turned to look at her. Her face was just a few inches from his. For the first time he noted there were flecks in her green eyes. The skin on either side of them was etched with deep lines. That all disappeared as the lights went out for a long second, then came back on.

"Your police won't be able to stop him," Caitlyn said. "Not without many dying. It's takes a good man who has walked the dark path to stop a bad man."

At Times Square/42nd Street several teenagers came in, loud and rowdy. When the doors shut, they turned toward Kane and Caitlyn and swaggered down the middle of the car. When they were close enough, Kane flipped aside his unbuttoned denim shirt, exposing the .45. He noted that Caitlyn hadn't turned to look.

The gang reversed course, searching for easier prey in the next car.

"I need more," Kane said. "They could be anywhere and attacking—"

She cut him off. "Kevin hates women."

"Right and—"

"Think, my friend. He hates women and wants to make a statement all of New York City will see."

"The Statue of Liberty."

"It would be in his style."

"Do you know or are you guessing?"

"When you're married to a man you know him. He's making more of a statement than just about the IRA."

Penn Station didn't bring anyone into the car.

"*Anything* else?"

"Kevin will sacrifice the others," Caitlyn said. "He cares about no one but himself. He won't be taken alive, though. He's sworn to die before prison."

"I'm not a cop," Kane said. "I don't arrest people."

She was just inches away. Her hands slid on either side, cradling his head. Tears were forming. "Do you feel my hands? That's the way I was holding that young lass's head. I cradled that child in my hands as she breathed her last. I saw the life leave her eyes as I felt her blood flow over my fingers." The first tears slid down her sharp cheeks. "She didn't go to a better life. She went to nothingness. To darkness. Send Kevin there."

"Where are they hiding?"

"They'd be close to the target."

"Come with me," Kane said. "I can protect you."

"No. I don't want protecting. I'm guilty too. Of waiting too long."

"What are you going to do?"

"If you fail, I'll go public with who they really are and what they plan. If you succeed, I'll go home."

"They'll kill you," Kane said. "The ones back there."

"They'll try. But I'll stand up and speak out."

The doors opened and the station was written in black tile on the white: 14th Street.

"My stop. Come with me."

She nodded and pulled her hands back. "All right."

They walked side by side to the doors and stepped out.

"Good luck, William Kane, with a K," Caitlyn said.

The doors began to shut and she slipped back inside.

Kane stood on the 14th Street platform and looked at Caitlyn, through a small clear spot of glass, devoid of graffiti. Her green eyes glittered in the flickering lighting inside the car. The train pulled out. He didn't move as the train disappeared into the dark tunnel, red lights diminishing and then abruptly disappearing as it rounded a curve.

The sound also faded until he was alone. He slowly walked toward the stairs to the surface.

GREENWICH VILLAGE, MANHATTAN

The tell was in place at the front door and Kane mentally debated whether to check the back, in case Yazzie had returned for a visit; or someone else as he seemed to be accumulating visitors with each passing day.

He unlocked the door without going around back, figuring one attempt on his life was enough for this evening. Terrible logic, he knew, and Charlie Beckwith had probably just sat bolt upright on whatever hard rock he was sleeping on at Fort Bragg, but Kane was too damn tired. He dead-bolted the door.

He did check all the rooms, but that took less than five seconds. His sleeping pad was under the shirts and pants hanging in the closet, a poncho liner haphazardly lying on top of it. Kane glanced at his bed, the top sheet and blanket loose from recent occupation.

"Fuck it," Kane said. He slipped off the denim shirt, pulled the .45 out of the holster and put it next to the pillow and got into bed.

He'd learned to sleep no matter what the circumstances during his deployments. Caitlyn's words faded and the last thing his conscious mind registered was the smell of Toni imprinted in his pillow.

Tuesday Morning to Afternoon, 9 August 1977

GREENWICH VILLAGE, MANHATTAN

Kane gently knocked on the front door, torn between not wanting to wake Pope up, and desiring to find out if his landlord had uncovered anything applicable to the current clusterfuck. The first tinge of dawn was touching the trees behind him and the sun would be up shortly. A cool breeze was blowing in from the west, bringing welcome relief.

There was no answer, but the door was unlocked. Kane opened it and stuck his head in. "Pope?"

No reply. He entered and heard snoring echoing down the short hallway. Pope was in the kitchen, sprawled in the arm chair, mouth agape. His reading glasses were still perched on his nose. The tea cup was upside down in its saucer. The top of the table was a scattering of papers and books and a map of New York City. Kane glanced at it. Pope had used a red marker to circle various buildings; whether he considered them targets or launch sites was difficult to tell and Kane quickly deduced the former reporter was out of his depth trying to do a target analysis.

Kane reached to remove the glasses, but paused, not wanting to wake him. An empty bottle lay on top of the trash bin. On top of other empty bottles. He glanced out back at the wilting plants in the garden Pope had once tended to with a passion verging on obsession, now struggling to survive.

Kane left, locking the door behind him.

MEATPACKING DISTRICT, MANHATTAN

Morticia deposited two meal tickets on Kane's table along with his coffee and water with two ice cubes. "Popular, aren't you?"

"I'm a man about town," Kane said as he unfolded them, revealing Thao's precise handwriting in five letter groups.

Kane pulled out his notepad and checked the trigraph so he could he decipher them.

TONIA TTENW INDOW SONTH EWORL DXXXX
MEETY AZZIE ATNOO NSAME BOATX

"Important?" Morticia was making a curving pass to the counter to pick up dishes.

"My dance card is filling up," Kane said.

"Save some space," Morticia said. "Thao just put some peppers on the counter."

Kane drew the .45 and rested it on his left thigh as Agent Shaw entered the Washington Street door.

"Should I dive for cover?" Morticia asked.

"I don't know," Kane said, "but get out of my line of fire."

"Righto." Morticia moved to the counter and retrieved meals for a pair of transvestites on the far side of the diner.

Shaw looked like shit and there weren't more agents following him as backup so Kane kept his finger on the outside of the trigger guard, while he turned on the tape recorder.

"I didn't know what Tucker was up to," Shaw said, standing at the edge of the counter and keeping his hands clear from his sides. "Can I sit?"

Kane nodded.

Shaw sat down, eyes red, deep pockets under them. He put his hands on the table. "They found Tucker last night. Seems he fell onto the tracks at 242nd Street up in the Bronx."

"Accidents happen," Kane said. "I don't think Tucker was sure of where he stood, so it's easy to slip and fall. Where do you stand?"

"Damon was Tucker's guy," Shaw said, the words coming fast and guilty. "I was against it from the start, but he was my partner. And then he set me up. Tucker told me it was a benny of the job. Some high-class hooker on Gramercy Park. I shouldn't have done it. I got a wife and kids. But, fuck, you know."

"You've got it backward," Kane said. "Tucker was Damon's guy. So were you."

"I don't know what he had on Tucker," Shaw continued. "But it was bad."

"What's going on with the Swords of Saint Patrick?"

Shaw frowned as if that was a strange question. "Shit, man, I don't know. Could have been bullshit by Damon."

"It wasn't," Kane said. He leaned forward. "Nothing Damon gave you two was ever sent up the chain of command, was it?"

"No."

"No paperwork at all?"

"No."

"No one at the FBI, other than you, knows about these Swords of Saint Patrick?" Kane asked.

"It was probably just Damon jerking our chain," Shaw tried, without conviction.

"Then why were you guys in the Bronx checking on it? Bringing me in?"

"Tucker was worried about you for some reason," Shaw said. "Then after going to the meeting at your lawyers, he started weirding out."

"Do you know a guy named Whitey Bulger in Boston?" Kane asked.

"Who?"

"Why the fuck are you here?"

"To tell you I had nothing to do with whatever Tucker was up to last night."

Kane leaned back in the seat. "You just went along with Tucker and Damon? You're telling me you had no idea what Damon was doing in his factory?"

"I didn't know anything about the place," Shaw said. "What I said at HQ was true. We never tailed Damon there."

"Because Tucker didn't want you to," Kane said. "Sofia Cappucci. Did you call her after I left HQ the other day?"

"I didn't. Tucker disappeared right after you. He was gone for a few minutes. He had all sorts of weird contacts."

"I'm going to give you one chance, Shaw. Did Damon or Tucker say anything about these Sword guys? What the target might be? Where they might be hiding?"

"I don't think Damon knew anything more, either, since he wasn't helping them."

"If I was you, Shaw, I'd turn in my badge and move to Montana and become a cowboy or a tree or more aptly, a rock. You're done in the FBI and you're done in the city. Go."

Shaw scooted out of the booth and scurried away.

"You don't look happy," Morticia chipped in as she cruised by. Then she brightened as the Gansevoort door opened. "Omar! Morning, sweetie."

"Morning, pretty lady," Omar greeted her as she pecked him on the cheek.

Omar took up most of the width of the other side of the booth from Kane. "Why do you have your gun out?"

Kane was startled and he holstered. "The FBI was just here."

Strong frowned. "You were gonna shoot the FBI, Kane? Even for you, that's a bit much."

"Did you get the donuts this morning?" Kane asked.

Strong looked up as Morticia put a cup in front of him and poured. "You're right. He's not funny."

"I know," Morticia said. "His mood seems to be getting worse. The usual, sweetie? Do you have time?"

"I do and yes," Strong said.

More customers entered and she moved off.

"To what do I owe the honor of your presence?" Kane said. "Do you come bearing more good news?"

"I wanted breakfast," Strong said, "and I was in the area."

"You tracked Son of Sam to the Village?"

"No. I was at headquarters." Strong lowered his voice. "We got a good lead. Real good. We're gonna nail the son-of-bitch in the next day or so."

"Congratulations," Kane said. "What was the break?"

"A parking ticket," Strong said. "At the last shooting. One of the witnesses reported seeing a uniform in the area writing tickets. When we checked, we didn't find anything filed. They were going to blow off the witness, thinking she was making it up—we've had lots of that—or confused. But I talked to every patrolman on duty that night in that precinct. Found the officer. He hadn't turned his in and was worried he'd get in trouble."

"Details," Kane said.

"Details," Strong agreed, but he didn't appear thrilled. "Of course, the boss just took the lead from me."

"Can't have the donut man making the bust?" Kane asked.

"More like can't have the junior black guy do it," Strong said, "since it's going to be the biggest story of the year."

"Fucked up," Kane said, but he had some doubts about biggest story of the year.

Strong echoed him the second time. "Fucked up, indeed. I just got told."

"Going to drown your sorrows in some pancakes?" Kane asked. "Let me ask you something, since you just came from the font of all police knowledge. Is there any buzz in the building about IRA terrorists in the city?"

Strong had the cup of coffee halfway to his mouth, but the hand froze. "What? What are you talking about?"

"Nothing," Kane said.

"Don't drop that in my lap and then nothing me," Strong said. "This have anything to do with the M-16s, Damon and the fire?"

"Partially," Kane said. "I don't think you want to know what I know."

"I'm sure I don't," Strong said. He took a deep drink of coffee, put the cup down. "But since you opened Pandora's box and unleashed your plague on me, you don't get to shut it. What's going on?"

Kane glanced to make sure Morticia was busy. He'd run this all through his mind enough times, that he was able to give Strong the quick version, in under two minutes, minus killings and other incriminating information. By the time he was done, Morticia arrived with his pancakes and bacon.

"You all right, sweetie?" she asked. She gave Kane a dirty look. "Did Kane ruin your morning?"

Strong forced a smile. "No. We're discussing the sad state of the city."

"Neither of you lie very well," Morticia said, "which is odd given your occupations." She waved a hand. "Go on. Conspire without my wisdom and insight." She walked away.

"There's not a peep of that on the force," Strong said. "We see everything on the Task Force. The IRA wouldn't do that here."

The brief summary had left out the IRA faction bit, so Kane filled that in. He withheld what Caitlyn had told him, because Omar would want to know how he knew it and of course . . .

"There's more to this," Strong said. "Stuff you aren't telling me. A reason you can't fire a flare."

"There is," Kane admitted.

"Fruit of the poison tree?" Strong asked.

"Fruit of the fucking-dead tree," Kane clarified. "My recent FBI visitor confirmed the Feebs are also clueless about this, for various reasons, mainly being fucked up."

"Without more, you won't be believed," Strong said.

"I know," Kane said. "But without getting that more, I wouldn't know much of anything. A Catch-22."

"Jesus, you *are* a plague, Kane." Strong's pancakes were getting cold.

Kane gripped the edge of the table. He leaned forward; his voice harsh. "Fuck you, Omar. You'd think someone would be happy there are less evil shits infecting the world with *their* sickness."

Omar sat back. Kane glanced to the side and realized Morticia had hovered into range for the last part. Omar looked at her also.

"Something wrong?" Morticia asked Strong.

"I'm sitting with Kane," Strong said.

"Ah!" Morticia moved off.

"You got a point," Omar said. "I don't agree with it, but you have a point. Do you have any proof of this? Something tangible?"

"No. And the FBI is a dead end." Kane checked his watch. "If this is for real, we've got twenty-nine hours. I have more information than anyone. If I can't track these guys down by tomorrow morning, you can send up a flare and I'll give you a target."

"We lose a day," Strong said.

"Of what?" Kane replied. "You've got nothing solid to report. Just some guy said something. And once we open this can of worms it goes to the Nabisco Factory, the FBI and Damon and a bunch of other shit that will muddy the waters so much NYPD could have a month and get nowhere and some good people will get hurt. It's taken you this long to get close to Son of Sam."

Strong's face tightened at the last comment. But then he nodded. "Yeah. You're right. They won't let me make this collar; they're not going to believe me with this. I'm not sure I believe you. As usual, you're keeping things from me."

"Best for everyone," Kane said. He looked past Strong as the Kid entered, *NY Times* in hand.

"Beautiful morning," the Kid said, sliding the paper in front of Kane, as he nodded at Strong. "Morning, officer."

"It was," Strong muttered.

"Hey," Kane said to the Kid. "You ever hear of a group called the Gentleman's Club?"

The Kid glanced at Strong, which was an affirmative and a question.

"You can talk," Kane said. "He's dependable. Right, Omar."

"Like a Rolex," Omar said.

Kane scooted over so the Kid could sit on his side.

"Rich guys," the Kid said. "Sometimes they hire people for parties."

"What kind of parties?" Kane asked.

"Wild and crazy," the Kid said. "I've never been to one, but the money is good. But scary. They're a bunch of mostly old men, but hey, nothing new there."

Strong was following the conversation.

"Where are these parties held?" Kane asked.

"Lofts or empty office space that hasn't been rented. They move around. No one knows beforehand and never in the same place. The people they hire get picked up by limos." The Kid frowned, glanced at Strong, then continued. "They especially want boys. The younger the better."

"Pieces of shit," Omar muttered.

"Thanks," Kane said. "You're smart to stay away from them."

"Makes one smart person at this table," Strong groused.

Kane peeled off a twenty and passed it to the Kid.

"Thanks. May the force be with you," but the Kid said it without the usual energy and left.

"Do I want to know what that was about?" Strong asked.

"You've never heard of the Gentleman Bankers?"

Strong shook his head.

"Rich homosexuals," Kane said. "Seems there's a lot of them. Very powerful."

"I picked up the homosexual part." Strong was lost. "And how does that have something to do with the IRA?"

Kane nodded. "That's why I've got to stop this. Too many moving parts for anyone else to get up to speed in time."

"He's living a dangerous life," Strong said, losing Kane for a moment. "Your newspaper boy."

"I've offered him a job here," Kane said.

"Magnanimous of you."

"Screw you."

"And if you fail to kill the fruit of this tree?" Strong asked. "What then?"

"Then it's NYPD's problem. You don't hear from me by tomorrow daylight, you'll know we failed. Everything we've learned will be in my apartment."

"Jesus," Strong muttered. He reached into his pocket and retrieved his card. "I'll be waiting for your call." Strong slid out of the booth. "I don't understand you, Kane." He paused and leaned close. "Be careful, all right?"

Strong wasn't out the door before Morticia zoomed by. "How come he never leaves happy after talking to you?"

"I'm the harsh rocks of reality," Kane said.

"Hey, your friend, Truvey?"

"Yeah?"

"She's okay," Morticia said. "We talked a bit. Did you ask your lawyer friend, Toni, about gigs for her?"

"I did," Kane said. "Do you want me to ask for you?"

Morticia froze. "What do you mean?"

"Thao said you're an actress. A singer."

Morticia folded her arms. "He did? You two talked about me?"

"We had some time on our hands," Kane said.

Morticia sat down across from Kane and her façade faded. "You don't talk much," she said. "At least not to me. And the other people that come in, half the time you're holding a gun. You kinda scare me."

Kane was surprised. "I scare you?"

"I can't believe Truvey thought we were an item. *And* you're my boss."

"Thao runs the place," Kane said.

"What else did he tell you about me?"

"That's about it. Oh. And that you live with a woman. Your friend whom Toni helped."

"Does that bother you?"

"Why would who you live with bother me?" Kane was having a hard time keeping his focus on the twists and turn of this conversation.

"It bothers most guys who find out," Morticia said.

"Right," Kane said.

Morticia hurried out of the booth and to her feet. "I'm sorry. I'm bothering you."

Kane gave an exasperated sigh. "You're not bothering me. I just asked if you want me to talk to Toni about your acting thing. Whatever. Not a big deal."

"It's not a thing. It's my life."

The way Morticia said it gathered Kane's focus. "What?"

"Singing. The acting is part of it on Broadway. And my son. That's all I've got."

"You have a son?"

"Remember?" Morticia said. "Woodstock? Second best moment of my life? My son being born was the best."

"He lives with you?" Kane was lost.

"No. He's with my father. This is my shot. My dream. My dad and I agreed and he's helping me as much as he can. My son is with him. I have two years to make it. If I don't live my dream, what kind of life can I show my son?"

Kane sat back, the new vinyl crinkling. "Okay."

A sparkle of anger in her eyes. "'Okay'?"

Kane put his hands up. "I got a lot going on. I'm sorry. I'll talk to Toni. I'll tell her to stop by here one morning. You see her, I'll have told her what it's about. Does that help?"

The anger was gone as quickly as it had come. "I'm sorry. I didn't mean to snap. It's just hard. Yeah. That helps. I wouldn't have brought it up, except I have to try everything I can. Go do what you have to do. Between the CIA, the FBI, the evil shits, and Omar, I have a feeling you've got something more important than my career going on." She left the booth and headed to the serving counter to swoop up plates.

Kane pulled out his notepad and made an entry to remind him of the conversation because he had a feeling a lot might happen before he made it to Toni's. He went to the payphone, dropping a dime. He checked his notepad and dialed Toni's new office.

Mrs. Ruiz answered promptly on the second ring. "Marcelle and Associates."

"Good morning, Mrs. Ruiz. It's Will Kane. Who are the associates?"

A chilly silence met his weak attempt at humor.

"Could you inform Toni that I'll meet her this afternoon at let's say three, same place, instead of ten this morning?"

"I will inform Ms. Marcelle." Two seconds ticked off. "Is that all?"

"Yes and—" the line went dead.

Kane replaced the receiver and went into the kitchen.

"Good morning, Dai Yu," Thao said.

"Morning."

"Do you wish for me to come with you to this boat?" Thao asked. "We can close early."

"No, I've got it."

"That Yazzie is very dangerous," Thao said.

"He said the same about you."

"If true, that would be a good reason for me to accompany you."

"I don't expect the meeting to be adversarial," Kane said.

"You told me you killed one of his men," Thao pointed out.

"Yazzie seems mission focused," Kane replied, but Thao did have a point.

"And when the mission is over?" Thao asked. "What will his focus be?"

"I'll deal with whatever happens then." He hesitated, then committed. "I might need your help tonight."

"Do you know what is planned?"

"I know the target," Kane said. "I've got to figure out where they're launching from, although I've got a good idea."

"And you will not be involving Sergeant Merrick?"

"I will not. That's why I need your help."

"I will be ready."

"I'll stop by here later today and we'll make a plan."

Thao slid an omelet onto a plate and added it to a couple on the serving wall. "You do not have one already?"

"Remember what Merrick used to say," Kane reminded Thao. "When you're up to your ass in alligators it's hard to remember you were in there to drain the swamp."

"Sergeant Merrick also believes *The Magnificent Seven* is a good template for mission planning," Thao said.

MARINA, BATTERY PARK, MANHATTAN

The water was calm and it was a smog-hazy sunny day. Under other circumstances this might be a leisurely cruise through garbage infested and polluted Upper New York Bay, as the boat cast off and headed south toward the Verrazano Narrows. Kane wondered if there was some sort of irony that it was the same one he'd been piloting when this mess began.

The Hard Flint Boys negated the pleasure crew aspect, once more reminding Kane of Captain Kidd and pirates. Yazzie had brought his step brothers. One was at the controls of the boat, two others in the rear cabin, where one was by the sliding door to the dive deck and the other standing behind the blindfolded, naked old man tied to a chair. Where the sixth one was, Kane had no idea.

Judge Charles Edward Clark's chest was sunken, covered with scraggly gray hairs. His arms were narrow and the skin drooped; he'd aged more than a decade since the film, probably a few years in the last couple of hours. There were several cinder blocks and loose rope next to the chair.

Kane took one look at that scenario, turned around and went up to the forward deck.

Yazzie joined him. "What's wrong?"

"Are you crazy? Did you ask him where Marcelle is?"

"Of course," Yazzie said. "He said he didn't know. I'm preparing to ask with more firmness."

"He's a federal judge," Kane said.

"We brought him here unconscious," Yazzie said. "He has no clue who we are."

"He might have a hint since you're asking about Thomas Marcelle," Kane pointed out.

Yazzie shrugged. "Marcelle has a lot of enemies. For all Clark knows, we're the IRA. You seem pretty big on that angle."

"You need to work on your accent then."

"I'm not worried about this guy," Yazzie said.

"Because you have a former federal prosecutor on your team?"

"Because Marcelle is dirty and Clark's connected to him."

Kane couldn't argue with that, although he didn't point out the obvious parallel with Crawford.

Yazzie explained the scenario. "Clark knows we're on a boat. Soon he won't hear any sounds of the city or land. Just the water. That will scare him."

"I get it," Kane said. Ellis and Liberty Islands were to the right while Governors Island was to the port side. Numerous anecdotes bubbled up, but Kane smushed them down. He stared at the statue, imagining what three TOW missiles could do to it. Which reminded him of Caitlyn and for a moment he was off balance.

"Did Clark give you anything?" Kane asked.

"He acknowledged knowing Thomas Marcelle. He did not acknowledge that they had any sort of relationship, but he was lying."

"We know that."

"Yes, but it gave me a baseline to know his tell when he's lying," Yazzie said.

"Somehow I think you did more than crawl through tunnels and speak Navajo in 'Nam," Kane said.

Yazzie ignored that. "He says it's been months since he last spoke with Marcelle and that it was over some legal matter. He was lying about that."

"Based on your baseline?"

Yazzie didn't reply.

Kane nodded to the port side as they plowed through Upper Bay. "Elvis left from there."

"What?" Yazzie was lost.

"Brooklyn Army Terminal," Kane explained. "Built at the end of World War I. During the Second War, over three million troops departed through it. Then later, Elvis for his Germany stint. Just think, for some of those leaving, it was the last time they were on American soil."

"Are you trying to distract me?" Yazzie asked.

"No. I'm just full of useless information and weird things trigger it," Kane said.

Yazzie was, as Kane had told Thao, mission focused.

"When we get to Marcelle," Kane said, "you've got to give me a chance to talk to him. He made contact with the Swords to set me up, so he knows something about them."

"After I get what I'm after," Yazzie said, "you can talk to him. But in the end, Marcelle must pay."

They passed under the bridge. The water spread out as they entered Lower Bay. A container ship went by, going in the opposite direction.

"Let's get the truth from Clark," Yazzie said as the boat angled to the southeast and open ocean.

Kane followed the Navajo to the aft cabin.

Kane waited by the bed as Yazzie went to the judge.

"Thomas Marcelle," Yazzie said. "Tell us where he is."

"You've assaulted a federal judge," Clark threatened. But he'd obviously had some time to think, because he was past the denial and anger stages of interrogation and into bargaining. "If you let me go now, I'll forget all about it. I don't know who you people are and we leave it like that. Nobody got hurt."

"Why do you think someone's going to get hurt?" Yazzie asked.

"I don't know what Marcelle was into—" Clark began but Yazzie interrupted.

"Wasn't he into you? Or were you into him? I never quite understood how that worked. Nor do I care to."

Clark blustered as much as a naked man tied to a chair could: "I have no idea what you're talking about."

Kane spoke. "We've got film of the two of you together."

Clark's head swung toward him. "Who are you?"

"I'm the only friend you have on this boat," Kane said. "You and Marcelle were lovers. Still might be. I saw the film."

"What are you talking about?" Clark tried to maintain his crumbling bluster. "What film?"

"Sean Damon's film," Kane said. "The one he used against Marcelle for the sweetheart deal in 1967. You knew about it. Marcelle flipped partly to protect you."

"Who are you people?" Clark's voice cracked.

"Do you want us to release the film?" Kane asked.

"You said you were the only friend I have on this boat," Clark said. "You're not sounding like it."

Kane pressed. "I've got a contact at the *Post*. They'd love to get their hands on the film. Probably put a still from it on the front page."

"I don't know where Marcelle is. I swear."

Yazzie jumped in. "Have you talked to him in the past week?"

Clark's shoulder's slumped. He nodded. "He called me Friday morning. He was scared. He said people were after him. I've never known him to be scared. Even with Damon, he wasn't scared. He was practical."

Yazzie had walked behind Clark. He leaned over and spoke close to his ear. "I'm the one after Marcelle. He has every reason to be scared. So do you. You've got two choices. Tell us where he is or we tie your chair to cinderblocks and send you to the bottom. We're far enough out at sea now."

"I don't *know* where Marcelle is. I swear!" There was dampness in the blindfold as Clark sniffled. He was past bargaining and into the depressing reality of his situation.

"Who would?" Yazzie asked.

"I don't know."

"You're lying," Yazzie said.

"He called you," Kane pointed out. "You couldn't help him, but who could?"

Clark was shaking his head. "I don't know."

"You're lying," Yazzie repeated.

"The Gentleman Bankers?" Kane asked.

Clark's head snapped in his direction.

"What? Who?" But the old man was rattled.

"The Gentleman Bankers," Kane said. "Are they hiding him?"

"Let's toss him overboard," Yazzie said grabbing one arm of the chair and his brother took the other. They lifted it up.

"Wait! Wait!"

Yazzie and his brother put the chair down.

"Yes," Clark said. "Yes. They're hiding him. He's one of us. We have to protect our own. And if I disappear, they'll search for me. They will find you. They're powerful. They'll crush you."

"Not likely," Yazzie said. "And even if they manage, won't do you much good will it?"

"Would they trade?" Kane asked.

"'Trade'?" Clark said.

"Marcelle's radioactive," Kane said. "He's always been linked to Damon and now things are coming out about that relationship that Marcelle can't come back from. Really bad things. Rapes. Murders. I've got those films. Marcelle is done. You're not. We'll be taking a liability off their hands and giving back an asset. Would the Gentleman Bankers trade you for him?"

Clark was silent, on the edge of depression and acceptance. Kane looked over him at Yazzie who gave a grudging nod of approval at the offer.

Kane took a step closer to the judge and lowered his voice. "You're weighing your emotions against your intellect." Kane kept dropping the volume of his voice as he spoke. "Your feelings for Marcelle. I knew his son, Ted."

Clark's head shifted, trying to hear. Kane's voice descended to a harsh whisper only Clark could hear. It took only a few seconds for Kane to impart what needed to be said. When he was done, he straightened.

Clark was shaking his head. "No. He wouldn't have. Not Tom. Not to his son."

"Think about the Gentleman Banker parties," Kane said. "The ones that are never held in the same place."

"I don't go to those," Clark snapped.

Kane glanced at Yazzie who gave him a quizzical look but nodded at the truth of that statement.

"But Marcelle does, doesn't he?" Kane put more pressure on the lever. "You loved him, still love him probably, don't you? But he doesn't return it. He can't. That's who he is. That's who his son, Ted, knew he was."

"No." But Clark's voice indicated the break.

"Will they trade Marcelle for you?" Kane asked.

"Maybe." Clark settled on acceptance. He firmed up, diving for the opening. "Yes."

"Is Roy Cohn a member?"

"Cohn? What's he have to do with this?"

"Nothing," Kane said. "But is he a member? So I can contact the Bankers through him."

"Yes."

"All right," Kane said.

"Tom didn't do anything wrong," Clark said, more to himself.

Yazzie and Kane exchanged a glance. Kane nodded toward the hatch. They went to the forward deck. Yazzie signaled to his man in the cockpit to turn the boat around.

"Not bad," Yazzie said. "You had some cards up your sleeve."

"Don't we both?"

LENOX HILL, MANHATTAN

"As I said on the phone," Kane said to Roy Cohn. "Judge Clark for Thomas Marcelle."

"I checked into you," Cohn said. "I know about your family. Your father. Your mother. Their little house in the Bronx. His pension with the Sanitation Department. How'd he like to lose that?"

"If you really checked," Kane said with forced patience, "you know I'm not close to my family."

"Everyone is close to their family," Cohn said, "even when they say they aren't."

"I'm here to make a deal," Kane said. "Not listen to threats."

"I don't like you," Cohn said.

"I'll take that as a compliment."

Kohn was in the same bathrobe. The bedroom/office smelled worse than Kane remembered; stale and sickly. A plate with leftovers of something was on the edge of the desk, a fly buzzing lazily around it. A window air conditioner was running somewhere in the background but making little headway.

"I got an idea who you're fronting for," Cohn said. "Somebody with DC connections. I can tell when I'm getting the blind. I haven't gotten a call about the money yet for the convention center."

"This is a different matter," Kane said. "A bit more urgent. Who has the authority to trade Marcelle for Clark?"

"'Who has the authority'?" Cohn laughed. "You're looking at him. Throw in a transaction fee. Let's see ten grand cash when you bring Clark."

"Sure," Kane said.

"You're not a very good negotiator," Cohn pointed out.

"I've been told that."

HUNTS POINT, BRONX

"You could have given him his clothes back," Kane said to Yazzie as a naked Judge Clark shuffled over the cobblestones to a white van, passing two men who were practically carrying a squirming, blindfolded and gagged, Thomas Marcelle between them.

He wasn't naked.

"I don't like these people," Yazzie said.

"Judges? Lawyers?"

Yazzie ignored him.

Marcelle was tossed in the back of the car where two Flint Boys secured him. Yazzie drove off without a glance behind. He drove through the wasteland of the South Bronx, negotiating abandoned and torched cars. Most of the apartment buildings on either side were burnt out husks.

Cohn had set up the swap with ruthless efficiency after Kane passed across the money supplied from Yazzie's leather satchel. Cohn had given the time and location in the Bronx to make the exchange.

Kane didn't say anything as they rode through a section of the city the rest of the country viewed as the epitome of the blight that was New York City. Kane had different memories of these streets from twenty years ago. His parents had lived here before migrating to slightly greener pastures of the north Bronx.

They passed underneath the Bruckner Expressway and entered Hunts Point. Hookers prowled in the afternoon shadows along with drug dealers and wanna-be gangsters mingled with real ones. Yazzie didn't continue to the Point where Fulton Fish Market bustled with business despite the decay. He turned into the large wastewater treatment plant.

Through it, past a couple of completely disinterested sewage workers, to an abandoned warehouse.

The sound of the wastewater plant next door was a throb of engines and pumps running, loud enough to drown out anything short of automatic weapons fire. The last of Yazzie's brothers was waiting for them and slid shut the large door they'd come through, leaving a bleak twilight of a few naked bulbs hanging on wires from the rafters.

Kane looked about, checking to see if there were any signs that this was Yazzie's patrol base, but the interior held only broken crates and scattered debris; no sign of long-term occupation. All five of the Flint Boys were here, in addition to Yazzie.

One of Yazzie's men dragged Thomas Marcelle out of the car and tumbled him to the dirty floor. The blindfold was ripped off and gag removed, but Marcelle didn't get to his feet. He lay on his back, blinking, disoriented.

He no longer looked like the man who ruled the top floor of the Broadway-Chambers Building, overlooking City Hall. His suit jacket was missing, his shirt was dirty and his shoes scuffed. He slowly sat up, looking around. His eyes locked onto Kane.

"William." Marcelle tried to smile as he got to his feet. "Good to see you, William." He took a shuffling step toward Kane, but Yazzie stepped between.

"I'm from Boss Crawford."

Marcelle reversed that step. "It's business, just business."

"Where are the deeds?" Yazzie asked.

Marcelle shifted gears and faced the Navajo. "You're going to kill me right after I tell you that. I've heard about his boys. Did he adopt all of you? What is it? Ten little Indians?"

"All I care about are the deeds," Yazzie said.

"You're not a good liar," Marcelle said. "I've worked with people who believed their own lies, they were so good. You're not good at all. I've got no incentive to give up those deeds."

Yazzie shook his head. "You misunderstand the situation. This is not a negotiation. This is you determining how much suffering you wish to undergo before you inevitably tell us what we will know."

One of the Navajo behind Marcelle drew a Bowie knife. Marcelle looked over his shoulder. "No need for that."

"You've got nothing to gain by not giving me the deeds," Yazzie continued, "and much to lose."

"We can make a deal," Marcelle said. "I've got information on people that's worth a lot of money. Powerful people."

Kane spoke. "The Irish. Do you know where they're hiding?"

"'Irish'?" Marcelle badly feigned ignorance.

"The ones you paid to kill me and Crawford and an actress whose name you probably don't even know."

"It was just business," Marcelle repeated. He screamed as the man with the Bowie knife slashed, the tip slicing through the dirty shirt sleeve and leaving a thin red line. He stumbled into Yazzie who shoved him away. The other Flint Boy drew a knife, a Marine Ka-bar, the edge of the blade honed to a silver razor's edge against the black of the shaft. He flanked Marcelle opposite Bowie.

"The deeds," Yazzie said.

Marcelle's eyes were darting back and forth, trying to track both knife men. "We've got to work out a deal for my safety. Then I'll tell you where they are."

"This is not a negotiation," Yazzie repeated.

"I'll help you," Kane said to Marcelle.

Yazzie turned toward him, face expressionless. Then he gave a succinct nod.

Kane stepped up to his best friend's father. "You scared Ted. He told me that in Beast. The first time I met you that summer, when you came to visit with your wife and Toni, you scared me. You were larger than life. Were."

A muscle in Marcelle's jaw twitched.

"You've done too much business with the wrong people," Kane said. "It's over. Where are the Irish? Where did you meet them?"

"I never met them," Marcelle said. "They called me."

"That's how you arranged to kill me? Over the phone?" Kane shook his head. "I don't believe you. You're not that stupid."

The anger was overwhelming the situation for Marcelle. "Walsh called and gave me a number. I went to a pay phone at a certain time and they called. No, I'm not that stupid, William."

"After you told them you wanted Crawford and me dead, did they tell you they wanted both of us on a boat?" Kane asked. "Was it their idea?"

"Yes."

"Did they tell you where they wanted the boat to go?"

"Yes."

"What else?"

"That's it," Marcelle said. "I passed it on to Selkis. Talk to him if you want to know anything else."

"He's dead," Kane said. "Things are spinning out of control. You know the Irish are going to do something tomorrow night, right?"

"I have no clue what they're doing here," Marcelle said. "They were looking for Damon and when they couldn't find him, they came to me. It wasn't like I could say no to them. Especially with Damon gone."

"You gave them money and in exchange they agreed to kill me and Crawford."

Marcelle had no response to that.

"They bought missiles with the money you gave them," Kane said. "They're going to blow something up. Do you care about that?"

Marcelle barked an abrupt laugh, fueled by his desperate rage. "Why should I care? Looks like I won't be around to see it, will I, William? Feel like a real man, right now? Ted was ten times the man you'll never be. You should have died on that hill."

"There are times I think I did," Kane said, but the words were wasted on the resurgent Thomas Marcelle.

"The deeds," Yazzie repeated.

"I'll give you the deeds," Marcelle said. "But this *is* a negotiation because you need them and you can keep cutting me and I'll never tell you. You don't think I was prepared for this?"

"I'm sure you were," Yazzie said. "And that's why we're going to extract every bit of preparation from you. I tried easy, now we go hard."

The two knife men had sheathed their weapons while Yazzie spoke. They grabbed Marcelle before he could react, handcuffing his hands behind his back. One ratcheted down a chain hanging from a pully, hooking it to the links between the two cuffs.

The chain was pulled and Marcelle was lifted off the ground as his arms rotated back unnaturally.

Kane gave him credit that he didn't scream as all his weight came to bear on his torqued shoulders via the arms. The toes of his shoes were just an inch from the floor as he hung angled forward. Marcelle was breathing hard, sweat on his brow as he slowly rotated in the air. A grimace of pain was etched on his face.

"How are you enjoying negotiating?" Yazzie asked.

"Fuck you," Marcelle managed.

"Cliché," Yazzie said.

"They may have given me up to you," Marcelle said, a gasp for breath between every few words, "but my friends will remember. They'll come for you. You don't fuck with the Gentleman Bankers."

"Your definition of friend and mine are different," Yazzie said. "And, if I was you, I'd leave fucking out of it when referring to those degenerates."

Marcelle tried to keep Yazzie in his gaze as he slowly turned. "I've got dirt on your Boss Crawford. I disappear, it comes out."

"You don't have anything," Yazzie said.

A bead of sweat slid from Marcelle's forehead to his chin, then dripped to the dirty concrete floor. "You don't know him." He looked at Yazzie and then the other Navajo. "None of you know him. *Boss* Crawford? You've all been played."

"The deeds," Yazzie said.

"Come here, William," Marcelle said. "Let me tell you something. Privately."

Kane glanced at Yazzie, who indicated his approval. Kane stepped up to Marcelle, staring into his beady eyes, less than six inches away. He put a finger on Marcelle shoulder to stop the slow spin.

Marcelle's voice was harsh and low. "He's going to kill me. I know it. You think you're the good guy in the white hat?" He nodded toward Yazzie. "You're on his side? You think him or Crawford are better than Damon?" He didn't give Kane a chance to answer. "Ted's footlocker. Get Crawford." He raised his voice to play to the audience. "Fuck you, William Kane. May you burn in hell." He lifted his head and spit into Kane's face.

Kane whispered his own secret back to Marcelle: "Toni was pregnant when Damon's goons raped her. She lost the baby." He stepped back.

Marcelle's eyes were wide in shock. "What? What did you say?"

"You heard me," Kane said.

"What was that about?" Yazzie asked.

"What?" Marcelle. "What?"

"It was personal," Kane said to Yazzie. "We have a history."

"Kane!" Marcelle screamed. "Kane!"

Kane walked to the door to the warehouse. As he exited, he heard Thomas Marcelle still shouting his name, then it was cut off by an inarticulate scream. He knew it wouldn't be the last.

TOWER ONE, WORLD TRADE CENTER, MANHATTAN

Toni was in the same seat at the bar in Windows on the World, similar drink in front of her. "You're late."

"I was busy," Kane said.

"Anything?" she asked as Kane sat down.

"The CIA, FBI and NYPD all seem disinterested in the potential threat," Kane said. "Actually, the latter is a little interested but they're close to Son of Sam so."

"Father," she said.

"I met Yazzie," Kane said. He was staring out the window.

"And?"

"He's negotiating with your father," Kane said.

"He found him?"

"Yazzie traded Judge Clark for your father."

Toni was trying to follow, so Kane briefly recapped Gentleman Bankers, Roy Cohn and the swap, stopping before events in the warehouse. It took less than a minute. Toni didn't appear happy about any aspect of it, nor was there any reason for her to be.

Kane was impressed when the bartender brought him a cup of coffee and a glass of water with two ice cubes in it. "You ever need a job," Kane told him, "there's a diner in the Village where one is waiting for you. Corner of Washington and Gansevoort. It's a classy joint. Interesting clientele."

"Thank you, sir," the bartender politely said before moving off.

"Where is father?" Toni asked, indicating the seriousness of the situation by forgoing a smart-ass observation on the job offer.

"I told you," Kane said. "He's trying to make a deal with Yazzie over the deeds."

"Did he give you anything on the Irish?"

"No. He doesn't know much about them. He just paid them to kill me." He gave a bitter laugh. "The ironic thing is this has nothing to do with the guns or the money that burned up with Damon."

Toni pursed her lips, but didn't say anything.

Kane turned from her and looked out the windows at the Statue of Liberty. The smog muted the view, but it was still spectacular. New Jersey, beyond, not so much as smoke stacks belched, contributing to the pollution. He spotted the latest construction amongst the swamps of East Rutherford, beyond the oil facilities. "I wonder why they still call themselves the New York Giants when they're playing over there in the Meadowlands."

"Don't fuck around with me," Toni said.

"I'm not." Kane turned back to her. "Toni, this is much deeper than your father. Much worse. I'm telling you up front that I'm not informing you of things that have happened in order to protect you but blood has been spilled. And more will be."

"No shit." She drained her drink and thumped the glass back down on the bar hard. The bartender swooped in with a fresh one as smoothly as he'd brought Kane's. "He gets me at least," Toni muttered. She began tapping a fingernail on the polished wood.

A refrain was chanting in Kane's mind: don't ask. "Hey, have you done anything for Truvey?"

"You're not good at changing the subject. I made some calls."

"You know Morticia from the diner?"

"How could I not? Hard to miss."

"She's also a singer and actress," Kane said. "She could use some help too. Stop by the diner sometime and talk with her, please?"

"Every waitress in Manhattan is an aspiring actress," Toni said, but listlessly, her mind on family. "Sure. Truvey and Morticia. Anything else."

Kane changed the subject. "Can you get on the roof of this building?"

"No," Toni said. "The observation deck is in the South Tower. The antenna mast is on top of this building. Why?"

Kane waved off the question. "Just thinking."

She didn't ask the direct question. "What are you going to do?"

"This is a tangled knot and I'm sitting in the middle of it."

"How are you going to untangle it?"

"Only thing I can do," Kane said. "Cut it." He paused, then said: "I'm sorry, Toni."

"Will you see my father again?"

"No."

"Will I?" But there was no indication she expected him to answer, nor did Kane volunteer one.

"Ted's footlocker," Kane said.

"Yes?"

"It's your father's emergency rally point. Yazzie is going to be coming to you for the deeds that are in it."

Toni was about to respond when the bartender approached, holding up the phone. He plugged the jack in and placed it in front of Toni.

"Yes?" she listened for a second, then hung up. "Yazzie's already here."

"Shit," Kane said. "There's other stuff in that footlocker. Dirt on Crawford that we might need. Probably stuff on a lot of other people."

"What do you mean 'we'?" Toni stood. "Come on."

Kane followed. As they got on the elevator he began to speak. "I'll distract Yazzie and you go in your office and get whatever's in there out. It's in--"

"Hush," Toni said.

Mrs. Ruiz wasn't smiling, nor was Yazzie.

Toni flicked a hand, indicating for Yazzie to follow into her office, negating Kane's aborted plan. The three trooped in, Kane closing the door.

Yazzie pointed at the footlocker. "Open it."

Kane inched his hand toward the .45. "Be polite."

Yazzie looked at him. "Did you tell her about her father?"

"I told her you were negotiating with him last I saw," Kane said.

"The deeds are in there," Yazzie said to Toni. "Give them to me and we're done."

"Are we?" Kane asked.

Yazzie ignored him.

"I've looked in it," Toni said. "It's just my brother's medals and some letters. His full-dress coat and hat."

"Tar-bucket," Kane automatically corrected her about the hat.

"There's nothing else—" Toni was cut off by Yazzie.

"Open it."

"You didn't say please," Kane said. "I told you to be polite."

"My brothers are waiting in the sky lobby," Yazzie said. "We can do this easy or we can do this hard. They'll be up here in ten minutes if I don't meet them with the deeds."

"Ah!" Kane said. "You're doing *Magnificent Seven*."

"Stop it, both of you," Toni snapped. She knelt in front of the locker and spun the combination on the old lock. It clicked and she removed it. She stepped away.

Yazzie flipped up both latches and pulled open the lid. He removed the top tray holding Ted's medals and letters, putting it to the side. He stared at the gray full-dress coat and its row of brass buttons for a moment, then gently removed it, along with the tar bucket.

It only took him a few moments to find what tactical officers at West Point had overlooked for four years, but he had the advantage of knowing it was there. He pried up the false bottom.

Yazzie straightened and faced them, a legal-size manila envelope in his hands. He looked inside of it. "They were here all along."

"Is your ten minutes up?" Kane asked. "We don't want your fellow warriors charging through the door with tomahawks. By the way, are you going to hang around and help me with the Irish situation?"

"That's your problem," Yazzie said. "They were after you, not Boss Crawford. It was Mister Marcelle who included him in the issue and that has been dealt with."

"Where is my father?" Toni said.

Yazzie walked toward the door, but paused by Kane. "I lied earlier when I said there wouldn't be repercussions for Johnson's death. I lied in order to achieve my goal. That is now achieved." He faced Kane and stared into his eyes. "Blood for blood. It is the way of my people."

"Can it wait a day or two?" Kane said. "I'm kind of busy."

"There's no time limit on blood vengeance," Yazzie said.

Kane moved forward, close enough that he could feel the warmth coming off the Navajo's skin in the air-conditioned office. "What happened to it having been a fair fight?"

"The vengeance will also be fair."

Kane stared into Yazzie's dark eyes. "Then I guess we'll eventually be taking a walk on the wild side."

Yazzie left without another word; the door swinging shut behind him.

Kane went to the footlocker and looked in. There was nothing else there. "Your father said he had quite a bit in here. Something on Crawford. He wasn't referring to the deeds. This was his cache. There had to be more than--"

He paused as Toni raised a hand. "I thought it was strange that my father shipped me Ted's footlocker. He's pissed at me, he won't talk to me, but he sends Ted's footlocker over?" Toni went to the wet bar, pouring a drink. She drained the glass, then refilled it. "Honestly, I didn't think to look until you mentioned my dad having his cache and, like I told you, I couldn't think of anyone he'd trust with it. Except Ted."

"He didn't trust you with it," Kane said. "He set you up with it."

"He did both," Toni said. "That was who he was. Always playing both sides. I knew Yazzie would get to him. Force him to give up the deeds. I removed everything else."

Kane noted she was using the past tense. "Have you looked at what you took out?"

"It's mostly on microfiche," Toni said. "I haven't had time to check it. What did Yazzie mean about blood?"

"Not important right now."

"But it's going to be," Toni said. "The bill always comes due. Father's certainly did." She took a drink, then pointed with the hand holding the glass at the footlocker. "Father put his stench on everything in our life. Even Ted's memory. He sent that to me knowing it was a ticking time bomb." She went to her desk and sat down. "Don't you have something to do?"

"Yeah," Kane said. "I gotta go."

*****

Kane took the express elevator to the 107th Floor of the South Tower. He ignored the indoor observation deck and followed the escalators to the roof. He exited facing east and the tall antenna of the North Tower was to his left front. The observation deck was set back from the edge of the building, with a suicide prevention rim below it, ringed with razor wire to prevent someone from climbing onto it and throwing themselves into the void.

The wind was gusting out of the south and the large American flag was snapping. The deck was crowded with tourists, who were more intent on snapping pictures than enjoying the view.

Kane earned a curse in German for walking between a picture taker and his subject, but ignored it as he made his way around, corralled by the white, waist-high fencing.

The ultimate in fields of fire.

As he walked south along the east side of the deck, the Williamsburg, Manhattan and Brooklyn Bridges straddled the East River from Manhattan to Brooklyn. Long Island stretched off into the hazy distance.

He reached the south edge. Governors Island dominated Upper Bay to the left. Ellis and Liberty Islands were smaller, with the Statue a toy figure from this height and distance.

He instinctively knew the Statue of Liberty was more than three kilometers away. Not by much, but he'd spent enough time on ranges and sighting in artillery fire that he had no doubt. Two miles at least, which was a couple hundred meters out of range. He'd estimated the same on the boat as they sailed out to sea with Judge Clark earlier in the day. The Tower seemed an obvious firing platform, but it was a distance from the water and would require getting the TOWs inside and up here; complications on top of complications. And out of range.

Kane commandeered one of the binoculars set on a fixed pedestal. He zoomed in on the Statue. Then he looked at Ellis Island, reminded of what Caitlyn has said: *They'll be close.*

"*'Lions and tigers and bears, oh my',*" he whispered.

Tuesday Evening,
9 August 1977

MEATPACKING DISTRICT, MANHATTAN

"The Statue of Liberty," Kane told Thao.

The diner was empty, the floor mopped, the tables clean. Kane had a map of New York City spread out on the counter, empty coffee cups holding it down.

"That would be terrible." Thao was appalled, a rare display of emotion and an indication how accurately Kevin Flanagan had chosen his target.

"It would be," Kane agreed.

"Where will they fire from?" Thao was looking at the map. "The Trade Center?"

"Out of range."

"New Jersey shoreline?"

Kane tapped a spot on the map. "They're on Ellis Island."

"How do you know, Dai Yu?"

"It's the smart place. It's where I'd be. And I saw their boat."

Thao raised an eyebrow. "You went to Ellis Island?"

Kane shook his head. "From the top of the South Tower. Their zodiac is pulled up on the island. It's covered by a tarp and in the middle of some bushes, but I know what it is."

"You are certain?"

"Yes. The island looks deserted," Kane said. "I called Pope and asked him to grab as much intel as he can. We're meeting him at my place."

Thao checked the legend of the map. "Around one thousand meters from Ellis Island to the Statue."

"Definitely in range," Merrick said. "If they aim for the torch or head. Three shots. They could make a mark. Perhaps take either one off." He paused.

"You're sure they're on the island?" Thao asked.

"We'll find out when we go there."

"But we are not doing *The Magnificent Seven*, correct?"

"More like *The Guns of Navarone*. Let's go to my place and plan."

GREENWICH VILLAGE, MANHATTAN

"People have it wrong," Pope said. "They think the first spot immigrants set foot in America was on Ellis Island, but the trans-Atlantic ships initially docked in Manhattan because the mooring at Ellis Island wasn't large enough for ocean-going vessels. The immigrants were then transferred to a ferry to be processed on Ellis Island. Most of them, that is. A handful who had the money to pay off the customs agents or the right connections already in the States, got released directly into Manhattan."

Kane and Thao sat across from Pope who had maps and documents spread out on the kitchen table. The old man had reached out to his friends, reporters and otherwise, and several messengers had delivered material for him to peruse and share.

"No one quite knows who has jurisdiction of the island," Pope said, "since the Feds shut it down. The governor of New Jersey actually commandeered a Coast Guard cutter in 1956 and sailed over there and claimed it for his state."

"Fucking New Jersey," Kane muttered.

"It's becoming an issue," Pope said, ignoring the commentary, "because the National Park Service is going to start renovating part of the island to open as a museum." He tapped the map. "The north side, where the Main Building is located. That part is known as Island One and is where the small, original island was. Ellis Island was developed in stages. Island One in the 1890s. Then Island Two, with a hospital in 1899. Island Three, with the contagion ward and some other buildings was filled in and built in 1906. Then the space between Two and

Three was filled in the 1920s, essentially making them all one island."

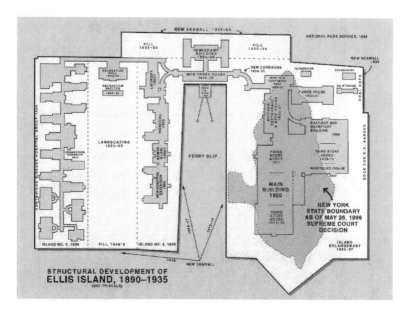

"Is there anyone on the island?" Thao asked.

"Not overnight," Pope said. "The Park Service might go over occasionally during the day. I didn't have time to get more accurate information on the status of the project but it's focused on the main building on Island One."

"The zodiac was here," Kane said, indicating the center of the fill between Two and Three, near the water. "Hidden amongst some bushes and covered. I could see the drag marks from the seawall."

Kane checked the map legend, then took a piece of paper and ticked off a distance. Moved it to Ellis Island then lightly traced a circle with a pencil. "The World Trade Center is in TOW range from all of Ellis Island. They could be firing at multiple targets."

Pope slid an aerial photograph out of a stack. "This is relatively recent. Friend at the *Post* had it for something he was working on and sent it over with the other material."

Ellis Island 1970s

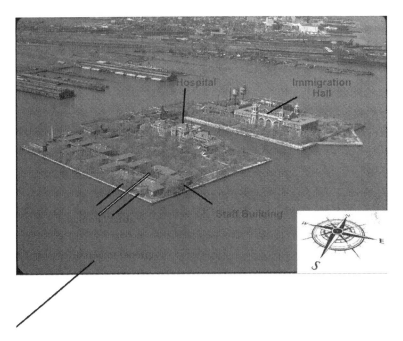

"These two water towers on Island One," Thao said, "would allow them to fire in all directions."

"But the boat is between Two and Three," Kane said. "They'd want to keep an eye on it. It's their only way to escape."

"And if anyone goes out there, they go to Island One," Pope added.

Thao held up his hands. "I agree. They are hiding in a building on Island Two or Three, most likely the latter. I was just considering possibilities. They could move to One after dark to fire."

"They could," Kane agreed. "But that's tomorrow night. We have the advantage of hitting them while they're encamped. But you're right, Thao, to look at the water towers as launch points. The TOW trails a wire when its fired and if that wire gets close to the water, it short circuits. However, firing from a height and angling up to either the Statue or the Towers, I don't think that will be a problem."

"How tall are these buildings?" Thao asked indicating the Contagious Disease Hospital.

"At least two stories," Pope said. "Some are three."

"That will work," Kane said. "Or the roofs." He stared at the map, doing what they'd always done during mission prep: putting himself in the shoes of the enemy. What would he do if he were them? "My source said there are six of them. One is wounded. They'd keep their perimeter tight. Not cover all of Ellis. Pulling shifts, they would have three at most on guard duty tonight. More likely two. If we're lucky, one."

"Hold on, hold on," Pope said, trying to follow. "Six? The two of you are taking on six?"

"At least half of them will be sleeping," Kane said, seeing the glass half full.

"Not if they see you coming," Pope pointed out.

"We'll have to make sure they don't," Kane said. "We've had worse odds."

"Not willingly," Thao pointed out. He didn't dwell on it. "We must factor in what they took from Boston. They will base their plan around their capabilities and available weapons."

"'Boston'?" Pope said. "What happened in Boston?"

"Nothing for you to worry about," Kane said. "Let's back up. Tell us about these buildings along the south shore on Island Three, facing the Statue."

Pope shuffled through the papers. "The contagious disease hospital has seventeen buildings with a connecting enclosed breezeway. They break down as follows: eight measles wards, three isolation wards which could be sealed off from the others, a mortuary, a lab, an admin building, a kitchen, a staff house and one, here in the corner that is a power house, sterilizer and autopsy theater."

Kane's took a piece of paper and tore it into small pieces and labeled pieces:

FIFTY

TOW

BOAT

He placed the last one where he'd seen the boat hidden.

"This is a version of a sand table," Thao informed Pope. "A way to depict the objective and visualize—"

"I get it," Pope said.

Kane was focused on the problem. "This last building in the southeast corner. What is it?"

Pope consulted his notes. "One of the three isolation wards. Patients with serious diseases were placed there. One and a half stories high. Two on the south side of the central corridor, one on the north. Nurses slept in the half story attics. The building on the north side of the central corridor and farthest to the east is the staff building. Two and a half stories and was where the higher-ranking hospital staff lived. Bedrooms on the second floor. Living and dining on the first along with a library."

Kane placed the FIFTY at the east end of the covered walkway that connected all the buildings on Island Three. The TOW on top of the southeastern isolation ward building. He glanced at Thao, waiting.

The Montagnard took his time, looking at the photo and the map. Then he nodded. "The most logical deployment. They can cover the sea approaches with both the heavy machinegun and TOW. The machinegun can also turn west and fire along the main ground avenue of approach. I'd put booby traps in the adjacent buildings and on either flank, north or south for anyone avoiding the central corridor, to channel attackers. The TOW can fire from a window at the Statue. Or even toward the Twin Towers if they move to an east facing window. They can keep their perimeter tight. If they have to retreat, the boat is within easy reach."

"Do you see a different deployment?" Kane asked.

Thao moved the TOW and FIFTY to the Main Hospital Building on the north side of Island Two. "How tall are these buildings?"

"Three and a half stories," Pope answered.

"If they desire to fire at both the Statue and Manhattan, this would be preferable. They could be on the top floor and fire north and south. They could also watch the ferry slip for visitors."

"A possibility," Kane said. "But they're farther from the boat and in a building facing the ferry slip where anyone visiting the island would come. Which brings up the issue of infiltration. Coming across Upper Bay is out." He pointed at the terminals jutting out from the New Jersey shoreline. "What are these?"

"The old Central Railroad docks," Pope said. "They're abandoned. The land to the south of them is just fill that was technically made into a New Jersey state park for the Bicentennial but no work has been done on it. Nothing much there."

Thao spoke his objections before Kane could even make his proposal. "There might be security guards in the terminal. The—"

"No," Pope said. "There used to be, but it's all abandoned."

"Scout swim infil," Kane announced.

"I did not go to this scout swim school you attended," Thao said.

"I know," Kane said. "Don't worry. I'll get you over there."

"I know you will get me there," Thao said. "But I will worry nonetheless. What about exfiltration?"

"Ah, the part headquarters always skimped on," Kane said. "We take their boat."

"How are you going to take their boat?" Pope asked. "You're going over there to make sure they're there?" He had to blink at his alliteration.

"We're going over there to kill them," Kane said.

Tuesday Night, 9 August 1977

LIBERTY STATE PARK, NEW YORK HARBOR

"Nice fucking park, New Jersey," Kane muttered as he and Thao picked their way across the barren landscape that had once been the terminus for a number of rail lines and was technically designated a 'park' by the State of New Jersey. Kane had the High Standard at the ready, while Thao held his crossbow. They both had rucksacks on their backs.

For a park, it wasn't much of one. The terrain was composed of landfill, dumped here by the rail lines. It had been designated so the previous year by the Governor of New Jersey in time for the bicentennial and thousands had lined the waterfront to watch the tall ships sail in and the fireworks. Kane doubted many had come here in the slightly over a year since, which was a small blessing as they were able to get to the waterfront without meeting anyone.

The air was foul with that peculiar odor of northeast New Jersey. A mixture of swamps, industry and pollution. Reaching the shoreline, Kane and Thao looked at Ellis Island. It was pitch black, the same as it had been the night of the boat tour. The Statue of Liberty's torch shone above and to the right, just shy of a kilometer from Ellis. Looking across the water to the left, the Twin Towers were brightly lit, aircraft warning lights strobing on top. To the immediate left on this shore, the terminals of the rail lines stuck out in the water, waiting for ships that no longer docked.

They turned in that direction. A fence surrounded the terminals but the rail lines went through, the gates long gone. Entering the southernmost building reminded Kane of the event that had started him down this, going into the Christopher Street Pier and photographing Alfonso Delgado, Sofia's deceased ex, in a homosexual act. This side of the river, though, saw no such action. The air was musty and still.

"I will not ask how this *Guns of Navarone* ends," Thao said in a low voice as they walked toward the end of the large, empty building. "But what was their mission?"

"A commando team lands on a German island. They have to silence two big guns."

"I see some similarity," Thao allowed. "Did they swim to the island?"

"I think they had a boat, but it sank."

"So they ended up swimming, anyway."

They reached the end. A wide door was open to the water. Ellis Island was three hundred meters away, southeast across dark, uninviting water.

Both of them dropped their rucksacks. Kane removed a poncho from his and spread it out on the ground.

Kane removed boots and socks, pants and t-shirt. Stuffed them, along with the .45 and commando knife from the belt, into a waterproof sack containing the High Standard .22 and Swedish K with folded stock. He added a plastic case containing a set of AN/PVS-5 night vision goggles. There were also a set of walkie-talkies he'd picked up from an electronics store on the way to Pope's from the diner. Kane tied the bag shut and put it in the ruck.

He looked up at the Statue of Liberty to the southeast. "I took 'lil Joe there."

Thao paused in stripping down and waited.

Kane frowned, searching his foggy memory. "I think it was just after Ranger School. He was such a small baby." Kane shook his head. "When I was growing up, the only time my family went to Manhattan was when we had visitors from out of state and we'd show them the sites we never went to and saw on our own." The frown deepened. "I must have brought Taryn and

Joe to my parents' house when I did that. I can't clearly remember." He collected himself and looked at Thao. "I'm gonna be pissed if they hurt the Statue."

"Let us make sure that doesn't happen." Thao finished getting undressed. He put his clothes, crossbow and the .45 from Kane, in his own waterproof sack. "You do, of course, remember that I cannot swim." He had the machete in a sheath attached to his back with a strap around his chest and waist.

"How could I forget?" Kane said. He proceeded to make a poncho 'raft' like he'd been taught at Camp Buckner at West Point and again in Ranger School. He put the bags inside their respective rucksacks and placed them in the center of the poncho. Then they covered it with Thao's poncho. The hoods were already tied off on the inside. They snapped the two ponchos together. Then they rolled them tight and tied off the ends with 550 cord.

Kane checked his watch. 10:24 PM. "Ready?" he asked Thao.

Thao didn't emanate enthusiasm, whether it was because of the water, or the objective, but Kane wasn't bubbling over with it either. They both knew if their target assessment was wrong and the Swords were on Island One, perhaps in one of the water towers, or even on the west side of Island Two or Three, they could be spotted. The sky was overcast, which wasn't unusual, as a good portion of it was smog settling in on a warm August night. The moon was a waxing crescent, barely a shape through the overcast sky.

Thao answered by edging into the water. Kane did the same, recoiling slightly at the chill and the oily sensation. He gently put the poncho raft on the surface and pushed it toward Thao, who grabbed hold of the tail end.

"Hang on," Kane advised. He was on his back, only his head above water. He began a slow kick, making sure his feet didn't hit the poncho raft or break the surface. He swam toward the dark mass of Ellis Island.

He had to turn his head every ten kicks to make sure they were on course. To keep the unoccupied part of his mind off the possibility of fifty caliber bullets spraying both he and Thao, he thought back to his naïve assumption when he applied to the Military Academy instead of the Naval Academy, which had pissed his ex-Marine father off greatly, that his lack of swimming ability would not be a factor in the Army. The fact he'd been issued a bathing suit on R-Day, his first day at the Academy in 1962, should have been a warning.

The roar of Manhattan was a distant echo. Faint car horns, sirens, but the sound of the water lapping on shore was louder.

Slowly they made their way across. Kane glanced over his shoulder to make sure they were on course, taking a swell in the face and swallowing polluted water. He fought to prevent hacking and coughing as he kept finning.

Less than a week into Beast Barracks, the training schedule had called for wearing the issued bathing suit, under sweats, and reporting to the archaic and labyrinthic gymnasium. To a pool. Where a weaselly old man in the black shorts and the monogrammed golf shirt of the Department of Physical Education, screamed: *"If you can't swim, go through that door!"*

Relieved, Kane had taken door number one.

He glanced over his shoulder once more, expecting to see the bright and large muzzle flash of the heavy machinegun from somewhere along the shoreline. Darkness ruled.

Behind door number one had been another pool and another crazed instructor screaming: *"Get in the water!"*

And thus, in order to graduate the Rock Squad, Kane had learned to survival swim.

Amazing how the Academy had so wisely prepared him for the future and this mission.

The dark bulk of Ellis was less than ten meters away and Kane focused. When he reached the rock seawall, he grabbed hold with one hand and pulled the poncho raft, and Thao, up to it. Thao clung to the rocks.

Thao didn't need to be told what to do. They'd been on so many patrols together years ago that the blood lessons of combat were ingrained into them. The Montagnard clambered over the sea wall, drawing the machete. Kane carefully climbed, pulling the poncho raft onto the seawall. He watched Thao's dark shadow disappear into the shadow of the powerhouse, the large building on the northwest side of Island One.

Three minutes later, Thao was back with an all clear. They hustled across the open space carrying the poncho raft into a gaping doorway and put it down on the floor. Silently they unwrapped the poncho and geared up.

Kane peeled back the wet Velcro and checked the time: 11:15.

Since Thao hadn't said anything, it meant that his clearing of the danger area had encountered no sign of the Swords. Kane slung the Swedish K over this back, the suppressed High Standard in hand. Thao had a .45 pistol in a holster on one side, the crossbow at the ready.

Kane allowed Thao to take point. The Montagnard wore rubber soled sandals and slid his feet carefully, head scanning, as they made their way outside the door and along the side of the building toward the Connector. When they reached the end of the attached bakery/carpenter shop building, they performed the crossing a danger area tactic Kane had first learned years ago in Ranger School. He provided overwatch with the K as Thao dashed across the open space to the dark bulk of the old Ferry Building on the Connector. Kane waited as Thao scouted the area. There was a brief flash of red light, Thao signaling with his flashlight. Kane hustled across.

They'd decided on the route during planning, going behind the main part of the Ferry Building, but between it and the western extension of the building. They reached the cross-building connecting the two. Thao found a busted door and went inside, Kane following. There was another door across the way. They were halfway across the Connector.

They moved slowly, allowing Thao the time to check for booby-traps. This was a much different environment than the last time they'd patrolled together in the jungle but the essence was the same. They reached the corner of the Ferry Building where the enclosed breezeway extended to Island Two and the hospital complex. They'd decided to stay out of the walkway if at all possible as it was the most likely place for an ambush or trap.

The walkway angled ahead and that was where they had decided to cut across it to get into the hospital since the field of fire in either direction would be limited. There was no door, but the windows had been broken out long ago. Thao slithered over the transom into the walkway. Then through a broken window to the other side. Kane followed.

The main hospital complex loomed. It was larger than it had appeared in the photograph and maps. Given Ellis Island had processed millions of immigrants he should have expected this. They entered the first of three buildings. Thao found the closest stairwell. Kane pulled the night vision goggles out of his ruck and powered them up. He slipped them over his head and took point from Thao. Everything was enhanced in various shades of green. The drawback was that he was viewing a two-dimensional display which negated depth perception. He slid the K on its sling over his back to rest next to the ruck and drew the High Standard. He led the way up the stairs, finger on the trigger of the pistol.

He reached the third-floor landing. Kane paused, a pain in the center of his chest. It took him a moment to recognize it: he hated hospitals. Nobody went into one because they were having a good day. It was as if the old, peeling walls were reflecting the pain and suffering that had occurred in here, even many decades ago. There was also the presence of death. Not every immigrant had made it off the island.

It was difficult to walk quietly given the amount of debris on the floor. Kane paused every few feet, listening. Thao was almost silent behind him and he was grateful for the Montagnard's presence.

He alternated rooms on either side of the corridor, clearing them one by one. There was no indication anyone had been in here in years. Kane knelt, checking the layer of dust on the floor and it was undisturbed. He moved faster, feeling the pressure of time. They moved on to the next building, then the final one.

The three buildings were empty of intruders. Kane turned off and pulled up the goggles. He checked his watch. 12:41 AM on a new day.

"What do you think?" he whispered to Thao as they halted in the last room in the third building on the third floor, facing south. From the window they could see the trees and brush in the empty landfill separating Island Two from Three.

"Let us observe," Thao said, indicating the dark buildings on the other side of the island. They could only see the row on this side, not the ones facing the water, which would be the likely lair of the Swords. Nevertheless, it was worth taking some time to observe.

Kane forced the ticking clock from his conscious mind. He scanned the buildings they could see with the off-center portion of his retina. After several minutes he put on the goggles and scanned again, alert for any amplified flicker of light. A cigarette would flare up like a searchlight in the goggles.

Nothing.

Kane signaled for Thao to follow. He took the southeast stairwell to the ground floor. The open area between Island Two and Three was overgrown with trees and bushes, which provided excellent concealment. Kane removed the goggles and pointed. "The boat is over there."

Thao took the lead through the vegetation. The sound of water lapping against the seawall grew louder. Thao held up a fist and Kane froze.

Thao pointed. Ten meters away, close to the seawall, a tarp covered the zodiac. The tarp wasn't layered in leaves or dirt, indicating it was newly emplaced. Kane had been worried that the Swords might have left the island to do some other task during the night, perhaps even search for Caitlyn at Kelly's.

Kane indicated the goggles on his head and Thao knelt, waiting. Kane slid them down and powered up. The Staff building was twenty meters away, the broken windows like dark eyes peering at them. Kane checked them, one by one. Darkness ticking away.

A freighter going by in the main channel let off a blast of its horn. High overhead a single plane arced to a late-night landing at one of the airports.

Kane turned the goggles off and lifted them. Waited as his eyes adjusted. Looked at Thao, who tapped the side of his nose.

Kane sniffed.

Cigarette smoke. Very faint, but distinct.

Thao pointed toward the closest building which Kane had been observing through the goggles. Kane nodded. Thao led the way to the north outside wall of the Staff Building.

Kane pulled the goggles down and turned them on. He carefully low crawled over debris toward the corner. His elbows slid over broken glass, denim shirt sleeve tearing, skin scraped. He ignored that, more concerned with not making noise. He reached the corner. Inch by inch he angled his view around the corner.

No sign of the Swords, but he also couldn't see the connecting corridor, since it ended where it branched off to the center of both buildings. Kane signaled for Thao to follow. He resumed the low crawl along the east side of the Staff Building. A bent nail on a board gouged his left knee. The southeast corner of the Staff Building was just a few meters away. His left hand touched something thin; a piece of line, two inches above the ground, extending left as far as he could reach and to a small pile of rubble at the base of the outside of the building. He felt Thao's hand bump into the bottom of his boot.

Kane traced the line into the debris, carefully removing pieces until he uncovered the pipe bomb. The line was attached to a simple fuse on the end of the metal pipe, but there was also a small green light indicating a remote detonator, a twin of the one that had been left on the boat. The Swords weren't relying only on passive measures such as the line, but were ready to remote detonate the homemade mines. Kane assumed the pipe was full of nails and screws, a poor man's Claymore. He glanced left. Given the size, if it went off, it would wipe out anyone coming between the Staff Building and the sea wall.

Kane calmly released the pressure on the line and extracted the fuse, disarming the device. He looked over his shoulder and indicated for Thao to remain in place.

He moved forward and reached the corner. He scooted inch by inch to see around. He spotted a glow, the edge of the halo from the tip of a cigarette. The smoker was standing next to a fifty-caliber machine gun mounted on a tripod. The muzzle of the large gun pointed toward a window in the end of the connecting corridor. But it was positioned far enough out that the fifty could be swung around and aimed toward the water.

The guard was staring down the breezeway. There was a low crackling noise and the man reached down and pulled a radio off his belt. "Three all right." He let go of the transmit. He had an M-16 slung over his shoulder and there was a pistol in a holster.

Exactly as Kane had expected. He couldn't see anyone else. He edged his way back until he was next to Thao. He nodded toward the direction they had come from. Like worms, they twisted around and low-crawled away. Once they were a sufficient distance, Kane whispered his plan to Thao and they prepared to make contact with the enemy.

Wednesday Early Morning, 10 August 1977

ELLIS ISLAND, NEW YORK HARBOR

Kane walked around the corner of the Staff Building, the High Standard held at the ready. The guard at the fifty didn't spot him until he was less than five meters away, which was too late. As he turned toward Kane and opened his mouth to shout a warning, Kane fired, the suppressed pistol making a light pfft sound.

The first bullet was slightly off, hitting the bone above the man's closest eye, but Kane was closing the distance and firing as fast as he could pull the trigger. The second round hit the target, powered through the eyeball and shredded the man's brain. He was nonfunctional before he hit the ground. Death would take a few more moments. Kane took no chances as he arrived, standing over the body and putting two more rounds into the bleeding socket. He shrugged off his backpack, placing it underneath the tripod of the fifty-caliber machinegun. He pulled the radio off the man's belt. He quickly retraced his steps, while pulling one of the walkie-talkies he'd purchased out of his pocket.

Thao was waiting for him at the corner of the building, his crossbow at the ready, scanning the Isolation Ward building on the southwest edge of the island.

"Sergeant Merrick would note one down and five to go," Thao said in a low voice.

"He would," Kane agreed. "Let's see how they respond. We know there are least two more on guard duty and they can't see the fifty."

It took ten minutes before the next radio check. "One all right," an Irish brogue announced.

"Two all right."

Kane and Thao exchanged a glance. Kane had the K in his left hand, the walkie-talkie he'd brought in his right.

"Hey, Jimmy?" The first brogue inquired. "Are you pissing or something? Jimmy?"

The other voice trampled on the end of the transmission. "Jimmy? You okay, lad?"

Kane and Thao watched the building. A flashlight came alive in one of the windows of the Isolation Ward. It flickered out toward the fifty, held by a man who leaned out and yelled. "Jimmy? Wake up, you fuck." The same man transmitted to the other guard: "He's lying down."

The first man radioed back. "Go kick him in the head."

The flashlight disappeared from the window. A few seconds later the man appeared in a doorway. "Jimmy, get yer fat ass up." He shone the light over the body. "Fuck!" He backed up a step and looked about, pulling the M-16 off his shoulder. He fumbled with the rifle and flashlight, then decided to go with the weapon, dropping the light. "Who's out there?"

"Shit," Kane muttered as his plan wasn't unfolding as he wished. He keyed the radio he'd taken from the guard and did his best imitation of a brogue. "Jimmy's hurt. He needs help! Get over here."

The man with the rifle looked down at the radio on his waist in confusion.

"What's going on?" the first unseen guard demanded.

The man with the rifle reached for his radio. Thao terminated that action, and him, with a bolt through the chest. The man dropped the rifle, one hand grasping the shaft sticking out of him as he dropped and the other still reaching for the radio.

"Get down here!" Kane brogued. "Get everyone!"

Thao shot him a look that indicated he was as impressed with *Guns of Navarone* as he had been by *The Magnificent Seven.* "Four."

A man came running out of a door on the side of the connector, M-16 at the ready. He halted at the two bodies and the machinegun. Kane glanced at Thao, as he tried to make a command decision.

The radio came alive. "Jimmy and Dan are dead!" The man grabbed the handles of the fifty, swinging it about on the tripod.

A reply from a new voice. "Keep whoever's attacking at bay. We're blowing the bitch's head off now!"

"Shit," Kane muttered. *Good idea, bad execution.* He pressed the transmit on his walkie-talkie, sending a transmission on the frequency Merrick's team had uncovered. The bomb he'd removed earlier and was in his backpack under the gun went off along with a half-dozen simultaneous blasts on avenues of approach all about the Isolation Ward building.

The man next to the fifty was obliterated and the gun was destroyed.

Kane and Thao ran through the smoke to the Isolation Ward. Kane had the Swedish K tight to his shoulder while Thao was sticking with his crossbow. Their ears were ringing from the explosions. The TOW had to be on the second floor, in a room facing the Statue.

Thao split off to the right on the first floor, while Kane went left. He took the concrete stairs at the end two at a time until he reached the landing. He halted, taking a deep breath. Double-checked that a round was in the chamber of the K, bolt pulled back. Thao would be on his end. No more time.

Kane stepped to the side, pieing his way to see down the hall, slice by slice until he could see straight down—to a door three meters away.

Isolation ward. Pope had said it could be sealed off. But the wood was old and Kane was pissed. He moved forward and kicked the door open, the K ready. A man was silhouetted in the hallway less that a meter away, one arm in a sling, a pistol in his good hand. He turned toward Kane, leveling the gun.

Kane lightly twitched the trigger of the K twice, both rounds hitting the man in the head.

There was a loud click which Kane recognized. The TOW had been fired, but there was a 1.5 second delay while the missile's gyroscope spun up. He dashed forward, almost to the door, when the missile launched. A flash of bright light exploded through the doorway with the backblast, followed by a loud whoosh of the missile leaving the tube.

Kane jumped, spinning in the air, firing on automatic, aiming at the bulky tracker unit on the side of the launch tube. The fact a man's head was pressed up against the optics and in the way was of no concern. Merrick's special 9mm rounds blew the head apart and Kane kept his finger on the trigger as he slammed into the floor, the bullets shattering the tracker.

At 280 meters per second, the missile had already covered half the distance to the head of the Statue of Liberty when the tracker was destroyed. The missile, no longer receiving commands from the guide wire, arced up into the sky and then down, splashing harmlessly into New York harbor.

The bolt of the Swedish K slammed forward, the gun empty.

The air in the room was thick with smoke from the initial launch of the TOW, a charge having propelled the missile out of the tube until the main motor had kicked in seven meters out.

Kane looked up at the muzzle of an M-16 pointing at his face. Holding the gun was a tall, thin, blond-haired man. He was dressed in black fatigues and wore an armband with an IRA flag on it.

"You fuck—" he began, but then Thao came through the door, fast, arm swinging, and his machete sliced through the man's right wrist, leaving the severed hand still grasping the pistol grip of the weapon as blood spurted from the stump.

The man didn't seem to comprehend what had happened for a couple of seconds. That was enough time for Thao to jerk the rifle out of his other hand and Kane to get to his feet and reload the K.

The man stared at the blood pulsing out of his wrist, but Thao was already at work, whipping a bandage out of his kit. He started to secure it over the bleeding, but the man's other hand went across his body for the pistol in the holster, so Kane grabbed it. He applied pressure until the bone snapped.

Kane shoved the last surviving Sword of Saint Patrick to the floor, his back against the wall. Thao struggled to fix the bandage in place. Kane placed his boot against the man's chest to keep him in position.

"What's your name?" Kane asked.

"Fuck you," the man said. "You coppers?"

"No," Kane said. "Are you Kevin Flanagan?"

The acknowledgement flashed in the man's eyes. "Who are you?"

Thao cinched the bandage as best he could. "I will have to put a tourniquet on the arm."

"No tourniquet," Flanagan said. He moved the stub toward his mouth, bit down on the bandage and used his teeth to rip it off. Blood flowed freely. "I'm not going to lock up." He put the amputated forearm in his lap. "I'm willing to die for a free Ireland."

Thao looked up at Kane, then slowly stood.

"You're going to," Kane assured him. The other two TOW missiles were in their cases, stacked against the wall.

"I am sorry, Dai Yu," Thao said. "I reacted. I should have—"

Kane waved off Thao's apology. "You saved my life." He looked down at Flanagan. "Do you have any last words for your wife, Caitlyn?"

Flanagan barked a harsh laugh. "'Caitlyn'? Why would I have any words for her? Are you daft, man?"

Kane shrugged. "I was just asking. You don't have much longer."

Flanagan's face was pale. He shook his head. "Caitlyn?" He repeated as if he didn't understand. "Why would you be asking me about her?"

"I talked to her last night," Kane said.

Flanagan began laughing, a manic edge to it, the dark realization of death tainting it, along with something else: "Poor Caitlyn's been dead for months, you sod."

Wednesday Morning, 10 August 1977

UPPER BAY, NEW YORK HARBOR

From the first immigrant, a 17-year-old girl from Cork, Ireland on 1 January 1892 to a Norwegian seaman in 1954, over 12 million have passed through Ellis Island, just a kilometer from the lady who had just narrowly survived decapitation.

From the Blackout the previous month, on top of the economic toll of the past decade, the city across the Bay, was also suffering under the fear of Son of Sam. In the dark waters to the south and east, past the Verrazano Narrows, at the edge of the Lower Bay, where the shelf dropped off into deep water, were six bodies weighed down by the very weapons with which they'd attempted to attack the Statue.

A victory of one sort in the midst of the gloom.

The Statue of Liberty's torch glittered in the darkness above a pre-dawn fog, a solitary beacon in the Upper Bay of New York Harbor as it had been ever since 1886.

GREENWICH VILLAGE, MANHATTAN

Kane took the steps down to his apartment, already having decided what remained of this night was worthy of sheet-breaking. He and Thao had spent hours loading the bodies and weapons onto the zodiac, taking them out to Lower Bay and dumping them. He'd left his Montagnard friend at the diner with instructions to call Strong and let him know the situation was resolved. Then he walked home.

He froze when he saw the Bowie knife impaled in his door, holding a piece of paper in place.

Kane pulled the knife out, holding the note in one hand. Block lettered:

A BLOOD DEBT MUST BE PAID WITH BLOOD

"Right," Kane muttered, crumpling the note. The tell was in place. He entered and locked the door behind him. On the far nightstand in the bedroom was *The Godfather*, open and face down. He smiled. Truvey had probably gotten about a dozen pages into it. Kane reached to get the book and relieve the pressure on the spine, but he stopped himself and let it be.

He lay down on top of the blanket, still holding the Bowie knife. He could smell Toni's perfume on the pillow. The knife was heavy in his hand. He lifted it and stared at the razor edge sharpness.

Kane got up, took his poncho liner and went to the kitchen. Grabbed a spool of fishing line and several empty soup cans from the trash. Went out the back door. Climbed the few steps to the garden. He quickly strung the wire around the perimeter of Pope's small garden. Hung the cans by their P-38 opened lids on the line and put pebbles in them. Stepped over the line and pushed into the weed infested, dying garden until he was out of site. There was a clear spot, just big enough for him to lie down in. He stretched out, covering himself with the camouflage poncho liner. He drew the .45 and laid it next to his left hand. He rested his right hand, holding the Bowie knife, on his chest. Stared up at glow of the city reflected back by the scattered clouds. A few stars glittered through a break, dulled by smog.

Utter exhaustion washed over him.

Oddly, his last conscious thought was of Caitlyn and her hand in his hair, holding his head.

THE END

Walk on the Wild Side continues Will Kane's story from
Lawyers, Guns and Money.
Walk on the Wild Side will be published on 9 December
2019.
An excerpt follows Author Information

The Green Beret series.
While this is part of the Green Beret series as book #11,
it's actually part of a prelude to the first book in the series,
Eyes of the Hammer, which features an older Dave Riley.
Books 1 through 6 feature Dave Riley.
Book 7, *Chasing the Ghost*, introduces Horace Chase.
Books 8 and 9 feature Chase but with Dave Riley as a
character.

Authors Note:
This story is framed around historical events, but the people
and details have been changed, except for significant
historical figures.
The West Point class of 1966 lost 30 members, the most of
any West Point class, in Vietnam. Four of the eight
assigned to the 173rd Airborne were KIA.
Roy Cohn was a controversial figure and many say he shaped
Donald Trump's vision of the world.
The 173rd Airborne was involved in numerous engagements
in Vietnam and the battles of Hill 1338 and Hill 875
occurred, but details and people have been changed.
Father Watters was awarded the Medal of Honor.
There was a Green Beret Affair in 1969 where a double agent
was executed. Colonel Rheault, the commander of the
Fifth Special Forces at the time, was the basis for Colonel
Kurtz in *Apocalypse Now*.
Son of Sam began his reign of terror on 29 July 1976. By
August 1977 he had killed 6 and wounded 7.
In 1977 the first tours of Ellis Island began. The bridge to the
island was not built until 1986.

Wednesday Morning, 10 August 1977

GREENWICH VILLAGE, MANHATTAN
"I could have killed you while you were sleeping."

Former Green Beret, currently exhausted, William Kane heard the words distantly, on the cusp between sleep and consciousness, not sure for a moment whether they lay in dream or reality, but based on his luck lately, odds were the latter.

He reluctantly opened his eyes to clarify. Night sky with clouds reflecting the constant glow of the City That supposedly Never Sleeps. The view was framed by wilting plants which fixed his position: lying in the midst of his landlord's garden in the back yard of the Greenwich Village brownstone. The thought that there were no 'front' yards in Manhattan flickered across his brain.

"May I have my knife back?" the intruder asked.

Definitely reality. Kane lifted his head from the dirt and looked toward the voice. A dark silhouette was squatting beyond his feet, backdropped by plants. The man pointed with one hand toward Kane's chest, while aiming a gun at Kane in the other.

Kane lifted hand from chest and extended the Bowie knife, spinning it so that the haft was toward the Navajo.

"Do you sleep out here often?" the man asked as he took the Bowie and checked the edge as if Kane might have dulled it during his slumber.

Kane remained on his back, considering limited tactical options. "Occasionally."

"It is good to be under the stars, although they are hard to see in this city."

"Yeah, I know," Kane said. "It's a cesspool. Yazzie and Johnson already told me."

Kane considered sitting up but he was still tired and he didn't know how far Navajo blood feud custom extended. Obviously, no killing a sleeping man which was damn considerate. But a man who sat up? He belatedly wondered why he'd given the knife back, then chalked it off to an autonomous obeying response hammered into him by four years at West Point. And there was the gun.

"Got your message," Kane said, referring to the note pinned to his door with the knife reading: A BLOOD DEBT MUST BE PAID WITH BLOOD. It was referencing Kane's killing of one of this man's Navajo 'brothers', Johnson, in the course of his search for a team of Irish terrorists trying to blow up the Statue of Liberty. His life was complicated.

The Navajo remained quiet.

Kane remembered he'd drawn his forty-five and put it just next to his left hand just before sleep. He also knew that it wasn't there, without having to reach. His Fairbairn-Sykes knife was in place, however, pressed against his spine in its sheath.

"Can I sit up?"

"You must stand so that we can finish this."

"I had a long night. I thought I'd have more time."

"We always think we will have more time," the Navajo said.

"Right," Kane said. "You know who I am, but I never caught your name on the boat or in the warehouse."

"Dale."

"'Dale'? I'd have thought you guys had names like Soaring Eagle or Man With Big Knife. Something like that. So far Yazzie, Johnson and Dale."

"We have the names we were given," Dale said. "They are honorable names because they are our fathers' names."

"Your real fathers," Kane said. "What happened to them?"

"They were code talkers and died in combat."

"And Boss Crawford adopted all of you," Kane said, knowing he was stalling. "At least he gave you your fathers' names but they sound Westernized."

"Our Navajo names remain within us and are not to be shared with outsiders."

Kane sat and glanced to his left. As expected, the pistol wasn't there. He could see that Dale wore khaki pants and nothing else. There was a single line of red smeared across his forehead. His skin was dark and smooth. He was in his mid-thirties and his body was lean, muscles like taut ropes. Despite the dim light, Kane could see several scars crisscrossing the man's torso. This wasn't his first knife fight. Kane had his own scars under his clothes and a nasty one on the side of his head from an AK-47 round, but it was mostly hidden by his thick, dark hair. He was lean, not as much as Dale, six feet tall, and after a busy week of tracking down and stopping the terrorist his face was dark with the first stage of a beard. He wore black jungle fatigue pants, a grey t-shirt and jungle boots. The denim shirt he usually wore was rolled in a ball as a field expedient pillow.

As Kane got to his feet, Dale also stood, putting the gun in the holster on his belt, keeping knife in hand. The first gray of dawn was permeating the air which meant Kane had been asleep less than an hour since returning from stopping the terrorists and disposing of their bodies and gear.

"BMNT," Kane said.

Dale inclined his head inquisitively.

"Begin morning nautical twilight," Kane said. "When the Indians traditionally attack which is ironic. I should have been on alert but I had a very long night." Kane looked past him. "Did you hit the wire and I didn't hear?" He was referring to the fishing wire hanging soup cans with rocks in them he'd put around the perimeter of the garden as early warning against an intrusion just like this one.

"The wire told me you were out here and not inside," Dale said. "Why put an alarm where you are not?"

"Right." Kane added that logical tidbit to his tactical repertoire.

"Where is the knife with which you killed my brother?"

"If I draw it, will that commence the fight?"

Dale readied himself, feet shoulder width apart, right slightly forward, Bowie held in front of his chest.

"I take that as a yes," Kane said. "What if I don't want to fight?"

"Either way you die. One path is honorable. The other the coward's."

Kane slid his right foot back. Then his left. He took another step back, pushing through the plants, sliding his feet. Another. Dale matched his retreat with advance.

"I don't want to have to chase you," Dale said.

"We'll need space to fight," Kane replied. "Plus, I don't want to ruin Pope's garden with blood and guts and all that."

"He has not taken care of his plants," Dale noted.

"He's had a bad couple of months," Kane said. "Got laid off from his job and he lived for his work." He knew he was being chatty, an anomaly to his nature, but talking delayed the fighting and Kane was still considering tactics because the scars, and the way Dale was moving and holding the knife, indicated he might have more prowess than the last Navajo, Johnson, whose death via Kane's blade had precipitated this blood vengeance.

Kane kept moving, slowly, steadily toward the edge of the garden and the open space between it and the brownstone. He drew the Fairbairn-Sykes fighting knife from the sheath in the middle of his back. The rear of his left leg hit the tripwire and the stones in the cans rattled loudly in the relative pre-dawn quiet of the city, against a backdrop of a distant siren and blare of a car horn. Kane paused, then lifted that leg to continue his retreat.

Dale attacked, a short slice of the Bowie at Kane's face, but it was a feint to get Kane off balance.

It didn't work as Kane jumped back, clearing the wire. Dale charged, hopping over the wire and slashing, three times, back and forth, closer and closer. Kane gave ground until they were both free of the plants.

Kane shifted and moved so that they faced each other in a five-foot-wide stretch of gravel and stone. Kane took a couple of steps back. The fence was just behind him.

"No more ground to escape," Dale noted.

Kane wasn't watching the knife, but rather the Navajo's eyes in the glow from the light over the back door and the gathering dawn. He spotted the decision a fraction of a second before Dale charged.

Kane threw the Fairbairn directly toward Dale's face with no hope of the point impacting at this close distance. It had the desired effect as Dale jerked his head to the side in the midst of his attack, slightly altering the angle of approach, even as he brought the Bowie down in an extended strike toward Kane's chest.

Kane blocked the thrust with his arms crossed in an X at the wrist just in front and above his face. He flowed, twisting, trying to lock down on Dale's knife wrist, but the Navajo surprised Kane with a punch to the throat with his free hand.

Kane staggered back, gasping, losing his tentative grip on the man's knife hand.

Dale was on him, free hand clenching Kane's throat, one leg sweeping Kane's feet from underneath him.

Kane fell hard on his back, knocking the wind out. He punched Dale in the face as the Navajo was on top of him, bringing the Bowie up for a final blow.

The knife came down and Kane used both hands to stop it, gripping Dale's wrist. The point was inches from his throat. Dale put his other hand on the hilt, lifting his body to put all his weight behind it.

Kane stared up into the Navajo's eyes. A drop of sweat from Dale's forehead fell onto Kane's.

Fraction by fraction the tip of the Bowie closed the distance. Kane tried to roll, but Dale's legs were spread wide, a stable platform with superior position. Kane jerked his knee up, slamming into Dale's crotch but there was no apparent effect.

The point touched Kane's throat.

Kane dug his thumb into Dale's wrist, deeper, finding the right place, then squeezing with all his strength. Dale grunted from the pain as a bone broke and the Bowie lifted because his own pressure was making the break worse.

Kane did a quick adjustment of his hands, thumb into the other wrist, digging. Dale's eyes widened as he realized he was going to lose use of both hands.

The tableau was interrupted by a familiar light pfft sound from behind Dale in concert with the slight mechanical sound of a pistol's slide functioning, ejecting the fired round and slamming forward, seating another.

A .22 caliber bullet ricocheted off the back of Dale's skull, but he remained on task, giving it one last attempt, the point reaching flesh and putting pressure on it.

The sound of the suppressed High Standard pistol firing was repeated and a round struck Dale in the back. The bone in the other wrist gave way to Kane's thumb and Dale finally let loose a grunt of pain, no longer able to maintain downward pressure on the Bowie. He made a quick decision, pulled back and slashed. Kane blocked it with a forearm on Dale's forearm.

Dale straightened, pulling the knife away from Kane, turning on his knees. The gun fired four more times in rapid succession, the small bullets hitting the Navajo but none striking a critical spot.

Kane used both arms to shove Dale to the side and rolled away. He jumped to his feet.

Pope was standing eight feet away, the gun at the ready, his eyes wide. If circumstances were different, he'd be a comical figure in his bathrobe and slippers, with stick like white legs ending in big, fuzzy slippers.

Dale was also getting to his feet, the .22 caliber long rifle bullets having distracted him but causing as much apparent damage as Kane's knee. Dale charged, knife in his good hand and Kane side-stepped, grabbed that hand and flowed it, down and in and around, the wrist completely snapping. The Bowie slammed into Dale's chest, breaking through the ribs, into the heart.

Dale reached for the knife, whose presence in his heart was actually sealing the wound and keeping him alive for the moment. He pulled it out, letting loose a spurt of dark red blood directly from his heart. He took a step toward Kane, who was retreating. Dale looked down at the blood pulsing out of his chest. He dropped the knife and looked skyward, whispering something in Navajo. He collapsed to the ground, blood still flowing from the wound as his heart gave a few last beats, pumping his life out.

"I shot him," Pope said. "I know I hit him."

"You did," Kane said. "You did good."

"I heard the cans." Pope's voice was a monotone, his mind still processing the shock of what had just happened. "I saw you fighting. Is he dead?"

Kane knelt next to Dale and checked the pulse in his neck while staring into the gathering cloud in the Navajo's eyes. "Yeah. He's dead."

"I killed him?"

"No," Kane said. "I killed him."

"I've never killed anyone," Pope said.

"You still haven't." Kane checked the body, finding the pager clipped to the belt. He wondered where the rest of Dale's clothes were? How did he get here? "Don't move," he ordered

Pope as he reclaimed his knife, sheathed it, and found his forty-five lying behind where Dale had been squatting. He partially pulled the slide to make sure a round was in the chamber.

Pistol at the ready, Kane climbed the fence to the next yard and ran up the narrow alley to the front of the row of Brownstones. A large dark car, the same make which he'd ridden in with Yazzie and the other Flint Boys, was idling out front. It burned rubber peeling away as soon as the driver spotted Kane.

It occurred to him the driver could have come with Dale, making it two on one and finishing the retribution. The Code. Kane shook his head, having had some experience with codes in his life.

Kane retraced his steps.

Pope was in the same spot, staring at the body. "I shot him. But it didn't seem to do anything."

"You distracted him," Kane said. "Twenty-two bullets are pretty small and these were low velocity. To do real damage there's a couple of key places to aim for. But you did good, Pope. I appreciate it."

"You killed him." Pope seemed to be having trouble processing that, but it was a positive shift from blaming himself.

"I did."

"Who was he?" Pope asked.

"The first."

"The first of what?"

"The first of six who've sworn a blood oath to kill me. Now there are five."

Monday,
14 April 1969

VICINITY PARROTS BEAK, SOUTH VIETNAM

Kane peers through the night vision scope at the tree line across the field. Nothing moving.

He turns it off and hands it to Thao, closing his eyes for a few moments to rest them from the strain. The small squad of Kane, Thao, the translator Ngo, and fifteen South Vietnamese CIDG—civilian irregular defense group-- have been lying in ambush since just after dark the previous evening. An intelligence report had warned of VC infiltrators and the goal is to ambush them before they get closer to the A-Team Camp and the South Vietnamese village, three kilometers behind them.

They are in the Parrots Beak, the portion of Cambodia that pokes into South Vietnam, just sixty-five kilometers from Saigon. Kane, who is fond of maps, isn't so fond of the arbitrary lines drawn on them delineating where he can fight and where he isn't supposed to go. Which is the tree line they're observing. It's in Cambodia and home to staging areas for Viet Cong and NVA to retreat in safety and regroup and launch cross border attacks.

Kane, and the other members of his A-Team stationed at Camp 4414 know that there are those very high in the U.S. military and government who do view the international border as arbitrary. Last month, beginning on the 18ᵗʰ of March, they'd heard the unmistakable sound of an Arc Light near the Fish Hook, which is north of their camp. B-52s carpet-bombing suspected enemy base camps in Cambodia. The bombings on the other side of the border have continued, on and off, for the past month. There's nothing about it on the news back in the United States because only a select few know. The B-52 crews only learn of their true target once they're airborne and all records are destroyed when they return to their air base at Guam. Oddly enough, the North Vietnamese aren't making it public either, given that their forces were in Cambodia illegally. A savage part of the war being fought in secrecy.

Despite the heavy ordnance from on high, it still requires, as it has throughout history, boots on the ground and that is why Kane, Thao and the others lay here in the jungle watching for movement.

Where and who the intel report came from wasn't part of the mission briefing, as it rarely is. A result of compartmentalization and other 'happy horseshit' as designated by Sergeant First Class Merrick, the team sergeant. The Americans spend as much time and effort keeping intel and operational status from the South Vietnamese as they do the NVA and VC. People back in the States might believe this war is being waged against communists, but there are sides within sides and angles not running parallel with the war effort. It is not as envisioned by those who see the world as white hats versus black hats and have watched too many John Wayne movies.

The intel also doesn't include pesky details such as size of the force, intent or direction. Often Kane wonders if these reports are generated by some REMF, rear-echelon-motherfucker, sitting behind a desk in a secure place who has a quota of such reports to meet and a vivid imagination. More often than not, they are bogus and a waste of time.

For Kane and Thao, this is a low-key mission as compared to illegally going cross-border by helicopter for a recon, but any trip beyond the wire is fraught with possibilities, all of them bad.

Two hours after midnight, Thao whispers: "Dai Yu." He passes the bulky scope.

Kane presses the rubber against his eye and spots what alerted Thao: movement in the tree line. Green shadowed figures flitting through the trees. They're moving on an angle which will take them in the vicinity of the camp and village. And they're crossing the border. At least squad sized, maybe more.

Kane passes the scope to the interpreter Ngo. He stares for a few seconds, then hands it back to Kane without comment. Kane's Vietnamese is limited, as is Thao's, so Kane relies on him to pass orders to the CIDG troops.

Kane grabs the handset for the radio. It's covered in plastic to keep it dry. Unlike his Infantry tour with the 173rd Airborne two years previously, Kane usually carries the radio, particularly when he's the only American on a patrol. His ruck containing it lies on the ground between him and Ngo.

He keys it. "Tango Victor Three, this is Six. Over."

The response is static.

"Tango Victor Three. This is Six. Fire mission. Over."

Kane wants the camp's mortars to initiate the ambush on a pre-plotted position right in the middle of the field. It's totally out of character for Merrick to be slow to respond.

Kane glances to his right at Thao. Looks through the scope again.

"Get ready," Kane whispers to Thao and then Ngo, who pass the word to the militia next to them and down the line.

Kane keys the radio. "Tango Victor Three. This is Six. Fire mission. Target Alpha-Two. Fire for effect. Troops in the open. Over." He gives where he wants the rounds on the off chance that the camp can hear him but he can't hear them. He'd conducted a radio check as soon as they were outside the wire and the commo had been fine.

Now? Nothing. Murphy's Law: what can fuck up will.

The first of the enemy are coming across the field, spreading out. Kane rolls left, slips the straps of the ruck over his shoulders. Turns back on his stomach, weapon at the ready. "Thao. Thump 'em."

"Roger, Dai Yu."

Thao takes the M-79 grenade launcher off the snap link connecting it to his LBE. Puts it to his shoulder.

"On the grenade," Kane orders and it's passed to the others, who ready their weapons.

The M-79 makes a popping noise as it launches the 40mm high explosive grenade. Thao is already reloading, breaking the weapon open like a shotgun, before the round strikes in the midst of the enemy. As it explodes, Kane and the others open up with their rifles, pouring bullets into the enemy. The VC in the field promptly drop down.

There is no return fire, which is unusual.

Kane fires his last round. He drops the magazine and inserts a fresh one. He stands. Fires three rounds. "Forward," he orders.

He's impressed as the South Vietnamese villagers follow suit, advancing with him on line. Thao hooks the M-79 back on his LBE and fires his M-16. Kane glances left and notes that Ngo isn't firing, but is doing something with his rifle, most likely clearing a jam.

Kane stops firing, but keeps advancing as he tries the radio one more time. No response from the camp.

The first green tracers scream out of the tree line, high, but that weapon is quickly joined by a chorus of others. Kane, and his patrol, hit the deck, returning fire. The chatter of a light machine gun joins the enemy firing, arcing a string of green just above their heads.

What sounds like a hellish racket to the uninitiated is a symphony of combat to Kane who can separate out the instruments. Two more light machineguns. At least two dozen AK-47s. He's outgunned. Not a squad. More a platoon.

"Fall back to the ERP," Kane yells.

Ngo translates the order. The militia have done all that can be expected of them and scramble back.

One of the South Vietnamese is hit. Kane grabs his LBE and drags him. Thao provides covering fire as the rest scamper back, through the ambush position and to the location Kane had designated the previous evening before they moved forward to the ambush site. It's a dike along the edge of a rice paddy, giving them a covered linear defensive position. Kane pulls the wounded man up and over the top.

The enemy fire lessens, then ceases.

Thao begins working on the wounded man. Kane tries the radio again; still no response.

Kane peels back the Velcro and checks the time. Several more hours of darkness. He decides its safer to hold this position than try to go back through the wire with no communication and an enemy unit afoot.

"What happened to your rifle?" Kane asked Ngo.

"Jammed," Ngo says. "Clear now, Dai Yu."

Kane slides down to Thao. "How is he?"

Thao removes his bloody hands from the soldier. "Dead, Dai Yu."

Kane returns to the dike. Scans with the scope. He's surprised to see at least fifty shadowy figures advancing across the field. A company? This is rapidly getting out of control.

Kane pulls a flare out, pulls the cap, putting it on the base, then slams it into the ground, aiming above and beyond the advancing enemy.

The red flare screeches up and over, then pops, bathing the field in its red glare. His estimate was low. There are at least a hundred VC. A company.

He shoots, the others joining in. The advancing VC return fire. There are many more green tracers coming their way then red going out.

One of the villagers screams in agony.

The VC have gone to ground, but continue to fire. Out of the corner of his eye, Kane sees the head of one of the militia punched back with a bullet through the forehead. The body tumbles down into the muddy water behind them.

Kane looks left and right. If the VC flank, enfilading fire will wipe him and his men out, besides being cut off from camp.

Kane tries the radio. No reply. He never planned on holding this position without mortar support, nor against such numbers. He knows what Charlie Beckwith would say about that.

Kane grabs Ngo's shoulder and shouts the order to be translated, while he points. "We slide right along the dike. That way."

Right is away from the camp and village; the VC won't expect that.

Kane leads with Thao taking trail. As he goes by, Kane grabs a villager, shoves him in the desired direction. Gestures to the others as Ngo relays the order. They leave behind two bodies. Keeping their heads down, they slither along the dike. The green tracers are concentrating on their former position, so the movement is yet unnoticed by the enemy.

A raised road is ahead, bisecting the dike and the rice paddy. It will at least give them cover in two directions. But just before they reach it, a squad of VC charge over the dike, a flanking element, as Kane fears. They are surprised to run into Kane and his men.

Kane fires first, killing two, then the two units are among each other in an all-out deadly brawl, every man for himself. Kane's M-16 is knocked out of his hands as a VC jumps on top of him; the two tumble to ground and roll into the rice paddy. The man is choking him, his eyes crazed. Kane is able to get to his knife with his right hand as he shoves his left into the enemy's face, fingers tearing at the man's eyes. Kane blindly stabs, feeling the blade go into flesh, strike a bone and angle inward. He punch-stabs several times in a frenzy, half-submerged, until the hands around his throat release.

Kane shoves the body aside and gets to his feet in knee deep, dirty water. He draws his forty-five. It's difficult to tell who is who. He sees Thao carving his way through the VC with his machete. Kane clambers up the slope. Shoots a black-pajamaed man entangled with a CIDG in the side of the head, producing a dark blossom of brain, blood and bone. There is screaming, grunting, cursing in Vietnamese, a cry for help, someone begging over and over and despite the language barrier Kane realizes the man is calling out for his mother.

As suddenly as the fight began, it's over, the surviving VC scurrying back over the dike and into the night. Kane turns to and fro, forty-five at the ready.

"Ngo?" Kane calls out. "Head count!"

Thao answers. "Six dead, three wounded, Dai Yu." He holds out an M-16.

Kane takes it. He fires a flare toward their old position. A green burst of light illuminates the night.

A desperate last-ditch message he'd coordinated with Merrick.

Within seconds comes the welcome sound of mortars popping rounds from the camp. Several seconds later they crump into the Emergency Rally Point which has been over-run by now farther down the dike.

The VC firing dwindles. The main body is also dispersing.

Several more mortar rounds impact.

Silence, except for the man calling out for his mother, although it's gone from a scream to frenzied murmur.

Ngo appears. "Dai Yu?"

"Where were you?" Kane asks.

"I was covering the rear," Ngo explains, pointing back the way they'd come.

Kane sees Thao kneeling next to a wounded man, holding a clamp knuckle deep in the CIDG's thigh. It's a slippery job, working entirely by feel to find the slender, severed blood vessel. There's no place above the wound to put pressure to stop the bleeding.

The man stops his maternal plea.

"He's dead," Kane says to Thao.

Thao continues to work.

Kane puts a gentle hand on Thao's shoulder. "Sergeant. He's dead."

*****

They return to the A-Team camp just after dawn. The bodies are wrapped in ponchos, attached to poles. It takes every man, including Kane, Thao and Ngo to carry them, given their walking wounded.

Women and children from the nearby village are waiting outside the wire. The families of the CIDG. Kane stops the patrol as women learn they are widows and children that they are orphans. Their cries of anguish pierce the morning quiet.

Merrick comes out of the gate to greet the patrol. He slaps the Captain on the shoulder, an unusual sign of affection for the gruff sergeant. "Glad to see you, Will. What the fuck happened?"

Kane nods. "Happy to see you too, Lew. What a clusteruck." He watches the grieving families. The team's two medics hustle the wounded inside the camp to the infirmary.

Merrick indicates the distraught families. "I'll take care of it." He has a wad of Vietnamese currency which he gives to Ngo to pay off the families of the dead men.

"How much is a life worth now?" Kane asks as Merrick comes back and the villagers carry off their dead.

Merrick ignores the question. "What happened? Never heard a peep from you. Once the shooting started, I was on the horn for hours trying to get the B-team to scramble the Mike Force. They couldn't send them 'cause they were engaged near the Fish Hook. I thought you'd been wiped out. Especially when I saw the green star cluster."

"I radioed all night," Kane says. "No reply."

"Bullshit?" Merrick shakes his head. "We had a five by five when you left the wire. I was on top of comms. Nothing. I ordered the mortars when I saw the green. Come on." Merrick indicates the gate. "Let's get inside."

Kane calls to the two members of his patrol who didn't live in the village. "Sergeant Thao, Ngo."

Kane and Merrick go to the commo bunker while two indigs go to their hooch inside the camp. Kane shrugs off his ruck. Merrick opens the top and checks the radio. "What the fuck! You're on the wrong frequency."

"Bullshit," Kane says. "You said it: we had a good commo check when I left. I never changed freqs. I didn't touch the radio."

"Look for yourself," Merrick says.

Kane believes Merrick but it's so outrageous he has to see. Wrong freq. "I don't understand."

"Who had access to the radio?" Merrick asks.

"No one," Kane says. "It never left my ruck."

"Did your ruck leave you?"

Kane has to think for a second after the melee of the night. "I put it next to me once we were in the ambush."

"And who was on the other side?"

Kane sits down, the adrenaline gone. Again, he has to think for a moment. "Ngo."

Merrick reaches out and Kane flinches, but he allows his team sergeant to remove something from his face.

A piece of brain matter.

New York Minute is a prelude to his 2 million copy selling Green Beret series, set in New York City in the summer of 1977.
Available HERE.
It's followed by the next book in this series,
Lawyers, Guns and Money
Th third novel featuring Will Kane, is **Walk On The Wild Side**

For free eBooks, short stories and audio short stories, please go to http://bobmayer.com/freebies/
The page includes free and discounted book constantly updated.

There are over 220 free, downloadable Powerpoint presentations via Slideshare on a wide range of topics from history, to survival, to writing, to book trailers. This page and slideshows are constantly updated at:
http://bobmayer.com/workshops/

Questions, comments, suggestions: Bob@BobMayer.com
Blog: http://bobmayer.com/blog/
Twitter: https://twitter.com/Bob_Mayer
Subscribe to his newsletter for the latest news, free eBooks, audio, etc.
Thanks to Beta readers: *Dalice Peterson, Kendra Delugar, Rich O'Neill, Brian Jenkins, Ken Kendall, Laurie Turner, Robert Mills*

ALL BOOKS

THE GREEN BERETS
Eyes of the Hammer   Dragon Sim-13   Cut Out
Synbat   Eternity Base   Z: The Final Option
Chasing the Ghost   Chasing the Lost   Chasing the Son

Will Kane Green Beret Books
New York Minute (June 2019)
Lawyers, Guns and Money (Sept 2019)
Walk on the Wild Side (9 December 2019)

THE DUTY, HONOR, COUNTRY SERIES
Duty   Honor   Country

AREA 51
Area 51   Area 51 The Reply   Area 51 The Mission
Area 51 The Sphinx   Area 51 The Grail   Area 51
Excalibur
Area 51 The Truth   Area 51 Nosferatu   Area 51 Legend
Area 51 Redemption   Area 51 Invasion   Area 51
Interstellar

ATLANTIS
Atlantis   Atlantis Bermuda Triangle   Atlantis Devils Sea
Atlantis Gate   Assault on Atlantis   Battle for Atlantis

THE CELLAR
Bodyguard of Lies   Lost Girls

NIGHSTALKERS
Nightstalkers   Book of Truths   The Rift
Time Patrol
This fourth book in the Nightstalker book is the team
becoming the Time Patrol, thus it's labeled book 4 in that
series but it's actually book 1 in the Time Patrol series.

TIME PATROL
Black Tuesday   Ides of March   D-Day   Independence
Day
Fifth Floor   Nine-Eleven   Valentines Day   Hallows Eve

SHADOW WARRIORS

(these books are all stand-alone and don't need to be read in order)
The Line   The Gate   Omega Missile   Omega Sanction
Section Eight

PRESIDENTIAL SERIES
The Jefferson Allegiance   The Kennedy Endeavor

BURNERS SERIES
Burners   Prime

PSYCHIC WARRIOR SERIES
Psychic Warrior   Psychic Warrior: Project Aura

STAND ALONE BOOKS:
THE ROCK   I, JUDAS THE 5TH GOSPEL

BUNDLES (Discounted 2 for 1 and 3 for 1):
Check web site, books, fiction and nonfiction.

COLLABORATIONS WITH JENNIFER CRUSIE
Don't Look Down   Agnes and The Hitman   Wild Ride

NON-FICTION:
The Green Beret Preparation and Survival Guide: A Common Sense Step-by-Step Manual for Everyone
Survive Now-Thrive Later. The Pocket-Sized Survival Manual You Must Have
Stuff Doesn't Just Happen I: The Gift of Failure
Stuff Doesn't Just Happen II: The Gift of Failure
The Novel Writers Toolkit
Write It Forward: From Writer to Bestselling Author
Who Dares Wins: Special Operations Tactics for Success

All fiction is here: **Bob Mayer's Fiction**
All nonfiction is here: **Bob Mayer's Nonfiction**

About the Author

Thanks for the read!
If you enjoyed the book, please leave a review as they are
very important.

Bob Mayer is a NY Times Bestselling author, graduate of
West Point and former Green Beret. He's had over 75
books published including the #1 series The Green
Berets, the Cellar, Shadow Warriors, Presidential, Area
51, Atlantis, and the Time Patrol.

Born in the Bronx, having traveled the world (usually not
tourist spots), he now lives peacefully with his wife and
dogs.

For information on all his books, please get a free copy of
the *Reader's Guide*. You can download it in mobi
(Amazon) Epub (iBooks, Nook, Kobo) or PDF, from his
home page at www.bobmayer.com

Thank you!